BREAK
the
RULES

LAUREN JACKSON

PENGUIN BOOKS

PENGUIN BOOKS

UK I USA I Canada I Ireland I Australia
India I New Zealand I South Africa I China

Penguin Books is part of the Penguin Random House group of companies
whose addresses can be found at global.penguinrandomhouse.com.

Penguin
Random House
Australia

First published by Penguin Books, 2024

Cover by Val at Books and Moods
Cover illustrations by Danny Hooks/AdobeStock (football x's and o's), Alexander Ant/Unsplash
(swirling background texture), Jazmin Quaynor/Unsplash (swirling background texture),
Ashley West Edwards/Unsplash (paint splodges), Kelli Tungay/Unsplash (paintbrushes and pots)
Author photograph by Lauren Jackson
Typeset in Sabon LT Pro by Midland Typesetters, Australia

Printed and bound in Australia by Griffin Press, an accredited ISO AS/NZ 14001
Environmental Management Systems printer.

 A catalogue record for this
book is available from the
National Library of Australia

ISBN 978 1 76134 885 3

penguin.com.au

*We at Penguin Random House Australia acknowledge that Aboriginal and Torres Strait
Islander peoples are the first storytellers and Traditional Custodians of the land on which we
live and work. We honour Aboriginal and Torres Strait Islander peoples' continuous connection
to Country, waters, skies and communities. We celebrate Aboriginal and Torres Strait Islander
stories, traditions and living cultures; and we pay our respects to Elders past and present.*

To the readers who turn to books to escape.
Let's get lost together.

Content Warning

Thank you for choosing to read *Break the Rules*.
I really hope you enjoy it!

Some of the content may be triggering to some readers.
Content warnings include profanity, explicit sexual scenes,
drug use, family violence and other types of violence.

I hope you enjoy the story.

PLAYLIST

'Do I Wanna Know?' – Arctic Monkeys
'Wrong' – MAX, Lil Uzi Vert
'Numb to the Feeling' – Chase Atlantic
'High Enough (RAC Remix)' – K.Flay
'Talk' – Retronaut, Salvatore Ganacci
'Suffer With Me' – líue
'Slow Down' – Chase Atlantic
'Lose Control' – Teddy Swims
'bad idea' – Ariana Grande
'Cravin'' – Stileto, Kendyle Paige
'Breathe' – Kansh
'Habits (Stay High)' – Tove Lo
'Lover' – Taylor Swift
'Greedy' – Tate McRae
'Woo' – Rihanna

For complete playlist

1

ANYA

BEING YELLED AT BY an incoherent drunk man isn't how I wanted to spend my Friday night. I also didn't particularly want to pack up my life and move an hour north because my boyfriend decided my best friend was a better option than me. I guess we all have bad days, though. Or weeks, in my case.

My heart hurts at the thought of Dylan – my now ex-boyfriend – and Phoebe, my ex-best friend, sneaking around behind my back and lying to me. Forcing them from my mind, I try to focus on the situation in front of me.

The man shouts at me again, spit flying from his mouth and landing on my face. Wrinkles line his forehead and fan out from the corners of his eyes. He waves his hands, swaying so much he almost topples over. I have no clue what he is trying to say, but I'm guessing I'm at the wrong place. I flinch away and sigh as I step back from the kerb, looking down at the address I saved in my notes, which is supposed to be the share house I'm renting a room in. This is where the maps on my phone directed me to.

The street is quiet, which makes the drunk man's voice sound ten times as loud. I'm positive I'm in the wrong place because a street full of student housing wouldn't be this calm. I turn, leaving the man to yell at my back as I retreat to the car. The first fall of rain hits my cheeks. Tilting my head back, I glare up at the darkening sky.

I slide into the driver's seat and retype the address into my phone and, this time, it tells me my destination is five minutes away. Exhaling, I pull away from the kerb, trying to keep my shit together, but the tiny thread of hope I'm holding on to is getting thinner by the second.

Tiredness gnaws at me as I battle to keep my eyes open. This is the last thing I feel like doing tonight, but I had to get away from there. From them.

I swing the car into a busy narrow street, littered with cars parked haphazardly in places they shouldn't be. Cutting the engine, I peer through the window at the small, weathered house I'm meant to be moving into. Neon lights shine through the windows, and music floats down the driveway as I wander up it. A guy sits on the front porch, his legs dangling from the railing as he blows out a cloud of smoke.

'Hi,' I say when he stares at me for a long, awkward moment. 'Are you Johnny?'

'Yeah,' he says wearily, a husky edge to his voice.

'Hi,' I say again. The rain is starting to fall heavier now, so I move onto the porch step, trying to avoid my shirt getting any damper than it already is. 'I'm Anya.'

'Who?' His brows draw together.

'Anya Stark? We spoke on Messenger. I'm renting room three.'

He raises an eyebrow, looking a little surprised. 'Not anymore.'

My heart does an awkward jolt in my chest. 'What do you mean, not anymore?'

'You were supposed to pay the two weeks of rent in advance, but you never did. The room has been rented to someone else.' His face fades into the stoic expression he was wearing before as he inhales a long drag from the cigarette between his fingers.

I blink at him. 'What are you talking about? The money left my account.'

'Never came into mine.'

'What?' I frown, reaching into my pocket and pulling out my phone. I log into my banking app and stare down at the red digits that indicate the withdrawn amount. I shove the phone under his nose. 'See?'

'It was withdrawn. Not transferred to me.' I stare back down at the screen, realising he is right. My heart plummets to my stomach. 'You also would've gotten a confirmation message from me once it went through.'

Swallowing, my shoulders sag in defeat. Once again, I'm furious with myself for giving Dylan access to my bank account because – as usual – he didn't have any money. He was meant to pay the deposit for me on the day it was due. A fiery ball of anger burns in my chest as I realise he stole from me.

'Well,' I say bitterly, stepping back into the rain. 'That's just great.'

'Yeah. That sucks,' he says flatly, flicking the cigarette to the ground in front of me before disappearing inside the house, slamming the front door behind him.

Running my tongue across my teeth, I try my hardest to stop the tears welling in my eyes from spilling over. I stiffly walk back to the car and exhale a shaky breath before I settle behind the wheel. I dial my brother's number. My left leg jitters restlessly as I listen to the phone ring out.

After a moment, a text comes through.

Zayden: Dodgy reception. Everything ok?

Anya: Are you home? Or if not is there a spare key?

My brother sends through where his spare key is kept, no questions asked. I sink my teeth into my lower lip, still trying not to burst into tears. After a ten-minute drive, I pull up at my brother's house. There are several lights on, and an unfamiliar black truck parked in the driveway. Maybe he's let a neighbour park there. After moving a few pots around, I exhale in frustration when the spare key isn't where my brother said it would be. Pressing my lips into a line, my eyes bounce from the truck in the driveway to the lights on inside.

Blowing out a hot breath, I knock on the door and step back. Just as a traitorous tear slips out, the front door opens. My breath gets trapped in my lungs when my eyes land on Mason.

My brother's best friend.

The boy I had always loved, until I hated him.

He's aged well. Really fucking well. He's tall, packed with muscle, and with broader shoulders than when I'd seen him last. His eyes seem darker, his jaw more defined, his hair longer. Tattoos that once painted only part of one arm now cover every inch of skin I can see, except for his face and some parts of his neck. He's dressed in all black; that's something that hasn't changed. The shirt shows off how big his biceps are and how defined his chest is. He had always been very attractive, and I'd hopelessly wished he would get worse with age. Damn. And after all this time he's seeing me dishevelled and crying on my brother's doorstep on a Friday night.

'What are you doing here?' I ask, my voice betraying me by coming out in a whisper. All the feelings and reassurances I've convinced myself of over the years flash before my eyes, and I realise how much of a lie they all were. Because I am very, very much still affected by this man, and he hasn't even said one word to me yet. In fact, I bet he doesn't feel a damn thing. That's where the problems began.

Those dark, whisky-coloured eyes settle on me, and I feel every inch of my insides curl in on themselves. My heart feels as if it's twisted into a ball of lead in my chest and plummeted into my stomach, knocking against everything in its path along the way.

He quirks an eyebrow, eyes scanning my face, as if reassuring himself it really is me standing here in front of him, shivering and looking on the verge of a mental breakdown.

'I live here.'

My eyes widen as dread spreads through my veins. His words ring loudly in my ears, repeating inside my head, as if stuck on a loop. 'Since when?'

'Since Leasa moved out.'

I hadn't considered the fact that my brother would have found a roommate after his girlfriend of three years moved out. I should have guessed Mason would be the replacement. It made sense, but in my defence I try my best not to think about the boy who ripped my heart out of my chest and stomped on it.

Could this night get any worse?

'Oh,' I mumble, attempting to swallow, but suddenly my mouth and throat are paper dry. My body has always had an extreme reaction to being near Mason, and it drives me crazy. It's as if he owns the remote to my body and knows exactly which buttons to press.

The corner of his mouth twitches as his eyes openly roam over me, not caring in the slightest how obvious it is.

'No "Hi. How are you? What have you been up to?"' He smirks, leaning on the door frame. My heart jackhammers in my chest at the familiarity of the movement. He used to do that exact thing in the doorframe of my bedroom.

I definitely don't want to be thinking about him and me in my bedroom right now.

'No, that wasn't my first thought when I saw you,' I say, hoping my voice sounds stronger than I feel.

'What was that thought, then?'

'I don't want to deal with this asshole.' I fold my arms across my chest, trying to look the opposite of how I truly feel.

Mason grins at me, flashing his teeth. Handsome smile lines appear around the edges of his mouth. The lines that I loved so much. The very ones I've trailed my fingertips over . . .

'Good to know you still have that giant crush on me.'

The memory shatters, and I'm forcefully jolted back to reality. My face must reflect my true feelings, because his smirk falters for a moment. I force a blank expression. As best I can, anyway.

'You wish,' I spit back, trying my best to mask my hurt.

'Mmhmm,' he murmurs, eyeing the bare bit of skin where my shirt has slipped off my shoulder. My stomach does a flip-flop motion. 'If you say so. Why are you here?'

'I've had a hell of a night. I need somewhere to crash,' I say, rubbing a hand down my face. 'Zayden didn't mention you would be here.'

'Would it have made a difference?' he questions, sounding genuinely curious.

I don't want to do this. I wasn't ready to face him, nor the feelings I've forcefully shoved deep down into a file labelled: Do not open. EVER.

'Can you just let me in?' I huff, shaking out the hair that has fallen across my face.

His dark-brown eyes – two smoky quartzes – hover over my glistening cheeks for a moment before he steps back, allowing me access through the door. I haul my bag inside and he reaches around me to grab it, easily slinging it over his shoulder. I wipe my cheeks and avoid his gaze as I scan the room, taking in what is possibly the cleanest place I have ever seen. My brother is not a clean person, and I imagine this is Mason's doing. It must drive him crazy, always having to clean up after my disaster of a brother. Hurricane Zay, my mother used to call him.

'Weren't you meant to be moving into some share house downtown?' he asks, gesturing to the stairs.

They talk about me? Interesting.

Sighing, I walk in front of him and start to climb, taking in everything around me. A lot has changed since Leasa left.

'My asshole of an ex really wanted to make sure the knife he dug into my back wasn't getting out easily.'

I feel the heat of his gaze on my skin as we trail down the upstairs hallway. I pause, seeing a photo of Zayden, Mason and myself. We're at the beach, and I'm holding my arms out, showing where a line of starfish is sitting on my forearm. Zayden is beaming at the camera, pointing to the starfish. Stepping closer, I squint, looking closely at how Mason's eyes are on me. I never noticed that before. His lips are tilted up in a crooked smile, his cheeks flushed from running down the beach. I remember that day so clearly. It was one of the last fun days we had before things got complicated. I stand so close to the frame that the tip of my nose grazes the glass.

Why did I never notice he was looking at me like that?

'Heard about Dylan,' Mason says, brushing past me and opening a door, revealing a neatly kept spare room. I startle, having been so focused on the photo, I forgot for a moment where I am. Shaking my head, I follow him inside the room. It looks different – bigger than I remembered, with a soft-looking brown comforter that is calling my name. 'And Phoebe,' he adds after a moment.

A sickening feeling washes over me at the mention of their names. The two people in my life who I love so much. Or at least, I did.

I have been extremely unlucky in the love department.

'You keeping tabs on me, Mase?' I exhale, bringing my hair over my shoulder, feeling how damp it is from the rain.

He lowers my bag onto the bed, and it groans briefly under the weight of it. The bag is practically bursting at the seams, and there are three more just like it in the boot of my car, but they can stay there for now.

'Of course, Blush.'

Heat burns my cheeks and races down my neck at the familiar nickname. Blush. Every time Mason looked in my direction when we were growing up, my cheeks would shine a bright, noticeable red, as vibrant as a neon sign above my head telling the world I was crushing on him. Since he loved to enjoy my misery and discomfort, he quickly nicknamed me 'Blush' to further torment me.

I haven't seen him since everything went down over two years ago. Or heard that nickname. As much as it was meant to be teasing, over the years it became something a little . . . flirty. Which is where the true trouble began.

And now we 're staring at each other, the air between us crackling. My cheeks warm impossibly more, and I step back from him, even though there is already two metres of space between our bodies. No distance is enough when it comes to him. His presence feels like a physical touch, and his hold on me is stronger than my will.

'So. You're back,' I say, just to say something, and I desperately hope he can't hear how loudly my heart is hammering in my chest.

His lips tilt in the sexy way they always have. 'Obviously.'

'How was Mexico?' I turn towards him, following him out to the hall, certainly not looking at how tightly his shirt clings to his back muscles.

He throws a smirk over his shoulder. 'Looks like you've been keeping tabs on me, too.'

If only he knew I had to block all his stories from my social media so I couldn't see anything. I couldn't bear seeing his face and crying over it, like I had so many times. I never went as far as blocking him completely. That would have raised questions from my friends and family that I had no intention of answering.

'More like the only person Zayden likes to talk about more than himself is you,' I point out.

'Uh-huh.'

My eyes roam over those delicious arm muscles, down to the ass that's been burned into my memory for years. Yup. Still as good as ever.

'Unusual for you to be in on a Friday night, isn't it?' I ask, padding into the kitchen and dropping onto one of the bar stools.

'Stalker, much?'

'Get over yourself.'

Mason effortlessly moves around the kitchen. He flicks the kettle on, withdraws two mugs from one of the cabinets and leans back onto the kitchen bench.

'You're not . . .' I start, a slow smile spreading across my face. Since Mason was at our house every weekend throughout high school, he would go out of his way to cook or do something helpful around the house. I assume it was a thank-you to my family for always taking him in. He knew his way around a kitchen, and often added unique extra touches on simple meals, making them somehow taste ten times better. And his hot chocolate was to die for.

'Making you the Mason Special? Why, of course I am.'

'Since when are you nice to me?' I narrow my eyes suspiciously.

His eyes look a little brighter under the kitchen lights, which cast a golden glow over his skin and a shadow across the slight stubble that's growing across his jaw.

'Since you've had a fucking terrible time lately,' he replies, way more honestly than I expected. His gaze lingers on mine for a heartbeat too long. 'But just tonight. Game over from tomorrow.'

I breathe a forced laugh, tugging the sleeves of my jacket down over my hands before I bring them up to cup my cheeks. I hate the fact that they are still extremely warm despite the cold temperature.

Just seeing his face makes me miserable. I thought I would feel angrier than I do, but I just feel crappy. I hate what he did to me, and I hate even more that I can't let go of all the feelings I've been harbouring for him all my life. I don't want to feel anything, but that's impossible when it comes to him.

'Wouldn't expect anything less.'

It's silent for a moment between us. Only the sounds of metal clanging on the bench top and his footsteps as he moves across the tiled floor fill the room. I try everything I can not to stare at him.

'It was amazing, by the way.'

'Hmm?' I murmur, drawing myself out of my thoughts.

'Mexico.'

'Oh,' I reply, my eyes slowly trailing down his tanned forearms and those swirling dark tattoos. 'That's good. How long have you been back?'

'Almost a month.'

'Just in time for a vacant room, hey?' I say with a tight-lipped smile.

'I've always had great timing.'

Ugh. Ouch.

'I know Zayden and Leasa had been rocky for a while, but I still feel like the break-up happened so fast,' I say thought-fully, desperately trying to stop my mind from thinking back to everything that happened between us as he turns and slides a mug across the bench top. 'Seemed like she was just up and . . . gone.'

'Pretty much how it happened, by the sound of it.'

'You must be glad to get your sidekick back,' I tease, circling my hands around the cup and embracing the warmth of it, even though I feel cold and empty inside.

'Zay falls head over heels for every girl he meets. He's a useless wingman.' Mason grins lightly. 'I'm just glad he seems happier.'

I don't know why I said that. The last thing I want to think about or discuss is Zayden being Mason's wingman. The thought of Mason with anyone makes me want to empty my stomach.

'He is?' I ask, leaning forward. 'Happy?'

Mason considers this. 'Honestly? I'm not sure. I think this break-up has been good for him in a lot of ways. They were toxic for each other in the end. But, no, I'm not sure that he is happy, just happier than he was.'

'They were always toxic,' I agree with a dry smile. My brother and his girlfriend had a relationship that made no sense to me. Powerful and passionate, but a whirlwind of extreme highs and the lowest of lows. 'The way they would scream at each other gave me nightmares.' Bringing the mug up to my lips, I take a small sip. An explosion of warmth and flavour takes over my tongue and I moan, having missed what used to be a weekly tradition.

I'm surprised to see Mason's eyes travelling down my body as he watches me. The tension from two years ago feels as strong as ever. I want to be able to look at him and not think about every-thing we once were, but it's too difficult not to.

'I've missed this,' I whisper, breathing into the mug.

I honestly don't know if I mean the hot chocolate or him. Both, really. Mason was a huge part of my life and then suddenly he wasn't. The hole he left behind is still gaping, as much as I tried everything to fill it up.

'Me too, Blush.' He offers me a small, sad smile. 'Me too.'

He turns, disappearing from the kitchen.

2

MASON

SEEING ANYA APPEAR ON my doorstep was like seeing a ghost from my past. A ghost who has grown into the woman of my dreams. I can't get the image off my mind – her white t-shirt plastered to her body like a second skin, practically see-through from the rain. When my eyes stayed trained on her ass the entire thirteen stairs it took to get to the top floor, I had to chant: *she's Zay's little sister, she's Zay's little sister, she's Zay's little sister.*

But *damn*, Blush isn't a kid anymore. She hasn't been for a long time. I know that better than anyone.

I blink back at my reflection, wondering what it must be like for her seeing me after all this time. After what happened. My hands shake as I grip the sink and grapple to even out my breathing. After taking a moment to steady my racing pulse, I head back into the kitchen, tapping my fingers against my legs.

My stomach tenses as I see her, and the feelings of guilt invade me. Thinking about what I did makes me sick to my stomach. My heart drums unevenly in my chest as I brush past her, reaching for the sauce bottles that Zayden has left out, our arms briefly touching. I retract my arm and move away from her, back to the safety of the cupboard.

Anya and I always had an intense relationship. I loved to tease her; she made it so easy. And she loved me. Whole-heartedly.

I loved her too, but I was too much of a coward to commit to her. To be the person she needed. She is two years younger than me. An age difference that means nothing now, but seemed a much bigger deal when we were growing up.

Regret swirls in my gut. I was never one to feel much towards anyone: Zayden and Anya meant the world to me, but everyone else was simply background noise. After all the drama, I could never stay in one place long enough to settle down with anyone. But maybe that's the whole point. The one person I wanted is the one person I can't have. No one else compares in my mind, so I never bothered trying after that. Whenever I had a partner in the past they knew, or at least suspected, my feelings towards Anya. It's always been a problem.

She sits across from me, her pretty emerald eyes gazing out the window. Her long dark hair spills down her shoulders in thick waves. Anya was always a bubbly, chirpy girl. But not anymore. Her eyes are darkened with a pain I know all too well: heartbreak. That shit hurts, and the bastard very much overstays its welcome.

Dylan Peterson. He is the definition of a douchebag. I never really liked him, and I liked him a whole lot less when he started hunting after Anya. Zayden had a very strict 'hands off' policy when it came to friends dating his baby sister, which many guys at school learnt the hard way. Since Dylan is two years younger than us and not in the friend group, he got away with upgrading from 'friend' to 'boyfriend' status, much to everyone's displeasure. Mine the most. We weren't around in Anya's final years of school to safekeep her either, so he slid straight in.

No one was good enough for Anya. No one ever would be.

Seeing her crying tonight made the rage uncoil inside me and threaten to detonate any moment. In the past, I wouldn't need much of an excuse to split my knuckles across Dylan's face. I used to struggle with my control issues when it came to that kind of thing, but I've worked really hard on breaking the cycle.

I'm not my father.

Honestly, I'd love nothing more than to never see or hear about Dylan again, but unfortunately since he plays on one of our rival's teams, we often see him or verse him in a game. He's as dirty a player as he is a person. If I want to get him where it hurts, I need to beat him on the field, where it really matters.

Bliss Bay, the small coastal town we all grew up in has a competitive football team: the South West Stingrays. They're known for being aggressive and often not doing the right thing. They're not a team I would be comfortable playing on. When I came back from Mexico, I joined Zayden at Stratton University. The reason Zayden moved an hour north, closer to the city, was to play for their team: the North East Sharks. It's a tough team to get into, and I'm honoured I made the cut. It's been incredible training with them, they're a great team and I have a lot of respect for our coach. He has a brilliant record and with the way he has been running our training, I can see why that is. He works his team hard, but he gets results.

'Are you going to tell me what happened tonight?' I ask her, leaning my hip against the counter. I twist the end of my rubber bracelet, needing something to occupy my hands now that everything has been packed away. When I feel the end unravel, I quickly let go of it, and reach for my mug. Anya's gaze is on the bracelet. Swallowing, I look away, trying not to think about the day she gave it to me.

Moisture gathers in her eyes once more and my grip around the mug tightens.

'Maybe tomorrow,' she answers softly. 'I'm really tired.'

I point a finger in her direction. 'I'm holding you to that.'

When she drains the remaining liquid in her cup, I lean over, taking it from her. Our fingers brush and I jolt in surprise at the coldness of hers. I glare at the sink, unable to meet her eyes as I wash and dry the mugs, then pack them exactly where I got them from. I study the mugs for a moment, making sure they're perfectly facing the front before closing the cupboard.

Anya shakes her head at me, a smile dancing around her lips. 'You're getting worse with age.'

'You have no idea,' I reply playfully.

She turns away from me and I see her cheeks redden, the familiar blush making me smile. She stands, stretching her arms over her head, making the shirt she's wearing rise, showing me her tanned stomach. I swallow as my gaze brushes over her skin.

We move upstairs and this time, I make sure to go first. I don't need any excuse to be checking her out. When Anya slips inside the guest room, I gather a towel and hang it over the rack in the bathroom. We meet at the doorway of her room, and I lean into it. I rub my hand across my jaw. I've been working on my coping habits for when I'm feeling anxious, but it feels like everything has completely unravelled now I'm back here with her.

'There's a fresh towel in the bathroom for you,' I say, quietly watching her as she wanders around the room, looking like a little lost lamb. My heart aches to comfort her, but too much has happened, and too much time has passed.

'Thanks.'

'Hey, Blush?' I say, striding over to her and placing a finger under her chin, forcing her sad round eyes to look at mine. 'We won't let them get away with this.'

3

ANYA

Three Years Ago

MY BEST FRIEND HUFFS beside me, drawing me out of my sleep. I blink groggily. We're sunbathing by the pool, and I must have drifted off at some point. Phoebe pushes to a seated position, stretching her long arms out in front of her. Her skin is tanned and smooth, and her hair so streaked from the sun, it looks like she's had highlights. She has the most startling blue eyes I have ever seen, and they're intimidating as hell when aimed in my direction.

'You have the best life,' she says, and I can't quite decipher her tone as she lowers her sunglasses, eyes skimming across the backyard before sliding them back up.

'I do?' I question, reaching for the iced latte perched at my side. The condensation has left a perfect ring on my towel. I bring it to my mouth and take a long sip. It's bordering on undrinkable, but I still enjoy it.

'Look at this pool. This house.' She gestures her hands in front of her. 'And, like, you hang out with the two hottest boys in school, and no one will ever give you shit because of that.'

'One of those is my brother,' I point out, wrinkling my nose.

'So? It doesn't change my point.'

'I am very grateful for what I have. You have a nice place too. You and your mum are literally best friends. Not many people can say that.'

'We live in a cramped two-bedroom apartment.' She scowls, lying back onto her elbows. 'Far from *nice*.'

Phoebe and I have different understandings of what makes a home nice, but I don't have the energy to argue with her. She argues just for the sake of arguing, I'm sure of it. Besides, we only have this house because my stepfather owns it. Before my mum was with him, we lived on the South Side, known for being the worst part of town, in a house that was falling apart around us.

I tap on my phone and the screen brightens. I glance at the time.

'I gotta go,' I say, practically leaping to my feet.

'Of course you do,' she says, and a look crosses her face that makes me pause for a moment. She shoots me a teasing smile, and I relax, wondering if I imagined seeing something.

'I did tell you I had plans before you invited yourself over.'

'Yeah, yeah.' She exhales, flopping onto the towel. 'I'll still be here when you get back.'

'Okay,' I reply. 'I'll bring us back some iced coffees.'

'Appreciate you.'

Making an excuse to get out of the house, to spend time with Mason, was fairly easy. Considering I spend most of my time reading or studying at the library, everyone is used to me being out. And he is often at work – conveniently located just up the road – so getting alone time together isn't much of an issue.

'Hello, Anya,' Mrs. Taylor greets me, her warm smile prompting one from me. Deep wrinkles border her eyes and the corners of her mouth. She is dressed in a fuchsia top with matching earrings and lipstick. Her wardrobe must be an entire rainbow with the vibrant colours she always wears.

'Hi, Mrs. Taylor.'

'You have some books to return?' she asks, putting down the book in her hand. Nodding, I shrug off my bag, and pull out the three I borrowed last week. She peers at me over her half-moon spectacles, giving me a pointed look. 'You have that young gentleman waiting for you at the back.'

A wide grin breaks through and I duck my chin, trying not to show my reaction, even though it's too late. 'Oh?'

'Mmhmm,' she hums, eyebrows raised. 'That boy never sets foot in here unless you're around, you know.'

My cheeks are flaming red as I step back and try to shield them with my hair. 'I'll be back soon. With more books.'

'I don't doubt it.' She smiles, her gaze burning holes in my forehead. 'Off you go. Behave.'

I basically trip over my own feet as I rush down the aisles, towards the right-hand corner of the library. My heart stumbles in my chest when I see Mason's long frame come into view. His messy hair is hidden with a black, backwards cap. He's dressed in the plain black clothing he wears to work. With the afternoon sunlight filtering through the blinds, his tall, muscular body perfectly proportioned and a book in his hand, he looks soft and casual, which is my favourite look on him. He gazes down at the book with a relaxed, unguarded expression, the usual tension in his shoulders momentarily gone. I wish I could frame this moment and hang it up on my bedroom wall. He is so damn attractive; I can barely function when I'm around him. I love that I get to see this side of him; I'm almost positive no one else does.

'Good book?' I question, leaning against the shelf, trying to appear nonchalant and most likely failing.

Grinning, he snaps the book shut. His eyes drag slowly over my legs, up my torso, before settling on my eyes.

'Yes, actually.' He takes a step towards me, and my heart thumps loudly in my ears. He holds the book out, and when I take it, his thumb runs up the length of mine. We're both single right now, and the tension between us is palpable. We have been fighting this pull between us – or at least he has been – but it's getting harder and harder to ignore. I don't want to ignore it. Not anymore. 'I read it and it made me think of you.' His fingers trail up my arm, and I shiver at the touch. He leans closer, and I breathe him in.

'What's it about?' I murmur, eyes fluttering closed as he inches towards me.

His lips move to my ear, and his warm breath brushes against my earlobe.

'A boy who falls for a girl he isn't supposed to,' he whispers, and I release a shaky exhale. 'But inevitably, they can't avoid falling in love.'

Swallowing, I keep my eyes closed, breathing hard. 'It sounds like a good read. Does it have a happy ending?'

He cups my right cheek in his hand, and I lean into it. He lightly presses his lips to my left cheek. He trails soft, lingering kisses across it, over my nose, and onto the other cheek. He loves doing that. Kissing my freckles.

'Yes, Blush,' he whispers, causing goosebumps to scatter over my entire body. 'It does.'

4

ANYA

THE SOUND OF FOOTSTEPS down the hallway stirs me awake. I yawn, rubbing my eyes and glancing at my phone, seeing that it's only 6 a.m. Someone walks past my room again, heading in the opposite direction, then there's a soft humming of pipes.

My brother never wakes this early, so it must be Mason. I'm not sure Zayden is even home yet. I lie in bed for a few minutes, trying to convince myself to get up. With a sigh, I throw off my blankets, the chilly morning air biting the exposed skin on my legs.

With another yawn, I shuffle out of the room. I run into something hard. And wet. I stumble back, and a strong grip prevents me from toppling over. I stare at a bare, muscled chest with water glistening across it before eventually moving up to meet the brutal intensity of Mason's eyes as he stares down at me.

'Good morning,' I whisper.

'Morning, Blush,' he says, lips curving into something that is halfway between a smirk and a smile, his voice raspy with sleep.

My skin warms under his hands. I wonder if this sizzling tension will ever let up. It makes even the simplest encounter feel like I've stuck my finger into a power socket.

'You're up early,' I observe, feeling heat rise up my neck because his hands are still on me, burning my skin. I haven't had this sort of a reaction to a guy in . . . well . . . ever. It's only ever been him.

'I'm always up early.' He releases me, stepping back and gripping his towel, which has slipped a little. I try hard not to stare at the prominent v-line between his hips and the hard muscles covering his torso. I curse myself when my eyes skim over his stomach and down to the bulge that his towel is covering.

I step to the left at the same time he does. Awkwardly, I step right. So does he. He reaches out again, spinning me so we swap places. He smirks at me before turning and strolling down the hall. My cheeks are on fire and I groan quietly, quickly rushing down the stairs just so I can breathe again.

After using the downstairs bathroom to freshen up, I gravitate to the kitchen to make coffee and breakfast. I'm absently licking Vegemite off a knife when Mason appears.

'That is a terrible habit,' he mutters in disgust, actually looking repulsed as he shakes his head, his dark hair falling across his forehead. 'You and your brother are so alike.'

'Sorry, Dad.'

Mason eyes me for a moment, then bumps me out of the way with his hip so he can make a coffee. It's such a familiar gesture that he's made countless times, but something I haven't experienced for so long, it makes tears randomly spring to my eyes. Blinking them away, I move out of the kitchen and take a seat in the lounge room. I feel as if I'm teetering on the edge of a breakdown and the tiniest thing will send me spiralling.

I watch his large hands make coffee. The last time I saw Mason was two years ago when he turned up with my brother for my eighteenth birthday.

Flashes of the night whirl around my mind. Drinking, dancing, his hands on my body, sliding underneath my dress and up my sides when no one was watching. We had been flirting on the line of danger for a long time. It had become obvious to everyone, including the girl he was dating at the time, even though neither of us would have ever cheated.

I can almost feel his hands on my thighs, travelling up them . . .

'What's going on in that pretty head of yours?' Mason asks, turning to face me. He raises a mug to his lips, peering over at me.

'Thinking about my eighteenth birthday.'

Mason chokes on his coffee. I coolly watch him turn a shade of dark red as he splutters, the hot liquid sloshing over the side of the mug. He hisses when some of it lands on him. He hurries to get his hand under the tap, clearing his throat awkwardly.

'You never reached out to me,' I continue after he finally gains his composure. 'You just left.'

He places his cup down and flattens his hands on the bench-top. He bows his head. Silence stretches between us, making the air thick, and it feels hard to breathe. I'm not sure I can do this. I've had enough heartache in the past few years to last me a lifetime. I don't need this.

And then the door opens.

'Anya!'

I drag my gaze from the man before me and a genuine grin takes over my face when I see my brother. I stumble to my feet and launch myself at him. He spins me around, hugging me so tight I fear a rib might crack.

'Hi!' I beam at him, reaching up and tousling his hair. 'You need a haircut.'

He reaches out, pinching the skin on my bicep with his pointer finger and thumb. 'You need to eat more.'

Since the break-up with Dylan and Phoebe, I've shed a few kilos. I've always been the same weight, never able to lose any with exercise or a change of diet, and yet in the past few weeks the weight has fallen off me.

'Who knew heartbreak was a great way to diet?' I say dryly. I wasn't in love with Dylan, as much as I tried to be, but the heartbreak of losing my friend feels as sharp as the pointy end of a knife.

The smile slips from his mouth, twisting into an angry snarl. I knew he would be beating himself up over this. He tried his best to prevent this very thing from happening. He has always been overprotective and, honestly, with some of his friends he had good reason to be. As much of a nuisance as it was at times, I've never despised him for it.

I softly squeeze his shoulder. 'It's okay, big bro. You can't protect me from everything.'

'I can still rearrange his face.' He scowls.

'I'll hold him down,' Mason interjects from somewhere behind me.

'It's settled, then,' my brother replies, turning to look at Mason.

Rolling my eyes, I step back, folding my arms. 'That's enough about all of that. I don't want to talk about him anymore. I just want to move on from it.'

'We'll see about that,' Zayden mutters under his breath, and I choose to ignore the comment. 'So, what happened with the share house?'

Exhaling noisily, I backtrack to the kitchen and drop into the bench seat as I give a quick recap. My brother's brows draw together as he listens. He lowers his sports bag to the ground; his white shirt is stained with dirt and mud – he must have been out playing football. That is the only reason my brother would get out of bed before nine.

Both Mason and my brother have always played. My brother is madly obsessed with it. He spends every spare moment he has practising, whereas Mason only goes to the scheduled trainings, unless my brother convinces him to do extra with him. Or at least, that's how it used to be. They're both exceptional players, but Mason is a bit more of a natural, which I think is why Zayden tries extra hard to keep up, to prove he is just as good.

'Again,' I repeat, eyeing my brother, whose expression is now looking particularly murderous. 'It's done now, I just need to move on.' He doesn't even know half of what Dylan has done to me recently. He would be out the door in the next second if he did. Especially about the money Dylan stole, but I'm going to try my best not to let that one slip.

A muscle jumps in Zayden's cheek, but he nods. 'It won't be done until my fist is in his face.'

Again, I ignore the comment. 'Would you mind if I crash here until I can find another place? I'll get out as quickly as I can. I just need . . . money. And a job. And some friends who don't sneak around behind my back with my boyfriend.' I let out a hysterical laugh and then groan, rubbing my face roughly, pressing my fingers into my eyes, as if pressing hard enough will force the tears escaping to go back in. 'My life is a disaster.'

'Stay as long as you need,' Zayden replies. I peer through the gaps in my fingers and he offers me a lazy, one-shoulder shrug. 'Or stay permanently. There's plenty of space and the rent would be even cheaper divided by three. Same with the utilities.'

I raise an eyebrow and glance at Mason, studying his reaction. He's staring at my brother with a serious expression, like he's thinking hard about something. I can't tell if he loves the idea or hates it. Possibly a mixture of both, considering that's exactly how I'm feeling.

'You don't mind, right?' Zayden asks, turning back to Mason. I'm not sure how he misses the tension between the two of us, but I suppose it's always been there. He is either totally oblivious or refuses to acknowledge it, since he assumes neither of us would ever act on our feelings. And we certainly shouldn't have . . .

'Not at all,' Mason replies smoothly, his voice deep and still a little raspy, which I have always loved. The best part of my day used to be his hoarse 'good morning, Blush' when I ran into him in the hallway. I remember how I sometimes dared to wear a skimpy night dress – I loved the way his eyes travelled over every inch of me whenever he saw me in it.

The tension between Mason and me is suffocating, and my stomach is in total knots. I twist the ring on my finger, trying to keep my breathing even. Mason's eyes track the movement, and my skin prickles with awareness. He was the one who bought it for me. I wanted to take it off, throw it out and pretend it meant nothing. But I couldn't. I could never let it go.

'I don't have a job I can offer you, but I can help in the friends department. Let's go to the university bar. We can meet and mingle with people. It'll be a good distraction,' Zayden says.

I refocus on what he is saying, since as usual, my mind has wandered off down Mason-lane. My brother and Mason have always been big on the party life, but they used to keep that side of themselves separate from me – I was always the 'younger sister'. Things have changed now, though, and it's nice to be included.

Perking up, I smile at them both. Going out and distracting myself seems like the perfect thing right now.

'Count me in!'

5

MASON

FLICKING ON MY LIGHT as the sky darkens, I run my hand through my hair, making it a little messy, but not too unkempt. I'm dressed in all black, with the sleeves of my shirt rolled up to my elbows. Finishing the drink I poured earlier, I make my way down to the kitchen for another. The price of a drink at a club is through the roof now, and the more we can pre-drink at home, the better.

I've lined up two rows of shots when Zayden trots into the kitchen. Dressed in a light-blue shirt – which I actually think is mine, as Zayden has taken all my coloured shirts, claiming I never wear anything but black – and with his hair combed back, he looks neat for once. His hair is a dirty blond, almost brown now, and so long he has to sweep it off his forehead all the time.

'Is that hair gel?' I raise an eyebrow.

'Mmhmm.' He nods, striking a pose. 'You like?'

'Sure.' I shrug, grinning at my best friend. 'Looks good.'

'You too, brother.' Glancing down at his watch, he sighs, calling up the stairs to Anya, telling her to hurry up.

I tap my fingers against the kitchen bench. I shouldn't be nervous. This is what Zayden and I always do – drink, party, go out. It just feels different with Anya here. After everything that happened when I was overseas, I want nothing more than to focus on school and get my head straight. The last thing I need is a distraction, and she is one gigantic distraction.

A few minutes later, I hear the distinct click of her heels descending the stairs before she saunters into the kitchen. My heart drops to my feet as I pause, my drink stopping midway from the bench to my mouth as I gape at her.

She looks stunning. And way too fuckable. Internally groaning, I track my gaze down her slender neck, curvy figure, and legs that run a kilometre long. She's dressed in a high-neck, figure-hugging white dress that leaves little to the imagination. She has always been pretty. And off-limits. But we're older now and it feels . . . different.

'You scrub up alright,' Zayden says casually over his shoulder. 'Let's do shots!'

She smiles warmly at her brother in that easy, affectionate way siblings who are on good terms share. When those doe eyes turn to meet mine, I realise every thought in my head is splattered across my face like a canvas. A smile tugs at her lips when she realises the effect she has on me. There is no point in denying it, the chemistry we have is off the charts. It always has been. Everything inside me tightens and I reluctantly drag my eyes from her.

Zayden shoves the shot into my hand and the other into his sister's.

'Cheers!' he shouts, and I throw it back. It burns every inch of my throat. Anya grimaces, and Zayden laughs at her expression, handing her another one.

Warmth spreads through my body and I feel my muscles start to relax. Me, drunk, and in close quarters with Anya, is a recipe for disaster. Flashbacks of her eighteenth slam into my mind and I feel dizzy for a moment, but I shove down all thoughts of that night and snap back to reality when Zayden launches a paper coaster at my head. I scowl, shoving the drink beside me onto it.

I'm the one who is always on his case about using them, but I was so distracted, I had forgotten.

'Another?' Zayden grins.

Bad idea.

In fact, it's a terrible idea.

'Pour it.'

After bar hopping for two hours, we end up at The Beach Club – by far the most popular club in the area. We used to drive an hour from our hometown just to come to this place. We would make a weekend of it: stay in a fancy hotel, spend the day surfing and drink way into the night.

The last few years have been a complete blur. A nostalgic feeling settles in my chest as I wade through the sweaty bodies. The music thumps so vigorously I can feel it under my skin. I did so much of this over the years, trying to rid her from my system. It worked, for a little while, but the booze and the blackout nights got old quickly.

Zayden yells something incoherent over his shoulder and dives towards a now-empty booth at the back of the club. I look behind me to see a tall man step in front of Anya, a leering smile etched onto his face.

Gritting my molars, I weave around him and slide my fingers through hers, pulling her after me. She lets out a squeak as I pull harder than I meant to, making her launch into me. The heat from her body seeps into mine and I rest my hands on her hips to steady her.

'You good, Blush?' I ask her. She feels small and fragile in my arms.

Looking up through long lashes, she steadily meets my gaze. 'Yes. Thank you.'

This is the moment where I'm supposed to step away. Her eyes drift down to my lips, and mine immediately move to hers. My thumb strokes her side, as if it has a mind of its own. She draws her bottom lip between her teeth, and I groan.

'You look beautiful tonight,' I murmur.

Even in the dimly lit room, I see her cheeks darken. 'There you go, being nice again.'

'Don't get used to it,' I tease, involuntarily tightening my grip on her.

'I won't. You generally don't stick around long enough to follow through.'

I step back as if she physically slapped me. She pushes my hands off her hips and continues trailing through the crowd. I stare after her for a few moments, shocked at her words, even though I shouldn't be.

Sighing, I follow her. She's seated beside Zayden at a small table littered with empty glasses.

'I'll get us a round of drinks,' I say, mainly to avoid sitting down beside her right after that awkward moment we just shared.

I wait in line for ten minutes before I get served. Placing the tray down back at the table, I hand the drinks to Zayden and Anya. I sit down beside her. Her bare thigh brushes my leg, and she angles her body to lean away from me. A muscle in my cheek jumps. I don't know why her attitude is bothering me so much.

Because she has always chased you, and now she isn't. And you don't like it.

Ignoring the annoying voice in my head, I throw my drink back. I'm starting to feel the effects of the alcohol taking place now and I welcome the warm, floaty feeling with open arms.

'Feeling any better?' Zayden asks, turning to face his sister.

They look alike. Same emerald-green eyes, with a dusting of freckles across their noses. Zayden's hair is lighter than Anya's, streaked blond from too many hours out in the sun. He towers above her, though.

I glance somewhere over her shoulder, finding it difficult to remain focused on her words and not get distracted by how incredible she looks. She was always pretty, but now . . . she's beautiful. *Very* beautiful.

'Yeah, this is a nice distraction.' She twists the straw between her fingers and smiles, although it's not quite meeting her eyes.

'Good.' He grins, not noticing the tension in her shoulders. Zayden is carefree and relaxed, with an easy smile on his face as he scans the room. I've been worried about him, but he is handling the break-up better than I expected him to. Although some days are better than others. 'This is the perfect place to get lost in for a while.'

'I have been here before, you know,' she points out.

'I'm ignoring that fact because in my mind you're still my sweet, innocent little sister who has never done anything I have done.'

Little does he know.

She laughs. It's soft and warm, unchanged since we were kids. 'Sure. You keep thinking that, big bro.'

'I can and I will.'

'How are you going with everything?' Anya asks softly, and I struggle to hear her over the music. 'With Leasa leaving?'

Zayden leans back. 'I miss her. A lot. I know breaking up was the right thing to do, but she was always there. Every day. Now she's just . . . gone. And we don't speak.' He shakes his head for a moment. 'She would send me engagement rings that she liked, and now we don't even follow each other on social media. It's kind of . . . wild how fast it all happened.'

'Break-ups are awful,' she says, offering him a sympathetic look. 'I'm sorry.'

He shrugs. 'It's whatever. We are going to be much happier. The both of us.'

'I hope so,' she says with a sad smile. 'Have you spoken to Mum at all? She's on my case about never hearing from you.' She wraps her lips around the straw and I gulp, looking away for a moment until I see her put the glass back down and rest her hands in her lap.

The teasing grin Zayden was wearing drops from his face, and he fidgets with his drink. My jaw clenches. I hate that I know the reason and she doesn't, but when Zayden confided in me I promised I would never breathe a word of it to anyone. We all promised each other there'd never be secrets between us, and yet we all break the rules sometimes.

'No.'

Anya opens her mouth to ask more, but Zayden raises his hand in a 'stop' signal.

'We're having fun tonight. And that topic is not an option.' His voice is firm, leaving no room for negotiation.

'Okay. Fair.' She relents – a little too easily in my opinion, but she is probably aware this is not the right time or place to be delving into such topics – and leans back in the seat. I absolutely don't notice the way the dress inches up her thigh. 'But I will be revisiting this.'

'Sure,' he retorts sarcastically. 'Can't wait.'

'Are you excited to be back on campus tomorrow?' she asks, and I scoot a little further down the booth, accepting the fact that she doesn't want to include me in this conversation. She hasn't seen her brother for a while, so I understand. It's my fault there's tension between us. I just wish we could go back to being friends like we used to be. There haven't been many people in my life who I've had effortless conversations with and felt completely at ease around, like I have with Zayden and Anya. I miss our hang outs.

Zayden twists his face into a frown. 'Classes don't start until Monday.'

'Yeah, but we have all the intro stuff.'

'I'm not going to that. I'm already playing football; I don't need anything extra added to my schedule. And I don't need any more friends.' Zayden glances at me with a cocky grin. 'Already got too many of them.'

I give him the middle finger and he grins.

'Whatever,' she says.

'Whatever,' he mimics. Looking over her head at me, he gives me a nod. 'I'll get this round.'

I'm feeling light-headed from the last one, but I don't discourage him. The amount we are drinking is tame compared to what we used to drink when we were first legally able to go out partying.

The overcrowded club is already hard to breathe in, and I struggle even more when I finally let myself look at Anya again. She is staring right back now that it's just the two of us.

'So, how was your gap year?' I ask. 'Well. *Years*, technically.'

She exhales. 'Tried to become an artist and discovered it's much harder than I thought.'

'Your paintings are incredible.'

'Not enough, apparently.'

'What do you mean by that?' I query, genuinely curious.

'No one wanted to put my art in their shows. I finally managed to get my paintings into the local markets, but I hardly sold anything.'

'Don't give up yet. This kind of thing takes time.'

She is silent as she gazes at me, looking tense. It seems I don't know how to talk to her properly anymore. Our conversations feel stilted and awkward, as if I'm not saying the right thing. That's never been a problem before.

'So, you're studying some sort of art major, I'm guessing?'

She nods. 'Yeah. A Bachelor of Fine Arts.' She swirls the liquid around her glass, eyes glued to it.

'Are you excited to start classes?' I ask her, just to say *something*.

'Yeah,' she replies, leaning forward and resting her arm over her knee. 'I can't wait for a fresh start.'

'Me too.'

She stills, narrowing her eyes. 'What do you mean?'

The corner of my mouth twitches and I lean forward, mirroring her position, placing our faces close to each other as I rest my arms onto my knees. She glances down at them. She once told me how much she loves tattoos, and since then I have been inking myself more and more. 'I enrolled at Stratton too.'

She blinks. 'You did?'

'I did.'

'Are you studying Exercise Science?'

My heart skips a beat at her casual question. She already knows what I want to study, despite us not talking for so long.

She remembers.

'Yeah,' I reply. 'I am.'

'That's good,' she says softly. 'You always wanted to do that.'

My heart is beating fast and I drag my eyes away from her, needing a moment to catch my breath and calm down. She makes me feel all over the place.

'And since you travelled . . .' she trails off, the crease in her forehead deepening as she puts two and two together. 'This will be your first year.'

'You're good at this.' I nod encouragingly, leaning even further forward and giving her a sarcastic grin.

Rolling her eyes, she takes a long sip of her drink. 'Therefore, we might be in some of the intro classes together.'

'Potentially, yes.'

'Great.' She forces a smile onto her face, as if the thought of sharing classes with me is the worst news she's heard all day. Maybe it is.

'Excellent.'

'Superb,' she counters.

'Swell.'

She snorts a laugh, which makes me laugh too. She has always done that.

'Since we're now roommates *and* classmates, we can carpool and study together,' I suggest with a flirty wink.

'You mean I would tutor you?' she asks sweetly, not missing a beat. She places her lips around her straw while maintaining eye contact with me.

Swallowing, I shift as the blood rushes to my groin almost uncomfortably. No girl has ever affected me the way she does and it's maddening.

'You wish, Blush. I could ace every test without attending a single lecture.'

She scoffs, shaking her glossy hair over her shoulder. I would do anything to be able to run my fingers through it one more time, holding her to me.

If only things were different.

'Whatever helps you sleep at night, party boy.'

'I sleep very well, thank you very much.'

'I'm sure you do. No thoughts in that small brain of yours to keep you up.' She sighs theatrically.

Grinning, I lean forward, so close I can see the freckles dotted across her nose and feel the heat of her breath fanning across my lips. 'Don't tell me my intelligence isn't a turn on to you, Blush. I seem to remember a very detailed journal entry—'

She squeals, smacking my arm and turning beetroot red. 'Oh my God!' Sinking back into her seat, she covers her face. 'You're such an asshole.'

Smirking, I lean back. 'Checkmate.'

'Fuck you.' She pouts.

'If you want.'

Her fingers open and she peers through the gaps. She slowly lowers her hands, staring at me for a moment. The cocky grin drifts off my face when the seriousness of our past presses heavily between us once more.

I hate this.

Her gaze shifts over my head and she pales, ducking quickly.

'Shit,' she half groans.

'What?' I ask, looking over to see Dylan striding in with Anya's ex-best friend. The very one he cheated on her with. Seeing him strut into a club, showing off his other woman, makes my blood boil and leaves a bad taste in my mouth. A slow, calm smile stretches over my lips and I lean close to her, latching my focus onto those soft emerald eyes I love so much.

'Be right back. I'm going to commit murder,' I say.

'Don't! Let's just go.'

'No way.'

'I can't have him see me here single and alone!'

'Am I invisible?' I raise an eyebrow.

'He's going to know I'm not *with* you,' she says with a groan, sinking even lower into the leather seat.

'How would he know that?' I counter, my stomach tightening at the thought of what I'm about to suggest.

'Hmm?' she asks, looking up at me.

'How would he know we aren't together?'

'Because you're Zayden's best friend.'

'But everyone has always noticed this.' I wave my hand between us. 'Every partner we've ever had, in fact. All our friends at school. Even our families.'

She looks surprised that I openly admit to this.

'You can't deny it,' I continue, and when I shift in my seat, my knee presses against hers.

'I'm not,' she says slowly, eyes darting to where our legs are touching. That's something neither of us can deny. The effect we have on each other is unmatched.

'Come on, then,' I say persuasively, tilting my lips into a smirk. 'Let's dance.'

'Zayden is here.'

Using my chin, I point in the direction of the back corner, where Zayden has his tongue down the throat of a blonde. Anya screws her face up, probably not having realised it's been a while since he left the table. My heart hurts for Zayden. He is desperate to forget his ex, and he thinks distracting himself with girls and booze is going to help. I hope it does, but I know it's like sticking a Band-Aid over a gaping wound. I know that more than anyone.

'I don't know about this,' she says, doubt clouding her face as she chews her lip, looking anxious. I hate that Dylan makes her feel like this. I can see the damage he has done, and it makes me livid.

Perhaps you're so angry he hurt her because you did too.

'Come on.' I grin, nudging her with my elbow. 'If you're not going to let me punch him, this is second best.'

She eyes me for a moment. I see the gears in her mind turning. Relenting, she shrugs and places her hand into my open palm. I pull her to her feet, wrapping my arm around her without a second thought. Holding her so close, her scent washing over me, feels so right. My heart skips a beat in my chest. Her scent, her presence, her touch – they're all much more intoxicating than the drinks I've been downing all night.

I see Dylan out of the corner of my eye. He stops suddenly, clearly seeing us, but I don't let on that we know he is here. Leading Anya to the dance floor, I step back and twirl her around.

She throws her head back and laughs. The neon lights splash across her skin, and heat spreads up my neck with every move she makes. Anya looks free and completely at ease as she dances, moving slowly and sensually.

She throws her arms over my shoulders, and I yank her closer, so close our noses graze. Her eyes lock on to mine, and a thrill shoots through my body. I've been numb for years, blocking out memories of her, and now they're all rushing back in full force.

She exhales, her warm breath blowing over my lips. I lean in, pressing her forehead to mine. She is warm, soft, and feels perfect in my hands. I have no idea what spell she has me under, but I'm drowning in it and, honestly, I don't care to be saved.

'You're a good actor,' she whispers.

I drag her closer, leaving zero distance between us. 'I'm not acting.'

My hands roam over her in ways they shouldn't. With every moment that passes a new fire ignites somewhere inside my body. I swear under my breath in longing, pressing her body to mine. I want to kiss her more than I have ever wanted anything.

For a few seconds, I completely forget about anyone else around us. My hands slide down the sides of her body and grip the ass that has been taunting me all night. I give her a sharp squeeze, earning a delicious moan from her.

Clearly, I have no fucking self-control around her. Considering how much I usually have, I should be shocked that it slipped so hard and fast. But if I'm honest, it really isn't a surprise. The alcohol has me buzzing. Light, careless, brainless.

Then suddenly, we are yanked apart, and Anya lets out an alarmed yelp. Dylan glares at her. She stares angrily back at him before he spins quickly, and a fist flies towards my face. Years of gruelling football games and training have thankfully taught me to react quickly.

So has being raised by my father.

I dance out of the way lightly, feeling the wind on my face as his fist soars past me. 'You missed.' I smirk, simply because I can't help myself.

'I always knew there was something between you two,' Dylan spits, his cheeks red, eyes glossy. Sweat beads across his forehead, and I wonder if he has taken something more than just alcohol tonight. It wouldn't surprise me; he used to deal back in school. Not that I think he ever told Anya that.

'You were right. For once.'

'Fuck you,' he growls, pushing my chest roughly.

I stay standing where I am, glancing down at his hands on me. My fingers twitch, the urge to react a delicious temptation, but I swallow it down. I am not him. I will never be *him*.

'If you actually cared for Anya, you wouldn't have done what you did.' Stepping back, I let my hands fall to my side.

Dylan's upper lip pinches into a sneer and he lunges at me. A hard shove throws me back and I stumble as Zayden moves in front of me. He thrusts his elbow in an upswing motion, connecting with Dylan's jaw. He yelps in pain, stumbling back and crashing to the ground. A few girls scream and dart out of the way just in time.

Dylan glares up at us, blood pooling in the corner of his mouth.

'That'll be the last time you ever lay a hand on Mason,' Zayden tells him in a low voice. 'And this is for Anya.' Slamming his foot down, he crunches his heel into Dylan's stomach. Dylan roars in pain, but the music drowns it out. I see the security guards rushing our way and I reach for Anya's hand automatically, pulling her close.

Adrenaline washes through me like a tidal wave, and I love the familiar zing it brings. Considering everything I've been through,

I know violence isn't the way to solve anything, but I can't deny it feels fucking good to see his blood right now. He makes me so angry I can barely think straight.

'We gotta go,' I say to Zayden. He turns, a wicked grin lighting up his face.

We push through the crowd and Zayden reaches out, grabbing some random girl's drink and sculling it. She shouts in protest, and he tosses it over his shoulders, whooping with glee as we fall through the door, laughing wildly.

Zayden has always been a wild one. We both had some issues with anger in the past, and I've dedicated a lot of time and energy to working on them, but Zayden still seems to be stuck in his ways.

I knew I needed help after one distinct incident. I got in a fight with a player from a rival team in a game a few years ago, when we still played for our home town. He made a comment about Anya to me, knowing it would rile me up. Everyone could tell there was something between us, even though I was determined to quash those rumours as best I could. When I tried walking away, he tackled me really hard – an illegal tackle – and I just lost it. I blacked out momentarily, and when I realised what I was doing, people were screaming. Blood soaked my hands and the grass around us. When I looked up and saw the fear in the onlookers' faces, I felt sick to my stomach. Because I was just like him. My father.

I never want to feel like that again.

I remember Zayden's face when I met his gaze . . . it will haunt me forever. He looked so disappointed in me, despite his own battles with self-control. He didn't have to say anything, but I knew exactly what he was thinking.

You look just like him.

Playing football means being among high-level tension and mind-consuming competitiveness, so it's a given that fights break out, but I've never raised a hand since. It was the wake-up call I needed.

We sprint down the street, passing people who stare at us in shock. When we are finally free we slow to a stop, leaning on the wall of a bakery, unable to catch our breath from laughing so much.

'That must have felt so good!' Anya says.

'Been wanting to do that for years.' Zayden grins, breathless.

'The look on his face!' Anya exclaims, wiping her eyes. 'It's imprinted in my brain now.'

My eyes drift to Zayden for a moment. I'm positive he didn't see us dancing, otherwise this night would be going in a very different direction. He has always been overprotective of Anya, taking on a father-like role, as their dad hasn't been around since they were young children – their stepfather not counting. But when it comes to me around her, he is *especially* overprotective.

'Hey!' someone bellows, and the three of us exchange quick glances before running off again. We dive into the first taxi we see in a tangle of limbs, hair and Anya's handbag, which smacks me in the face.

'Go!' Zayden yells at the poor man trying to eat his sandwich.

He jumps in fright and quickly starts the car. It jolts forward and I fly into the back of the seat, my head connecting painfully with the leather headrest.

'Ow,' I mutter, leaning back and rubbing my head.

'I can't believe Dylan dropped like that.' Anya laughs so hard a whistle escapes her nose, making me laugh too.

'He folded like a lawn chair!' Zayden calls from the front, and the driver winces at his volume.

We erupt into more laughter and the taxi driver frowns at us, his bushy grey eyebrows bunching together to form one. He doesn't seem too impressed with our behaviour, but the more we try to stop laughing, the harder it gets. Zayden slaps money into his hand once we stop in front of the house. He glowers at us as we climb out, muttering under his breath. I'm glad it wasn't an Uber, otherwise he would have given us a bad rating.

As we walk up the path, Zayden throws his arms around our shoulders.

'Always a good night with my two best friends,' he sings. He stumbles into me, almost knocking all three of us over in the process, but I manage to right us again. He gives us a wobbly smile. 'Love you guys.'

I reach out, ruffling his hair. 'Right back at you, bud.'

When we make it inside, Zayden walks two steps before collapsing onto the lounge. I go to help him and realise my own movements are a bit wonky. I give him a quick once-over and confirm he's okay, then make my way up to my room.

Turning, I go to talk to Anya, but she is already gone.

An hour later, Zayden is passed out face-first on the lounge and I am sitting on the kitchen bench, handfeeding myself cereal. Anya wanders into the kitchen, dressed in a hoodie and sleep shorts.

'Well, that was a good time,' I say, leaning back on my free hand.

Rolling her lips into her mouth, she leans against the counter. I offer her the box and she takes a handful. Now that we're semi-sober, the reality of tonight is starting to sink in.

'Thank you,' she murmurs. 'For what you did.'

My eyes sweep over her rosy cheeks to the pretty freckles that I love, then up to those round eyes.

'Any time, Blush.'

The corner of her mouth tilts up. She peers over at her brother, rolling her eyes. 'He'll have a sore head tomorrow.'

'Definitely.'

There's silence between us for a few moments, and I'm a little sad that what happened tonight hasn't really made things easier for me, regarding my feelings towards her and the tension between us.

Tucking her hair behind her ear, she doesn't meet my gaze as she turns.

'Night, Mason.'

'Goodnight, Blush.'

6

MASON

Three Years Ago

IT'S BEEN A SCORCHING hot day. Rubbing my eyes, I drag my feet along the pavement that leads to my house. No lights are on, but a flicker coming from the living-room window has me pausing. I listen, trying to gauge what is going on inside. Dread fills me at the thought of going in. After a long shift at work, then a gruelling practice, I feel dead on my feet.

Crashing at friends' houses works out most of the time, but right now I'm down to no clean clothes. I've been saving madly for my overseas trip, which means I've been stuck living at home far longer than I ever wanted to. But I work all day, every day, and my savings have been climbing. I'm close to getting the fuck out of here.

Round, green eyes appear in my mind, and my heart splinters at the thought of leaving Anya and Zayden. They have been such a big part of my life; I honestly have no clue what it would look like without them in it. I'm not planning to go away forever, but long enough that their absence is going to hit me hard. Zayden and I do everything together. And I mean *everything*. If I'm not with Zayden, I'm with Anya. If I'm not with them, I'm probably still at their house. They've become more than best friends to me. They are my family.

Twisting the handle, I slowly ease open the front door. Sound from the TV floats through from the living room and I wait a beat before stepping inside. I walk on tiptoes, trying to reach the bottom of the stairs in silence. My stomach sinks when I don't see my father's sleeping form on either the recliner or the lounge.

Something hard crashes into the back of my head and I curse, flying forward and landing on my knees, my skin dragging painfully across something stuck in the carpet. My father's hand clutches the back of my shirt, yanking me to my feet. He spins me around, then rams his shoulder into my gut, and the air exits my lungs. I choke on a breath as I stumble back. I throw my hands out.

'Dad! It's me!'

'Get. Out. Of. My. House,' he seethes, blindly reaching for the baseball bat he keeps behind the lounge. I move it all the time, but whenever I return home again, it's always back there. Once, I even tossed it in the bin right before the rubbish truck collected it, but he went and bought a new one.

'*Dad.*'

I step back from him, trying to meet his stare, but my father isn't there. His eyes are glazed over and red-ringed. He lunges at me, and this time I crash backwards into the coffee table. Glass shatters around me, and a large piece slices my skin, digging into the back of my hip. I howl in pain, kicking out and striking Dad in the chest. He falls backward, landing in a sprawl.

Despite being out of his mind, he still has insanely fast reflexes. He's up again and swinging the bat at me as I scramble to my feet. I feel the whoosh of air, and the bat smashes into the side of my face, forcing me off my feet and into the wall. Photo frames crash around me, and I stagger out of the room, black dots dancing across my vision.

I'm in such a rush to get out the door, I trip over my own feet, falling down the front-porch steps. I roll and push myself up, then limp down the path. The pain is everywhere. Reaching back,

I touch my hip and hiss. I can feel the glass wedged in deep, but I can't bear to pull it out.

My father was always a little unhinged, but since my mum left, there's been a serious decline. That's when he started drinking and taking other substances. Whether he blames me for it, I don't know, but she left both of us, and I'll never forgive her for it. I'll never forgive him, either, for the monster he became in her absence.

I could close my eyes and make my way over to their house by pure instinct. When I get to the end of their driveway, Zayden's car isn't there. His words from earlier resurface in my mind – he's out with Leasa.

Gritting my teeth, I limp down the side of the house, trying to be as quiet as possible. I breathe a sigh of relief when I try the glass door and it opens. I slip inside and pad down the hallway. I hear the murmur of conversation coming from the kitchen and sneak up the stairs. I get to Anya's bedroom door and open it.

She's lying belly-first on her bed, headphones in, a book in her hand. Her mouth falls open when she sees me. My breath comes easier now I'm here with her. The anxiety fades from my body as her presence wraps around me like a warm blanket.

'Oh my God, Mase.'

'I'm sorry,' I choke out, realising how much of a mess I must look. I don't know why I even go back home; this has happened far too many times now. But then he has good days, and I forget how bad things can get. 'I don't have anywhere else to go.'

'Was it him?' she whispers, inching towards me, scanning my injuries with a petrified look on her face.

A tear slides down my cheek before I can stop it. 'Yeah.'

Placing her hands either side of my face, she swipes her thumb across my cheek, collecting the tear. 'You're safe now,' she murmurs. 'I've got you.'

I fall into her arms, burying my face into her neck. 'I can't go back there.'

Rubbing soothing circles over my shirt, she makes a soft hum of agreement. 'You don't have to.'

Reluctantly, I release her and step back, those emerald eyes meeting mine again. God, this girl. I love her. I've always loved her.

The one girl I want. The one girl I can't have.

'Come on, I'll get you cleaned up.' She slides her fingers through mine. 'No one has to know.'

My eyes close for a brief moment, pain radiating through me to the point where I feel I might pass out. My relief and appreciation for this girl swells in my chest. 'Thank you,' I murmur, tightening my hold on her. 'I don't know what I would do without you.'

Squeezing my hand, she smiles up at me through her own tears. 'You'll never find out because I'll be here. Always.'

7

ANYA

THE NEXT MORNING, it isn't until I'm about to open my bedroom door that I remember what happened last night. I danced with Mason. Mason *felt me up*. In front of Dylan. And it felt fucking amazing. I hope the betrayal tasted as bad as what he made me feel.

Turning, I lean my back against the door, closing my eyes and letting myself relive the moment when those haunting dark eyes watched me dance, remembering the way his firm hands felt running over my body. I have wanted to feel his hands on me ever since my eighteenth birthday. A part of me is angry with myself for giving in and letting him break down the walls I spent so long building. The other part is floating on cloud nine from the small taste of his attention again.

I have always wanted Mason, and clearly, he still wants me too. But I can't forget everything that's happened. We might be older now, but that doesn't change the fact that he's my brother's best friend. If things were to not work out for us – like last time – everything would be difficult. I was okay with pretending the rift never happened when he wasn't around, but now he's back and settled in, for at least the next four years of school.

Things have always been complicated when it comes to Mason.

Expelling a breath, I turn, banging the back of my head against the door. I feel a headache forming behind my eyes; it isn't even eight a.m. yet. Pressing my ear against it, I confirm that there's no noise coming from the other side. Stepping out of my room, I walk down the hallway and into the kitchen. My shoulders relax when I see that no one is there. I make myself a coffee before hightailing it back to my room.

I'm in such a rush to get back unnoticed, I don't see Mason walking just as quickly out of the laundry. We collide and I scream when the hot coffee splashes across the front of me. I fly backwards and land in a painful sprawl.

'Ow,' I moan.

'Jesus!' Mason exclaims, yanking out his AirPod. He pulls me back to my feet and stares down at me. 'Are you okay?'

'I just got fucking burned!' I snap, blinking away the tears that are stinging my eyes.

'I didn't hear you, obviously,' he bites back.

Sighing, I slowly peel my shirt from my skin, whining in pain. I tug it over my head and stare at the red welts across my chest. Mason clears his throat, and it dawns on me that I'm standing in front of him in a lacey white bra that reveals more than it covers. A flush spreads over my cheeks. Swallowing, I look up at him. Those bottomless eyes of his quickly dart away from my chest.

Scowling, I wrap my arms around myself and march into the bathroom. I inspect the damage, wincing as I run my fingertips over the marks.

'Can I get you anything?' he calls.

'No!' I yell back, hissing as my nail scratches the burn. Huffing, I peel off the rest of my clothes and step into the shower. The cool water helps soothe the burning sensation flaring across my skin. When I return to the hallway, Mason is nowhere to be seen and the mess is cleaned up.

I need to move house. Immediately. I can't live in a house with him. I feel like so much has happened already, and I haven't even been here for two days. It's always been like that between Mason and me. From zero to a hundred. Back and forth, up and down. The flirtation and games may have been exciting and fun when we were teenagers, but we're adults now, and I don't have time for this. It's exhausting.

Dressing quickly, I get ready and basically sprint out the door.

Fifteen minutes later, I'm at the university carpark. Since I'm early, I manage to find a park easily and make my way to the coffee shop. I order myself a large cappuccino, hoping it will magically cure my headache. I head to the courtyard, suddenly experiencing first-day jitters.

Sweat dots my forehead, and I dab the back of my hand across it. Having moved from a coastal town that was more often windy than not, being further north means the weather is a little more tropical than what I'm used to.

The only other person here is a girl who is seated at one of the tables with a kindle in one hand and a takeaway coffee in the other. I squint, trying to read the stickers on the back of her e-reader.

Hot Coffee & Anti-Heroes

Grinning, I walk over to her.

'I love that sticker,' I say, pointing to the back of the kindle. 'My kindle says: "BRB, reading smut".'

The girl lifts her eyes. She is gorgeous in a very in-your-face kind of way, with long, brunette waves, crystal-blue eyes and smooth, pale skin. I realise we are wearing an almost identical outfit: Vans and a black t-shirt tucked into ripped jeans.

'Sorry,' I say quickly. 'I get excited when I see someone reading.'

She smiles, and I feel my shoulders relax a little. The run-in with Mason this morning has rattled me, and I don't need to make an idiot of myself in front of this stranger to top it off, but thankfully, she seems friendly.

'Bookworms are the best type of people.'

'Definitely. May I?' I ask, gesturing to the empty seat.

She nods, clicking her kindle off and taking a sip of her drink.

'I'm Anya,' I say, dropping into the seat and flicking my long hair over my shoulders. It's way overdue for a cut. Dylan used to pester me about it and say I should cut it off, so now I want to grow it out *really, really* long.

'Nora,' she replies. 'First semester too?'

'Yeah. I just moved here.'

'Oh, me too!' Nora replies, perking up. 'I'm living on campus.'

'How are you liking it?'

'I live with four other people who I didn't know before I moved in. It's definitely going to be a party apartment.'

'Are they nice at least?' I ask, and briefly wonder if I should investigate on-campus housing. Last I checked it was full, but maybe there is a cancellation list they can put me on. People drop out of uni all the time. I'm sure something would pop up eventually.

'I've made friends with one of the girls. She's coming to this too, but she'll be late. She's late to everything.'

'I just moved in with my brother and his best friend. I was meant to move into a share house, but my stupid ex-boyfriend screwed that up for me.' I let out a huff at her curious eyebrow raise. 'Long story.'

'I'd love to hear about it one day.'

'Maybe we could have dinner later,' I say, wanting any reason to avoid the house and Mason, then I laugh at myself. 'Wow, that felt like I just asked you out on a date.'

'Sounded like it.' She smiles, two splotches of red appearing on her cheeks. 'I'd love to go to dinner.'

A few other people are starting to arrive now. A guy who doesn't look much older than us calls out, asking everyone to gather around him. Nora and I head over to where he is, and a girl rushes up to us, her hair covering her face. She hastily throws it over her shoulders as she does her lipstick.

'You made it!' Nora exclaims, looking relieved that the girl turned up on time. 'Cami, this is Anya.'

'Hey!' she says brightly. 'I'm Camilla.'

Camilla towers over both of us, with long tanned legs that seem to never end. She is stunning in every single way. Her dark complexion and features are striking, only enhanced by the red top she is wearing. Dainty gold jewellery glitters on her wrists and fingers. She has more earrings in one ear than Nora and I have combined.

'Nice to meet you,' I say.

'Anya just moved here too,' Nora explains.

We fall into a brief conversation. I start to feel at ease the more we talk. They both seem kind and genuine, which is exactly what I need right now. The guy commands our attention once more and the group falls silent.

'Hey everyone. I'm Jeremiah. I'm going to give you a campus tour to show you the ins and outs. Hopefully you'll meet some new people along the way.' He beams, clasping his hands together. 'Let's get started.'

My mother once told me that one good friend is worth a thousand bad ones. After spending the last few hours with Nora and Cami,

I've decided there's some truth to that. Already I feel so at home with these girls compared to my friend group back home.

We've been talking nonstop for hours about anything and everything. A day like this was something I desperately needed. We have been taking advantage of Happy Hour at the uni bar. I feel warm and floaty as I follow the girls down the busy walkway through town. Cami has taken us off-campus, to show us the other place a lot of students go to, since the uni bar can get quite crowded.

'And here it is,' Cami says, gesturing towards the building with a wide sweep of her hand. A bright-orange neon sign flashes above the door: The Illusion.

'Looks swanky,' Nora observes.

Cami shoves the door open, and we follow her inside.

'It's a fun place to work. I've been here for almost six months. We're hiring, by the way,' Cami says over her shoulder while she struts through the room, waving and greeting each person she passes.

It's a dimly lit place, with lots of high tables and dark, patterned couches scattered throughout the room. My eyes drift towards one of the many poles situated throughout the dance floor and a shiver of *something* runs down my spine. I would love to know what it feels like to dance on one of those.

As if reading my mind, Cami smirks at me. 'You game?'

'Hmm?'

'Give it a go.' She raises a hand towards the pole closest to us.

A blush kisses my cheeks and I shake my head. 'I am not coordinated enough to look good doing that.'

'Practice makes perfect.' She winks.

'Can you dance?' I ask.

'I was dancing before I could walk.'

'Do you compete?'

'Not as much as I used to, but yeah. I mostly cheerlead now.'

'Can you pole dance?' Nora asks, eyeing the pole to her right with a curious expression on her face.

'Yeah, I pole dance a lot.'

'Show us!' Nora and I exclaim at the same time.

Shrugging off her bag and kicking off her sandals, Cami climbs onto the stage. She circles it, placing her hand onto the pole and sending us a wicked grin. 'Watch and learn, ladies.'

Elegantly, she twists, her leg extending before wrapping around the pole. She tosses her head, bends her arm behind her and arches her back in a way that I could never. The way her body moves and twists looks effortless. My eyes widen in awe as she climbs up higher, flipping so that she hangs upside down. She shimmies down the pole and finishes her performance in the splits. She extends her neck, and her gorgeous black hair tumbles down her back. When she stands, she bows towards the men who are now hollering. She leaps off the stage and beams at us.

'Dancing is my happy place,' she says, enjoying the fact that our jaws have practically divorced our faces.

'You're incredible at it!' Nora gushes, squeezing her arm.

'I go to a class every Thursday night for it. You both should come!'

Nora's face falls and she steps back. 'I couldn't do that.'

'Why not?' Cami demands, a crease appearing between her brows.

Nora lazily flicks her hand towards her body.

'You're both gorgeous as fuck and would have a great time at the class. If you want to come, it's at the dance academy studio every Thursday at seven.'

Turning her back to us, she strides towards the bar. We exchange glances before following her. We order our drinks and find a secluded booth at the back of the room. The bar is bigger than I expected, and busy for this time of afternoon. Everything about this place is ultra-modern and chic.

'Okay,' Nora says as she sits down opposite me. 'Spill the beans on the brother's best friend.'

Cami gasps, swivelling to face me. She takes a long, obnoxious slurp of her drink. Leaning forward, she smirks. 'Brother's best friend? Tell me more.'

Groaning, I sink into the seat. 'It's a giant complication that I don't have the energy for.'

'Spill the tea, sis!' Cami urges, tapping her hand impatiently on the tabletop, her bracelets jingling together.

'Basically, I've always been into him. It was embarrassingly obvious to everyone when we were growing up. But as we got older, he seemed to return my feelings. Whenever we were seeing other people, we both had the same problem – our partners always had an issue with Mason and I hanging out.'

Nora's lips stretch into a smirk. 'Sexual tension – check.'

'He would flirt with me, convince me that he liked me and then deny it to everyone else. Basically, he made me feel like I wouldn't ever be good enough to have him.'

'Sounds like an A-Grade asshole,' Cami mutters, shaking her head. She brings her hands up in an 'X' shape in front of her and makes a buzzer sound. 'It's a no from me.'

'Then he broke up with his girlfriend – Zayden said he never really liked her, but I don't know. It was a whole big thing. He came to my eighteenth birthday and things got heated. I don't want to go into it but, basically, he hasn't been around for ages and now he's back and we're living together. I don't really want anything to do with him now, but I also want him to fuck my brains out. I have complicated feelings.'

Nora spits her drink across the table and Cami shrieks when

half of it lands on her. I burst out laughing and hastily grab a napkin, dabbing it on her arm and then the table.

'Sorry,' Nora chokes, slapping her chest. 'I didn't expect you to say that.'

'You just need to show him that *he* is the one who isn't good enough for *you*.' Cami points a shiny, black-nailed finger at me.

'Mmhmm,' I mumble, reaching for her hand to inspect the dainty tattoos covering her fingers. I have been wanting to get a tattoo for ages, but Dylan always told me he hates the look of tattoos on women. 'I'll get right on that.'

I take a long sip of my drink. My head is feeling a little light, and I decide then that I need to slow down. I don't make great decisions when I drink, and since Mason will be at home, I need to have a clear head and be on my best behaviour.

'The hottest of hot just walked in,' Cami whispers, running her tongue across her teeth as she not-so-subtly checks them out. Nora and I both turn to see.

I scoff, turning to glare at my drink. 'Gross.'

'Gross?' Nora exclaims with wide eyes. 'Are we looking at the same guys?'

'That's my brother,' I mutter. 'And Mason. Aka, the best friend.'

Cami and Nora gasp, then turn to stare at the boys walking over to the pool table. My hands curl into fists seeing Mason. He is too damn sexy for his own good. It makes it hard to hate him. It honestly feels like having an ex, but we never even had the relationship part. Can you have a 'one that got away' when you never got to have them in the first place?

'Damn, girl.' Cami waves a hand near her face, fanning herself. 'I get it now.'

'Get what now?'

'The infatuation.' She blows out a breath. 'That boy is so hot, it's criminal.'

'Right?' I sigh, leaning my head back against the seat. 'I'm so screwed.'

'Also, your brother . . . wow.'

'Ugh,' I groan, reaching for my drink – my earlier decision disintegrated the moment the boys entered the bar.

Nora not-so-subtly stares at the boys, quietly sipping her cocktail. She quickly looks away and shoots me an apologetic look. 'Oops. I think they saw us.'

The girls sit up straighter in their seats as the boys approach. I suddenly find the table fascinating and glare down at it.

'Looks like they let anyone in here.' My brother smirks at me. His hair is messy, and his shirt looks two sizes too big, but that's standard for my brother. He rocks the 'just rolled out of bed' look no matter what the occasion, but to be fair, it does work for him. If I attempted that, I'd look like I just stepped out of a hurricane. 'Must be cool by association with these lovely ladies.'

'Ugh.' I scowl, but it's half-hearted. 'Don't flirt with my friends.'

He raises his hands innocently, and I notice some new tattoos lining his wrists. At this rate, he will have more tattooed skin than not. Our mum will have a fit when she sees him. She was horrified when he got his first one, and now he has two sleeves. 'I'm simply here to say hello to my dear sister.'

'Hi,' I say unenthusiastically, avoiding the searing eyes of Mason. I squirm in my seat, hating how the temperature seems to increase whenever he's close by. 'You can go now.'

Zayden's eyebrows rise and I sigh.

'This is Zayden,' I deadpan.

Zayden grins, extending a hand to Nora. She smiles up at him as he shakes her hand and then repeats the procedure with Cami, who is looking at him like he's something she wants to eat. Mason smirks at me when I finally turn to look at him.

'What?' I snap rudely.

'Aren't you going to introduce me?' Mason asks, leaning onto the booth and looking way too good right now.

Grinding my molars, I wave my hand at him. 'This is Mason. My brother's annoying friend.'

'Ouch.' He smirks, placing a hand over his heart. 'You wound me, Anya.'

'You have to have a heart for it to hurt,' I mutter.

'Someone is grumpy,' Mason says, shooting me a sweet smile. 'Did you forget to take your happy pills today?'

'Go away.'

'I'm Cami,' Cami interrupts our banter. 'This is Nora.'

'Pleasure,' Mason replies, but his eyes don't leave mine.

'Pleasure is all mine,' Cami chirps.

I lightly kick her foot, and she yelps, scowling at me.

'If you're free tonight, we're having a party,' Zayden says casually, leaning forward, pressing his palms flat on the table. His eyes shift towards Nora. 'You should come.'

'Huh?' I ask, raising an eyebrow. 'What party?'

'Our party.'

'Where?'

'At the house, obviously,' Mason pipes up unnecessarily.

'Since when are we having a party?' I frown.

'Since always,' Zayden says, flashing his trademark playboy smile at my new friends. 'Anya can give you the address.'

'Cool,' Cami says. 'We'll be there.'

Zayden leans over and takes a long sip of my drink, slurping it obnoxiously as he finishes the last of it.

'Hey!' I exclaim.

'Hay is for horses.' He flicks me on the nose. He glances at my friends, looking cockier than ever. 'See you later, ladies.'

When I look up at Mason, his eyes are already on me. My stomach clenches. His gaze hasn't left me the entire time he's been here. He smirks.

'See you tonight, Blush.'

My heart slams painfully in my chest, like it always does when he says that familiar nickname. Offering him a sarcastic smile, I raise my middle finger, hoping my face doesn't betray how I'm really feeling. He blows me a kiss before turning to follow Zayden.

'You're in so much deeper than you realise.' Cami gives me a pointed look. 'You two have such hard-ons for each other that it literally made me uncomfortable.'

'Oh my God,' I squawk. 'We do not.'

'Did he call you Blush?' Cami smirks. 'He has a nickname for you. Ugh. That's hot.'

'Go away,' I mutter.

Both of them are looking far too happy right now, considering what I told them earlier about my situation with Mason. They're meant to be helping me get over him, not fall even more in love with him. Not that I'm in love with him anymore. That's the old me. I made a vow to myself to no longer fall for boys who are only going to break my heart.

'Don't get me started on you.' Cami points at Nora. 'You and Zayden.'

'What?' Both Nora and I exclaim.

'He was looking at you like you're a little mouse' – she grins – 'and he's the lion trying to catch you.'

Nora's face erupts in flames. 'I don't even know what you mean by that.'

'Mmhmm.' Cami rolls her eyes. 'Let's go back to campus. We needed to start getting ready, like, yesterday.'

I exhale. I feel like another drink, since my brother so kindly finished mine off for me. Despite living with him now, I was hoping to keep to myself as much as possible, to try my best to avoid crossing paths too much.

Looks like my plan to avoid Mason is off to a great start.

8

MASON

WHEN WE WERE KIDS, Zayden and I would make pinky promises as a sacred form of trust. We never broke our promises to each other. Until the night of Anya's eighteenth, that is. I promised to protect her, to be there for her and to treat her like I would Zayden – like she was family. She *is* my family. Of course, I've never seen her as my sister – despite that being my excuse to everyone who questioned me about her – but as someone I love and care for. Someone I would do anything for and never let down.

But I did let her down.

And I'll never forgive myself for it.

This thought weighs on my mind as I move around the bodies gathered in the lounge room. 'Do I Wanna Know' by the Arctic Monkeys plays through the speakers. As the sun sinks into the horizon, it casts an orange glow through the space, complimented by the neon lights bouncing from the corners of the room.

I've spent the last hour on the move, searching for her, but she still isn't here. Is she avoiding me? She certainly didn't seem happy to see me earlier today. It's always been effortless between us. That's something I always loved about her. But now it's strained and awkward. I want to fix it; I just don't know if she'll let me.

The only people I really know here are the football guys. Though clusters of people fill the house, they're all two years

ahead of me at university. While I was travelling, everyone formed
their groups. Other than Zayden and the few guys I've met at
football practice, I haven't really found my friend group yet. The
one dude that I really like, Parker, only turns up to half the practices, and when he does, he leaves immediately after. There's only
one other guy from the team who seems decent and who Zayden
is close with. I spot him hovering near the pool table, a red plastic
cup in his hand.

'Hey,' I nod at him.

'Hey, man.' Christian smiles, clapping his hand into mine and
pulling me in for a one-armed hug. 'This is a great house for a
party.'

'Yeah, it's a good set-up,' I agree. My eyes roam the room and
I crane my neck to get a view of the front door.

'Looking for someone?' Christian asks, his lips curving into
a knowing smirk.

Am I that obvious?

'Hmm?' I ask distractedly. 'Oh, um, Anya. Zay's sister. She
lives here, but I haven't seen her. We didn't give her much notice
about the party, and I didn't realise Zay had invited so many
people.'

'Zayden has a sister?' Christian arches an eyebrow. 'He's kept
that under wraps, hasn't he?'

'For good reason,' I say.

As if I manifested her arrival, the door swings open and she
walks inside, followed closely by Nora and Cami. I can't stop my
gaze travelling down her body.

Goddamn.

Our eyes connect, and I send her a wave. She flips me off in
response.

Christian lets out a low whistle. 'Okay, yeah, I get why now.
The team will be all over her.'

Clenching my jaw, I attempt to appear nonchalant. My death-grip on the cup in my hand causes it to crumple. He eyes the cup and then my face for a moment, his teasing smirk morphing into a full-blown grin.

'Oh, gotcha. She's with you.'

'What?' I snap, narrowing my eyes at him.

Christian smiles even wider, enjoying my reaction a little too much. 'She's yours. Got it.'

She's yours. I like the sound of that far too much.

'I don't know what you're talking about,' I mutter, bringing the cup to my lips and taking a hearty gulp. I'm meant to be cutting down on the drinking and partying, after everything that happened when I was overseas, but it's the easiest way to mingle around here, and it helps with the anxiety. Not that it makes me feel good the following morning. I always forget that part when I start the night.

Ignoring Christian's smirk, I push off the wall and weave through the throngs of people, trying to get to her as quickly as I can.

'Anya,' I say. She turns, and those gorgeous eyes land on me, making my heart feel like it's beating sideways. She may have grown, but I still tower over her, which makes me feel like a giant. To be fair, I've always been the tallest one among my friends. I actually used to get bullied for it when I was younger, until everyone else started catching up. 'Hey. You made it.'

'I live here,' she says flatly.

I clench my jaw, realising how stupid that sounded. My brain and my mouth don't seem to cooperate when she's around.

'Obviously,' I snap back out of habit, since we bicker more than not these days. 'You could have stayed out, though, if you didn't want to come.'

She gives me a weird look. 'What do you want?'

'I just wanted to say hey, I guess. I didn't realise the party was going to be this big.'

'Okay?' she says, waiting for me to say something else. There's a beat of silence, and her frown creases further. She even has the audacity to eye me up and down with her nose screwed up, as if I might be sick or something.

'Why are you being a bitch?' I huff, feeling the heat in my cheeks.

'I can't keep up with your mood swings, and I don't really want to hang out with you. I need a drink.'

'Don't get drunk,' I say quickly.

She glares at my hand, which I didn't realise is on her arm. She scowls and pulls away, as if I burned her. I feel sick over the recoil.

'You have no right to tell me what I can and can't do.'

Exhaling, I realise I won't win this fight.

'Okay, fine. I'll get you a drink.'

'No, Mason,' she growls, anger flashing across her eyes. 'Just leave me alone.'

Turning on her heel, she storms towards the kitchen. Nora sends me a sympathetic look before trailing after her. Cami's eyes are narrowed as she surveys me for a few seconds. She then follows her friends without a word to me. I blink after them, unsure what to do.

My head is a fucking mess. I want her. I've always had this hunger for her. An uncontrollable ache. An itch that never quite got scratched. But I fucked it up that night. I lost her trust, I lost her love . . . I lost *her*.

I'm the one chasing her. I've never chased someone before. Realising now how much it sucks causes my stomach to tighten as I think about what she must have gone through for years.

The thing is: as much as I do want her, I know I can't have her. I made a promise to Zayden, and I want to do right by them both. Yet whenever I see her, all rationale leaves my body. There's a constant battle being waged inside me. Groaning, I finish my drink and toss it into the first bin I see.

Whoever said falling in love is the best thing to happen to you is a fucking liar.

9

ANYA

Three Years Ago

FINALLY, THE LONG WEEKEND has arrived. I've been counting down the days because my parents are going away for the weekend, and Mason and Zayden have planned a party.

Things have been really tense at home. Zayden won't stay in the room if Rod – our stepfather – enters, and Mum and Zayden aren't speaking, which has never happened before. No one will explain what the hell is going on, but Mum and Rod can't seem to get away quickly enough, and Zayden can't contain his excitement about having the house to ourselves.

A warm breeze blows as I walk outside, and the humidity makes my hair stick to my forehead. After sweeping the back patio and putting away all the pool gear – as per Mum's request – I head back inside for a drink of water.

Two large hands land on my shoulders, and I flinch in surprise.

'Sorry to scare you,' Rod apologises, brushing past me as he moves through the kitchen. He turns and offers me a smile. 'Going for a swim?'

'Yeah, I think so. It's unusually warm today.'

'It sure is,' he comments, spreading out his hands and leaning forward onto the kitchen bench. 'That's why I wanted to get on the road nice and early – to beat the traffic and the heat. But you know your mother; she'd be late to her own funeral.'

I snicker. 'You're probably right about that.'

'Do you think that bikini is getting a bit small for you?' Rod asks me.

I glance down at my chest; my boobs certainly grew in the last six months. It seemed like they just appeared overnight and, suddenly, none of my tops looked the same on me. I flush under his scrutiny. 'Oh,' I mumble, shrugging. 'I don't know. It feels comfortable enough.'

He opens his mouth to say more when Mum bustles into the kitchen like a whirlwind.

'Okay, okay,' she says, whipping past me and grabbing her vitamins from the kitchen counter. 'I'm ready.'

'Finally!' Rod deadpans. 'I'll get the car started.'

'Have a good time!' I tell them.

Rod points a finger at me. 'Keep the boys in line.'

'I will.'

He winks at me as he disappears out of the kitchen.

'Love you, miss you already,' Mum says, planting a wet kiss on my cheek. 'Don't stay up all night reading, I'll know!'

I roll my eyes. 'Bye!'

The front door slams shut and suddenly, the house feels empty and still. I drum my fingers against the kitchen counter, surveying the space. I pack away anything of value into cupboards and move the furniture back against the walls to create room for people to dance. I don't know who the boys have invited, but since they're the star football players – kings of the school, as they like to call themselves – I imagine the guest list will be quite long.

Once I've finished all the jobs Zayden ordered me to do, I head outside to dip my toes into the water. The coolness instantly makes my hot skin feel better, and I slide the rest of my body into the pool. There's a calmness under the water. A sense of peace

I don't get anywhere else. It's quiet down here and, in this moment, it's just me and the water.

I'm climbing out of the pool when the boys return home. I meet them inside and help Mason with the bags he's holding. Liquid heat pools in my stomach when his eyes drink in my exposed skin. He brings his lower lip between his teeth. Something flutters between my legs, and I clench my thighs at the feel of it.

Zayden heads back out the front door to get whatever else is in the car, and Mason glides towards me. I back into the kitchen counter, and he plants his arms either side of me, caging me in. I feel the heat of his skin near mine as he looks down at me. Excruciatingly slowly, he leans forward, then drags his tongue up the side of my neck.

'Mm,' he murmurs, and it feels like my insides are dripping. 'Salty.'

Rod is insistent about using salt water in the pool. I must admit, I do enjoy it – chlorine used to irritate my eyes and skin when I would spend hours and hours in the pool. I'm certainly appreciating it *right now*.

'Is it?' My voice is barely audible as I struggle to inhale and exhale.

He tucks my wet hair behind my ear, his breath fanning over my lips. He leans in close, barely brushing his lips against mine, when we hear Zayden's footsteps approaching. With a wicked smirk, Mason pushes back, creating distance between us. I feel like every inch of me is on fire, despite the water dripping off me.

Once everything is set up for the party, we decide to take a break. We spend the next half hour swimming, and then make homemade hamburgers to eat out the back. We sit around the table, the latest hits softly humming from the portable speaker.

My phone rings, interrupting Mason and Zayden's argument about something I'm not paying attention to. I glance down at it, seeing Zeke's name across my screen. When it finishes ringing, a beep comes through, indicating a text. Then another.

Zeke has asked me out twice now. I've said yes both times, only to pull out the day before, making up some stupid excuse not to go. He's kind, and I know we would have a good time, but it's hard to think about dating someone when I know my heart belongs to Mason. It beats for him and only him. My friends insist I'm too young and naive to know that Mason is 'the one', and that I'm wasting away my teenage years crushing on him, but the heart wants what it wants. They don't understand what we have, or the depth of our relationship. Our friendship. Whatever the hell it is at this point.

My friends tease me for wanting all my firsts to be with Mason; they don't understand why I'm holding out. They can tease me all they want because I know it will be truly special.

One night when we were sharing a bottle of vodka we found, giggling and hiding in the shadows at the back of the house, he promised me that when I was eighteen I'd be old enough for us to take things further. I'm not sure he even remembers the conversation, but I certainly do. When I'm eighteen, and he's graduated, and there isn't the pressure of school, classes and my brother's watchful eyes – we will be together. He promised me. Once I'm eighteen . . . everything is going to change.

We got in an argument only yesterday when I tried talking to him in front of his friends and he brushed me off. I hate it when he does that. He acts all sweet when we're alone, but too cool for me when others are around, but I know it's because he is waiting to graduate before starting anything between us. He's saving for a trip, and then once he's back, we are going to be together.

'Are you going to answer that?' Zayden asks, quirking an eyebrow.

'Nope,' I answer.

'Who is it?' Mason asks.

'No one.'

They exchange a glance before Zayden dives for my phone. I let out a squeak of protest, swiping for it, but Zayden is too quick. He leaps to his feet, easily dodging me. He looks down at the screen, and I sink into my seat.

'Zeke,' he says loudly, looking up at me. He clears his throat, putting on a high-pitched voice that sounds *nothing* like him. 'Heyyyy. Heard your brother is throwing a rager tonight. Do I get to be your plus one? Would love to see you.'

My cheeks grow hot, and I feel Mason's glare land heavily on me. My food suddenly tastes dull as I chew it, refusing to look his way.

'Is Zeke your boyfriend?' Zayden teases.

'No,' I mutter.

'Zeke who?' Mason asks, and I wince at the severity of his tone.

'Yeah, Anya. Zeke *who*?' Zayden probes nosily.

'No one. It's nothing. Just drop it.'

'Ohhh.' Zayden smirks, glancing at Mason. 'I think she likes him.'

I close my eyes briefly. When I open them, Mason is staring at me, his expression unreadable. It's hard to tell what he's feeling, but I'm assuming he's pissed. I groan inwardly.

'Stop being an asshole!' I complain, shooting daggers at Zayden, who has a stupid, smug grin on his face. 'It's just a guy in my class who asked me out, but I didn't say yes. Okay? Happy?'

Zayden considers this. 'Yes. I am. No dating until you're twenty-five.'

I snort. 'Yeah. Okay.'

When I sneak a glance at Mason, his easy expression has returned, and I feel the tightness in my chest loosen. It matters to me that he knows how unimportant Zeke is. Or anyone is, for that matter.

An hour later, I'm showered and sitting in front of my mirror, doing my makeup. Mason strolls into my room, sitting on the edge of my bed. I half turn, glancing over at him.

'Can I help you?' I ask in a snippy tone, but my smile betrays me.

'Zeke, huh?' Mason says, folding his arms across his chest, his biceps bulging deliciously as he does so.

I give him a deadpan stare. '*No.*'

'No?' He raises a brow.

'No,' I repeat.

'There's nothing there?' he questions.

I shake my head. 'Like I said, no.'

'Okay,' he says.

My heart jerks in my chest. 'I thought you wouldn't care.'

'I don't.'

'Seems like you do.'

His jaw ticks. 'Maybe I do.'

Neither of us breaks the stare for several long moments. Eventually, I turn back to the mirror and continue applying my eyeshadow.

'Did you answer his text?'

'Yes.'

'Why?'

I meet his eyes in the reflection. 'Because he's my friend.'

'Is he?' Mason asks, his voice frosty. 'And what did you say to him?'

'I said he's welcome to come if he wants to. It's an open invite party.'

Mason's eyes narrow. 'Right.'

'Since you're too cool to talk to me in front of your friends, it shouldn't be a problem anyway.'

'It isn't,' he quips.

'Good.'

'Great.'

'Excellent.'

Mason leaves my room, and my door bangs shut behind him. Exhaling, I lean forward, my face against my palms.

That boy will be the death of me.

I've been dancing for hours and my legs are beginning to burn. Phoebe's hands hold mine as we move to the beat. The house is packed with people, a lot of whom I recognise as already graduated, making the party feel a little more mature than the other high school ones I've attended.

For a long time, I stuck to my introverted ways, but Phoebe really brought me out of my shell. She is quite possibly the most outgoing person I've ever met. I don't think the word 'no' is in her vocabulary when it comes to invitations. I'm grateful, because she's made me step out of my comfort zone.

People who I've seen around school for years have come and said hello to me for the first time, and two boys have asked for my number. It's definitely because of the dress I borrowed from Phoebe – a spaghetti-strapped emerald number that matches my eyes. Since I've filled out more, we can finally share clothes, as Phoebe matured a lot earlier than I did. She's wearing a cute matching crop top and skirt set that she saw advertised in a magazine and just *had* to get. Her long hair, which was perfectly straight at the start of the party, is tangled in messy waves from all the dancing.

'I don't know how you do it,' Phoebe shouts at me.

'What?' I ask, leaning towards her.

'Have guys falling over their feet to get your attention all the time!' She rolls her eyes, shaking her head.

'I don't think you're one to have any complaints in that department, Phoebs,' I laugh, lightly squeezing her arm. I'm not sure how she doesn't see her own beauty, or why she always has to compare us, but sometimes I don't think she knows how truly gorgeous she really is. 'Boys fight for your attention!'

'Never the ones I want.'

'What?' I ask, pulling my hair back behind my shoulder, as if that will help me hear her better over the loud pop song blaring from the speakers.

She waves her hand dismissively at me, ending the discussion, and I go back to dancing, enjoying the beat.

The floor beneath my feet is vibrating, and suddenly I feel lightheaded. I signal a time-out gesture, and Phoebe looks annoyed before turning to join the group beside us. She is wildly popular and friends with everyone, although she insists she dislikes all the girls who claim to be her close friends – except me.

Heading to the bathroom, I take a moment to sit in silence and pull out my phone. I stare down at the screen, smiling and reading through Mason and my last conversation. I was feeling confident, wanting to flirt with him like I often do, ignoring our earlier disagreement.

Anya: I think you're hot

Mason: Yeah?

Anya: Veryyyy

Mason: I think you're hot, too

Anya: For real?

Mason: For real, for real

Anya: What do you like, in particular?

Mason: Everything

Anya: Yeah?

Mason: You know this already

Anya: Just realised I actually texted the wrong person

We love playing this game. It's dangerous, but I don't want to stop.

I go to the kitchen and snag a bottle of water from the fridge before heading out the back. The cool night air washes over me and I can breathe again. I'm surprised by how cold it is tonight, given the heat we had throughout the day. Making my way around the side of the house, I find that this part of the yard is deserted. Leaning against the wall, I gaze up at the dark, starry sky.

'You should be careful out here all alone,' a voice murmurs.

Turning my head, I see Mason. He flashes me his trademark smile – the one I fall in love with more and more each day.

'I needed a breather,' I admit. 'It's so loud and busy inside.'

'It is,' Mason agrees. 'Are you having a good time?'

'Sure,' I say. 'Are you?'

'I am now.'

Pressing my lips together, I peel my gaze away from him.

'You look beautiful, Blush,' Mason murmurs, sending a shiver down my spine.

'What are we doing, Mase?' I ask, a little exasperated. 'You tell everyone I'm like a little sister to you. You deny anything ever going on, but here you are, telling me that. Kissing my freckles. Getting angry when boys show interest in me.'

He's quiet for a long moment. Digging his hands into his pockets, he sighs. 'We can't be together right now. Your family has become my family, and Zayden is everything to me. There's a lot going on for the both of us right now. We just have to wait it out a bit longer.'

My heart crumbles, but I nod. It's always the same answer. Every time I tell myself to stop asking, to walk away. But I never do. 'Right.'

'But,' he murmurs, stepping closer to me. 'I'm unable to stay away from you.'

Gulping, I risk a glance in his direction, and the heated look in his eyes makes everything inside me clench.

'I don't know what that means,' I confess in a broken whisper. 'You're confusing the hell out of me, Mase.'

'I know.' He sighs. 'I'm sorry.' He moves in front of me. Capturing my hand in his, he brings it to his mouth, kissing it. He pulls it to his chest, and I feel how hard and fast his heart is beating. Swallowing, I lift my eyes to his. I wonder if he feels the same way I do.

I splay my fingers across his muscles, letting them roam his chest, then sink lower to his stomach. He applies a little pressure on my hand, giving me encouragement to go further. My fingertips brush the top of his waistband. His gaze connects with mine, his eyes appearing darker in the dim lighting out here, as my hand skates across the bulge in his pants. I'm barely breathing at this point, too scared to blink and suddenly wake up, realising this has all been a dream.

This time, he is the one who is breathing heavily.

He is affected by *me*.

Applying a little more pressure, I move my hand. He closes his eyes, his other hand slamming against the wall near my head. He presses his forehead into the side of mine.

'I want to touch you,' he groans, his voice hoarse and rough, like when he first wakes up in the morning. 'But I know I shouldn't.'

'I want you to,' I whisper.

'We can't,' he chokes out. '*I* can't.'

I move my hand once more and he groans softly, before gripping my wrist and forcing me to stop. He releases a shaky breath and slides his fingers between mine, gripping me so hard it almost hurts. I've never seen him shaken like this.

His lips move against my hairline, skimming across my cheekbone. He kisses across my freckles, down my jaw, and then, his lips are on mine.

Warm, soft, *perfect*.

He tastes like coffee, mint chewing gum and a slight hint of something else. Beer perhaps, but I know he isn't drunk. Neither of us have drunk much at all tonight, too stressed and on edge about something going wrong at the party, given that it's our house and all. Well, my family's house, although he's here just as much as Zayden and me.

Our lips move together, slow and soft at first before moving into something a little more desperate. His hands are in my hair, combing through it, and I whimper into his mouth, loving the feel of his hard body against mine. His lips move across my chin, down to my neck, and he softly bites my skin there, making me moan. My hands run down his sides, then slide across his torso.

I trace the hard lines of his stomach. His hand moves from my hair, carving a line down my neck and moving to my breast. He gently palms it, and I arch my back, pushing myself into him.

'Fuck, Blush,' he groans.

His mouth is on mine again, sucking my lower lip between his teeth. A thrill shoots through me at the sensation. The kiss is deep and hungry, and our hands move across each other's bodies, exploring our touch properly for the first time.

'Do you know how hard it is not to kiss you every moment of every day?' he pants, his breathing ragged.

'Yes,' I whisper. 'Because I fight the same urge.'

'Beautiful,' he keeps murmuring between kisses. 'So, so beautiful.'

A shriek startles us both, and then the sound of glass smashing on cement jolts us from our trance. Breathing heavily, he steps back, combing a hand through his hair.

'That doesn't sound good,' I pant, needing to fill the tension-laced silence, my head spinning from what just happened.

'No.' He shakes his head. His eyes drop to my wrist, and I realise I'm playing with the end of my leather bracelet. 'That's new,' he says.

'Um,' I whisper, my throat suddenly dry. 'I actually got it for you.' My cheeks grow warm. 'I'm not sure if it's something you'd like . . . or even wear . . .'

His brilliant smile lights up his face. 'You got that for me?'

I nod. 'Yeah.'

Slipping it off, I hand it to him. He trails his fingers over it, before unknotting it and tying it around his wrist. His eyes linger on it for a moment. The leather weaves in a crisscross movement, fitting him perfectly.

'I love it,' he says. 'It's even more special knowing it's from you.'

My heart trips in my chest as I beam up at him, thrilled. I felt confident when I bought it, but was too scared to give it to him, as I was worried he would think it's juvenile.

Moving my hands up the sides of his neck, I thread my fingers around the back of his head. His eyes lock on mine.

Reaching up, I press my mouth to his for one more moment before we step away from each other and pretend nothing ever happened.

10

ANYA

EVEN WITH MY EYES CLOSED, I can see the vibrant flash of coloured lights throughout the room. Long slender arms wrap around my waist. I shimmy down Cami's body, bounce a few times, and slide back up.

I've been fighting off the flashbacks tearing through my mind. Me dancing, Mason nearby, those whisky eyes boring into mine. The way his mouth moved against my lips so passionately, so hungrily. Shaking the thoughts away, I desperately try to focus on the reality I'm in now, rather than the moments my mind is begging me to revisit.

A loud whistle draws my attention to a guy in the corner of the room. He has champagne-blond hair and an arrogant smirk twisted onto his lips. He is tall and packed with muscle, so I assume he is part of the football team. He beckons me over with his fingers, but I pretend I don't see it. I don't have the energy to deal with boys tonight. Instead, I turn and reach for Nora, pulling her close. We move to the beat. The bass is so loud the walls shake. The rational part of my brain is concerned about the neighbours, but the other part of me just wants to let loose and have fun.

A succession of vibrations against my thigh makes me pause and fish for my phone. When I pull it out, I see Dylan's name across the screen. I frown at it, the alcohol making my thoughts slow. The screen goes black.

A moment later, it's ringing again. Ignoring the call, I shove the phone back into my pocket, but the warm buzz I was feeling a moment ago has dimmed. My stomach churns as his face flashes through my mind. I can't believe they did that to me. My boyfriend and my best friend . . .

'I'm getting a drink!' I shout to the girls, holding up my now-empty cup. They both nod.

Instead of heading to the kitchen, I rush up the stairs. I pause when I see my door, which was closed, slightly ajar. Stalking towards it, I pull it open to see two guys bent over my dresser. One of them steps away and tilts his head back, a finger pressed against one side of his nose.

'Get out of my room,' I snap, grinding my molars together when I see they've knocked over some of my photo frames.

They both startle and turn to face me, one of them holding a rolled up note in his hand.

'Sorry,' the other says, sniffing and rubbing the back of his hand across his face. 'Just borrowing the space for a minute. Want one?'

'No, I want you to get out,' I say through gritted teeth, a headache starting to form behind my eyes. I might bring up all the alcohol I consumed this afternoon, which is a sight I don't want anyone to witness.

They don't argue. They step around me and, seconds later, Mason barges into my room, as if he has the right to be in here. He lost that long ago, although he seems to be forgetting the way he left things with us.

'Why are two guys leaving your room?' he demands, a muscle in his jaw twitching as his eyes dart around, inspecting my bed before jumping back to me and narrowing a little, even though the bed is neat and tidy, unchanged from when I made it this morning.

Groaning, I turn my back to him. 'Stop stalking me.'

'I'm not stalking you,' he scoffs.

'Seems like it,' I mutter.

My phone vibrates again. I look down at it and ice fills my veins. Dylan sent through a message. A single word.

Dylan: Slut.

A cold, numb feeling spreads through me. I don't know why I haven't blocked his number. He never has anything nice to say.

A part of me has been worried about what Mason said to Dylan when we saw him at the club. Dylan has this delusion that Mason and I were up to no good together while I was with him, and the other night Mason basically admitted that was true. It wasn't – Mason wasn't even in the country when Dylan and I dated – but with what he said, I'm sure Dylan has twisted it in his mind and convinced himself he's the victim here. He's exceptional at that. It would explain the sudden calls and texts from him, but I could be completely wrong with that theory. I don't want to think about any of it. I don't want Dylan in my life at all.

'What?' Mason asks, noticing the colour draining from my face.

Closing my eyes, I lean back against the wall, feeling like all the energy in my body has suddenly evaporated.

My phone is yanked from my hand, and my eyes pop open to see Mason glowering at it, as if it's personally responsible for the message it's displaying.

'Obviously he didn't learn his lesson,' he grounds out, looking furious.

'Seems that way.'

'You know he's full of shit, right?'

'Right,' I reply, but my voice betrays me, coming out as deflated as I feel.

Concern fills Mason's face, and he steps towards me. 'Don't let him get to you, Blush. You're better than him and he hates it. He knows he isn't going to get someone like you again, so he needs to tear you down to his level.'

'Yeah,' I murmur, looking at my feet. 'I'm sure that's it.'

His finger presses underneath my chin, forcing my gaze to his. 'You're an extraordinary person, Blush. Don't let anyone ever convince you otherwise.'

His words warm my heart, but I struggle to draw breath under the intensity of his gaze. If he truly thinks that, then he would have given into this thing between us long ago, saving us both the longing and torture we've been enduring for years. But the damage is done, and there is no going back.

But he steps closer, and my thoughts become more and more cloudy by the second.

There is no going back to how we once were. Right?

'Hey, I have an idea,' he murmurs, and I blink back to reality, that stunning face only inches from me. He brings my phone up to face level with the camera open. He steps behind me, pressing my back to his chest. He wraps his arm around me, so that his forearm is resting against my throat. I watch through the front-facing camera, curl my fingers around his arm, and look back over my shoulder at him. I hear the distinct click of the camera going off.

Glancing back at the photo, I see him smirking. My insides coil. This photo is the exact representation of my relationship with Mason: me adoring him – it's so damn obvious, written across my face in bold lettering – and him being his usual, cocky self, treating this as a game. I watch as he presses send. Within seconds, we see

Dylan's read receipt. Usually, I would never encourage something like this, but Dylan hurt me so badly and so viciously, I don't care if it makes him sad or angry to think of me with someone else. Especially Mason, who was always a major threat and argument-starter in our relationship. What Dylan and my best friend did to me was much worse.

Wordlessly, I pull my phone from his hand and shove it back into my pocket.

'Hopefully that shuts him up,' he says, pushing a hand through his dark hair, looking completely unfazed, as usual.

I say nothing. The scent of him lingers around me. It's somehow comforting and discomforting at the same time. Longing and love mixed with heartbreak.

'It's because of that night, isn't it?' Mason's voice drops low as a pained expression settles across his face.

The fierceness of his gaze is so strong, I feel it like a physical touch. I keep my eyes trained on a spot on the wall above his shoulder, refusing to return his stare.

'It's why you don't want to be around me.'

I can barely make him out over the loud beat of my heart in my ears. My chest is rising quickly, as if I'm short of breath.

'Admit it, Anya.'

'Yes,' I mutter through clenched teeth.

'I'm sorry,' he whispers. His voice breaks and it hurts to hear. I harden my jaw to the point that it's painful. Tears betray me and burn my eyes, but I hold on tight, determined to push them away. 'I didn't know how to handle everything. I was a coward.'

My face crumples and I roll my lips into my mouth, biting down hard to stop myself reacting.

'I know this doesn't make it right,' he says softly, his fingers threading through the dark strands of my hair. 'But I need you to know.'

'It's too late.' My voice cracks and I close my eyes, wincing.

'I know,' he murmurs, his fingernails scraping gently across my scalp. Unintentionally, I tilt my head back into his touch. 'But I want you to know I think about it all the time, and I regret every minute of it.'

I inhale sharply. 'You regret every minute?'

The pressure of his fingers deepens, and I groan slightly at the feel of his hand working through my hair. He slides his fingers down the back of my neck, then traces a line between my shoulder blades.

'I don't regret you.' His mouth is suddenly against my ear, his hand travelling lower down my back. 'I only regret myself. My actions. My behaviour.' His breath is hot on my skin. 'Never you, Blush.'

I should move away. Push his hand off me. But I'm frozen. His words wrap around me, the warmth of his hand searing through the thin fabric of my dress.

'I have to go,' I say thickly. 'Back to my friends.'

He turns me, cupping my face in his palms. 'Don't hate me, Blush. I can't handle it.'

Slowly, I let my eyes flutter open. Those gorgeous eyes stare back at me, framed by long, dark lashes.

'I could never actually hate you,' I whisper. 'No matter how hard I try.'

When the last of the party-goers stumble from the house towards their Uber, I sag against the wall. I had a lot of fun with my new friends. We talked a lot, laughed loudly, danced until our feet hurt – and I had the best time doing it. I haven't felt this connected to friends in what feels like a lifetime.

Avoiding Mason was extremely difficult when his mission was to find me. I appreciate what he said to me, and his apology. I do truly think he regrets what happened, but it doesn't change the fact that it *did* happen.

Pulling out the piece of paper in my pocket, I stare at the digits scrawled across it. Kai Adams – total playboy and charmer – spent most of his time trying to get my attention. I finally relented towards the end and danced with him. He left with a kiss to my hand and his number in my pocket. The last thing I want right now is a new relationship – if that's even what he's looking for. If he only wants a hook-up, then I'm not the girl for him. I've never been able to casually date.

'What's that?'

I jump in surprise at the deep voice. Forcing out a harsh exhale, I shrug. The effects of the alcohol are still in my system, but I'm feeling partly sober now. 'Nothing.'

'That better not be what I think it is,' he warns. Mason folds his arms across his chest. His biceps bulge as he does, but I don't let myself enjoy the view. The way he stalked around the party with stormy eyes once he saw me dancing with Kai was almost comical. I must have forgotten the part where what I do impacts him.

'Stop,' I glare at him. 'Stop with this overprotective, possessive bullshit. I'm not a kid anymore, you have no right to dictate anything in my life.'

'Don't call him.'

'Are you listening to me?' I ask in exasperation.

'I'm serious,' Mason bites back. 'This isn't about me. This is about him. He's not a nice guy, and you need to be careful.'

Making fists of my hands at my sides, I even out my breathing before I cause a scene and alert my brother to our argument. Twisting on my heel, I march up the stairs. His footsteps follow me, so I walk faster.

I stride into my room and slam the door. I hear it bang against his hand as he throws it back open.

'Fuck *off*,' I snarl through gritted teeth. 'I mean it, Mason.'

He's suddenly right in front of me. He gently pushes me so that my back hits the wall. I inhale so sharply I nearly choke. He wedges his knee between mine, holding me in place. His fingers dig into my pocket and pull out the piece of paper.

'This isn't a *I-can't-have-her-so-no-one-can* thing,' he growls, the heat of his skin searing against mine. 'I'm doing what's best for you.'

'You have no right to pick and choose what's best for me!'

He steps back and rips the piece of paper in two. My jaw drops as I gape at him. Without breaking eye contact, he crumples the paper in his palm.

'You're such an asshole,' I seethe.

'I'm warning you, Blush,' he says. 'Don't talk to him.'

'I've changed my mind; I do fucking hate you,' I whisper, furious tears welling in my eyes. I don't even know why I'm upset, it's not like I'm head over heels for the guy I met tonight, but Mason always brings out the worst in my emotions. He makes me feel too much, too intensely.

The left side of his mouth tilts upward. His gaze drops to my lips. 'We both know you don't.'

11

MASON

THE FOOTBALL SLAMS INTO my chest and I let out a breathless gasp.

'Pay attention!' Zayden snaps at me, shooting a frustrated look my way.

Sighing, I toss the ball back. I can't stop thinking about how I acted last night. Stalking Anya like I have some sort of claim on her. Ripping up Kai's number like a possessive freak. I'm a fucking idiot. But I just can't watch Anya get hurt by someone like him. She has been through enough – and I acknowledge my part in that. This is me making amends, even if she doesn't see it that way. She doesn't know him like I do.

Zayden is the one going through a break-up, but he seems a hell of a lot more put-together than I do. The last few nights, I heard him talking on the phone, but could never quite make out what he was saying. Part of me is convinced he and Leasa have started calling each other again, but he hasn't mentioned anything about it.

When my head is a mess, football is usually the one thing that re-centres me, but not today. That girl is embedded in my mind, body and soul. I just can't shake her, no matter how hard I try. She makes me irrational.

'Take a lap, Jameson!' Coach calls from the sidelines, giving me a displeased frown. His cap is firmly placed on his head, casting a shadow across his eyes. He grips the whistle hanging around his neck so tightly his knuckles are white.

'What?' I exclaim in shock, forcefully yanking myself out of my thoughts and back to what I'm currently doing. 'Why?'

'Your head isn't in the game. Lap. Now.'

The anger surging inside me is a tidal wave, destroying anything in its path. Gritting my teeth so hard I might crack a molar, I nod stiffly, knowing better than to argue with him. 'Yes, Coach.'

Pushing myself into a jog, I run past the rest of the team. Zayden sends me a confused look, which I ignore. He's the only person I confide in, but about this, I can't. If anyone acts crazy when it comes to Anya, it's him. He's even worse than me.

I have been throwing myself into football since returning from Mexico. I was a slack player in the past; I did the absolute bare minimum. But I'm working hard this time around to do better, and it's paying off. Coach and I had a few one-on-one meetings about strategies for games, which makes me feel like an essential part of the team, and that he values my opinion. Since Anya moved in, though, my laser-sharp focus has been wavering. I can't let my control slip. This is important to me, and I want to stay focused, but it's hard when my mind is consumed with her. The wind is cold and harsh on my flushed cheeks. I pick up the pace, chasing the burn in my lungs. I need the numbness that practice provides me.

I focus a little better through the rest of training, but everyone keeps giving me looks as if they know I'm off my game. They're making it worse. When Kai tackles me so hard I see fucking stars, it doesn't help. It takes every bit of my self-control not to pummel him into the ground. Flashes of him dancing with Anya, his hands on her hips, make me so insufferably mad I want to scream.

Dragging my feet, I walk to the locker room. I peel off my

sweaty clothes and step into the shower, desperate to feel the warm water run over my wound-up muscles. Leaning on the tiles, I rest my forehead on my hand. It's too early in the year to be feeling this out of whack. I finish showering and dress quickly.

Zayden is by my car when I head outside. Every part of my body hurts.

'Took your time,' he says, eyes glued to his phone. 'What's up with you today?'

'My head is all over the place.' I sigh. 'I can't seem to get it straight.'

'Everything okay?' he asks with concern, leaning back onto the car. His eyes are hidden behind his sunglasses, but I can tell he's studying me.

'Fine.'

'Has he called you?'

Drops of ice slither down my back. I turn, sliding into the car and starting the engine.

'Mase,' Zayden says.

'No.'

Zayden sighs. My grip on the wheel tightens. He has no right to get angry with me about not wanting to discuss family shit. He is the worst one for it.

We're silent as we drive to the burger place we often go to after practice. Coach has us on a strict diet, but none of us stick to it. Asking a bunch of university students to not drink alcohol or eat junk food is pointless, in my opinion.

Pushing open the door, I see some of the other guys are here, including Kai Adams. My expression sours. I didn't feel much for him until he showed interest in Anya, but I hate him now. With every fibre of my being. I know his type; he isn't good for her. I might not be good for her either, but he is a hell of a lot worse a choice than me.

He saw me come out of her room the night of the party. I don't know what his game is, but I don't like it. He targeted me in training today. I'm sure of it.

'Hey, boys.' Zayden nods.

I barely acknowledge them as I drop into the booth beside Zayden.

'Are you feeling better now, Princess?' Kai coos, leaning over and pinching my cheek between his thumb and pointer finger.

Grimacing, I slap his hand away. 'Fuck off.'

Zayden flashes a warning look at Kai, effectively telling him to back down. Kai rolls his eyes and leans back on the seat, resting on his elbow. Zayden has an air of command about him – he's a friend to all, but he earns their respect.

My mood is even worse now. I feel hostile and agitated. I want to be at home relaxing, not suffering through the presence of these assholes. I have to see them three times a week already for training, and they're in a bunch of my classes and at every party. There's no space to get away.

'Good party, fellas.' Angus grins, slapping his hand on the table. The salt and pepper shakers fall over on impact, spilling across the surface. 'When's the next one?'

'Always down for a good time,' Zayden replies. 'We can host the victory party after our first game.'

The boys cheer and whistle at that announcement. The first game is next week. A mixture of excitement and dread fills me at the thought. I've been excited to play ever since I enrolled. This type of football is bigger and better than what we played in high school, and even the competitions after. I just hope I can sort my shit out before then. I *need* to.

'Move over.' Zayden nudges my arm. 'Gotta take a piss.'

I let Zayden out of the booth, wincing when my muscles protest. My legs hurt from all the running. In the end, I did twelve laps because I couldn't focus. I tap my fingertips together as I mull over Coach's words from earlier today. He held me back after training to ask if everything was okay. He then proceeded to tell me that he wants me to be team captain. A part of me is honoured and thrilled at the opportunity; the other part of me is petrified to admit this to anyone, since I'm one of the new guys on the team.

Coach Kennedy has seen me play countless times before, though – he scouted me in school. Even when I didn't attend university straight away, the offer from him was still waiting for me when I returned. I was put straight into the top team, without working my way up like most do, and I can tell it's made some of the guys bitter, since they spent the last two years working on landing their spots.

The bathroom door has just shut when Kai turns to the group, smirking.

'You see the ass on Zayden's sister?' he asks in a hushed tone, leaning forward, his face looking way too punchable right now. He curls his hand and bites it, making a high-pitched moan sound that has my blood boiling.

'Fuckin' oath,' Andy agrees, half-turning and shaking the shoulders of Angus next to him. 'Angus is still wiping the drool off his chin.'

'That's not the only thing he's wiping off.' Gav snickers.

'I bet you fifty bucks I can bag her before the first game.' Kai sneers.

My fists slam down on the table, silencing the group. 'Not another fucking word about her,' I snarl, glowing with white-hot anger. 'If I see one of you so much as lay a hand on her, I'll make your life a living hell.'

The boys exchange surprised looks and lean back in their seats. Kai levels his gaze to mine, running his tongue down the inside of his cheek and fighting with the smirk trying to take over.

I swallow the fury welling in my throat and lean forward, interlocking my fingers.

'Go on,' I say, a sadistic smile stretching across my lips. 'Keep talking. I dare you.'

Kai's shit-eating grin broadens, but he doesn't say anything else. He leans back once more and takes a long sip of his beer.

'This just got a little more interesting,' he says smugly glancing at the other boys around the table.

12

MASON

Three Years Earlier

I'M ALREADY SPRINTING AHEAD when the ball lands in my hands.

A guy lunges for me and I slice past him, my lungs burning as I take off harder and faster down the field. Heavy footsteps pound behind me. I slide across the ground, touching the football down past the line. Cheers explode from the crowd, and I push to my feet.

Zayden is in front of me in an instant, gripping my forearm and yanking me towards him. He wraps his arm around me in a brief hug, clapping me on the back. Glancing up, my eyes scan across the clusters of people. They land on Anya, and a smile is stretched across her face from ear to ear. I can't help but smile too. My eyes drop to her body, and the wind is knocked out of me.

She is wearing my jersey.

Even from this distance, I can see the pink in her cheeks and the dark hair tumbling down her shoulders. She is in a short skirt and dark, patterned stockings that make her legs look impossibly long. My God, she is stunning. In every single way.

'Earth to Mason?' A voice to my left says, and I blink back into focus, realising that everyone has moved back, and I'm the only one left at the goal line. Shaking the hair from my eyes, I jog down the field, trying to regain some sort of focus.

It's been a week since the party. A week since the kiss. *Multiple kisses*. I'm doing my best to avoid her, but given I'm staying in her family home, that is a difficult challenge. I can't believe I let my self-control slip like that. I can't be that guy for her. I can't lead her on when I don't know what my future looks like right now. I can't do this and risk ruining everything.

Rubbing the sweat out of my eyes, I try to rid my mind of all thoughts of her.

I manage to get through the game, and we finish with a significant lead. We have been unbeatable this season.

'What the fuck?' Zayden mutters, and I look up to see him glaring at the stands. Following his line of sight, my stomach lurches when I realise who he's staring at. Zayden's lips spread into a thin line. 'Why is Anya wearing your jersey?'

Chewing the inside of my cheek, I frown up at the stands, acting as if I've only just noticed myself. I offer a non-committal shrug. 'Don't know.'

Zayden's stare burns into the side of my face as I run my fingers through my hair.

'There better not be anything going on, Mason,' Zayden snaps, and I flinch at the bite in his tone. 'I swear to God, I will kill you.'

'You think I'd do that?' I counter, feeling a flush sweep across my neck at the blatant lie. Guilt grips my stomach in an iron fist. We don't lie to each other. *Ever*.

'You tell me.'

'There is nothing going on,' I say, and the self-hatred I feel hits me like a tonne of bricks.

'She is everything to me, and you are everything to me, and if anything was to ever happen . . .' He trails off, looking at me intensely as he tries to read my expression. 'I would never forgive you for fucking everything up.'

'Jesus Christ!' I retort hotly. 'Nothing is going on. I'm sick of people fucking grilling me about it. How many times do I have to say she is like a little sister to me? She means everything to me too, man. Don't fucking forget it.'

His eyes take on a stormy look before he jerks his chin in a sharp nod. 'Good,' Zayden says coolly. 'If I find out you touched her,' he says, stepping so close the ends of our noses almost touch. 'We're done. Got it?'

The weight of his words slice into me like tiny bullets, hitting my vital organs. The pressure builds behind my eyes, and I want to scream. It's always been like this. I can't have one without hurting the other. And yet, I can't lose either of them.

Swallowing the lump in my throat, I exhale, realising what I have to do. 'Got it.'

13

ANYA

I'VE BEEN AVOIDING MASON like the plague – I'm still furious with him. I've been doing anything I can to fill my afternoons and nights to reduce the chances of us being home at the same time. He requested to follow me on all my social media last night – since I removed him from everything in anger after the party – but I didn't accept him. His obsession with me makes my pulse race, of course it does; it's all I've ever wanted. But I'm not giving in. He hasn't earned it.

Mason spent so much time promising me things he didn't deliver on, and as much as I do care for him, I can't let him in. I can't be hurt like that again.

Nerves bubble in my stomach as I walk into Dance Academy. The room is dim, lit only by neon purple stripes that line the skirting boards. A crowd of girls is gathered in the centre of the room, clad in classy, sexy lingerie. I glance down at my oversized off-the-shoulder jumper and faded booty shorts, feeling like I didn't get the dress-code memo. We drop our things on the bench where everyone else's belongings are and meet the other girls in the middle of the room. Cami introduces us to everyone, and Nora and I follow her stretching routine.

I used to dance and do gymnastics as a kid, but stopped when I started high school. I got too embarrassed to perform at the concerts, fearing someone from my class would happen to be there. It's ridiculous to think that now. I wish I'd stuck with it. Watching the girls around me bend and twist so flexibly and elegantly has me regretting my decision to stop.

The instructor, Amelia, is a tall, beautiful woman with raven-black hair and long, slender limbs. She is a ball of energy, hyping everyone up as we warm up and stretch. I feel myself relaxing the more I move. Everyone is happy doing their own thing, no one is paying attention to me half as much as I thought they would, and if they do look my way, they offer me enthusiastic smiles and thumbs-ups.

'Okay, new girls – allow us to show you the most recent routine we've been learning. Once you've seen it, we'll go over the steps.' Amelia beams, gesturing for Nora, me and two other girls to stand by the mirror in the corner.

'Sex' by JVLA starts playing, and the girls strut to their positions. The lights change to a deep red, and the dancers start moving in sync. I'm completely mesmerised.

'Oh my God,' Nora breathes beside me. 'They're incredible.'

'I am *not* going to look like that.' I blink, watching them glide around the room in heels I can barely walk in.

When the routine is finished, us girls who were watching join in. We spend the next thirty minutes learning the steps. By the end of it, I'm exhausted. I'm glad we didn't do any pole training today – I want to start with baby steps. Everywhere hurts already, and I'm sure I'll wake up feeling even worse.

Even still, when we spill outside after class, I feel amazing. Sweat sheens across my skin, I'm breathless, but I feel fucking *good*. I needed this.

Cami convinces us to go to The Illusion for a drink.

'That was so much fun,' Nora gushes as she pushes the door open. It's packed inside, much busier than when we were here the other day.

'Right?' Cami smiles encouragingly. 'Told you.'

Loud hollering snaps me back to reality. I look over to see a few familiar faces by the bar. Kai Adams and some of the other football boys have spread out across two booths that back up against each other.

'Ugh,' Nora mutters under her breath, glancing down at her exercise clothes. We're all sweaty and flushed.

I force a friendly smile onto my face and follow the girls to the last empty booth. The tabletop is scattered with empty bottles; the people who were seated here must have only just left.

Kai finishes his drink and pushes off the bar, beelining for me. I hope I'm not grimacing as much as I think I am. He slides easily between me and the booth, preventing me from taking a seat. He smirks at me, eyes dipping over my outfit. I straighten, feeling extremely self-conscious in my oversized clothes.

'Hi, gorgeous.'

'Hi, Kai.'

'How are you?' he asks.

My skin feels prickly where his eyes walk over my shoulder, lingering on the exposed skin there. 'Fine, thanks.'

'You never texted me,' he says.

I knew that was coming. 'I accidentally put the piece of paper through the wash,' I lie, feeling my cheeks heat under his scrutinising gaze. 'I . . . er . . . wanted to message you.'

'Oh,' he says, looking a little relieved that I didn't intentionally blow him off. 'That's cool. Give me yours and we can start over.'

I feel torn. I don't particularly want to give Kai my number; he seems a little sleazy and arrogant. But on the other hand, why not? I'm single. I'm entitled to some fun. Besides, I won't be committing to anything. He may not even text me, and even if he does it probably won't lead to anything.

I rattle off my number and he punches it into his phone, then sends me a message so that I have his. I'm instantly relieved I didn't give him a fake one, since he stares down at my phone and waits for it to light up with his text.

'I'll be in touch,' he says. 'Let's hang soon.'

'Sure.' I smile. 'Sounds great.'

He winks at me, and I bite the inside of my cheek to stop the laugh threatening to escape. I'm not sure if he truly thinks that was smooth. He probably does.

He returns to his friends, and I do the same, my heartbeat loud in my ears. Guilt gnaws at my insides. I feel I'm betraying Mason somehow, even though I'm not. He has no claim to me, and I don't owe him a single thing. I shake off the feeling and sit down opposite Nora and Cami.

'Did you just agree to go out with Kai?' Cami asks, her eyebrows so high they almost disappear into her hair.

'Yeah.'

'What about Mason?' Nora asks, exchanging a look with Cami.

'Wait.' I narrow my eyes, pointing between them. 'What was that?'

'What was what?' Cami asks in mock innocence.

'That little . . .' I move my hands to emphasise the look between them. 'Whatever you just did. As if you've been talking about me.'

'I like him,' Nora admits, casting me a sheepish look. 'He seems sweet and really into you.'

'Sweet!?' I protest, eyes widening. Then I realise I never told them what happened all those years ago. 'Sweet' is a fair evaluation, I suppose, since they've only ever seen him as he is now. If they knew how he made me feel – repeatedly – they would have different opinions. Especially if they knew what happened after.

But that's in the past, and maybe the chapter needs to end. We are both different people now. Maybe I need to move on from it.

'He didn't look at anyone else the entire night,' Cami agrees. 'There's something there, girl. Whether you're ready to face it yet or not.'

'Going out with Kai is going to be more confusing,' Nora adds, leaning forward and tucking a piece of her hair behind her ear. 'Unless you're into him. Are you?'

'My head hurts,' I mutter. 'I don't know what I want.'

My mind flashes back to Mason crumpling up the piece of paper Kai gave me. The audacity of that man. It is definitely not *hot* when he's so possessive of me.

It's not.

It's not.

It's *not*.

Nora's hand rests lightly on top of mine. 'It will work out how it's meant to.'

'Sure,' I agree weakly. 'Let's hope so.'

14

MASON

I'M ALONE FOR THE drive back home. Zayden stayed with the boys, who were wanting to go for a drink. I thought he might try to pressure me into staying, but even he could tell I needed to go.

It's only a fifteen-minute drive back, but with my mind so deep in thought, it feels I get there in seconds. Swinging into the driveway, I kill the engine and peer out at the darkening sky. As I get out of the car, raindrops bounce off me. It was an unusually humid day today, which means it will most likely storm tonight.

As a child, storms filled me with so much anxiety I would throw up for hours. It was all because of him: my father – a schizophrenic alcoholic – who was terrified of storms. As a little boy, he got caught outside in the middle of a bad thunderstorm, and lightning hit the tree he was cowering under. Whenever the storm clouds started to roll in, which was often, he would board up the house, unplug all the electronics and scream at me to hide. I would lie in puddles of my own vomit for hours until he unlocked my door. No other kid I knew had a bedroom door that locked from the *outside*.

When I started staying semi-permanently with the Starks, I couldn't believe the difference. Their mum and stepfather would sit out the back of the house, share a drink and watch the storm pass over. It was a surreal moment when I realised I didn't need to be afraid, unlike I always thought. Every time it storms, my mind reels back to childhood and everything I used to deal with. I hate it. I wish there was something I could do to forget it all.

The rain starts to fall harder. I dash inside and kick off my now-wet shoes. Shaking out my hair, I shrug off my jacket and hang it up to dry. 'Numb to the Feeling' by Chase Atlantic is playing softly through the speakers. Curiously, I wander into the kitchen and see a cocktail-mixing kit on the bench.

A splash draws my attention to the pool outside. Anya emerges from the water to float on her back. Rain splatters down on her, and she smiles up at the sky. Her dark hair billows behind her in a long coffee-coloured stream. Her navy bikini is tight over her body, showing off everything that's been consuming my mind for the past few days.

Marching across the room, I yank the screen door open, casting a nervous glance at the almost-black sky.

'Are you crazy?' I shout.

Unfazed, she turns, paddling towards the edge. She wraps her fingers around her cocktail glass and takes a sip. She smiles. 'What?'

'It's storming!'

'No, it isn't.'

'It's raining.' I point at the sky, as if she hasn't noticed the wind slapping against the plastic pool cover piled up on the side.

'So? I'm already wet.' She shrugs, a coy smile dancing on her lips.

I internally groan. I really don't need my mind to go there right now.

'Either join me or go away.' She shrugs again, the teasing grin on her face remaining as she stares up at me.

I raise an eyebrow, surprised at being invited to stay, considering she asked me to leave her alone after the party. I watch her for a moment, then turn to the sky, which is darkening by the second.

'Fuck it,' I mutter. Peeling off my shirt, I toss it on the ground. The tiles are cold and slippery as I walk to the edge of the pool. The raindrops hit my shoulders and slide rapidly down my back.

Anya's entire body is under the water. Her stare doesn't leave mine as I step into the pool. With the low lighting and her dark hair pooling around her, she looks as terrifying as she does remarkable.

The water is surprisingly warm. Moving towards her, I don't stop until I'm just inches away. She stays where she is, silent and watching. God, she is beautiful. No matter if she is dressed to the nines, in her pyjamas or head-to-toe covered in water.

'How was your day?' I ask. A droplet slides down her forehead, between her eyes, before sinking below the water's surface.

'Good,' she answers. 'Had classes, then went out to lunch with Nora and Cami.'

'They seem nice,' I say.

'They are.' She smiles, moving forward just the slightest bit.

'Do you like your classes?' I question, wading my hands softly through the water, causing small ripples across the surface.

'Yeah. They're very different from high school. So far so good. Do you like yours?'

'They're fine.'

'And your day?'

'Terrible.'

'Why terrible?' she asks curiously.

'I want things I shouldn't want. It's messing with my head.'

'What things?' she murmurs, dipping a little further under the water. Her eyes are a piercing dark green in this lighting. Goosebumps scatter across my skin, and not because of the cool wind.

'I think you know.'

'Where's Zayden?' she asks, her arms slowly drifting underneath the water.

'Out,' I whisper, even though there is no need to be speaking so quietly.

'Why aren't you out?'

'I wanted to be home,' I reply. 'I wanted to see you.'

Her expression doesn't waver. She's changed. A lot. She used to be an open book, but now I find it very difficult to guess what she's thinking. Instead of telling me off – like I assumed she would – she tilts her head, staring openly at me with those gorgeous eyes of hers.

'Why?'

'Because I want you,' I murmur, the words falling from my mouth before I can stop them. When I was growing up, I had to shut people out and keep my thoughts hidden to survive, but I'm tired of that. I don't want to play this cat-and-mouse game with Anya anymore. After being separated for so long, and knowing I can't fill the void she left, I want to be honest and real with her for the first time in my life. 'Even though I shouldn't.'

'I see.'

Pausing, I wait in case she is going to elaborate. She doesn't.

'You used to want me,' I choke out, and the weight of her gaze hits me like a sledgehammer. I feel it everywhere, all at once, settling deep in my bones. She is truly embedded in me. I don't know what the fuck is wrong with me, and why my love for her has twisted into this all-consuming obsession. She was on my mind from the moment I left the country, of course she was – she was ingrained in my thoughts for a long time before then – but ever since she turned up at this house, the obsession has been getting worse with every day. 'Tell me, what do you want now?'

'I want to be happy,' she tells me earnestly. 'I want to focus on myself. Achieve the goals I've set, make great friends and memories, and be truly, genuinely happy.'

'I want that for you too,' I agree, the water lapping over my chin as I sink lower, losing my concentration on treading water for a moment. Those long legs of hers softly kick under the surface, and they're extremely distracting.

'Good,' she murmurs. 'Then stop all of this.'

My heart sinks. 'All of what?'

'This chasing and possessiveness, when you probably just want one night of fun to get me out of your system.'

My jaw drops open at her words. I wait for her familiar smile to appear, or her warm laugh – one of my favourite sounds in the world. But her face remains impassive. This stoic expression, which she wears constantly around me now, isn't her. This isn't the Anya I remember. Hurt and betrayal shine in her eyes, and I want nothing more than to rid her of these feelings, but I know I'm one of the people who caused them in the first place.

'You think that's what I want?' I ask, incredulously. 'One night with you?'

She releases a bark of laughter. 'Of course that's what you want, Mason.'

'Why the hell would you think that?' I exclaim. Part of me is furious she thinks so little of herself, but mostly, that she thinks so little of *me*.

'Why do you think?'

I swallow. 'You think you mean as little as one night in my bed? You really think that of me?'

'Yes, I do, Mason.'

'Are you lying to me right now?' I breathe hard as we face each other. Her dark, cool eyes bore into mine, making me feel as if a tendril of ice has wrapped itself around my heart, squeezing it until the pain punctures a hole inside my chest.

'No.'

Closing my eyes, I clench my jaw, trying to process what she is saying. I know I hurt her, but I didn't realise the extent of it until this moment. And I feel crushed all over again.

'Look, Mase,' Anya says after a minute, exhaling a sharp breath. 'There's a lot of tension and history here. I'm not denying that I was in love with you, but I'm a different person now, and too much time has passed. We live together and share some classes. Zayden is your best friend. We will always be in each other's lives because we both love Zayden more than we love ourselves. I know that was my main reason for never letting my love for you consume me, but you never loved me like I loved you, and I'm sick of you acting like you did now that years have passed. What happened can't just be swept under the rug and forgotten. You hurt me, more than I could have ever imagined, but I'm over it. Let's just . . . call a truce.'

I stiffen, hardly able to breathe any air into my lungs. The fact that she's still gazing at me with that expression of *nothing* speaks volumes. I'm truly hearing her. What I did caused irreversible damage, and that knowledge is going to eat at me until there's nothing left.

Usually, I have to stoop a little to look down at her, but here in the water, we're eye-level, and it's making this conversation much more confronting. Her eyes haven't left mine, and I have no idea how my face looks right now.

'A truce,' I repeat, unable to digest all the other words she just threw at me.

'Yeah. Let's just . . . go back to being friends.'

'Friends.' I don't recognise my own voice.

'Yeah. Since that's all we ever were, anyway,' she says. 'Right?

That's what you used to tell everyone.' She leans in close, her cold, empty smile looking all kinds of wrong on her pretty face. 'I'm just a little sister to you. Remember?'

I flinch. I have never felt like this. Reduced to absolute fucking ruin. The silence is thick and suffocating. After a moment, she gives me a stiff nod, looking satisfied with my lack of response.

'Yeah,' she murmurs, rolling her lips into her mouth. 'That's what I thought.'

She moves away from me, and I'm too stunned to do or say anything.

I have never regretted anything more in my life than how I treated her. And I will never forgive myself for it.

15

ANYA

Three Years Earlier

I'VE BEEN SITTING IN the living room for an hour now, snapping my head up to look at the doorway whenever I hear footsteps. I keep waiting for Mason to appear, but he doesn't. He has been spectacular at avoiding me over the last two weeks.

Dread clamps down on my stomach as I recall the hotter than ever kiss we shared, only for him to practically ghost me afterwards. On game night, I thought things were going to change. The shine in his eyes and the genuine, handsome smile that lit up his face when he saw me in his jersey filled me with warmth and hope. And then, radio silence. I thought showing him I wasn't afraid of accepting this, accepting us, would be a good thing, but clearly it wasn't the right approach.

I'm hoping to catch him when he comes home after practice. I'm going to ask if he will watch a new horror movie with me. I read online that it's one of the most gruesome movies to hit the screens in over ten years, and I can't wait to watch it together. Zayden thinks we're insane when we sit here laughing at traumatic scenes, but it's something we enjoy doing together. It always has been. Whenever things get tense, this is how we get back on track.

Sighing heavily, I look at the time. Maybe he's staying somewhere else for the night, or he's out with the boys after practice.

I sent him a message earlier, but it's been left unopened, even though I can see he's been online.

Sinking back into the pillows, I pull up one of my social media apps and begin scrolling through my friends' stories. I open Zayden's, and my stomach hits the floor when I see a girl with her arms snaked around Mason's shoulders, circling her hips and grinding sensually on him. Everyone is whooping their encouragement. I squint, leaning so close to the phone my nose hits the screen. They're at a party, and since everyone is gathered in a circle, I assume they're playing some sort of drinking game.

Tears well in my eyes and I drop the phone, burying my face into my hands.

My heart is shredding, and the feeling burns through me as the tears flow. I quickly scramble for my phone and re-watch the story over and over, cementing the truth into my brain.

Posted an hour ago.

I've been sitting here this whole time, waiting for him, while he's been getting a fucking lap dance from some girl.

Inhaling sharply, I type in his number – of course I know it by heart – then listen as the phone rings. I straighten in my seat when he answers. The background is loud, and I can barely make out his rough voice, 'Anya?'

I open my mouth to say something – I don't even know what – but nothing comes out. I draw in a shaky breath, unable to stop the sob escaping my throat. There's a long beat of nothing, and then a low curse. The phone makes sharp sounds of static, and then everything is quiet.

'Anya,' he says quietly.

'What the *fuck*, Mason?' I cry out, hot tears spilling over, racing down my cheeks.

'I'm sorry,' he whispers. 'I'm sorry, I'm sorry . . .'

'Why?' I choke out.

'We can't do this. We can't be together. I thought this was the easiest way to tell you . . . I'm a fucking idiot. I handled this all wrong.'

'Huh,' I bite out, my voice edged with fury. 'Yeah. Could've maybe had a fucking conversation with me.'

'I have, Blush,' he says quietly. 'We've had this conversation countless times.'

'So then why do all of this?' I shout into the phone, not caring if my parents can hear me. I don't even know who else is in the house at this point – my mind has been consumed with him, as usual. 'Why kiss me? Why act like you fucking care?'

'I do care. I care a bit too much, which is the problem.'

'There is no problem. I like you; you like me. It's simple.'

'It's anything but simple.'

'Mase . . .' I begin, but my words fall short. I don't know what to say. I don't know how to move on from here. We can't go back to how things were. We can't go forward.

I can't lose him. Not like this.

He takes a deep breath, and I feel the resignation it holds. It washes through me, burying deep into the marrow of my bones. I can't contain the cries that escape me. I double over, sobbing into my thighs. His own shaky exhale meets my ears, making me cry harder.

'It has to be this way,' he eventually says, his voice raspy with sadness, and my heart squeezes at the thought he might be crying too.

And then the line goes dead.

16

ANYA

THE FIRST THING I do once I go inside is head straight to the kitchen, where I make myself another drink. One that's even stronger than what I made earlier, which was borderline too strong, but right now, my hands are trembling, my eyes are burning, and I want to feel *none* of it.

How the hell I said any of that without sobbing or breaking down right in front of him is simply astonishing. I mentally pat myself on the back for holding it together. I climb the stairs, dressed in only my bikini and carrying my cocktail glass, with tears tracking down my cheeks.

What a sight.

The drink is consumed by the time I get to the bathroom, and I peel the wet swimmers off my body, tossing them onto the tiles with a *splat*. I get in the shower and turn on the speaker that's suctioned to the wall, cranking up the music. Pressing my forehead to the glass, I let myself sob – the chest-wracking kind of sobs that hurt but feel sort of good at the same time.

My eyes are puffy as hell when I step out of the cubicle, but I feel better for letting it out. I couldn't hold it in any longer, and saying what I did to Mason has lifted a weight off my shoulders. It's done now. We just have to move on and forget about it as best we can.

My phone vibrates and I tense, wondering if Mason is trying to reach out to me. The dread turns to cement that rolls through my body like a bowling ball when I see Dylan's name on the screen.

> **Dylan:** Do you think about me when you're with him?

Scoffing, I click into his contact and block the number. As *if* he thinks that. If he does, he's completely delusional, and more in love with himself than I thought, which is really saying something.

Hardly daring to breathe, I inch the bathroom door open. I'm relieved Mason is nowhere to be seen. I tiptoe down the hallway and disappear into my room. Throwing on an oversized tee, I crawl into bed, feeling exhausted and drained from the day.

When I close my eyes, tortured whisky eyes blink back at me.

Squinting down at my phone, I increase the brightness on the screen as I walk to class, taking my time as I'm a few minutes early. Pulling my sunglasses down the bridge of my nose, I bring the phone so close to my face it probably looks like I'm about to make out with it.

> **Unknown:** Blocking me isn't going to stop these messages.

A shiver runs down my spine as I read those eight words. I don't understand why Dylan is doing this. *He* is the one who cheated on *me*. He played the leading role in ruining our relationship; I don't get what he thinks harassing me is going to achieve. There's no chance in hell I would ever go back to him, and even if I did want to, there's no way Zayden would approve.

Unknown: Can you tell me one thing?

Unknown: How many times did it happen while we were together?

I blink down at my phone, confused. I shake my head. I have no idea how he can believe I cheated on him with Mason, when Mason wasn't even in Australia while I was with Dylan. Unless Dylan thinks we were contacting each other, which I'm guessing he does. I honestly don't even know when Mason came home. I should ring Dylan to try to clear the air, but the thought of hearing his voice literally makes my skin crawl. I don't want anything to do with him, and I don't owe him anything.

Unknown: I saw the photo. Don't bother denying it.

My skin prickles with unease. I quickly glance around my surroundings, suddenly feeling like I'm being watched. My eyes flick back to the screen, and I stop walking.

I can't help but remember the last time I received a text from a number I didn't recognise. Mason, whose number I deleted during one of my heartbroken meltdowns, sent me an old photo of us, with the message 'I miss you' attached. I never even responded to it because it sent me spiralling for days.

'Tall cappuccino, with an extra shot.' My throat tightens at the sound of a voice in front of me. I jerk my head up, seeing Mason's hand extended towards me, holding a takeaway coffee. Not that I show it in any way, but I feel relieved that he's here right now. Those texts have my mind spinning. I have no idea what the hell is going on, but I don't want to deal with any of it.

'What are you doing?' I ask with a sigh, locking my phone and shoving it into the pocket of my jeans quickly, hoping he didn't see anything on the screen.

'Being a good friend,' he replies, offering me that annoyingly adorable smirk that's seared into my brain for eternity. 'Isn't that what we are?'

Giving him a deadpan expression, I take the coffee. 'Okay, Mase. Sure.' I take a long mouthful, trying to hide my smile. He remembers how I like my coffee. 'Thank you.'

'I'll walk you to class.'

'I don't need a chaperone, Mase. I'm a big girl,' I say, re-adjusting the sunglasses on my nose. 'I appreciate the offer, though.'

'Ah, but I'm in the same class. So it makes sense to walk together.'

Stopping, I turn to face him, and he grins boyishly down at me.

'How do you know what class I have right now?' I ask, my voice laced with suspicion.

'I memorised your schedule. The one on your wall.' He shrugs, shoving his hands deep into the pockets of his hoodie. 'I'm going to walk you to the classes we share. Because that's what friends do.'

'Oh great,' I grumble, shaking my head and resuming walking, trying desperately not to show how much I'm screaming on the inside.

He memorised my schedule.

I always wanted this kind of attention from him. I craved it all my life. But now that I'm finally getting it . . . it seems unreal. Like at any moment he's going to turn around and tell me that I've been Punk'd, that he was just waiting for me to fall into his trap first.

The only sounds between us are our breathing and the light shuffling of our shoes on the footpath. I glance over at Mason, who is staring ahead and looking completely relaxed, as if we didn't have a conversation yesterday that completely shifted the way we're supposed to act around each other.

'Why did you come back?' I blurt, my fingers tightening around the strap of my bag.

Mase turns to look at me, surprised at the question. 'Why? Did you want me to stay away, Blush?'

'Answer the question,' I say, ignoring his deflection.

'Well. I didn't want to come back,' Mason admits after a few moments. 'Didn't really want to face everything I left behind, but I had to.'

'You had to?'

He exhales. 'Yeah. Something happened.'

'How awfully specific of you,' I reply sarcastically. 'Really painted a picture for me.'

'I was held at knifepoint, tied up and robbed,' he says flatly.

I stop walking. Mason's shoulders sag as he turns, looking at me wearily. My mouth hangs open as I gape at him.

'I didn't really tell anyone,' he continues. 'Didn't want people to worry.'

I close my mouth, then re-open it, but nothing comes out.

'It's fine,' he says. 'I'm fine.' He swallows, his jaw twitching as he looks away. 'It's done now.'

'Jesus Christ, Mase. I had no idea.'

'I know.' He runs a hand through his hair, looking a little agitated.

'Are you okay?'

'Yes.'

I blink at him, seeing him in a different light suddenly. Maybe this is the reason why he's acting so differently. Maybe having a close call with death changed his perspective on life.

Reaching out, I touch my hand against his arm. 'I'm sorry that happened to you, Mase. That must've been really scary.'

He looks down at my hand, then covers my small one with his much larger one. For a moment, I relish being this close to him.

'I appreciate you telling me. And for being open about your feelings. I know that doesn't come easy to you.'

His thumb runs a line back and forth over mine. He nods and gently removes his hand.

'I'm trying this new thing where I don't fuck things up when it comes to you,' Mason says.

I smile. 'So far, so good, Mase.'

He returns my smile, and we fall back into step with one another. I let go of some of the resentment towards Mason that's been building inside me. At this moment, I just can't hold on to it. I've always wanted him in my life. More of him. But after everything that went down, thinking about letting him back in scares the hell out of me. I can't deny the change in him. The way he is, but also the way he acts towards me now.

Despite this fear, I feel my resolve crumbling inch by inch as each day passes.

17

MASON

IT'S A FRIDAY NIGHT and I'm sprawled across the lounge watching reruns of *Brooklyn Nine-Nine*, a show I've seen so many times I can basically recite it word for word. The old Mason would be ashamed of me, wasting a perfectly good evening and chance to be out partying.

'Mason!' Zayden whines, throwing the football at me. I backhand it away from my face, and it crashes into the coffee table, knocking over the bottle of water I had sitting on it. 'Come on, man. I need this.'

Damn it.

We promised each other we would never ditch a night out if the other bro needs it. His smirk inches wider as he notices my glare and into a full-blown grin when I exhale, pushing myself off the lounge.

Going out is the absolute last thing I feel like doing right now, but Zayden is dealing with the loss of his long-term girlfriend, and I want to support him through it. He wouldn't hesitate to do the same for me.

'Okay,' I relent.

Zayden fist-pumps and lets out a whoop. Exhaling, I trail after him towards the stairs.

'Hang on . . .' Zayden mutters, turning to face me and giving me a narrowed stare. 'Since when do I have to drag you out? You're usually the life of the party.'

A muscle jumps in my jaw and I shrug. 'Just tired.'

'You sure?' Zayden asks, his eyes burning holes into the side of my face. 'Is it your dad?'

'No, Zayden,' I say, harsher than I intend to. 'I don't want to talk about him. I'm just fucking tired. But you want to go, so let's go.'

He jerks back at my words, and guilt instantly floods me. Sucking his teeth, he doesn't say anything as he trudges up the stairs.

'Sorry,' I mutter when we reach the hallway. 'I really am just tired.'

Zayden nods, clapping a hand on my shoulder. 'We don't have to go.'

'No, it's fine,' I say, though even my voice lacks any sort of enthusiasm. 'It'll be fun.'

Twenty minutes later, our Uber drops us off outside the front of the university bar. Loud music thumps through the door and a security guard stands in front of us, assessing Zayden and me. Once he concludes that we're not drunk, he waves us through.

It's busy tonight – so crammed that every table is full, as well as the dance floor. Neon lights dart wildly around the room, and I squint, trying to find a clear path to the bar. Zayden yanks on my elbow, towing me after him as we wade our way through the bodies.

When two fingers pinch my ass, I turn back in surprise to see a leggy blond winking at me. I smile back politely and feel even worse about coming out tonight. Zayden will most likely find a girl to swap spit with, and I'll be stuck by myself. Usually, I don't have any issues mingling and letting the night take me wherever it does, but the last thing I want right now is to make idle chitchat.

Zayden orders our drinks. He's already leaning against the bar talking to a girl when the bartender slides our drinks across to us. Sighing, I take the drink and lean back, surveying the room. It looks like a typical Friday night at a bar dedicated to hosting university students. I used to love these kinds of nights. I don't know what's wrong with me.

Pulling my phone out from my pocket, I bring up Anya's number. I casually asked Zayden for it – for emergencies – as she changed her number since I last had it, and she's removed me from all of her socials.

> **Mason:** Hey. It's Mason.

After a few moments of staring at the screen, I go against my own never-double-text rule and start typing.

> **Mason:** What are you up to?

A minute goes by. And then another. Frowning, I exit the message thread and pull up the Messenger app, since she forgot to remove me from that. It shows that she's active, which means she *is* on her phone, but ignoring me. Excellent. Scowling, I pocket my phone and stare out sourly at the growing crowd.

The door swings open and I glance over. My heart beats sideways in my chest when Anya walks inside, laughing at something one of her friends says. I spy her phone in her hand. My scowl deepens. Cami and Nora are with her, but Kai Adams also appears from behind her, throwing his arm around her shoulder. My teeth grind together so hard my jaw hurts.

She has to be delusional if she thinks Kai Adams is a nice guy.

Looking deliciously sinful in a red dress that fits her like second skin, she lets him walk her towards the bar. Three of Kai's friends also enter after a moment, making me wonder whether it's a coincidence they're all here at the same time. Cami and Nora have drifted off to the side, deep in conversation with the other guys, but Kai hovers close to Anya. Too close.

I'm moving before I realise what I'm doing. She stiffens when she clocks me, and Kai's smirk widens when he notices my pissed-off expression.

'Hi there, Mason.' Kai nods at me.

I don't even look at him. Instead, I direct my glare at Anya, who looks just about as pleased to see me as I am her.

'What are you doing here?' I mean to ask casually, but it comes out like a demand.

'Having fun,' she deadpans, upper lip twitching as she fights off a sneer, clearly not appreciating my tone and attitude right now. I wouldn't either if I were her, but I can't keep a lid on my self-control when it comes to Anya. 'Like you.'

'Trust me, I'm not having fun,' I mutter bitterly.

'Well, I am,' she says, lifting her chin in that new defiant way of hers that makes me miss the old us with every fibre of my being. 'And *friends* don't ruin each other's nights.'

My hands ball into fists at my sides, and I take a deep breath. Like always, she's right. Nodding stiffly, I step back. 'You're right,' I say in defeat, unable to meet Kai's eyes. That cocky smirk he's wearing will be imprinted on the back of my hand if I do. 'I guess I'll see you later.'

Turning my back to her, I stalk off to the bar and slap my hand down. 'Two shots.'

Zayden nods in approval, his signature grin taking over his face. Reaching for the glasses, I hand one to Zayden and throw back the other. I grimace at the burn that runs down my throat.

My eyes flick over to Anya. Anger surges inside me as she leans back against Kai and his hands rest on her hips.

'I don't like that,' I grunt.

Zayden follows my gaze and blows out a breath. 'As much as I hate it, she's old enough now to make her own choices. Even if we both know it's a mistake.'

I blink, startled. Turning to face him, I give him a deadpan stare. 'After what she's just been through, I would've thought . . .'

Zayden's hands land heavily on my shoulders. 'Mase, I appreciate you and how much you care about her, but she isn't a kid anymore, and if she wants to be out having fun, she can. With whoever she wants. As long as she's happy, that's the main thing.'

My mouth falls open. Since when have we done a complete role reversal?

I slide my phone back out and type out a text to her, unable to help myself. Our texts, the games we played, they used to be such a fun part of our relationship.

> **Mason:** What are you doing here with him?

> **Mason:** You'd have a better time with me.

Never taking my eyes off her, I watch as she glances at her phone. The blush that kisses her cheeks is visible across the room. She opens her mouth, looking shocked and, admittedly, a little impressed, before she shifts her face into a stony stare that she swiftly directs at me. I smirk at her, and she narrows her eyes into slits, turning her back to me.

'Hey!' a voice says, and Zayden turns and grins.

'Hey, yourself.'

'Hi,' the girl says again when I still haven't acknowledged her. I wait a beat, collecting myself before I face her.

'Hey,' I say distractedly, my eyes bouncing back to Anya, hoping she will reply. We used to always text these kinds of messages, *especially* in a crowded room like this, when we certainly shouldn't have. My heart sinks a little when she makes no move to reach for her phone.

'You wanna buy me a drink?' the girl asks, her voice low and sultry.

'He sure does,' Zayden says when I fail to reply. He claps his hand on my back, making me flinch. I shoot him a narrowed glare, which only makes his smirk widen. He melts into the crowd, and I glower at him as he disappears.

'I want a screaming orgasm,' the girl chirps, brushing her arm against mine as she casually leans on the bar. 'Think you can handle that?'

Heat inches up my neck as I repeat her order to the bartender. Even though I only ordered one, he reappears with two. I hover my phone over the payment machine and once it chimes in approval, I pocket it and hand the girl her drink.

'Rachel,' she says. 'And you?'

'Mason.'

'Look at that, both of us have had orgasms and we haven't even gotten back to your bed yet,' she says flirtatiously.

I admire her confidence, but my head is a mess, and this means nothing to me. My eyes drift, landing on Anya, who is staring hard back at me. She excuses herself, striding towards the bathrooms.

'Hey, why don't you grab us a table, I'll be right back,' I tell Rachel, holding out my drink for her to take.

'Sure thing,' she replies.

I practically chase Anya down the hallway. I stick my foot in the bathroom door before it slams shut. I grit my teeth, and she whirls around, narrowing those pretty eyes at me.

'What are you doing?' she hisses.

Stepping inside, I close the door, thankful that the bathrooms here are private, so no one can overhear us accidentally. The light overhead dims in and out of brightness, and for a moment, I wonder if we're about to be blanketed in darkness.

'You look mad.'

'I'm not mad,' she retorts with a huff. 'You were having fun. I'm having fun.'

'I don't want to be here. I don't want to be doing this. I just want to spend time with you.'

'Right. And that's why you bought that girl a drink.'

'Trust me, I didn't have much choice in that situation.'

'Okay,' she says, disbelief clear in her tone.

'Wait,' I say, folding my arms across my chest, unable to fight the smirk threatening to take over my face. 'Are you jealous, Blush?'

Two splashes of colour brighten her cheeks. 'No.'

'Yes, you are.'

'If you need to tell yourself that, then fine,' she argues, running her tongue across her teeth as she stares down at her feet.

'Why are you here with him?' I ask, stepping closer to her. Her gaze lifts to meet mine, and I see her throat move as she swallows. 'With Kai?'

She curves an eyebrow. 'You're the one who sounds jealous, Mase.'

'That's because I am.'

Her lips part in surprise. Raising my hand, I trace my fingers down the side of her cheek, and I swear I can hear her pulse drumming. Or maybe it's just mine.

'Don't make decisions because you're angry at me,' I say. 'You know your worth. Remember it.'

Her eyes drift closed, and she leans into my palm. My thumb strokes across the soft lips inviting me in for a taste.

'You need to go,' she whispers. 'You have someone waiting for you.'

'I don't care.'

She lets out a soft laugh, her warm breath spilling across my thumb. 'You should care.'

'Well, I don't. I only care about you.'

'Mase . . .' She trails off, shaking her head. 'This isn't very "just friends" of you.'

'You're kidding yourself if you think we can be just friends.'

'Mase,' she says patiently, stepping out of my hold. She circles her small hands around mine, squeezing them. 'I want you to always be in my life. I have always loved you. But too much has happened. We aren't destined for anything more. Please . . . just leave it be.'

'Why are you saying this?' I demand, a strange mix of fear, anger and urgency welling inside my chest. 'I know what I did was shit. I screwed up. But I'm here now, and I want to make it right.'

'It's okay, Mase,' she says softly. 'You don't know everything, and it's okay. Just . . . let me go.'

'I don't know everything?' I echo. 'What does that mean?'

Yanking her hands from mine, she shakes her head and darts around me. She opens the door and slips out of it so quickly that when I reach for her I grasp empty air. Shoving through the gap in the doorway, I stumble into the hall, where Kai is standing, watching Anya and me with growing interest.

'I was wondering where you ran off to,' Kai says to Anya, even though his eyes don't leave mine. 'Guess there's my answer.'

'It's not what it looks like,' she says weakly. 'I don't feel well, I'm going to head home. I hope you have a nice night with your friends.'

Kai's cheek spasms as he finally drags his gaze from me down to Anya.

'I'll take you,' he says.

'It's fine,' I cut in, stepping so close my chest hits Anya's back. 'I'm leaving now. I can take her.'

Kai nods slowly. 'Yeah. Sure. I bet Zayden will love hearing all about that.'

Ignoring his comment, I push around him, and Anya follows closely behind. We are silent as we make our way through the crowded room. Zayden is leaning on the bar, talking to the girl who I bought the drink for. She was probably looking for me, and I feel a little bad about that, but it looks like she is enjoying Zayden's attention. He won't even realise I'm gone. Deciding to text him later, I lead Anya out onto the street. The crisp night air washes over me, relieving me momentarily of the anxiety that is swirling in my chest.

'Wait, do you even have your car here?' she asks.

'No,' I reply. 'But I didn't want you going with him.'

She rolls her eyes. 'How are we getting home?'

I wave my hand, showing her my phone screen. 'I just ordered an Uber.'

'You don't have to leave,' she says.

'I want to.'

'Did you have a lobotomy when you were overseas?' She raises her eyebrows, looking at me curiously. 'You're not the Mason I remember.'

'That's what I've been trying to tell you,' I murmur, stepping so close that our hands touch. 'I've changed. For the better.'

Chewing her lip, she stares down at the proximity of our hands, deep in thought. Headlights swing onto the street, and the Uber stops in front of us. Wordlessly, we climb into the car.

The tension between us is simmering as we take the short trip back to our house. My eyes are glued to her bare thighs. She faces away from me, gazing out the window, her knee bouncing up and down. My hand drifts towards her, skating across her shoulder. She shivers as my fingertips drag across her bare skin. Wrapping a dark piece of her hair around my finger, I gently play with it.

'Mase,' she whispers, closing her eyes.

I continue my soft caress until the Uber pulls up out the front of our house, when I reluctantly pull my hand away. My skin burns where it made contact with hers.

When we get inside, Anya walks into the kitchen.

'What are you up to?' I ask, watching her pull out ingredients for a hot chocolate. Every part of my body begs me to close the distance between us and hold her, but I know I can't. She isn't ready for that, and I need to come to terms with the fact that she may not ever be again.

'Having a drink. Want to join me?' she asks, her voice surprisingly calm and collected. She seems so unaffected by the tension between us, whereas I feel it in every bone of my body. Was this how she felt all those years? It must have been torture.

'Sure.'

'Then I'm going to watch a movie.'

I bite the inside of my cheek. That was something we used to do together all the time. I nod, leaning my elbows onto the kitchen bench as she prepares the drinks.

'Can I watch it with you?' I ask.

'If you want to, but I'm choosing the movie.'

'Of course.'

'You're okay, right?' she asks softly, pausing for a moment to meet my eyes. 'Should I be worried?'

'I'm okay, Blush.'

'You'd tell me if you weren't?' I watch her grip the handle of the jug tightly as she waits for my response.

My eyes are fixed on her. I can't help but admire her beauty every time I stare at her. It's as if she grows even more stunning with each day. I've always cared deeply for her, but this feels different. Like an unscratchable itch that is burning a hole in my chest.

Even when life was bleak and things were hard, she was always there for me, and I was always there for her. How did it get so screwed up?

'You're probably the only person I would tell.'

Her eyes soften, and she offers me a timid smile. 'Okay.'

'I'll make my special hot chocolate for you, if you want to go pick a movie?' I suggest, feeling the need to occupy my hands before they start wandering towards her. Again.

'Sure,' she replies.

As she brushes past me, I get a wave of her sweet perfume, which lingers in the air as she exits. Despite her changing so much over the years, her signature scent has remained the same: jasmine with a hint of vanilla. My heart trips in my chest at the familiarity of it.

Flashes of embracing her, tangling my fingers through her hair as she buries her face into my chest swarm my mind. Now, as I walk into the lounge room, both of us are tense, subtly side-eyeing each other, gauging the other's reactions. I hate this.

I hand her the mug and collapse onto the lounge, draping a blanket over my legs. I rest my feet up on the coffee table and sip at the hot chocolate I made.

It's clear from the start that whatever movie she's chosen, it's a horror. Grinning, I turn my head to face her.

'A horror? You're so sweet. Thank you.'

Rolling her eyes, she smiles. 'You made me my favourite drink. I put on your favourite genre. It's only fair.'

'*Our* favourite genre,' I correct her.

Avoiding my eyes, she takes a generous gulp of her drink. Smiling, I settle back into the lounge, making myself comfortable.

Hopefully this is the start of things getting back to how they used to be.

18

MASON

Three Years Earlier

'YOU AND CHELSEA?'

Exhaling heavily, I turn to face a smirking Zayden. The plan has worked almost perfectly. I need to let Anya go. She deserves better than what I can offer her, and I can't risk jeopardising my relationship with my best friend. All of it makes my head hurt. And my stupid, damn heart. I can't wait to get out of here for a little while. I feel as if I haven't breathed fresh air for weeks now.

Shrugging off his hand, I mutter something incoherent. It's not fair on Chelsea either, but I don't know how else to keep my mind off Anya. She needs to be hurt and angry to move on. As much as it kills me, it's how it has to be.

The laughter and chatter in the locker room drowns out our conversation, but it doesn't go unnoticed that I don't want to discuss this.

'Come on.' Zayden grins, lightly backhanding my shoulder. 'Give me some goss. You two have . . .?' He makes a barbaric hand gesture, and I screw my face up.

'Drop it, will you?' I grunt, stomping into my boot.

Zayden pouts. 'You're no fun.'

He eventually moves over to the other guys, and my shoulders sag at the relief of being left alone. I've been in a depressive, anxiety-riddled state for weeks – ever since the conversation with Anya that broke both our hearts.

'I hear my little bro is planning to ask out your sister,' I hear JP drawl, and my head snaps up at his words. He leans against his locker, a crooked smirk on his lips.

Zayden's eyebrows rise as he blinks at JP. 'I don't fucking think so,' Zayden snarls.

JP shrugs, and I want to wipe that smug look off his face. 'That's what he reckons.'

'Your brother is a dirty dog,' Zayden mutters.

JP barks out a laugh. 'That he is.'

I feel the urge to empty my stomach onto the floor, but I force myself to stand, swallowing down the bile climbing up my throat. I'm the last to leave the locker room, and everyone is already spreading across the field as I jog out.

I look upwards, admiring the afternoon sun. It's been a sweltering Australian summer, with lots of humidity and afternoon storms, but as we're moving into autumn now, there's a refreshing coolness in the air.

I've been throwing myself into football; I'm living and breathing it. I'm barely even spending any time with Chelsea, her dislike for which she makes clear any chance she gets, but it's the only way I can tire myself out and ease the thoughts racing through my mind.

Now that's been ruined too. Because every time I see JP's face, I picture his smart-ass younger brother – Dylan – and rage uncoils in my chest, threatening to detonate at any moment.

Swallowing the anger, I push through practice, going harder than I have all week, and I'd already amped it up. I notice Coach's eyes on my back more than a few times. He's probably wondering what's going on with me, but since I'm turning up to every game and delivering every single thing he asks for, he isn't complaining or asking after a reason, which I appreciate. My commitment to the team comes and goes depending on where my head is at, but I'm working on getting better at that.

Sweat drips down my forehead by the time we finish, and I swipe it away with the back of my hand. Fatigue rattles my bones; I'm starting to feel the week catching up with me.

Zayden wanders over and nudges my side. 'Hey, you okay? You've been quieter than usual.'

I shrug. 'I'm fine.'

'Your dad?' he guesses. 'Have you been back to see him?'

I shake my head. 'No.'

'What is it, then?' he asks, forehead crumpling in concern. 'Not into Chelsea?'

'I don't know.'

'You're crazy, man. That girl is *hot*.'

I breathe a half-scoff, half-laugh. I feel like shaking him and saying, '*She's not Anya*.' But I'm too tired and drained from thinking about all of this. I have spent the last week contemplating whether I should just confess everything to Zayden and hope he forgives me, but the anger that simmers in those eyes at the mention of anyone being with his sister is enough to make me second guess that idea. He says he doesn't trust anyone with her, which only confirms even further that Anya deserves way better than me – I've already broken her trust. I just have to man up and accept that, as hard as it is to do.

I understand why Zayden feels the way he does. Both of us have struggled with controlling our anger. My father is a violent man, and their stepdad has anger issues as well. We're both certainly traumatised by them. We've struggled with this for a long time, but I'm working really hard to break the cycle. Neither of us are anything like our father figures, but we still want better for Anya, because that's what she deserves.

Zayden sings off-key the entire drive back to his house, and I try to relax and enjoy spending time with my best friend. The bass is so loud, it rattles the doors. He swerves into the driveway and as we pile out of the car, I swing my sports bag over my shoulder.

My chest tightens when Anya steps down from the porch. Her long, tanned legs are smooth, and the dress she wears clings to her tightly. My hand clenches the strap of my bag.

'Where are you off to, dressed like that?' Zayden queries, pulling off looking curious and stern at the same time.

'I have a date, if you must know.'

My eyes close briefly, and I want to bang my head against the side of the car, hoping it sends me into a coma.

'A date?' Zayden echoes, a pinched expression appearing on his face. 'With who?'

'Zeke.'

Both of our heads whip up. Zayden's eyes narrow. 'I heard a rumour you and Dylan were an item.'

'He asked me out too.'

Of course they both did. She is stunning and kind. The boys would be biting at her heels to get her attention.

'I don't approve of this.' Zayden frowns.

'Good thing you're my brother, not my *dad*,' she says snarkily. She brushes past me, and I clench my jaw when a wave of her perfume hits me. Delightfully sweet, like her. Well, most of the time.

'Don't be out late.'

'Don't tell me what to do,' she tosses over her shoulder just as Zeke pulls up at the end of the driveway. She disappears inside the car, and he throws a wave in our direction before flying down the street, the car's loud exhaust drilling inside my skull.

'Fuck this shit, I need a drink,' Zayden mutters.

'Me too.'

We go inside, and I'm feeling glum as fuck. I'm pissed as hell too – with her, with Zeke, with Zayden and, most of all, with myself. Better Zeke than Dylan, but I don't want her with either of them. With *anyone*.

I stumble into the bathroom and slide down the wall. Black dots swallow my vision and I choke on my breath just trying to inhale. Pushing to my knees, I throw my head inside the toilet bowl and retch, waves of nausea rolling over me as the anxiety eats its way through my body.

When will this fucking end?

19

ANYA

THE STEADY RHYTHM OF my feet hitting the pavement calms my mind, which feels as if it's been spinning for the entire last month. There's a slight breeze, which moves the two tendrils of hair that have fallen in front of my face. I run harder and faster until the burn spreads into a feeling of numbness that trickles through my body like icy-cold water.

I used to run all the time, and when Zayden told me about the perfect running track that goes from our house down to the beach, I decided to force myself out of bed this morning to see it for myself. Running used to clear my head, and that's something I desperately need right now.

Stumbling to a stop, I lean over, pressing my hands against my knees as I heave, but nothing comes up, since I haven't eaten for what I realise is an unhealthy amount of time. My heart gallops in my chest and my vision swims. After a few greedy gulps of the fresh morning air, my pulse finally starts to slow as I catch my breath. I've already run the track in full and have pushed myself to do it a second time, even though the length of one lap is certainly enough.

My head is so full. I can't stop thinking about Dylan, and Phoebe, and the fact that they may have been together for most of the time I was with him. My best friend let me confide in her, only to betray me in the worst way, lying right to my face.

And then there's Mason, who makes my heart hurt in a different way. Longing, lust and resentment, all bound tightly into one aching ball lodged in my chest. I can't think straight when it comes to him. I spent years building walls around my heart to protect myself from him, and he's doing everything in his power to rip them back down.

Tears burn my eyes, and I sag to the ground, drawing my knees to my chest and burying my face. It all hurts. No amount of running or distraction can stop my mind from going over everything, like a song stuck on replay.

'Blush.' Mason's voice, deep and raspy, makes me jolt in alarm. I snap my head up to see him looking down at me in concern. He looks handsome – as always – in a sleeveless black shirt, and a backwards cap that pushes his dark hair away from his face. His sweat glistening across those bulging, tattooed biceps makes me question my strength. 'Are you okay?'

'Yes,' I exhale, shakily getting to my feet. 'Just went a little too hard.' Surreptitiously wiping the tears from my eyes, I clear my throat, levelling him with a suspicious look. 'Are you following me?'

'I run this path every day,' he says flatly. My eyes track the movement of his chest rising and falling; his shirt clings to his hard, muscled torso. I tear my eyes away.

'Oh.'

'Which means you're the one following me, technically?' He smirks.

'I am not.'

'Okay.'

'What do you want, Mase?' I sigh, planting my hands on my hips.

'Just checking in on you.'

'Well, I'm fine.'

'Okay, then.'

His eyes stay trained on my face for a heartbeat too long before he turns and starts jogging away. I spend way too long watching him effortlessly run down the exact path I was planning to head down myself. My saliva feels thick as I swallow and turn to go back home, feeling too drained and lightheaded to continue the run.

Zayden is in the front yard when I arrive, and he throws the football he's playing with at me. I catch it with a slight *oomph* as it collides with my chest. He holds out his hands, and I launch it back to him.

'Morning.'

'G'morning,' I mumble.

Wordlessly, we throw the ball back and forth a few times before I make a time-out signal. Tucking the football under his arm, he strolls over to me.

'I didn't realise you were running again.'

I shrug. 'Trying to get back to my old self.'

'How are you doing with everything?' Zayden asks, raking a hand through his mop of dirty-blond hair. He rests his foot on the bottom step of the porch and starts lightly tossing up the ball and catching it.

'I don't know,' I answer honestly. 'Some days I'm totally fine. Some days I'm really sad.' Clearing my throat, I survey the yard and gaze out to the road. 'And you?'

Zayden nods. 'Much the same, I guess. Trying to keep myself busy and distracted. Sometimes it works, sometimes it doesn't.'

'That's the best thing to do.'

'Mase is worried about you,' he says.

I whip my head to face him, surprised. 'He said that?'

Zayden nods. 'Worried about you and Kai Adams.'

I'm surprised Mason raised this concern with Zayden, since the topic of me can be quite sensitive between them, especially when it comes to dating.

'Is he now?' I deadpan.

'We hear and see shit that you don't,' Zayden points out. 'He's a total douche. But I said to Mason that it's up to you to make your own choices.'

I straighten, widening my eyes at my brother. Since when is he reasonable?

'Just be careful.'

Smiling, I reach out and touch his arm. 'I will.'

After I've showered and dressed for the day, I set up in a spot in the backyard that's sheltered by a giant chestnut tree. Sitting with my legs folded beneath me, I spread my paint supplies out across the rug and place a blank canvas in front of me. One of my upcoming assignments makes up a huge part of my grade, and the top three students get the chance to have their art featured in an exhibition. I'm working with a few ideas and have been trying to figure out exactly what I want to paint.

As I swipe my paintbrush over the canvas, I feel the knots in my back unwind. This is one of the only things that relaxes me. Especially since it's still and quiet in the backyard, the air warm. Music hums softly from my phone, and I get lost in the painting. I don't realise hours have passed until my alarm goes off, startling me.

Stepping back, I admire my work. It's one of my more colour-ful paintings, since I've been making a lot of dark ones lately. I pack up my things and place the canvas on the back deck to dry.

I follow the sound of voices and peer out the kitchen window, where I see Zayden and Mason throwing the football back and forth in the front yard. I trot upstairs to get ready for my afternoon classes. By the time I'm good to go, Mason is leaning against the wall beside the front door, twirling his keys in his hand.

'Ready?' he asks. He looks handsome dressed in all black, his hair damp from the shower. He must have done that quickly, as I didn't even hear him come up the stairs. When his mouth tilts into his familiar lopsided smile, it feels like a fist is tightening around my heart.

'Ready?' I repeat, confused.

'You have Intro to Communication, right?' His eyes travel down my body, and my breath hitches in my throat, as he doesn't try to hide it one bit.

'You're such a stalker.'

'You didn't answer my question.'

'It sounds like you already know the answer.'

His lips twitch. 'Come on. I'm taking you.'

Deciding not to argue and instead be grateful I don't have to drive myself, I follow him out the door. I always get stressed trying to find a park, so I appreciate it when someone else offers to take one for the team.

Climbing into Mason's truck, I try not to stare at him, but it seems to be getting more and more difficult to keep my eyes off him. It's like he's a magnet, always drawing me in.

'I'm glad you're still painting,' he says conversationally as he starts the engine.

'It's my form of therapy,' I say quietly. After Mason left, I was convinced he took all my inspiration with him. It was like all the creative, fun ideas I once had flowing out of me dried up – nothing I painted seemed to compare to my older stuff. But now that Mason is back in my life, it seems my creative streak has returned. I'm trying to convince myself that the two aren't connected, but obviously he impacts me in more ways than I care to admit.

'Like mine being football.' He nods. 'We all have something.'

Turning my head, I gaze out the window. My fingers furiously pick at a loose thread in my skirt. For months, I gave myself countless mental pep talks in preparation for potentially seeing Mason again. I had it all planned out. I was meant to be cool, calm and unbothered. Like he always was. Instead, I'm a tightly coiled bundle of nerves who feels like more of a mess than anything whenever he's near me. And since he's made it his mission to insert himself into my everyday life, whether I try to avoid him or not, it doesn't seem like he'll be going away any time soon. A part of me is holding my breath, though, and waiting for him to run away again, like he did before.

Each inhale is filled with him. A pleasant, comforting mixture of his body scent, coffee and the mint body wash he's used every day for as long as I remember. It reminds me of warmth and the sense of his arms around me. The feeling of having his attention and the forbidden nature of our touches and kisses. I don't want to be reminded of all this. I spent so long squashing it deep down, but no matter how hard I try, it keeps trying to resurface.

I focus on inhaling and exhaling, the knot in my chest tightening with each passing moment. Does he feel this? The crackling tension between us? The air thickening to the point it hurts to breathe? Is this all in my head?

'If you pull any more on that thread, you're going to rip a hole in your skirt.'

I blink back to reality. My eyes dart to his, then down to my denim skirt, where the thread has unravelled way more than I realised. 'Oh,' I say.

'You seem nervous.' The truck smoothly comes to a stop as we idle at the traffic lights.

My throat is dry when I try to swallow. I feel the heat of his gaze on the side of my face. 'Being around you makes me anxious,' I blurt out before I have the chance to stop it. I mentally cringe at the statement, wishing I could take it back.

My words hang heavily between us, and even when the light changes, Mason is still staring at me.

'The light is green,' I croak out, gesturing in front of me.

After a beat, the truck moves forward.

'I'm sorry,' he says quietly. 'I don't mean to make you anxious.'

I chew my lip and reach for the thread, internally cursing when I realise I can't pull on it anymore.

'If it's any consolation, you make me anxious too.'

'I do?' I whisper.

'Extremely. My head is all over the place when it comes to you.'

I inhale sharply, facing the front again.

We're just friends. That's all we can be.

My cheeks are hot to the point they're burning. I drum my fingers rapidly on my thighs. Why does this fifteen-minute trip to the university feel like it's taking an eternity?

My shoulders sag in relief when the car park comes into view. We manage to snag one relatively close to the walkway, which means I don't have to climb a series of stairs, like I would have if I were driving. I always play it safe, parking way back in 'no-man's-land', as Mason and Zayden call it.

By the time I get around to the boot of the car, Mason has my bag slung over his shoulder and my extra textbooks lazily held between his chest and forearm.

'Thanks, Mase, but I can carry them,' I say, reaching for my items, but he steps back. Frowning, I swipe at them, but he holds them above my head. I'm tall, taller than the average girl, but at six foot two, he towers over me, and easily holds the books out of reach. Grumbling, I step back, shaking my head. I'm not annoyed in the slightest, but I act like it regardless.

'Not on my watch,' he says dismissively. He walks off in the direction of our building, and I have to jog to keep up with his long strides.

I push the sleeves of my top up to my elbows as the warm air, combined with the excessive walk to class, has me feeling hot. I regret thinking a long-sleeve shirt was a good idea.

'I'm going to take a trip back home next weekend, to catch up with some people,' Mason says. 'If you want to come, you're welcome to. Zay probably will.'

'Oh, sure,' I reply, reaching back to tighten my bun, since my hands refuse to sit still. 'Would be good to see everyone. Well, not everyone . . .' I trail off, realising that going back would mean facing the problems I ran away from. Growing up in a small town, it's hard to avoid people. The last thing I want to do is run into Dylan or Phoebe, but I would like to see Mum and the few friends I do keep in touch with. 'Maybe I won't go.'

'Forget about them.'

'Easier said than done,' I say, exhaling. 'Will you go see your dad?'

Mason visibly tenses at the mention of his father. His jaw locks, and he turns his head away so I can't see the expression on his face.

'Maybe,' he eventually replies.

'Would you like me to go with you?' I question, tucking a loose piece of hair behind my ear, which the wind keeps blowing it into my eyes. 'To see him?'

Immediately, Mason shakes his head. 'It's not safe for you to visit him. The fewer people, the better.'

My heart squeezes. I can't even imagine how it would feel to be in Mason's situation. It must be awful. As much as my stepfather is stubborn and set in his ways, I don't believe I've ever felt unsafe around him. Sure, he's odd, and makes strange comments here and there, but he doesn't seem malicious. He's fourteen years older than my mum. It didn't seem obvious when we were younger, but now with his grey hair and wrinkled face, the age gap between them is clear as day. It was extremely embarrassing when one of my friends assumed he was my grandfather.

We reach class, and I expect us to go separate ways, but he trails behind me and collapses into the vacant seat beside mine.

'I'm starting to think you're attached to my hip,' I joke.

'In my dreams I am.' He winks, and I realise he took my comment completely out of context.

'Did the dream only last five seconds?' I ask sweetly.

His jaw drops. 'Excuse you?'

'Sorry,' I concede, my voice dripping in sarcasm. 'It was more like three seconds.'

He lets out a dark laugh, running his tongue against the inside of his cheek. 'Trust me, Blush, the next time I fuck you, you'll be screaming my name and seeing stars.' He leans forward, and the heat of his skin seeps into mine. 'And believe me, it will be longer than three fucking seconds.'

My ears are ringing and my face is on fire as his dark eyes bore into mine. I gulp, facing the front of the room, unable to form a response to that. The lecturer strides in at that moment, saving me from having to scramble for something to say. I sink low into my seat, hating that I can sense the smirk on Mason's face, even though I'm not looking at him.

I can't focus for the entire the lesson. I feel extremely unsettled and flustered because of what Mason said, and the fact that our arms keep brushing as we take notes. I was supposed to become immune to his charms and the unwavering effect he has on me. How the hell has it gotten even *worse*?

By the time class ends, my notes are in shambles, as well as my mind. Slowly, I begin to pack up my things as the room starts to empty.

'Coming?' Mason smirks, and I hate the ripple of desire that inches down my spine when he says it, the double meaning like a prickle on my skin.

'I need a minute,' I mutter. 'You go ahead.'

'Our next class isn't for another hour.'

'Exactly. I'm good here. Run along.'

'Is that what a good friend would do?' Mason asks, pushing to his feet and turning to lean against the desk.

I gulp when I realise the last person just left, the door swinging shut behind them with a deafening bang.

'Mason,' I breathe. 'I'm trying very hard to keep a hold of my self-control right now, and you're not helping.'

'Helping you hang on to that control is not exactly my intention, Blush.'

I scramble to my feet and begin shoving my things into my bag, wincing as my notebook bends when I press down on it aggressively.

He steps closer, his warm breath fanning across my neck as his hard chest rubs against my shoulder. 'Let me relieve the pressure,' he murmurs, his voice smooth, melting my insides into a pool of hot liquid. His mouth is millimetres from my ear, sending shivers racing through my body.

I exhale, closing my eyes and clenching my thighs. I love his dirty mouth. 'I don't want to fall for you again,' I whisper. 'I don't want you to hurt me.'

'I won't hurt you, Blush,' Mason says, his voice firm. 'I promise.'

'Promises don't mean shit when it comes to you.'

'Blush,' he murmurs, his lips brushing my ear. 'I know you want me as badly as I want you. I want to make you feel good.

To make up for . . .' He pauses. 'For our first time.' Pushing my hair back over my shoulder, he leaves a soft, lingering kiss on the delicate flesh of my throat. 'Only if you want it, of course.'

I'm panting at this point, gripping the desk like it's the only thing keeping me upright. We are doing this. We are acknowledging what happened, and he wants to make up for it. Is this really happening right now?

'Tell me to stop, and I'll stop,' he whispers.

My lips remain shut.

'You want me to touch you, Blush?' Mason asks, sending a rush of tingles through my veins. 'You want me to taste you?'

'Oh, God,' I whimper.

'That's not an answer.'

'Y-yes,' I stammer, legs buckling.

Wrapping an arm around me, Mason spins me around, hoisting me onto the desk. He pushes my thighs apart as he steps closer, towering over me, his broad chest in line with my eyes.

'Tell me what you want.'

'I want you,' I breathe.

'You want me to what?'

'Mason,' I groan, throwing my head back as his warm fingers trail up my thighs.

'Yes?'

'I want you to touch me,' I whisper.

'And what else?'

'Fuck you,' I hiss, but my breathlessness gives away my true feelings. I'm loving the touch of his hands on me.

'Come on, Blush. Tell me.'

'I want you to taste me.'

'Okay,' he murmurs. I inhale long and hard, relishing in his scent, and let myself finally enjoy his closeness. Goosebumps erupt across my skin as his lips caress mine, so tender and soft that I end up gripping the back of his neck and pulling him to me, roughly kissing him with all the pent-up emotions I've kept locked away. He groans into my mouth, kissing me back just as hard.

I don't know why all rational thought has evaporated from our brains, but at this moment, I really don't care. I don't care if I'm weak, or stupid, or downright fucking insane. I just want him, and that's all that matters.

We kiss long and hard, and I'm breathless when we break apart. He leaves a trail of kisses along my mouth, across my jaw and down my throat. He bites into my neck and I hiss in delight, arching my back, pressing my body into his, even though there's no space to close between us. My hands roam wildly over his muscled back, his shoulders, across his chest, the hard outline of his abs.

'What if someone walks in?' I whisper, not daring to open my eyes and ruin this moment.

'They can enjoy the show.'

His body slides down mine, and he leaves hot, open-mouthed kisses up my inner thigh. My chest is heaving at this point, and I sink my fingers into his hair, wrapping the unruly dark strands around my fingers.

'Look at me, Blush,' he murmurs.

Swallowing, I force my eyes open, and stare down at him. He's wedged between my bare thighs, on his knees, those dark eyes fixed on mine.

'I've wanted to taste you for a very long time. Do you know that?' he asks.

I shake my head, words escaping me.

Moving his hands underneath my thighs, he hoists them over his shoulders, simultaneously dragging me forward to the very edge of the desk. Eyes darting back up to mine, he licks his lips.

'You want this?' he murmurs.

'Yes,' I whisper.

'How much?'

'So fucking much,' I whisper, tears springing to my eyes as the aching need intensifies.

His cheek spasms. 'Okay, okay. You don't have to beg me.'

'You're such an asshole.'

Grinning, he slides his hand down my leg, hooking the lace fabric of my underwear. He yanks them down my legs, tossing them over his shoulder. He glances up one last time before he dives between my thighs. A sound I don't recognise leaves my mouth as his tongue runs straight down the slit of my entrance. His tongue circles over my most sensitive area, making my legs tremble on his shoulders.

'Eyes on me,' he murmurs. My eyes shift back to meet his, and I feel the heat of a blush race up my neck and jump onto my cheeks.

As his tongue circles and teases my clit, I jerk under his hold, barely able to withstand the intensity of it. He spends a generous amount of time down there before he leans back for a breather and to sink a finger inside me. When a second finger enters, curling at just the right angle, I know I'm about to come undone. A desperate part-moan, part-yelp tears from me, and my fingers slide down his neck, sinking into his flesh as I buck and writhe my hips, grinding against his tongue and fingers.

The sensation is building, coming on fast and hard, making me tense. When I feel my orgasm explode, I let out a shriek, his name leaving my lips. An intense throbbing sensation courses through me in waves before I slowly come back down from the high, feeling like my soul is detached from my body and I'm floating overhead, watching this all take place.

Leaning back onto his calves, he runs his tongue around his glistening mouth. His cheeks are deliciously flushed, his hair a total mess, and my wetness coats the complete lower half of his face.

'I knew it,' he murmurs, sucking his bottom lip into his mouth. 'I knew you'd be the best damn thing I've ever tasted.'

20

MASON

ANYA PUSHES TO HER feet and combs her fingers through her hair, which has completely fallen out of the bun she had it piled up in on top of her head. Her entire body is shaking as she quickly redoes it and pulls her skirt down. Pupils dilated, her face a stunning peach colour, she moves desperately around, trying to find something.

'Looking for these?' I ask, a smug smirk dancing across my lips.

Her eyes zero in on the scrap of white fabric I have clenched in my hand. Her jaw drops open before she manages to neutralise her expression, straightening her spine in an attempt to look me in the eyes, even though she only comes up to my chest.

'Yes, actually,' she says curtly, holding out her hand.

'Nah, I think I'll keep these.' I grin, pocketing her underwear and enjoying the reddening of her cheeks. 'You know, for the memories.'

'Mason!' she snaps, eyes wide in panic. 'Absolutely not.'

'You can try to get them from me,' I dare her, smirking.

Letting out a huff, she glares at me, knowing that what I've just said is fact. With my height and quick reflexes, there's no chance of her hands even coming close.

'Fine,' she hisses. 'Keep them.'

'I will.'

She spends more time than necessary fixing up her outfit, and I can't help but smirk, enjoying how much I've ruffled those perfect little feathers.

'So,' I drawl, leaning forward and trapping her against the desk once more. 'Did you like it?'

Gritting her teeth, she glares somewhere over my shoulder. 'It wasn't too bad.'

I let out a low chuckle. 'You came all over my face, Blush. I think it's safe to say it was better than "not too bad".'

'Oh, God.' She lets out a high-pitched laugh, covering her face with her hands. 'I can't believe we just did that. In our *class-room*.'

'Pretty hot, wasn't it?'

Peering at me through the gaps in her fingers, she eventually lowers them, finally breaking free the playful smile that I love.

'Yeah. It was.'

I help her gather her things, then we exit wordlessly. I offer to get us both coffees and much to my surprise, the effortless-ness between us seems to be back. At least for now. Probably still wrapped up in her post-orgasm high, Anya doesn't hate me right now and isn't afraid of letting me in. I'm going to enjoy every moment of it.

I order our coffees, and we make our way to one of the tables. I desperately want to talk to her about us, about what she wants, what I want, but I don't want to push my luck. For this brief moment, I have her back, and I'm not going to fuck it up. I just need to know that she's all in, and we can face Zayden's reaction together as a united front. I don't want to hurt anyone any more than I already have.

'Zayden told me you've started dancing,' I say once we're both seated.

'Yeah, with Cami and Nora. It's pretty intense, but it's fun.'

Thinking about what we just did, and now picturing her in minimal clothing, dancing sensually in a dimly lit room, I have to adjust myself in my pants. Anya sips her coffee and eyes me for a moment, enjoying my obvious discomfort.

'Something wrong?' she asks innocently.

'No,' I grunt. 'Just . . . enjoying the visual in my head.'

Her smile widens. 'I see.'

'You think I might get to see some of your moves one day?' I can't help but ask, my blood thickening as the pressure in my body increases.

'Maybe,' she replies coyly. 'If you're lucky.'

After what happened earlier today with Anya, and now with the intensity of this practice, I feel riled up and on edge.

'Again!' Coach Kennedy shouts, bits of spit spraying from his mouth and landing on the poor sucker who managed to stand a little too close. Gav grimaces, but doesn't dare wipe his face until Coach blows his whistle, turning his back on us.

I sprint hard across the field. When I get to the line, I bend down, touching my hand to it, before propelling myself back in the other direction. My lungs are on fire as I slow down. My feet have barely touched the line when the whistle pierces the crisp air.

'Again!' he yells.

'Who pissed in his cereal this morning?' Zayden mutters as a collective groan spreads throughout the team.

I don't have the breath or energy to reply. With my head down, I push forward, knowing that the more we complain, the worse it will get. He's been especially hard on us this week as the first game is on Friday, and everyone is feeling the tension and nerves.

We have a strong team, since anyone above eighteen can be part of it, meaning Coach can select from all the most powerful and athletic players. We have some in their mid-twenties who are strong and equipped for defence, as well as some younger late teens who are lean and quick on their feet. Half of us – more specifically Zayden and me – fall in the middle of the two groups, possessing a good mixture of both qualities. As strong as some of the players are, the team still needs to improve on working together – knowing where our teammates are and what they are doing. We'll get there, it's just going to take a bit of time.

What feels like an eon later, Coach eases on us, letting us spend the final ten minutes passing back and forth. My heart rate finally slows, and the ache in my chest begins to ease. When he finally calls an end to practice, relief ripples through me in warm waves. Zayden and I partner off to start our end-of-practice stretching routine. My eyes sting and my body aches as I try to relieve some of the knots in my muscles.

When we walk into the locker room, everyone is covered in a layer of sweat and dirt. I peel off my shirt and shoot it into my bag like it's a basketball. Zayden is the first one to beeline towards the showers. He's barely disappeared around the corner when Andy turns to face Kai, wiggling his eyebrows.

'Update on banging his sister?' He grins, and my stomach clenches in an iron fist. Anger circles deep in my gut at the mention of the stupid bet Kai has on sleeping with Anya before the first game.

Kai glances over at me, his notorious smirk smeared across his face. 'It's a work in progress.'

Calmly, I gather my towel and other necessities before I head towards the shower. I ram my elbow into Kai on my way past, and he slams back into the metal lockers with a bang that thunders through the room. Everyone glances over as Kai struggles to gain his footing.

'Watch it,' I threaten, narrowing my eyes into slits and swinging my glower to Andy. He steps back out of my way as I walk past, not looking back.

My head is still mulling over what happened yesterday when I arrive at the local bookshop. It's Anya's favourite place. It stocks all the latest and greatest in fiction, but also has an entire attic full of second-hand books. With a coffee shop tucked around the corner at the back, it makes the perfect place for studying, since the library can get crowded. When I suggested meeting here for a coffee and to study, I thought Anya would either not reply or blow me off, so when she replied instantly, agreeing, I was shocked. Especially after what happened between us yesterday.

I linger at the door, taking in a deep breath and working on keeping my heart rate steady. Growing up with my father, I always experienced anxiety. It's been ever-present, though growing stronger the older I get, but it's always been manageable. Since the attack I endured overseas, however, the anxiety has settled deep in my bones, burrowing itself so deep inside me, it's threatening to take over. I know I should do something about it, seek help, but I don't want to acknowledge it or give it any more power over me. I'm trying to get better control over it, it's just harder than I expected it to be.

It's been a long day: my morning run, classes and gruelling training, but when I see her, the pressure on my chest lifts. Tucked into a corner booth with her legs folded beneath her, she scribbles something down in her notebook, eyes on the textbook in front of her.

It's dimly-lit inside, and the smell of books washes over me. Candles burn and flicker as I pass, making my way through the gathered groups of people and over to Anya. Sticking her pen behind her ear, she taps on her phone, as if checking the time. Probably because I'm a few minutes late.

'Hey, Blush,' I say.

She jerks her head up, not having heard me approach the table. Her dark bangs fall across her face, and she flicks them out of the way. A warm smile lights up her expression and I smile back, relaxing my shoulders when I see that her eyes don't hold the hostility they have recently.

'Hi, Mase.'

'Have you ordered anything yet?' I ask, shrugging off my bag and sliding it across the leather seat.

She shakes her head. 'No, I was waiting for you.'

'I'll go get it. Do you want your usual?'

'Yes, please.'

'Hungry? Want something to share?' I ask. 'Do you want me to see if they have those muffins you like?'

Her lips part in surprise. I've noticed her bring in a muffin a few times since she's moved in. I always take note of these things, so I don't know why she's shocked. I remember all the little things she likes and all her quirks. We were best friends for years before our relationship developed into something more. Sometimes, I think she's convinced the crush she had all those years was totally one-sided. I mean, sure, for a while it was, but for an even longer time, it wasn't.

I like her like this. Soft and casual. Clad in tight yoga pants, a singlet and a cardigan that slips off her shoulder. Her blue-light glasses are perched on her nose and, despite their size, her doe-eyes are not hidden behind them. If anything, they stand out more. My gaze roams her face, taking in her rosy cheeks and the little freckles on her nose. I want to kiss each of them, like I used to.

'Sure,' she replies, a little hesitantly. 'Sounds good.'

I'm all too aware of how date-like this seems, but it has always been this way between us. If anything, I'm glad it's happening again. It gives me hope that not all has been lost between us.

Making my way over to the counter, I order and lean on it. I sift through the books that are sitting in the trolley, waiting to go to their places on the shelves. I read a little while I was away, but have gotten out of the habit since being back. Grabbing a thriller that piques my interest, I pay for that as well, and by the time I'm putting my wallet away, my order is ready. Returning to the table, I place it down.

'You bought a book?'

I shrug. 'Yeah. I want to get back into reading.'

She picks it up, surveying it for a moment, before flipping it to read the blurb on the back. 'Let me know how it is. I'll borrow it if you like it.'

'Sounds good.'

She slides the book back over and I reach for it, our fingers brushing. She quickly yanks her hand away, placing it in her lap, as if she's afraid if she left it there something disastrous might happen. Like we might *hold hands*. Smiling, I lean back, slightly enjoying how flustered I make her. She's been doing a fantastic job of appearing unaffected, but I can see the cracks in her facade appearing, especially since my tongue was inside her yesterday. As if I said my thoughts aloud, her cheeks blush their usual red.

I take a long sip of my coffee, then split the muffin in half. I scoop a piece onto my spoon and take a bite.

'Good, right?' She smiles.

'Delicious,' I reply. 'Like you.'

She groans. 'My God, Mase. You can't just say things like that with a straight face.'

'Why not?' I grin. 'I enjoy watching you squirm.'

'Oh, I know you do.'

I pull out my laptop and open it up. Clicking on the latest document I saved, I scan through my notes. They're riddled with spelling errors and sentences that make zero sense.

'What?' Anya asks, noticing the pinched expression on my face.

'My notes never make any fucking sense,' I say. 'I don't know how we can take notes when they talk and go through the slides so quickly.' I peer over the top of the screen. 'You know, you're freakishly fast at typing.'

'I've had a lot of practice. Turn your AirDrop on, I'll send you some of my notes.'

'Oh, thanks. Appreciate that.'

'No problem.'

Her notes appear on my screen and, of course, they're much neater and more polished than mine. We work in silence for the next few minutes and soon the coffee is long gone, the plate that held the muffin is empty and my eyes are starting to hurt from staring at the screen. I've never been big on studying before, but I'm trying my best to improve in every area of my life that was lacking in the past. Turning up and trying are big priorities. Attending all my football practices is another. Then there's the other area, the one that's the most difficult: Proving to Anya that I'm here for her, and I'm not leaving anytime soon.

'Are you coming to the game on Friday?' I ask.

'Of course,' she answers. Closing her laptop, she rests back against the seat. Pulling her glasses off, she rubs her eyes. 'I never miss a game, you know that.'

'Good. Just checking.'

'You'll be too focused on the game to notice whether I'm there or not,' she teases.

'I always look for you.'

My comment catches her off guard, and she blinks at me. 'I'll be there. Wouldn't miss it for the world.'

Warmth spreads in my chest. I don't know what it is about her attending my games that gives me some sort of reassurance, but she's like a confidence boost. Her absence would only distract me and leave me unfocused.

'I'm going to leave early Saturday morning to head home. Are you coming?'

'Yeah. Are you staying the night and coming back Sunday?'

'That's the plan. Do you know if Rod is going to be there?' I ask, purposely shifting my gaze to the table as I pack away my things.

'I believe so, why?' she asks, looking adorably confused by the question. I never bring up the topic of her stepfather, so it makes sense for her to be thrown by it.

'Just wondering. Zay suggested getting an Airbnb for the night.'

'Really?' she questions, a frown tugging at her lips. 'Why wouldn't we just stay with Mum?'

'Er.' I shrug. 'It's a bit crowded, I guess.'

She looks puzzled for a moment. 'Um, well, okay then. I suppose, if that's what you both think.'

'Might be easier if we're coming and going, especially if we go out on Saturday night.'

She considers this. 'Okay. Sure.'

'I'll book something cheap and close to town.'

'Sounds good.'

'So, how are you dealing with everything?' I ask, leaning my forearms on the table and clasping my hands together.

She's quiet for a moment, and I wonder if she is contemplating whether to tell me the truth or not.

'It's been difficult,' she admits. 'I feel really stupid that I didn't know it was going on right under my nose.' Exhaling, she sinks further into the seat, a sad, faraway expression on her face. The urge to wrap my arms around her and protect her from everything is almost overwhelming. If it wasn't for me and my stupidity, none of this would have happened. If I hadn't run away, we could have been together. We still *would* be together.

'I don't miss him. I don't think I was ever really happy with him,' she continues. 'But I miss Phoebe. She was my best friend. We did everything together. She helped me through some really hard times, and for her to betray me like this . . .' Tears fill her eyes, and my heart plummets into my stomach at the sight of it. 'It just really sucks.'

Collecting her delicate hands in mine, I squeeze them. 'She doesn't deserve you or your kindness. Neither of them does.'

'Well,' she smiles wearily, sniffling, 'they have each other now.'

'Birds of a feather.'

'Yeah.'

'Have you spoken to her since?' I ask, running my thumb up and down the curve in her hand.

'No. I don't think she can face me, but I also blocked her on everything.'

'You know, I never really liked her.'

Anya's eyebrows rise. 'What? Since when?'

'Since always.' I press my lips into a thin line. 'She made a pass at me once.'

Anya freezes. Her mouth drops open as she stares at me. 'She *what*?'

'Since you were best friends, she knew about us. About our history.' I pause. 'About how you felt.'

Her hands fall into her lap as she stills. 'You never told me.'

'I didn't want to cause any drama. I shut it down, and she never tried anything again. I never would have expected her to do what she did with Dylan, even though I didn't like her much.'

'I feel like I didn't even know her at all,' Anya whispers, shaking her head and looking perplexed.

'She was envious of you.'

Anya scoffs. 'I don't think so.'

'It was obvious to everyone but you, Blush.'

'What on earth would she be jealous of?'

'Your beauty, your intelligence, everything that you have and she doesn't.' I shrug.

'My relationship with you,' she murmurs, her gaze connecting with mine.

I nod. 'And that. Pieces are falling together in your mind, aren't they?'

Anya pulls her hand back, covering her face. 'Wow. I must be super self-absorbed to have never noticed any of this. Maybe *I'm* the problem.'

'No,' I assure her. 'Trust me, you're not.'

'Thinking about any of this makes my head hurt,' she confesses. 'Tell me some good news. Something positive.'

'Okay,' I say, sitting a little straighter. 'No one knows this. Not even Zay.'

Anya looks at me with growing interest. 'Okay . . .'

'Coach wants me to be captain. They haven't replaced Will since he graduated.'

'Oh my God!' A smile breaks out across her face, and it's one of the most beautiful things I have ever seen. I love her smile. 'That's incredible, Mase. Especially since you just joined.'

'Well, that's what I'm concerned about. There are guys on the team that have been around a lot longer than me, and I don't think they'll appreciate me swooping in and claiming the title.'

'Well, it's not their decision. The coach obviously values your strength – not only as a player, but as a leader. That's a really amazing achievement, Mase. Forget about what the others might think. This is for *you*. You're always the best player on any team you're on. You deserve this.'

There she is. The girl from my memories. The one who has an unwavering belief in me and my dreams. I always feared that she put me on too high a pedestal, but in moments like this, I truly appreciate her faith in me. Despite everything else that's happened, that hasn't changed. The way she is smiling at me right now makes all the worries and concerns I have about the promotion fade away.

'Thanks, Blush. You've just made me feel a lot better about it all.'

'When are you going to tell Zay?' she questions, a loose strand of hair falling across her face. My hand twitches with the urge to reach over and push it back, just to have an excuse to get closer to her. She pushes it out of her eyes and leans back before I get a chance to act on the impulse.

'I don't know. I wasn't sure what to do. I hope he isn't going to be annoyed that I was asked.'

'He would be happy for you, Mase.'

'He works so hard. If I turn it down, what if they offer it to him? He would be so happy for the chance.'

Anya's face softens, and she looks at me as if she's truly seeing me for the first time in a long time.

'It's moments like these that remind me why I fell so hard for you,' she whispers, and her eyes have a deep, sad look in them that I don't understand. My heart jerks in my chest at her words. *Fell. Past tense.* 'He doesn't work harder than you; he works hard to be your equal. You challenge him. Honestly, you're probably the best thing to ever happen to him in that regard. He would be far too complacent if he didn't have you making him rise to his full potential. He knows this. He would be so happy for you, Mase. He would be shattered that you think that he wouldn't be.'

Her words hit me hard, and I realise she's right. Zayden would be happy for me, just like I would be happy for him. When it comes to us, there's no competition. Sure, we always have a playful rivalry going on, but not when it truly matters. Zayden might not be my blood, but he is family to me, and I'm disappointed in myself for thinking he wouldn't have my back on this.

'You're right.' I nod. 'I needed that reminder.'

'Anytime.'

'At the risk of ruining everything,' I blurt, the words tumbling from my lips before I can stop them. 'In the bathroom the other night you said I don't know everything. What did you mean by that?'

This time, she's the one reaching for my hand. She places her fingers over my knuckles, tracing them. My skin is on fire where she touches it. The cool metal of the ring I bought her rubs against my skin, and I glance down at it. I'm glad she didn't throw it out; I spent weeks saving up for it.

'It doesn't change anything now. Don't worry about it.'

'I am, though,' I insist, gripping her hand. 'I want to know.'

An alarm blaring from her phone startles us both, and she quickly scrambles for it, shutting it off. 'Gotta go. Dance class.'

Disappointment sinks in my chest. I was so close to getting answers, only for them to be torn away again. I'm desperate to know what she meant.

Anya gets to her feet, collecting her things. Touching my shoulder, she smiles down at me.

'I had a good time with you this afternoon. See you later.'

Chewing my lip, I spend an insurmountable length of time watching her walk away, feeling as if I've been left with far more questions than answers.

21

ANYA

Three Years Earlier

MY TIRED EYES READ the same sentence over and over, none of it transmitting to my brain. A silver lining of this unofficial break-up with Mason is that I have thrown myself into my studies like never before.

As hard as we both try to avoid each other, it's pointless. The tension is worse than ever, and I can barely breathe when he's nearby. It's not fair on me, it's not fair on him and it's not fair on anyone else who gets involved. Three times in the past two weeks I've heard Chelsea and Mason arguing about me, and I barely even make eye contact with him when he's in the same room. The tension is completely dialled down compared to what it usually is, so if she's still able to sense it, then I don't know what else to do.

'I want everyone to have read up to chapter eight by class tomorrow, as we'll be having a quiz on it,' Mr. Dawson states, and there's a quiet groan in response. The bell blares loudly overhead and there's a collective sound of textbooks snapping shut, chairs scraping against the linoleum floor and chatter breaking out.

'What are you up to over the weekend?' Phoebe asks, looping her arm through mine as she guides us around the desks and out of the classroom.

'Undecided,' I answer.

She side-eyes me. 'Meaning?'

'I haven't given him an answer. About the date.'

Phoebe's lips tilt. 'Which one, babe?'

I groan. I should be flattered that there are two nice, attractive guys who want to go out with me. Both of them are great. They're fun, athletic, we share common interests, and they truly seem to be very nice guys. I'm starting to question my own sanity for having less than zero interest in either of them.

'I think I'm broken, Phoebs,' I say hopelessly, dragging my feet.

She scoffs. 'You are so young and so beautiful, my girl.' She leans over, brushing her lips against my cheek. 'Drop the loser older friend, and start focusing on the very, very hot boys right in front of you.'

'Hey!' Dylan greets us, his long floppy hair falling across his forehead. He sweeps it off his face, only for it to fall right back in the same spot a moment later. He turns to face Phoebe and nods. 'Phoebe.'

'Dylan.' She smiles coyly, grazing her shoulder against his arm as she sidles past him, shooting me a wink over her shoulder.

'Hi, Dylan.' I smile politely, feeling my shoulders tense as he beams at me. I don't miss the way his eyes dart down to my legs. 'How are you?'

'I'm excellent. How are you?'

'Good, thanks.'

'Walk you to English?' he offers, falling in stride with me. A part of me wonders whether he asked Phoebe how to get my attention and if she suggested this, because he seems to be popping up everywhere, offering to do things for me. It's really nice, but my head is a mess. It's hard to focus on anyone other than Mason.

'Sure.'

'Have you given any more thought to the weekend?' he asks, and my stomach tightens with nausea at the thought of going on a date with anyone who isn't Mason. I would love to say yes to

Dylan, but it wouldn't be fair on him when my mind is consumed with someone else.

'Look, Dylan . . .' I sigh.

He holds his hands up. 'Don't say it, Anya. I'm patient. I'll wait. For when you're ready.'

I release a breath as I smile, feeling instantly relieved he isn't being pushy like I thought he would be. Again, I have a niggling feeling he's had a conversation with Phoebe about me. 'Thanks, Dylan.'

'Any updates on your party?' He wiggles his brows.

My birthday is fast approaching, and I feel a flutter of excitement in my chest. I have been counting down the days until my eighteenth for *years*. Mason had always promised me that once I turn eighteen, things would be different. He promised me that, if I still feel the same – even after everything that's happened – we can be together. It's been a long time coming.

'My house. Anyone who is anyone will be there.'

He grins. 'It's going to be epic.'

22

ANYA

I HATE RUNNING LATE.

I should already be on my way to the game, but I was so engrossed in my book I lost track of time. As this is a regular occurrence for me, I live by setting multiple alarms throughout the day to keep me on track, but, somehow, I forgot to set this one.

Jumping up and down, I yank on my leggings and almost topple over in the process. I slip my satin top over my head, shimmy into it then detour into Zayden's room. I switch the light on, and I make a repulsed face at the piles of the clothes scattered across the floor. I eye the six empty water bottles lined up on his bedside table and the box of condoms that looks nearly empty. Classy, big brother.

Stepping over the mountain of clothes, I yank open his closet door and peer inside. I huff in frustration when I don't immediately find his jersey; I always wear it to the game. I once wore Mason's, but Zayden got a bit weird about it, and with everything that's happened since, I don't feel comfortable doing that now. Groaning, I jog down the hall and into the laundry. Opening the washing machine, I look down into it and see a pile of wet clothes sitting in there. I sift through, finding his jersey plonked at the bottom of the machine. I pull it out and wince at the feel of the damp material.

My eyes travel to Mason's doorway, and I chew the inside of my cheek. For a moment, I consider wearing his jersey instead, before shaking off the idea.

'Anya!' Nora hollers from downstairs. 'We have to go!'

'Coming!' I call back, rushing to my room and swiping up all my last-minute things.

Hastily making my way down the steps, I head out to Nora's car. The fresh night air stings my skin and I curse under my breath, wishing I had gone back to find something else to wear, but it's too late now.

'Hi, hi, sorry!' I say breathlessly, throwing myself into the passenger seat.

'You're going to freeze in that!' Nora exclaims, eyeing my bare arms that are pebbled with goosebumps.

'It's fine, let's just go before we end up missing the start.'

The car park is full when we arrive, and we end up parking in a small grassy area that I'm positive is not somewhere we're permitted to park, but Nora does it anyway. The roar of the crowd is deafening, even all the way back here. Cheers erupt, and people stomp on the ground beneath them, shaking the grandstand.

'Would you kill me if I said I have to pee?' I whisper, sending Nora an apologetic look.

'Go, I'll find us a seat,' she replies with an eye roll.

'Won't be long.'

Running to the bathroom, I'm relieved to see there isn't a line – everyone has probably found their seats by now, as the cheerleaders are either about to perform or already are. I hope we haven't missed any of it, since Cami is performing and has been gushing about it all week.

I'm looking down at my phone as I exit the bathrooms, trying to understand where Nora is sitting from her jumbled text message.

'Hey, you.'

I yelp in alarm, jerking back. Kai smiles down at me.

'Oh, Kai,' I exclaim, placing a hand on my chest. 'You scared me. Aren't you meant to be in the locker room, enduring a long-winded pep talk or something?'

'Yeah.' He shrugs, looking somewhere off to the distance. 'I come and go as I please.'

I try to control my reaction as he says that, wondering if he thinks I would for some reason be impressed. I've heard Mason and Zayden talk about the team, and I know Kai is someone who doesn't contribute as much as the others, both on and off the field. My brother can see the good in everyone, but he is also a great judge of character, so when I hear him talk like that, I take his word for it.

'Okay,' I say eventually, when it appears he isn't going to say anything more.

'You haven't replied to any of my messages.' Kai's eyes are focused on mine, and I bristle a little at the intensity. 'You're starting to hurt my feelings.'

'Sorry, I've been really slammed this week.'

He nods. 'Sure. I get that.' His eyes bounce down to my arms. 'Where's your jacket?'

'I was in a rush. Accidentally left without it.'

'Wait here,' he says, quickly disappearing.

I should take this as my chance to flee, but to be fair, I really am cold, just like Nora said I would be. Stepping towards the grandstand, I hesitate, torn between rushing away and waiting for him to return. He makes the decision for me when he reappears, holding out his jersey. My throat feels dry as I blink at it.

'Here,' he says.

'Oh, I couldn't,' I quickly say.

'Why not? You're cold; I have a jersey.' He extends his hand. 'Take it.'

The crowd hollers again, and I shiver as the cool wind chooses this moment to remind me that we're at the beginning of a long game, and it's only going to get colder as the night goes on.

'Thanks, Kai,' I say, reluctantly reaching for it. Though I'm unsure what his true intentions are, I don't have another option right now, or much time to argue. 'I'll return it to you after the game.'

'No stress,' he says, as I slip it over my head. 'Looks better on you anyway.'

It completely envelopes me, landing mid-thigh, the sleeves stretching way past my hands. It feels wrong, and the scent is not the one I'm used to. It's not Zayden's.

It's not Mason's.

'Good luck tonight. I hope it's a good game.'

His smirk widens. 'Oh, it will be.'

I love the atmosphere of the game.

The excitement in the air, the thunderous stamping on the cement beneath our feet, the cheers and whistles erupting every few moments. When Cami struts out onto the field, Nora and I leap to our feet and scream so loudly the group in front of us turns back and gives us a dirty look.

The football field is gigantic. Much bigger than the ones we had back at school. This has a more professional feel to it, with the cheerleaders and the high-rise stands bordering the edge of the field. I get so caught up in the hype of the game and all that comes before it, my earlier worries evaporate from my mind.

Nora and I hold one side each of a sign we made. I used neon pink and sparkles to paint Cami's name in big, bold letters. I can't take my eyes off her as she performs, hitting each move perfectly in time with the beat.

'She's incredible!' Nora murmurs, looking as awe-struck as I feel.

The cheering has barely subsided when the guys start jogging onto the field. An excited smile spreads across my face as I take in the long, even strides of Mason. A flutter of *something* swoops through my stomach. His head turns, those whisky eyes sweep through the crowd, landing heavily on mine. His lips tilt, and warmth rushes through me.

After a few minutes, the game begins. I love watching Zayden and Mason play. The way they can silently communicate has always made them such a deadly combination. I'm on the edge of my seat as a player launches himself at Zayden. He flings the ball out to Mason barely a second before he gets tackled hard into the ground. Mason is like lightning. He weaves in and out of the players with an electric speed that has made him legendary in past games. Shooting forward, he runs half the length of the field before launching himself across the line. I'm on my feet, screaming before my mind can even catch up. Mason's best move is always getting the first try, and he never fails.

'Damn,' Nora mutters, looking impressed as she claps. 'He's fast.'

'Yup.' I smile, feeling proud. I watch Zayden clap him on the back as they exchange a moment of victory.

Zayden and Mason are both incredible players, and it baffles me that Mason thinks Zayden works harder than him. In the past, Mason definitely let himself get distracted, but I've noticed a big difference in his commitment since he's been back. He is training harder than ever, showing up to every practice, and it's delivering tonight. He is playing fiercely.

The crowd calms down through the next play, and when it's

back to our turn, I can't keep my eyes off Zayden and Mason as they pass back and forth, outplaying the opposing team with an ease that comes from years of playing together.

Parker – another brilliant player, although I don't know him personally – gets the ball and makes a run for it. He quickly throws it to Mason before getting slammed into the ground, and Mason slices through the defence, executing another massive run down the field. I feel giddy with happiness when he slides across the line, the crowd screaming so loud it actually makes me wince.

'Far out!' Nora comments, shaking her head. 'He's bloody amazing!'

'I know.' I grin, feeling my cheeks grow hot.

After the team finishes jumping all over each other in excitement, he swings his gaze to me, smiling. I smile back at him as he jogs to position. His eyes drop to my chest, and the colour drains from his face. He stops running, causing the person behind him to slam into him. My stomach hits the cement at my feet when I see his expression. I look down, reading Kai's number in a striking white, branded right smack in the centre of my chest. Zayden frowns at Mason, following his line of sight, and the slight curve of his mouth flattens. My insides shrivel under the scrutiny, and I mentally berate myself. I knew this wasn't a good idea.

Kai rams his elbow into Mason's side, nods his head towards me and says something over his shoulder before jogging away, looking happy with himself. My cheeks flare with unbearable heat as I realise that was his plan all along. To mess with Mason.

Because he knows how we feel about each other.

The tension is high for the entire first half, and the tight feeling stretching across my chest only seems to increase as each minute inches by. All of a sudden, Mason is off his game. He went from playing powerfully to fumbling the ball and being tackled, when he's usually notorious for slipping right past other players' outstretched hands. I can't help but feel the blame rests heavily on my shoulders. The first game of the season, ruined by me.

'Shit,' I say. 'I've just cost them the game.'

'Quit being dramatic,' Nora says softly. 'You accepted a jumper because it's cold. It's not a big deal.'

'Yeah,' I mumble, picking furiously at my nails.

'Seriously. If Mason wants you to wear his, he needs to man up and ask you out.'

'It's not that simple, Nora.'

She offers me a sympathetic smile, touching my shoulder. 'I know. Sorry.'

When the game ends, they're up by four, thankfully, but the fun atmosphere has died down. For me, at least.

Nora and I make our way back to her car quickly, since Zayden told me last minute that we're hosting the after-party. I already dread tomorrow's post-party clean-up, having done it far too many times. But I can't think about that right now, or what kind of mood the boys will be in after the game.

Within the hour, the house is full. I weave through the groups, joining Nora and Cami at the beer pong table.

'Who's next?' shouts a guy I have never seen before, gesturing to the beer funnel in his hand.

'Me!' Cami volunteers.

'Pause,' Nora says to the two boys at the other end of the table.

Cami strolls towards the guy as everyone claps and eggs her on. She drops to her knees – thankfully someone thought to put a plastic tarp over the carpet – and the guy begins to pour a steady stream of beer into the funnel. She flips the nozzle on the side and the liquid disappears so quickly that I blink, and it's gone.

'Goddamn,' one of the guys mutters. 'I think I just met my future wife.'

Nora giggles, and we exchange a look as we clap and whistle, praising Cami.

'New record to beat!' beer-funnel guy hollers, and there's a loud whoop from the dude who made the wife comment.

'Relax!' Cami says, gripping my shoulders and gently shaking me. 'Loosen up. It's a party!'

I offer her a weak smile.

She thrusts a cup into my hand and I take it, downing the contents. It's my first drink of the night, but I don't feel like partying. I just want to make sure things are right with Mason.

Neon lights swing around the room, lighting up at least fifty faces I don't recognise. I assume they're all people from school. I always wonder how word gets out about a party, but I suppose when one of the footballers is throwing it, everyone hears about it.

Feeling jittery, I continue to scan the party, constantly assessing whether anyone is doing anything damaging to the house or our things. Surprisingly, everyone seems pretty tame. I see two girls from my class making out against the wall, with everyone ogling them. One of the girls bumps into a photograph of me and my mum. I turn away. I'm not going to look at that picture the same again.

'If I get this in, you have to kiss me on the lips,' the guy at the end of the table comments, and I desperately try to remember what his name is. He has a charming, confident smile on his face, focused on Cami as she narrows her eyes at him.

'Hmm,' she contemplates, tapping her chin. 'How confident are you?'

'I don't miss often,' he teases.

'Okay.' She shrugs. 'Why not?'

Grinning, he aims and elegantly shoots the ball straight into the cup. Cami rolls her eyes as she strides around the side of the table. Planting her palms on either side of his face, she stands on her tip-toes and presses her lips to his. As she goes to pull back, he wraps his hand around the back of her neck, securing her there as he kisses her harder.

'Oh my God.' Nora laughs.

The two spend the next minute making out, oblivious to everyone watching them.

'What's his name again?' I ask.

'Er – Jake? Jim?' Nora guesses, looking as clueless as I feel.

The front door bangs open, and loud whistles flood the air as the football team enters. My throat feels dry and I step away, attempting to fade into the background. Cami and Jake/Jim finally detach from each other, and she has a playful smirk on her lips as she struts back around to our side.

'Get it girl,' I say teasingly.

'Well played, Jack,' she says.

Nora and I look at each other.

'Oops,' Nora says. 'I was close.'

Purposely keeping my eyes off the team, I focus on the game, anxiety simmering underneath my skin and churning in my gut as if I've eaten something bad.

After a minute or so, I nervously peek a glance. Fire ignites inside me when I hit Mason's cold stare, already in my direction, as if he pulled my gaze to his like a magnet.

'Oh dear,' Nora mutters, casting me a worried look. 'He's pissed.'

'Yup,' I reply, my blood turning to ice in my veins.

'Fuck him.' Cami snorts dismissively, tossing her shiny hair over her shoulder as she turns her attention back to the game. 'You did nothing wrong.'

I wish her words were a comfort to me, but they're really not.

The volume of chatter in the room increases tenfold now the team is here. A migraine throbs behind my eyes. Quietly, I step away from the group and duck my chin as I hurry through the room, beelining to the stairs. I manage to sneak up them uninterrupted. A couple are heading towards my room and I shake my head.

'No,' I snap, stepping in front of them. 'My room is off limits.'

Scowling, they resume the hunt for privacy down the hall. I dart inside my room and lean against the wall, placing a hand on my chest. Not a moment later, it swings open, and I close my eyes, feeling Mason's presence like a physical touch.

'What the *fuck* were you doing wearing his jersey to *my* game?' he seethes, and a bolt of electricity runs down my spine at the rough raspiness of his voice.

Swallowing, I force my eyes open and track his long strides as he eats the space between us, towering over me.

'The only jersey that belongs on your body is *mine*,' he murmurs, his warm breath kissing my cheeks.

I tilt my head back, lifting my gaze to meet his. 'Since when?'

'Since always.'

With that, he presses me back against the wall and kisses me. His lips press into mine, desperately and urgently. I kiss him back just as hard. His hands run down my sides, then cup my ass as he lifts me, turning us and stumbling forwards. We fall back onto my bed, and I wrap my legs around his waist.

He pulls back from the kiss; our foreheads stay pressed together; our breaths mingle as one as we both exhale.

'It's me and you,' he whispers, breathless. 'I'm not fucking around this time. Me and you. You got that?'

'Me and you,' I murmur.

His mouth is on mine once more, and I groan into him. Arching into his hard body, I explore the rigid muscles of his back with my hands. Curling my fingers around the hem of his shirt, I yank it up over his head, throwing it somewhere on the other side of the room.

I thread my fingers through his hair, and we kiss long and hard. I suck his bottom lip into my mouth, savouring the sweet and salty taste of him. His hands are everywhere – skimming over my back, tracing my curves, dancing across my stomach. Flipping him onto his back, I pepper kisses across his face, the same way he has to me a million times.

'I like that,' he breathes, his voice husky, his chest rising and falling underneath me. 'You're kissing my freckles.'

'They're faint, but they're there,' I murmur.

Moving down to his neck, I run my tongue across his skin, tasting the minty freshness of his body wash and the signature spice of *him*. I wish I could bottle it to keep for myself. My lips trail across his collarbones, gliding down his hard chest. My tongue snakes across his nipple, and his hands tighten on my hips. He pushes upwards, his erection pressing against my stomach as I move lower, dragging my tongue along those sculpted abs I love so much.

'Fuck,' he mutters when I pop open his jeans with a quick flick of my finger. He lifts his hips as I pull his pants down, never breaking eye contact with him.

'Okay?' I whisper.

'Okay,' he croaks.

Moving my hand across him, over the fabric of his underwear, I encircle his thick length. His breath stutters, and a shooting sensation spears through me at the sound of it. Peeling the fabric back, I keep my eyes on his as I circle his head with my tongue. He hisses, moving a hand to my hair and scraping his fingernails against my scalp, and I moan at the harshness of it. Moving my lips over his length, I take him as far down my throat as I can.

The sound that leaves his lips has me clenching my thighs together as heat threatens to consume me. I suck softly and gently at first, getting used to his size, before taking him further and deeper.

'Blush,' he says through gritted teeth, fingers moving to the back of my neck and curling around it, the other hand gripping the sheets so hard his knuckles are bleached white. 'I'm not going to last long if you keep doing that.'

Smirking victoriously, I repeat the action once, twice, and then hot liquid spurts onto my tongue as he lets out a guttural groan, hips jerking as he spills his release down my throat. After swallowing every single drop, I peel back, licking my lips. His cheeks are tinged a delicious pink, and his eyes are dark and lustful as I move back up his body.

'You're incredible,' he drawls, fingers curling around my hips, tugging me close. 'It's . . . never like that for me.'

'The feeling is mutual, Captain.'

The dark storm in his eyes flares up. 'Say that again.'

'Captain,' I whisper, lightly tracing the lines of his stomach.

And then we are kissing again, wild and desperate once more. I lose all sense of time and reality as we kiss like the world is ending tomorrow and these are our last moments together. It feels like that, after waiting for so long. The feeling of his hands and mouth all over me is something I never want to forget. Despite everything, it just feels so *right*.

My door handle begins to jiggle, and then a loud knock jolts us out of our trance. I roll off him, panting, and hastily brush my messy hair out of my face. The person moves on quickly, but my heart is still in my throat as I push to a seated position and press my fingertips to my pulsing lips.

'Do you forgive me?' I ask, sporting a coy smile.

He looks at me with his trademark crooked grin on his face.

'Yeah, Blush. I think so.'

23

MASON

MY EYES ARE ON her as we re-enter the party like the world hasn't just tipped on its axis.

She rejoins her friends in the corner of the room, and I reluctantly go in the opposite direction, finding the football guys gathered in the kitchen, a line of shots spread out across the counter.

'Where have you been?' Zayden asks, an eyebrow curved. He quickly assesses my messy hair and flushed cheeks, and smirks. 'Ah, you dirty dog. Who was it?'

My stomach hardens into cement as the guilt hits me with the force of a B-double truck. 'No one.'

Rolling his eyes, he claps his hand onto my back. 'Okay, keep your secrets, then.'

I exhale, feeling even worse. I don't keep secrets from Zayden, and this is one giant secret that has the potential to combust and detonate everything in its surroundings. Swiping the shot in front of me, I throw it down my throat, growling at the bitter taste it leaves in my mouth.

I can still taste her lips on my tongue.

My mind gets so hazy around her; it's like I become someone possessed. Like I have no ability to control my emotions. Or my mouth. Or my hands.

Those glimmering emerald eyes, locked on mine, as she moved up and down my . . .

Fuck. I'm in trouble. As usual, I acted on primal instinct without considering the consequences. But fuck the consequences. They've been a threat all my teenage and adult life. I just want her, that should be enough to eradicate all this other bullshit.

'You good?' Zayden's voice snaps me back to reality and I blink, his concerned face coming into focus in front of me.

'Uh,' I say, 'can I talk to you for a sec?'

'Sure.'

We move off to the side a little, and anxiety swells inside my chest to the point my head starts to spin. Swallowing it, I take a deep breath, refusing to let it overcome me.

'So, here's the thing . . .' I trail off as movement over Zayden's head captures my attention. Kai has Anya cornered in the living room, and it's clear from all the way over here how uncomfortable she is.

Zayden turns, seeing the same thing. We look back at each other.

'Nope,' we both say, pushing off the counter and storming over to them.

'Come on,' I overhear Kai say. 'Just a quick walk around the block. You owe me.'

'She doesn't owe you shit, Adams,' I bite out, and Kai stiffens. He whirls around to face us, the smirk vanishing from his face.

'What's going on here?' Zayden demands.

'Kai is trying to pressure Anya into going for a *walk*,' Cami fills in, dramatically forming quotation marks with her fingers, making it evident what she thinks Kai's true intentions are. 'And Anya is too polite to tell him to fuck off.'

'Fuck you, bitch,' Kai snaps.

'Hey!' Zayden snarls, taking a threatening step in Kai's direction. 'You don't speak to anyone like that in my house. If Anya doesn't want to go, then she doesn't want to go.'

'You always going to fight her battles for her, big bro?' Kai taunts, his slimy, leering smile etched on his face.

I'm moving before I realise what I'm doing.

'No!' Anya blurts, throwing her hands out and slamming them into my chest. 'Think, Mase.'

'I am thinking,' I reply, my stare locked on Kai's face.

'Don't blow your chance of . . .' she starts, and then stops.

'Chance of what?' Zayden asks.

'Yeah, chance of?' Kai says. 'Looks to me like you're bitching out.'

A low rumble emits from my throat as I sidestep Anya.

'Don't blow becoming captain on him!' she whispers, but she may as well have shouted it with the way everyone looks at us.

'What?' Zayden asks quietly, his eyes ping-ponging between Anya and me. 'Who? Captain?' He's not making any sense as he processes her words. 'Coach asked you to be captain?'

Kai's jaw is practically touching the floor as he gapes at me. He scoffs, taking a step back and holding up his hands. 'Sorry there, *Cap*, didn't mean to step on your toes.' I bristle, heat inching up my neck as he glances suggestively at Anya. 'Bitch doesn't put out, anyway.'

I see red.

It takes everything inside me to hold back and not react to his words, even though that's exactly what he wants me to do. My fingernails dig into my palms as I form fists with my hands, fighting for control. Meanwhile, Zayden's fist launches straight into Kai's face. His head snaps back, and he drops to the floor like he weighs nothing. His six-foot frame sprawls across the carpet, and the music comes to a screeching halt as everyone turns to see what's going on.

'Get the fuck out of my house,' Zayden grounds out, an eerie calm settling across his face and shoulders, blood spread across his knuckles. My stomach roils at the sight of it. '*Now*.'

Kai releases a dark laugh as he stumbles to his feet, blood trickling down his face and onto his white t-shirt. He shoves a finger in Zayden's face, but I step in front of him, and his finger jabs my chest.

'You're going to regret that,' he seethes, a sinister look in his pale eyes. His gaze lifts over my head, boring into Zayden's. 'Both of you.'

'Yeah, I'm fucking shaking,' I retort sarcastically. 'You heard him. *Get out*.'

Spitting blood, Kai shoves his way through the crowd and kicks over an esky full of beer. Ice scatters across the floor and beer cans tumble out as Kai slams the front door shut, rattling the walls so hard a photo frame falls down.

Zayden's lips are pressed together in a hard line, and I can see the disappointment in his eyes as he looks at Anya. He hates that he struggles with anger, especially in front of her, given everything their stepfather has done.

Exhaling, I rub my hand along the underside of my jaw, exchanging a weighted glance with Zayden. We both know that Kai is not someone to be underestimated.

The next morning, after hours of clearing out rubbish and cleaning, we are finally in the car on our way back to Bliss Bay, the small coastal town we all grew up in.

My thumb taps the steering wheel absently as we cruise down the highway. Zayden is sunk down in his seat, shades on. His head already lolls to the side as he sleeps, despite us being only ten minutes into the drive. As the one person in the car who actually *partied* last night, he now has the honour of nursing a hangover. Anya's eyes meet mine in the reflection of the rear-view mirror, and I feel heat slithering through my veins as flashes of last night spin around my mind.

The rustling of a wrapper snaps my attention back to the girl behind me. She slowly twirls a lollipop in her fingers before placing her tongue on it, running it in a circle. I sit up a little straighter in my seat. Her lips twitch momentarily before she sucks the lollipop into her mouth, hollowing out her cheeks, before she releases it with a wet-sounding *pop*. I'm pretty sure all the blood flowing in my body is rushing to one spot right now.

Shaking my head, I force my eyes back to the road before I do something stupid.

The Airbnb is perfectly located close to town. Nudging Zayden awake, we pile out of the car and gravitate towards a room each, as there are three to choose from. It's a relatively small place, but with the open-plan layout, it doesn't feel cramped. Yanking open the windows, I let the warm air spill in. The beachy cosiness of it all reminds me of Anya and Zayden's house. Crowded and rustic, but homey and comfortable. My safe place. Or maybe it was just Anya and Zayden who were my safe place.

'Shotgun the biggest!' Zayden whoops childishly as he zooms past Anya and me, disappearing down the hallway.

'I'll take the small one,' I offer.

'You're used to small things,' Anya teases, smiling sweetly.

Leaning down, I press my lips to her ear. 'You didn't think it was small when you were choking on me last night.' I feel the whoosh of her breath as she exhales. Stepping back, I smirk down at her, smug.

Undeterred – or at least pretending to be – she steps away from me, brushing her hair from her eyes. 'You mean gagging from repulsion?'

'The way I remember it, you gladly swallowed every drop.'

'I don't recall that,' she says dismissively. 'Mustn't have been very memorable.'

'That's okay, Blush.' I flash her an easy grin. 'I can remind you again tonight, if you like.'

Rolling her eyes, she dips into the room closest to us. Grinning to myself, I make my way down the hall and dump my things into the other room. I quickly rush to put music on when I hear Zayden start singing and soon we're all lounging in the living room and it feels like old times.

I'm reminded of just how much it is like *old times* when the longing stares shared by Anya and me grow more heated by the moment. I'm highly aware of every movement she makes. Each brush of her hair, each stretch, each flicker of her eyes as she moves her gaze away when I catch her staring.

'We better go soon,' Anya says, glancing at her phone for the time.

'Where are we going?' Zayden asks.

'To see Mum.'

Zayden's expression hardens and he looks away from her, back at the TV, which is currently showing the film clip of a new rap song he is obsessed with. 'I'm not going.'

'What?' Anya asks, frowning. 'Why not?'

'I don't want to.'

'I know you guys had a big fight before you moved out, but I'm confused. What's going on? Why don't you speak anymore?'

My chest tightens uncomfortably. Zayden's jaw tenses as he glares ahead, refusing to meet her eyes. 'Don't worry about it.'

'I am,' she snaps, getting to her feet and planting her hands on her hips. 'Tell me.'

'Drop it,' he hisses, eyes flashing angrily. 'Besides, I'm going with Mason. To see his old man.'

'No,' I say, shaking my head. 'It's all good.'

'What the fuck is going on right now?' Anya protests.

'You're going to see Mum, and we are going to see Mason's dad. End of discussion,' Zayden retorts hotly.

Throwing her hands up, Anya stalks out of the room.

'Don't,' Zayden warns as I open my mouth. 'Not a word.'

Pressing my lips into a thin line, I nod, holding up my hands in surrender. After a moment, I get to my feet and slip into Anya's room, where she's shrugging into a denim jacket.

Brow furrowed, she turns to me. 'Tell me what's going on with him.'

'I'm not involved,' I say.

Her eyes narrow. 'So you do know.'

'I'm not involved,' I repeat. I hold out my arms to her, and she pauses for a moment before falling into my chest. I press a kiss to the side of her head.

'Is he okay?' she whispers.

'I don't know,' I admit. 'I think he's trying to be.' Inhaling the sweet scent of her perfume, I hold her close for a few more seconds before releasing her.

She steps back and adjusts her ponytail, a concerned look on her face. 'So, you're going to see your dad,' she says.

'I have mail to collect,' I answer.

'I know you don't like anyone knowing anything about your dad, but Zayden going with you is a good idea. Just to be on the safe side.'

I nod. 'Yeah. You're probably right.'

'You don't have to talk to him. If it's too much.'

'Yeah. I know.'

Sliding my hands down the sides of her face, I stare at her for a long moment, taking in her round, emerald eyes, the freckles dusted over the top of her cheeks, her cute-as-a-button nose.

'What?' she whispers. 'Why are you looking at me like that?'

'I hope you know this isn't just physical for me,' I say, my voice raspy.

Her lips part and she steps back from me, forcing me to release her. Folding her arms over her chest, she looks down at her feet. 'That's all it can be, Mase.'

My heart plummets into my stomach. 'Why?'

'I can't give my heart to you, not after everything.'

'Blush . . .' I trail off, teetering on the edge of losing control. 'I know I left last time, but things are different now.'

'It doesn't really feel different,' she admits, pulling her bottom lip between her teeth. 'I'm not making any decisions about anything right now. I don't want to jeopardise hurting Zayden and mucking everything up, just in case this . . .' She waves a hand between our chests. 'Isn't serious.'

'It's serious,' I say firmly.

'I have to go,' she murmurs, touching her hand to my arm. 'Good luck with your dad.'

Exhaling, I step back and watch her walk out the door.

I don't know how to feel about this awkward limbo we are in. We both want each other. We have no interest in anyone else, even if we lie to ourselves about it – that's always been consistent. And same as before, there's the sneakiness and forbidden nature of being together while no one knows about it. But unlike last time, I want to face this head on. I'm ready to own our relationship and take it on with everything I have. I just need her to be on the same page, so we don't ruin everything.

I lean against the doorframe, unease nestling in my chest.

Within the hour, I pull up out the front of my childhood home. The house seems as if it has aged a lifetime since I left. The paint has peeled off in large chunks. The lawn has grown to the point it is almost knee-height and the pavement is cracked, with weeds sprouting through the gaps. The gate hangs off its hinges and is so rusty, it looks like one gust of wind would tear it apart.

'Jesus,' Zayden comments, peering out the windscreen. 'This place has gone to shit.'

'Was it ever not?' I counter dryly.

'You okay?'

'I'm fine.'

'You're always fine,' he says quietly.

Unclipping the seatbelt, I hesitate a moment, mentally preparing myself for what I might be walking into. Given that Dad's car is parked in the driveway, I'm guessing he's home. He's always home.

Zayden unbuckles and I look back at him, shaking my head.

'No,' I say. 'Stay here and don't come inside, even if you hear him yelling.'

Zayden stares at me before shifting his gaze to the house and then back to me. He offers a slow nod as he reaches for his belt, clipping it back in.

'I'm right here,' Zayden says. 'If you need me.'

Heading first to the letterbox, I open it, sighing when I see that it's empty. Of all the chores he completes around the house, or lack thereof, why must collecting the mail be the only thing he does? Trepidation fills me with each step I take. Hovering near the door, I can hear the faint rumble of the TV. It's never switched off, no matter what time of day it is. Rapping my knuckles against the door, I wait. After knocking two more times to no avail, I blow out a breath and push the door open, stepping inside.

The room is dark and smells stale, as if it hasn't breathed fresh air for months. Dust is settled on every surface in sight. Empty bottles are scattered across the floor, many of which have cigarette butts jammed down their necks. I shudder in repulsion. My heart squeezes, and I brace myself against the wall, feeling the panic rising.

Breathe in and out, in and out, I tell myself, not letting the anxiety of being back here overwhelm me. I need my mail – stupidly important mail that can't go ignored – and then I'm out of here. Now I'm back in Australia, all my mail comes directly to me, but when I was travelling, I didn't think about it. I should have redirected it to Zayden and Anya's house.

'Tony?' I call out. 'It's me.'

A shadow moves, gaining my attention, and my father steps out from the hallway. I flinch involuntarily, taking in his over-grown, scruffy appearance. He's gained a significant amount of weight, and he looks as if it's been days since his last shower. His eyes are glassy and red-ringed. He peers at me, swaying on his feet.

'You ain't welcome here,' he snarls gruffly.

Oh, I think, my grip on the wall tightening. *He knows who I am today.*

'I need my mail, and then I'll be gone,' I say.

I wait a beat, to see what else he might throw at me, but to my surprise, he stays silent. Stepping back, he gestures towards the kitchen bench. A large jumble of envelopes is strewn across the surface. Moving slowly, without taking my eyes off him, I walk over to it and start quickly sifting through. There are more than I realise. I stack them into a neat pile and fold them in half, jamming them into my back pocket.

I don't even hear him move. He shoves me hard, slamming me into the bench and sending dirty kitchen utensils flying onto the floor with a loud *clang*.

'Fuck,' I grunt, feeling him slice one of the knives across my stomach.

Gritting my teeth, I push as hard as I can and manage to get out from underneath him. I'm lunging for the front door when he yanks the hood of my jumper, reeling me backwards and off my feet. His fist slams into the side of my head, and black dots soak my vision as I blink rapidly, trying to stay conscious. His fists keep coming, harder and faster than I expect from him.

'Dad!' I shout, bringing up my arms to protect my head. 'Stop! I'm going!'

'You nothing, no good, piece of shit,' he gripes, swatting my hand away. Curling his meaty hands around my throat, he squeezes. Blood drips into my eyes as I desperately try to pry his hands off me.

Two hands clamp down on my dad's shoulders and pull him off me. Zayden swings, landing one solid hit on his nose. My dad staggers back, hitting his head on the corner of the bench before collapsing on the floor. Blood oozes down the side of his face and he groans, spitting onto the dirty ground. Then he gazes ahead, looking dazed.

Zayden pulls me to my feet and quickly inspects me, wincing at what he sees.

'Come on,' he says urgently. 'Let's go.'

Dragging the back of my hand across my face, I glare down at the man who was supposed to raise me. To mould me into a man worthy of being in this world. I feel sick to my stomach staring at those sunken eyes. My hands shake as I yank out a bunch of paper towels. When I hold them out to him, my father blinks at them, then at me, as if he doesn't even know who I am. Maybe he doesn't. It's hard to tell.

'You need help,' I spit, sucking my teeth, tasting blood. 'Take a good look, because you'll never fucking see me again.' As much as I hate myself for it, I wait, staring down at him, hoping he will say something. Apologise. *Anything.* 'Did you hear me?' I demand, closing my fists, attempting to reduce the trembling. 'I'm *never* coming back here.'

The corner of my dad's mouth twists. 'Don't let the door hit you on the way out.'

All the air leaves my lungs, and my heart breaks a little more. This is it. This is the last time my father and I will be in the same room. The man I'm supposed to love, respect and look up to. A scowling shell of a man who can't even look me in the eye as I say goodbye.

I let Zayden steer me out of the house. I take in the faded wallpaper, the broken photo frames and my childhood paintings for the last time. I've said it many times before, but this time, I mean it: I'm not coming back.

I feel numb as I collapse into the passenger seat of my truck. Leaning forward, I cradle my head in my hands, the throbbing growing worse as the adrenaline fades.

'Fuck,' Zayden says softly, touching a hand to my back. 'I'm so sorry, man. No one deserves that shit.'

'Thank you,' I exhale shakily. 'For not listening.'

'That's the one thing I'm good at, you know.'

I can't help but smile, but the pain that radiates through my head makes me feel I might pass out.

'I think you should go to hospital,' Zayden points out, gesturing to my side.

Pulling up my shirt, I look down at the cut. I shake my head. 'Looks worse than it is. I'll be fine.'

Zayden gives me a dubious look. 'I'm not sure I agree with that.'

'I'm fine. Trust me.'

Pressing his lips together, he nods, searching my face for a few long moments as I shove my shirt down and lean my head back.

'Your mum leaving never had anything to do with you,' Zayden says quietly. 'Deep down, your dad knows that. He just needs someone else to blame.'

'Yeah,' I reply. 'It's whatever.'

'It's not whatever, Mase.'

'I don't need her, or him. You and Anya are my family. You're all I need.'

Zayden nods. 'Always here for you, brother. No matter what.'

The rush of love and appreciation I have for my friends almost overwhelms me. But I clench my jaw and nod, holding in all the emotions threatening to release.

Turning my head, I take in the house for the last time.

24

MASON

Three Years Earlier

'WHO'S BLOWING UP YOUR PHONE?'

Following Zayden's gaze, I look down at my phone. I shrug. The locker room is eerily quiet. It's not often there isn't at least one other person in here. 'Probably a group chat.'

'We're in all the same chats, dude,' he replies, waving his phone around. 'No notifications for me.'

I shrug again. 'Check yourself if you must know.'

Zayden leans over, swiping my phone from the bench. He lets out a low whistle. 'Oh, boy, you're in trouble.' He hands it over to me.

Twelve missed calls. Ten unread texts.

'Shit,' I mutter, dropping my head into my hands. 'I was meant to go to dinner with Chelsea tonight.'

'How late are you?' Zayden asks, looking at his watch.

'Forty-five minutes.'

He winces. 'You better buy her flowers or something. That's not cool.'

'I lost track of time.'

'I'm convinced you don't even like this girl.'

I rake my fingers through my sweat-drenched hair. This isn't fair on her. The fights and arguments have become too much. She's convinced there's something between me and Anya, and we haven't been able to move past it. Trying to ignore my feelings for Anya was the whole reason I agreed to go out with Chelsea. I've tried my best to forget about her and push the feelings aside, but it obviously isn't working.

'You're right,' I mumble. 'I need to break it off.'

Zayden offers me a sympathetic look. 'Sorry, man.'

I bang my head back against the lockers behind me.

I need to get out of this damn town.

25

ANYA

I'M LAZING ON THE LOUNGE, a cool glass of lemonade in my hand. The ice clinks against the glass as I lift it and take a sip. The heat of the sun warms my skin. Being back home is making me feel content.

'This time next week, you'll be lounging back, enjoying your cruise.' I grin, looking over at my mother, who is basically already doing that, but in our backyard instead of on a boat.

'I can't wait,' she breathes, her face lighting up with excitement. 'I can't remember the last time I went away with the girls. It's been years.'

'It will do you a world of good, Ma,' I say, smiling.

'I hope so. I'm looking forward to relaxing for a while.'

'Make sure you take lots of pics of the islands you stop at!'

'I will,' she assures me. 'So, where's your brother?'

I peek over at her. Her mouth is pinched with disapproval. She looks similar to me, but her hair has gotten lighter with age and the highlights she's added to it.

'With Mase,' I reply. 'Have you tried calling him?'

'I call him almost every day.'

I glance at her in surprise. 'And he never answers?'

She shakes her head, looking out at the pool, shoulders slumped. She looks tired; there are dark circles under her eyes, and her normally lightly tanned skin is pale.

'What was the fight about?' I question, thinking back to the time I arrived home to find Zayden marching out the front door, a duffle bag clutched in his palm, while Mum sobbed from the door, begging him to come back. He grabbed me by the arm and dragged me to his car. He didn't tell me what the fight was about, but he refused to let me back inside.

She tenses, but it's subtle enough that I question whether I truly saw anything.

'I don't want to get into it.'

'It must have been bad. Neither of you will discuss it, and your entire relationship has broken down over it.'

Folding her arms, she stares ahead, stony-faced. The way her jaw clenches reminds me so much of Zayden. They both have fiery personalities and are extremely stubborn, too alike for their own good. Growing up, I was always the peacekeeper. It helped having Mason around – he centred my brother and always brought light-heartedness into the house.

'I can't help if I don't know what's going on,' I press. I glance down at her arm, where a long bruise sits. 'That looks sore. What did you do?'

'Hmm?' Mum replies, looking down at her arm. 'Oh, nothing. Must have bumped into something.'

'Must have hit it hard.' I frown.

'Well. You know me. I'm a klutz.'

'I inherited that from you.' I roll my eyes. 'So, you're really not going to tell me what the fight was about?'

When Mum doesn't reply, I exhale and rest my head back, giving up. We spend the rest of the afternoon catching up, and when the sun starts sinking into the horizon, I make my way back to the Airbnb.

*

I drop my keys on the floor when I see Mason's face. Tears spring to my eyes as I rush over to him. Taking his face between my hands, I inspect it, before remembering Zayden is in the room. Dropping my hands, I step back, feeling the weight of Zayden's gaze on me.

'Fuck,' I murmur. 'I won't ask how it went.'

'Thanks,' Mason says dryly.

'I'm sorry.'

'Me too.'

'Can I do anything?' I ask. 'Is there anything you need?'

'I just want to relax, honestly.'

'Relax.' I nod. 'We can help with that.'

'I was keen to go out for dinner,' Zayden states. We both turn to stare at him. 'Not go out,' he quickly adds. 'Just dinner. Casual, quiet dinner.'

Mason and I glance at each other.

'It's up to you, Mase,' I say. 'Are you feeling up to it?'

He shrugs. 'Dinner sounds good.'

'Alright, then.'

'Yay!' Zayden claps enthusiastically, and we ignore him.

Once we're all ready, we head into town, deciding that dinner at the local pub will do. It feels like old times being back here, especially since I recognise every single face. Smiling and waving as we pass, we make our way to a table out in the beer garden, away from the noise of the TAB and pokies.

'Oh, shit,' Zayden mutters, rubbing his face. He looks tired. 'Be right back, I'm going to go hide in that corner and pretend I don't exist.'

Raising my eyebrows, I look up to see Leasa in line at the bar. I wince. 'Have you spoken to her since the break-up?'

'She liked my Instagram story the other night,' Zayden replies thoughtfully, avoiding my question. 'What do you think that means?'

'Depends. What was the story of?'

'I was holding a beer in front of the sunset.'

I shrug. 'I don't know. I wouldn't think much of it.'

Zayden's eyes linger on his ex-girlfriend for a moment longer before he drops into the seat, purposely sitting with his back to the bar.

'Why did I think coming home was a good idea?' he mutters.

'You should go out tonight,' Mason says. 'You came back here to catch up with everyone.'

'But you don't feel up to going.'

I smile. My brother is so dependent on Mason.

'You can still go,' Mason says, leaning back in his chair.

Zayden chews his thumbnail, turning to face me. 'What about you?'

I shake my head. 'I'm happy with an early night. I just came to see Mum.'

Zayden nods. 'Well. Alright, then. If you're both sure.'

He's barely finished his dinner when he starts pushing his chair back and getting to his feet, having already made plans to meet with others. I'm silently relieved. All I want to do is go back to the Airbnb and relax.

'Call if you need me,' Zayden says, gesturing to his phone.

'We will. Have fun!' I reply.

'Ready to go?' Mason asks me, his fingers pressed against his temple, looking like he's nursing a headache.

Nodding, I push to my feet.

Zayden tosses a wave over his shoulder as he disappears out the back. Leasa notices Zayden walk past her and she downs her drink, following him.

'Oh, God,' I mutter. 'That's not going to end well.'

'Nope,' Mason agrees.

We make our way to the exit, and my heart plummets when I

see Phoebe walking towards us, eyes trained on her phone. I stiffen, attempting to sidestep her and go unnoticed, but she glances up and startles in surprise. My throat instantly turns dry. My eyes sting with the threat of tears, but I swallow down the pain, lifting my chin as I slowly exhale, refusing to let her see how much she broke me.

'Anya . . .' she whispers, taking a step towards me, having the audacity to look as if *she* is the one about to cry.

'Don't,' I warn her, shaking my head.

'I'm sorry . . .' She trails off, cheeks reddening. She looks pale, and thinner than I remember. It never occurred to me that she would be having a hard time with our falling out as well, since *she* was the one who betrayed *me*.

'Why?' I demand, my voice coming out sharper and firmer than I expected it to sound. 'Why did you do it?'

Her eyes close, and tears glisten on her cheeks. 'You had everything I wanted. I just . . . I'm sorry.'

'That's fucked up,' I hiss at her, jabbing my finger in the air towards her. She flinches, recoiling and covering her face with her hands, as if scared I might start swinging at her. If I was angrier, I probably would, but I'm hurt and lost because of this. I thought she was my best friend for life, but, obviously, I meant nothing to her. 'That is nowhere near good enough of an excuse for what you did.'

'I know,' she whispers. 'I'm sorry, Anya.'

'Good, I hope you are,' I say, drawing in a breath and meeting those icy-blue eyes of hers. 'I'm moving on from all of this. You should too.'

'Just wait . . .' she says, reaching for me.

'Don't,' I snap at her, and she flinches. 'It's done now. We will never be friends again. Let's both move on.'

The sound of her crying makes me close my eyes, the pain washing through me as if I've just heard about it all over again for the first time. The sting of her betrayal, of losing her, feels as sharp as ever.

'Come on,' Mason says, throwing his arm around my shoulder. My heartbeat is loud in my ears and, suddenly, I feel ice-cold, despite the warm breeze around me. 'Let's go.'

I let him steer me past her, and we walk out the exit. Her eyes remain on us until we round the corner. I turn, pressing my forehead into his shoulder.

'Fuck,' I whisper shakily, pressing a hand to my heart. 'It hurts to see her.'

'I know,' he murmurs, rubbing soothing circles on my back.

'Please get me out of here.'

Mason takes my hand in his, bringing it up to his mouth and kissing the top of it carefully, his lips soft and warm on my skin.

'Here for you,' he says, just like we always used to. 'Always.'

I smile sadly. 'Always.'

'*Psycho*?'

'We've watched that one too many times,' Mason counters.

'*Get Out*?'

'We watched that last time.'

'Oh, yeah,' I agree. '*Alien*?'

Mason shakes his head. 'Not tonight.'

'*The Invisible Man*?'

'I watched that one last month.'

'*A Quiet Place*?'

Flicking his hand into a finger gun, he aims it at me. 'Bingo.'

Switching off the light, I wander over to the lounge. Mason is settled right in the centre of it, with his arm slung over the back. He glances up at me, patting the spot beside him. I flop down and nestle into his side, feeling myself relax in his hold.

He presses his lips to my temple, making my pulse race.

Focus on the movie.

Being here with him, just like this – it feels so right.

'I want this every night,' he whispers, lips still pressed against the side of my head.

I turn towards him, our lips coming dangerously close to meeting. My heart is thrumming, steadily increasing in pace as we inch closer and closer. He nuzzles my cheek, the slight stubble across his jaw tenderly rubbing against my chin, and I close my eyes at the feel of it. My favourite look of his is when he has a little stubble.

'Always?' I ask softly.

'Always. Me and you.'

'Me and you,' I murmur, feeling warm, safe and content here in his arms.

'Think about it,' he says. 'About me, you and what you want.'

'Okay.'

'It will work out as it should.'

'I hope so.'

Kissing me gently once more, he turns his head, facing the TV. Burrowing my face into his chest, I snuggle in close as we watch the movie.

When the credits start rolling, neither of us moves.

'Are you okay? After seeing Phoebe tonight?' he murmurs, fingers playing with my hair.

I shake my head. 'If everything she did was out of jealousy . . . that's disgusting.' Releasing a shaky breath, I hold my hand up in a 'stop' signal, as if that will help my mind from detouring towards the past. 'I'm not letting myself think about her or give any of my energy to that situation.' Swallowing, I wipe the corners of my eyes. 'Let's talk about something else.'

'Do you remember that night we stargazed?' he asks quietly. 'And we made wishes on shooting stars?'

'Yes,' I breathe.

'When I was overseas, I often lay outside, looking at the stars. I always thought of you. I was so scared that you hated me, and my heart hurt.'

'My heart hurt, too.'

His thumb runs across my knuckles. 'And then we fell asleep outside.'

'I had the *worst* mosquito bites,' I groan. 'I even managed to get bitten on my ass!'

He chuckles softly. 'I don't blame that mosquito one bit.'

Lightly, I shove him, then push to my feet, stretching. A few bones in my back crack, and I rub my eyes.

'You want first shower?' I ask, trying to shake off the growing need building inside me. More specifically, between my legs.

His dark eyes travel slowly down my body before he shrugs. 'I don't mind.'

'You go first.'

Unhurriedly, he stands. Leaning down, he presses his lips to my forehead and holds me for a moment. And then, he is gone.

26

MASON

WITH MY HANDS BRACED on the bathroom sink, I take a long inhale as the room fills with steam. My body feels a little sore and tender after today, but not as bad as I expected it to. I glance down to the cut in my side. Thankfully, it isn't very deep.

When I look back at my reflection, my mind wanders towards Anya. My heart thuds loudly. My skin feels hot. My need for her fills me so intensely, I feel myself growing hard at the thought. Screwing my eyes shut, I push off the vanity and walk towards the door. Opening it, I poke my head out, but the hallway is empty.

I shut the door.

I open it again.

Exhaling, I leave it open and step back, staring at the gap between the door and the doorframe. After a moment, I turn and step into the shower.

Breathe, my inner voice directs me.

This want for her. This *need* is taking over my life.

This time, I'm doing it right. Because she deserves the world.

The hot water runs over my skin, sliding down my body as I think about her. Those eyes, that mouth, the curves that haunt my dreams. Curling my fingers around my length, I move my hand up and down, picturing the other night at the party, when she had those pretty lips wrapped around me.

'Ah, fuck,' I groan, not caring how loudly it slips out, as my hand begins to move faster.

I'm so hard, it's almost painful. Each pump has me twisting and jerking, as I imagine her underneath me while I move in and out of her. The sound of the water hitting the tiles mixes with my laboured breathing as I thrust my hips forward, picking up momentum.

'Anya,' I say through gritted teeth.

'Yes?'

My head jerks up, and my eyes snap open. Those round, innocent eyes peer back at me through the fog, and my mouth falls open in shock as she smiles at me slowly, her gaze dropping to where my hand is.

'You're here,' I say.

'You left the door open.'

'I did.'

'You wanted me to come.'

'I do want you to come,' I agree, smirking.

Biting her lip, she shimmies down her skirt and panties and steps out of them. Swallowing, I continue moving my hand up and down my length, my fingers tightening as my gaze roams over her tanned, bare thighs.

Leaning back onto the bathroom sink, she places a foot on the edge of the bathtub beside her, opening her legs. A coy smile dances around her mouth as her hand slides across her stomach, dipping between her thighs, and sliding across her slit.

'You drive me fucking crazy, Blush,' I croak.

'Do I?' she whispers, fingers glistening as she slides them teasingly across her entrance, before sinking a finger inside herself.

Groaning, I press my forehead against the glass as I continue to work myself, my movements becoming harsh and jerky as she begins to finger herself.

'Touch your clit,' I instruct her.

'Yes, Captain.'

Oh, fuck.

She does as she's told, and I almost come undone right then, but I am so desperate to ride this out longer. I'm so highly turned on, so deeply in love with this girl that I can't see straight.

'Does it feel good?' I ask, hardly recognising my voice.

'Yes,' she replies, her lips parting as her head tips back. 'But not as good as when you do it.'

This. Is. Torture.

'Will you come?' I ask. 'For me?'

She nods.

'I want you to think about what I want to do to you,' I say. 'All the dirty things that have been on my mind for years.'

'Such as . . . ?' She trails off, breathing heavily as she works her hand faster.

'I want to kiss you,' I whisper. 'I want to lick every inch of that perfect body.'

'What else?'

'I want to taste you on my tongue every morning.'

'Anything else?'

'I want to be inside you again. I want to be so deep inside you that I ruin you for anyone else.'

A moan falls from her lips, and her fingers move faster, in the same rhythm my own hand moves.

'You ruined me for anyone else long ago, Mase.'

'Oh fuck,' I say, breathless. 'Come for me.'

A cry leaves her, and her legs shudder as her head falls back, hitting the mirror behind her.

'Good girl,' I murmur, dragging my tongue across my lower lip as I drink her in, knowing I will *never* forget this moment.

Shakily, she pushes to her feet. She yanks her top over her head and unclasps her bra. Her breasts tumble out of their hold, bouncing slightly as they release. A sound mixed between a groan and a whimper leaves me at the sight of it. Stepping inside, she gets down on her knees, the water spraying across her skin.

'Blush?' I question, tensing, as my release is drawing nearer by the second.

'Come on me, Captain.'

Barely a second later, my come shoots out, painting her face as I release harder and more intensely than I have in what feels like forever. I do a few quick pumps, making sure every last drop is out before I sag forward, breathless. The sight of her on her knees, covered in my release, feels so sinfully wrong, but so damn right. Deliciously sexy and forbidden, and fuck I want to do it again.

Curling my arm around her, I help her to her feet, and she lets me rinse her off. Leaning down, I kiss her deeply and slowly. We stay like that for a long time: kissing and touching in lazy, long strokes. We're so desperate to be close, and neither of us wants to break this moment.

'I don't want this to stop, but Zayden could be home any minute.' She sighs wistfully, stepping back and pushing her wet hair from her face.

I nod, knowing she's right. 'Yeah. And he won't be impressed if we use all the hot water.'

'Good point.' She laughs.

Reluctantly, I turn the tap and we step out, both towelling off, and managing to not touch each other long enough to get dry. As much as I yearn for her, I don't want to rush this. Not like last time.

After Anya is settled in her bed, I fall into mine. My eyelids hang heavily, exhaustion sweeping through me so intensely. I fall into a deep sleep, thankful that for once, no nightmares plague my dreams.

*

I am in love with Anya.

All my life – or so it feels – my common sense has told me this isn't a good idea. I've had friends tell me. Zayden, who I consider my family, has told me. I've tried and I've tried to resist this, but when I breathe, I feel her. When I close my eyes, I see her. She's embedded in me, and I can't stop this anymore. I don't want to.

On the trip home, I'm settled in the driver's seat, Anya has her feet perched on the dash as she reads, and Zayden is sunk low in his seat in the back, eyes closed, resting his head in his hands.

Once Anya decides a relationship with me is what she truly wants and she's ready to go all in, I am going to speak to Zayden, and make him see why Anya and I being together is right – and basically inevitable at this point. He will understand. He has to. Once he realises how serious we are about each other, he won't be able to not support this. Right?

My eyes shift to the mirror, and I wince at the bruises on my neck: thick, unmistakable finger marks. After not moving all night while I slept, I'm really feeling the injuries from yesterday. My muscles feel sore, and the bruises look worse than I expected.

'What have you decided to do about becoming captain?' Anya asks, placing her book on her lap.

'I'm going to take it,' I say, tapping my fingers against the steering wheel. 'You talked me into it.' I glance at the mirror, seeing Zayden's neck bent at an awkward angle and his mouth open as he sleeps. 'Besides, I really like it when you call me Captain.'

Her lips twitch. 'Glad to hear it.'

'I just hope I don't ruffle too many feathers with this,' I admit, leaning my elbow on the door.

'That's on them if they can't be happy for you.'

'Hm.' I make a noise of agreement, even though I'm quite positive this new development will create tension among the team. Tension I don't particularly have the time and energy to deal with.

The rest of the day is spent lounging by the pool at home, and it feels like old times. Soon enough, everything that happened with my dad fades into the background. Anya and Zayden are great at distracting me.

Anya pushes to her feet, and I glance up at her.

'Where are you going?' Zayden queries, placing his arm behind his head as he leans back, crossing his ankles together.

'Cami has convinced Nora and me to go to an off-campus party with her.'

She's dressed only in her black bikini, and I find it extremely difficult not to let my eyes trace over those curves and long legs I love so much. My sunglasses are perched on my nose, shielding my roaming gaze, but I still feel it's obvious that I'm unable to take my eyes off her.

'That sounds fun,' I say.

'Yeah. I'm not going to have a big night tonight. I might even drive.' She shrugs, seeming to avoid meeting my eyes as she gathers her rubbish.

'Okay,' Zayden says as she strolls towards the door. 'Make safe choices!'

My eyes linger on her back as she disappears through the sliding doors.

'She's doing okay,' Zayden observes, eyes remaining on the door. 'Her life literally got turned upside down. The two people who were by her side when we couldn't be betrayed her in the worst way possible. But she kept going. She's okay.' He turns to face me, a proud smile on his face. 'Our girl is strong. Isn't she?'

Our girl.

'Your sister is the strongest, most beautiful girl I know.'

The words are out before I can stop them. A beat of silence stretches between us, and Zayden nods.

'She's lucky to have you.'

'Me?' I question, surprised.

'You'd do anything for her, and it's not often you can say that about someone. She feels safe around you, and that's something I don't take lightly, my friend. I appreciate you.'

I blink at my best friend, in shock for a moment, unsure how to process everything he just said to me. He isn't someone to speak like this, especially to me, about Anya, and I am utterly speechless. It warms my heart to hear his words and makes me feel as if maybe he would accept us being together.

I think my trouble with anger in the past was the main reason Zayden never wanted his sister involved with me. Other than disrupting our trio's dynamic, he was worried trauma from my dad would somehow emerge, but I've worked hard on myself and I don't ever want to be like him.

Zayden groans as he stands, stretching his arms over his head.

'I love her, you know,' I say quietly, and I barely dare to breathe as he turns to face me, sliding his sunglasses into his damp messy hair.

'I know,' he replies, clapping a hand on my shoulder. 'Like a sister. I love you for that.'

I tense, watching Zayden walk away, my heart sinking to my stomach.

27

ANYA

Three Years Earlier

MY HEAD IS LIGHT as I move about the room, swaying my hips, throwing my hair over my shoulder. Mason's gaze hasn't left my body since he walked through the front door, and electricity is sizzling underneath my skin.

Most of the crowd has gravitated out the back, hanging around the pool. Beer pong and other drinking games are set up out there, leaving the living room as the designated dance floor.

Scanning the room, I search for Mason. He and Chelsea broke up, and I know it was because of me.

'Watch out.' His voice is right in my ear, his hot breath blowing my hair across my eyes. Goosebumps erupt over my body, and I shiver at his proximity. 'Little Blush isn't so little anymore.'

Because this tension between us has been driving me wild, I press my ass back into him, slowly grinding. He groans, hands tightening on my waist. We have been tiptoeing this line for far too long now, and I'm sick of not giving in to the aching need between us.

His words ring inside my head. Words he whispered to me one night when we were in the shadows of the house, pretending to be asleep. *If you still want me when you're eighteen, I'm yours. It's me and you. Always.*

'You're right about that, Mase,' I murmur.

I twist around in his arms, and he takes a step back, eyes darting about, looking to see if the coast is clear. He's totally checked out recently, due to the break-up, but I also know he's been avoiding me. Because he can't deny this anymore.

I want him. I always have. And he wants me, too.

Squeezing his eyes shut, he takes a further step back, but I inch closer.

'What did you get me for my birthday?' I whisper, so close that our breath mingles as one. His smell overwhelms me. The warm, familiar scent that has always been Mason.

His gaze lifts briefly from my mouth to my eyes before his hand finds mine and drags me into the hallway. A few people glance in our direction, but mostly they don't even notice us.

Gently, he pushes me into my room, kicking the door shut behind him. My breath hitches as he slams his palms against the wall, caging me in, a wild smirk on his face.

'You wore that for me, didn't you, Blush?' he drawls.

I barely manage to tear my gaze from his as I look down at my tight black dress. It shows off every bit of my body, leaving nothing to the imagination. He was there when I bought it, and the look on his face at the time told me everything I needed to know.

'Yes.'

He groans, pressing his forehead into mine, his hand tangling my hair. 'This is for you.' He pulls out a small velvet box from his pocket and places it in my hand.

Flipping it open slowly, a sharp gasp leaves me when I see a silver ring sparkling up at me. Removing it, I spin it slowly, reading the word *Always* engraved on the inside. My teeth sink into my bottom lip as I try not to burst into tears.

'Mase,' I breathe through a watery smile. 'I love it so much.'

'You do?' He grins, looking thrilled.

'So much.' Sliding it on my finger, I beam up at him. Stepping onto my tiptoes, I move my mouth towards his. He presses his forehead into mine, breathing heavily.

'We can't do this.'

'You're not with her anymore,' I whisper.

'It's never been about that,' he says, and then immediately winces. 'I didn't mean for any of that to happen. To hurt you. To drag her into it . . .'

'I know.'

'You're Zayden's baby sister,' Mason murmurs, twirling a piece of my hair around his finger.

'No,' I say, so close now that our lips lightly brush. 'I'm Anya fucking Stark, your friend.' I exhale. 'I'm more than your friend.' Moving my gaze upwards, I fight the coy smile off my lips. 'I'm eighteen now, and I still want you.'

Growling, he closes the minuscule gap between us, claiming my lips hungrily with his. I tilt my head back, allowing him to kiss me deeper. I sigh into his mouth. I've wanted this for so long, my mind can't process that it's actually happening. This is it. The moment I've been waiting for. We are going to give in, and we are going to be together. Everyone will know he belongs to me, and I belong to him.

His lips move messily from my mouth across my jaw, as his strong hands push my dress up around my waist. When his hands skim over my bare backside, a sound I can't quite describe escapes him.

'Anya,' he groans, voice low, raspy and a little tormented. His thumb possessively strokes my hip bone, bordering the area that has greedily wanted his touch for as long as I can remember.

My pulse jumps. 'Please,' I breathe.

He knows what I want. The pace of his breathing increases as he presses closer, his tongue making a pattern across my neck, making my thighs clench. The ache building between them is unbearable.

'Blush . . .' He exhales. It's partly a warning, but murmured in a tone of longing.

'No one has to know,' I whisper, pushing my hips into his. 'Not right now.'

'Fuck.' His hand slides across my skin and I shiver, white-hot desire pulsating through me in waves. 'If your brother ever finds out, he will kill me.'

'It'll be our secret, until we're ready.'

His thumb runs across my slit and I moan. He slips his fingers inside me and lets out another curse as my wetness coats his fingers.

'You'll be the death of me,' he chokes out hoarsely, before sliding a finger over my clit. I throw my head back, hitting the wall, my eyes closing. His finger moves tantalisingly slowly before he enters me again.

My grip tightens around his shoulders, bunching his black shirt under my fingertips. I shamelessly grind into his hand as his finger slides in and out of me, a faster rhythm with each stroke.

'We can't do this,' he whispers. 'Can we?'

I slide my hands up his neck and pull his face to mine, kissing him hard and passionately, letting all the pent-up feelings I've harboured for so long pour between us. We moan into each other's mouths as he glides another finger in, simultaneously adding pressure to my clit.

'We can,' I answer breathlessly. 'Me and you.'

'Always.'

'Always.'

We kiss for a long time. It's deep and fiery, overflowing with all the tension and longing that has been building for years and years. We are so close there's no space between us, but I drag him impossibly closer, desperation coursing through me.

His fingers work inside me, hooking and bending in a way that has my legs trembling. A half-moan, half-whimper climbs its way up my throat, escaping my lips as I throw my head back. His mouth is on mine, his tongue clashing with mine deliciously. A powerful, thrilling sensation overtakes me and I break from the kiss, sinking my teeth into his shoulder as the orgasm crashes through me.

His mouth is back on mine as he hoists me up. My legs wrap around his waist as I tug at his pants. We're both desperate to get them down, and when I wrap my hand around him, he hisses, pressing hard into it, then sliding across my entrance teasingly. He pulls back, eyes dark, glistening with lust and adoration as he gazes down at me, his lips tilted in that sinfully sexy smirk of his.

I grip him in my hand and line him up, and then he pushes inside. He groans and I wince, tightening around him. He sinks further into me, thrusting a little hard, making me whine in pain, but also in pleasure. My insides stretch and curve around him, and I try to relax my muscles, wanting to take him deeper. He does a quick thrust, slamming me hard against the wall, and I choke out a moan, tears springing to my eyes at the rawness and fullness of the pain. Mason's fingers bite into the soft part of my backside as he pumps in and out of me, a little rougher than I expected, and I choke on a gasp as the pain worsens.

'I'm sorry, Blush, but this is going to be quick,' he groans, shifting me so that when he thrusts, it feels as if a spear runs through me. He uses one arm and the weight of his upper body to hold me in place, the other hand tangled in my hair. 'Next time, I will treasure every inch of your perfect body, and devour it piece by piece.'

I moan, feeling pressure building again, and squeezing my legs tighter around him as I attempt to relax and revel in the pleasure.

'Fuck,' he groans, releasing a guttural growl as he spills inside me, pumping hard and fast a few more times before sagging against me, his hot breath fanning across my neck.

A loud knock bangs against the door, and my heart leaps to my throat as I startle in alarm. Mason's eyes widen in panic.

'Hey, Anya? Are you there? We're about to do the cake!' My brother's voice floats into my room from the other side of the door, and it's as if an icy-cold bucket of water is thrown over us. I sit up, the lust-filled trance breaking instantly.

Mason wrenches away, sliding out of me painfully and practically dropping me to my feet. I yelp at the sensation and the lack of contact with him. A few traitorous tears spill down my cheeks. I hastily wipe them away, and wince at the soreness between my legs.

'Yes!' I call out, voice shaky and high-pitched. 'Just need a minute.'

'Okay! Be quick!'

I bite my lip, my heart sinking at the expression on Mason's face. He's not looking at me, but down at himself, and the blood smeared across his length. His hands tremble as he blinks down at them, completely rigid.

'Oh my God,' he says slowly, taking a step back and blinking furiously in shock. 'Anya . . . I'm so fucking sorry. I didn't . . . you're a . . . of course you are.' He backs up further, looking distressed, pushing his hands through his hair. 'Jesus Christ, I just went straight in, I wasn't even gentle . . . fuck . . . are you even on birth control?'

I stare at him, realising that he is not sober. Not at all. I could taste alcohol on his tongue, but I didn't know he was this drunk.

I'm tipsy – most definitely – but he is *drunk*. How did I not notice this before? My lips tremble as my eyes fill with tears.

'Are you?' he demands, cheeks reddening with what looks like anger.

I shake my head, a tear falling, and he curses. Despite the blood, he yanks his pants up, shaking his head.

'I'm a fucking idiot,' he mutters, looking anywhere but at me.

He strides from the room, banging my bedroom door shut behind him, rattling the walls. My entire body shakes as I stand there, trying to process everything that just happened.

Everything I wanted for so long . . . to be ruined in a matter of seconds.

I can't believe that just happened. The moment I'd been waiting for . . . the moment I thought I would treasure for the rest of my life. The special thing I wanted to experience with Mason for the very first time. The promise of being with him, completely and openly.

It was meant to be special.

Instead, it was everything it shouldn't have been.

My hands are trembling violently as I stumble towards the bathroom. I wash my hands and use my towel to pat my face dry, fixing my makeup and hair as best as I can. It hurts when I walk and I wince, dreading the burn I know I'm going to feel when I pee.

'Anya!' Zayden barks at me, and I whirl around, fearing that he's found out what just happened here. 'Can you hurry the fuck up? Everyone is waiting!'

'Can I pee?' I huff, keeping my hands busy, hoping he doesn't notice how badly I'm shaking.

'Do it after!' he demands, leaning forward and yanking my elbow, almost tipping me over, since my heels are gigantic. 'Come on.'

Another tear slides down my cheek as he leads me out of my room. I glance over my shoulder at the wall, the space I lost my virginity, and my heart.

And here I was, thinking this was going to be the best night of my life.

28

ANYA

TWO HANDS GRIP MY waist and yank me harshly backwards. I collide with a firm chest.

'Anya,' the voice rumbles, and I tense, quickly stepping out of the hold.

'Hello, Kai.'

Some sort of techno song I've never heard blares out of a speaker not far from me, and I step further away from it, and from him. He moves in front of me, blocking my path. I grind my teeth, frustrated.

'Can we talk?' he asks.

'No!' Cami shouts at him, appearing out of nowhere. Reaching for my hand, she drags me off the dance floor and towards the bar. She screws her face up, throwing a shady look in his direction. 'That boy really rubs me the wrong way,' she grumbles, shaking her head. 'You okay?'

'Fine.'

'Let me get you a drink.'

'I'm not drinking tonight,' I say for what feels like the hundredth time. I don't feel like being here right now, surrounded by all this noise and all these bodies. I want to be home, watching a horror movie, in the arms of the boy I have loved all my life.

'You're not having fun,' she states, frowning.

'Sure I am.'

Her brows rise. 'Not sure who you're trying to convince there, but either way, you did a terrible job.'

'Don't worry about me. Go.' I lightly shove her in the direction of a group of guys who keep looking over at us. 'So many people want your attention right now.'

'I don't care,' she protests. 'I want to hang with you, and make sure you're having a good time.'

'I love you for that. I really do. But I want you to go mingle and have the best time. I'm going to get some water and chill for a bit.' She opens her mouth, and I give her a look, nodding towards the group. 'Go. Please.'

'Fine,' she relents, leaning in to plant a kiss on my cheek. 'Call or text if you need me, okay?'

'I will.'

She squeezes my hand, then shoots off in the direction of the group. Nora ended up bailing to study, and I don't know how she managed to get out of it, but I didn't want to leave Cami hanging when I knew she really wanted to come.

Pulling out my phone, I bring up Mason's contact details.

> **Anya:** I'm here at a party, surrounded by people.

> **Anya:** But all I want is to be with you.

Raking my fingers through my hair, I chew my lip, waiting for his response.

> **Mason:** Say the word, and I'll come get you.

Anya: Please.

Anya: I want to see you.

Mason: Leaving now.

Anya: I'll meet you out front.

Smiling, I look over my shoulder to see Cami being led to the dance floor by a guy who I swear must be almost seven feet tall. I shoot her a quick text, saying I'm heading out, but to call me if she needs a ride later. I pocket my phone, and finally the line at the bar moves. I reach the front, and a girl leans towards me.

'Hi, can I get some water, please?'

'The water station is over there!' she shouts at me then turns, serving the person next to me.

Running my tongue across my teeth in irritation, I leave the line and stride over to the cart. Groaning, I stare down at the empty tray that is supposed to hold the glasses for me to fill up.

'Sorry, gorgeous, I think I took the last one.'

Closing my eyes, I exhale noisily through my nose before turning to face Kai, who smiles down at me, holding a glass of water in his hand.

'I don't believe that you're not drinking,' I say a little hotly as I stare up at him. 'I've never seen you pass up the chance to party.'

'You never took the chance to know me, how can you even make that assumption?' Kai retorts, his eyes flashing with anger briefly.

Pressing my lips together, I turn, planning to leave, when he reaches out for me.

'Hey,' he says, face softening. 'I'm sorry. For the dumb shit I said at your house. I didn't mean any of it. I really like you and

I didn't handle the fact that you don't really like me back. It was rude. I'm really sorry.'

I blink at him in surprise. 'Oh.'

'Look, we have years of university left. Games, parties, classes. I don't want you to feel like you have to avoid me all the time. I really am sorry. I hope we can just forget any of it happened.'

'That sounds good to me,' I admit, feeling my shoulders slump in defeat, not wanting to drag this out either. He makes a valid point. The campus is big, but not that big. With Mason and Zayden on the football team, too, we're bound to run into each other often, whether we like it or not. 'I'm sorry my brother punched you.'

'I deserved it.'

I smile. 'Okay. Well, thanks for that.'

'Here,' he says, thrusting the glass towards me. 'You can have it. I'm going to get the staff to refill the glasses.' He pushes the glass into my hand and swerves around me, stalking towards the bar, looking like he's on a mission.

My throat is paper dry, begging me to relieve it. Sighing, I take a long sip, and end up draining the entire cup.

29

MASON

I SWEAR TRAFFIC IS always the worst when you're in a hurry. Tapping restlessly against the steering wheel, I continue to inch down the street. Anticipation rises in my chest as I think about the message Anya sent me. This feels like old times, and I'm so happy for it.

I pull up, managing to snag a park, and my eyes move to the door of the club as it pushes open. My fingers tighten around the steering wheel as Anya appears with Kai, who's touching her elbow as he guides her out the door. Her foot stumbles and she lurches forward, hitting her knees on the cement. I jerk in surprise, jumping out of the car. Kai roughly yanks her back up to her feet, shouldering most of her weight as he begins to push her in the opposite direction to me.

'Get the fuck off her,' I snarl, storming up to him.

I curl my hand round his arm and yank it back so hard, he loses his footing, stumbling backwards. Anya falls onto me, and I wrap my arms around her, pulling her close. Her head rests heavily on me, and my heart plummets to my stomach.

Something is wrong.

Pushing the hair back from her face, I touch my hand to her cheek. 'Anya?' I whisper, brows pinching together. 'You good?'

Her breath comes out heavily, but she doesn't speak.

'What is going on?' I demand, staring down at her. Her eyes are closed, her lips parted, and she can barely keep herself upright. Rage fills me, potent and raw. My glare swivels to Kai and I glower at him, a look of panic crossing his face. 'What did you do to her?'

'Nothing, she's wasted,' he spits, clambering to his feet.

'Bullshit,' I seethe. 'She was sober.'

'Clearly not,' he snaps back, gesturing to her. 'She's a fucking mess, and I was looking after her.'

I scoff. 'Yeah. You're just that nice of a guy.'

Making fists with my hands, I turn, searching for the two police officers I saw walking down the other end of the street as I drove in. My eyes land on them as they approach their car. I shout at them, and they startle, whirling around before quickly racing across the road. Kai curses, ready to make a run for it when I slam him against the wall, one arm around Anya, the other now pinned across his throat.

'What's going on?' one of the officers demands.

'My girlfriend texted me to come pick her up, and this asshole was dragging her out the door. I think he's slipped something into her drink,' I quickly explain, and despite everything going on, it feels good to call her my girlfriend.

A sharp intake of breath captures my attention, and then Anya collapses against me.

The last few hours have been a blur.

Anya spent the night in hospital as they monitored her, restoring her hydration and everything else the drug affected. She was sent home sometime this afternoon, feeling a lot better now and managing to keep down some food.

As I suspected, Kai spiked her drink. I shudder to think about what his plans were with her. He insisted to the police that it was a harmless prank, only meant to scare her a little. He pleaded with them, saying he didn't mean for the dosage to be so high. Considering the strength, and the history of fights between our group and Kai recently, the matter isn't being treated lightly. I spoke with an officer, who said that Kai will be going to court.

Closing my eyes, I exhale heavily. It was a close call, and I can't be more thankful she made it out safely. Thank God she messaged me when she did. I dropped everything to meet her. Things could have been very different if I hadn't.

'Can I get you anything?' Zayden asks her, hovering near the lounge like he has been all afternoon. He has dark circles under his eyes and looks as if he hasn't slept at all in the last week.

'I'm fine,' she says with a weak smile. 'Thank you.'

'I'm so mad, I could kill him.'

'Justice will get him, Zay. Don't you worry about that,' I grunt, cracking my knuckles as I glare at the floor, jaw tense.

'Thank God you were there, and that the police were just down the street.'

The street with all the nightclubs is heavily monitored by police, and I'm thankful they weren't too far away from us when it all went down. If anything, it was one of the worst places to try something like that, considering how much police gravitate to the area.

'I don't want to talk about it anymore. Please,' Anya whispers brokenly, rubbing her eyes, probably feeling drained after everything.

I collapse onto the couch next to Anya, and Zayden does the same on her other side. She rests her head on my shoulder, and I place a hand on her arm, softly rubbing my thumb over her skin. Zayden leans against her.

'Thank you,' she murmurs softly, curling into me. 'I feel safe being between the two people I love most in this world.'

Kissing her hair, I let my own eyes drift shut, and after a moment, we all fall asleep.

Sweat stings my eyes. Shoving my hair back from my face, I run forward. Zayden zips the ball to me and I race ahead, feeling the wind on my face and the presence of others chasing me.

Launching over the line, I slide across the ground as the ball hits the grass. I'm back on my feet within a second, whirling around to face the team. We've split into two, and the players on my side wander over, slapping me on the back.

'Alright,' Coach calls out, blowing his whistle. 'Good. That's enough game for today.'

The rest of training is winding down, and I'm eager to hit the showers. The cool water runs through my hair, feeling incredible, and I spend longer than I probably should cleaning myself. Stepping out, I curl the towel around my neck and wander towards my bag.

'Every time I watch you play, man, you remind me why you're the best on the team,' Zayden says, a lopsided smile on his face. 'You're just a natural.'

'Thanks, man,' I reply, a rush of warmth filling me. 'I appreciate that.'

'You know, in the past, you let yourself get distracted, but you've really got your head on straight now. You deserve to be captain.'

Pressing my lips together, I stay silent for a moment, guilt coiling in my gut. I was so worried about how Zayden would feel if I became captain – whether he would wish it were offered to him, whether he might've thought I don't deserve it – but here he is, proud of me. He's so stoked for my achievement, and I'm repaying him by sneaking around with his sister.

I need to talk to him about it. I know how he feels about men, and anger, and the trauma that comes from that. The dynamic between us is also something he doesn't want screwed up, though I already technically did that. I understand all this, but I've grown up. We both have. I just need to know that Anya is all in, otherwise, this entire thing is pointless.

'You good?' Zayden asks, frowning at me.

'Er – yeah, sorry. Just thinking.' I clap a hand on his shoulder. 'I'm really working on being the best I can for the team. So I appreciate you saying that. Means a lot.'

Zayden nods. 'Any time.'

Turning his back to me, he disappears through the door, and I lean back against the locker, eyes tilted towards the ceiling.

I don't deserve him.

30

MASON

THE UPSIDE OF HAVING a pool and living with the girl I'm in love with is that I get to see her in a bikini regularly. The downside – not being able to look at her or touch her the way I crave to – is that it's unbearable at times.

On this specific occasion, I'm able to stare. Zayden is out with some of the team, meeting them for lunch. I was honest with Zayden, telling him I didn't want to leave Anya alone after everything, but that he should go. He seemed reluctant, but we basically forced him out the door. We both knew he wanted to go. He's been by her side ever since it happened, and she is doing fine. Or at least she says she is.

Cami and Nora are coming over later today to spend the evening. They've been around a few times, having movie marathons, eating junk food, gossiping about anything and everything. I'm glad she's found good friends. She deserves them, after the last ones she had.

She's been painting a lot, and every time I'm reminded of how gifted she is. It blows my mind that she didn't paint much while I was away, since she's constantly doing it now. She's incredibly talented, and I hope she does something with it in the future. I wish I had a creative mind like she does.

'What are you thinking about?' she asks, dropping beside me

and dipping her feet into the water. I exhale, watching the water ripple for a moment.

'Nothing,' I reply, my gaze catching hers. 'Everything.'

The slight breeze blows her dark hair over her eyes. Reaching out, I push it back. My eyes roam her face. Letting my hand fall, I face the water again, my heart beating painfully in my chest.

'Everything?' she repeats softly.

'I've, um, decided something.' My chest constricts, and I curl and uncurl my hands, trying to stop the anxiety from climbing its way up my body like it's trying to.

Her brows furrow. 'Okay. What is it?'

'If you decide you don't want to pursue this' – I wave a hand between us – 'if you don't want a relationship, then I'm going to move out. Give you some space. I think it would be easier on both of us.'

Shock registers in those pretty eyes of hers. 'No way. You were here first. If things reach that point, then I will be the one to leave. I'm the one who invaded your space.'

'You didn't *invade* my space.'

'I sort of did.'

Cheers erupt somewhere in the background. I glance up at the TV, where a re-run of one of our games is playing. Zayden always puts them on to watch and he never remembers to turn the TV off when he leaves a room – or turn off any of the lights. It drives me mad.

'Either way, I've made my decision. It's on you now.' I swallow, glancing at her and then away just as quickly. 'No pressure. Just wanted it to be clear to you that I'm all in. There is no one else for me.' Running a hand down my face, I scratch my jaw. Turning to face her, I gather her hands in mine. 'You're my person. You always have been, and I regret all the shitty things I did in the past. I'm sorry for everything. I love you. I've always loved you. I'm ready to do this. If you are.'

A tear slides down her cheek, and I bring her hands to my mouth, pressing my lips to them.

'Okay?' I say.

'Okay.' She nods.

'I was so scared of losing you and losing Zayden. My response to what happened and the decisions I made were childish. I was a coward. I'm so sorry, Anya.'

'I know you are,' she replies softly.

Letting her go, I get to my feet and help her up. She rolls her lips together, staring down at her feet.

'Last one inside has to make the other dinner,' I tease, wanting to break the tense air around us. She launches forward, and I wrap my arms around her waist, yanking her back and throwing her into the pool. I hear a gasp just before she lands with a splash that sprays my legs. Jogging to the back door, I put one foot inside, just for the win, before I run back out and cannonball right next to her, sending a giant wave in her direction.

Spluttering, she releases a laugh and wipes her hair back. Shoving me, she dunks my head under the water.

'You idiot!' She shakes her head, a smile curving her lips.

'An adorable idiot?' I smirk.

She rolls her eyes. 'An adorable idiot.'

'So, what are you going to make me for dinner?' I question, paddling up to the side of the pool and resting my forearms on the tiles.

'Tacos,' she replies.

'Tacos sound good.'

'They are your favourite, after all.'

'Aw, you remembered.'

'I remember everything,' she whispers, smiling.

'Everything?'

'Everything.'

'When's my birthday?'

She scoffs. 'Give me a hard one.'

'Okay. Middle name?'

'I said a hard one!'

As she treads water, I get distracted by her long legs before mentally shaking myself, focusing on the conversation. 'Hmm. What's my favourite colour?'

'Black, and you don't care that it's' – she brings up her fingers for air quotes – 'a shade, not a colour.'

'Favourite snack?'

'Barbecue Shapes sandwich with chocolate in the middle,' she replies without missing a beat. 'Which is *disgusting*, by the way.'

'Don't knock it till you try it.'

'You've made me try it. Countless times. Those two snacks are perfect on their own. They're simply not two things you mix together.'

'I beg to differ,' I argue, splashing her, only for her to send a more forceful wave back at me, causing water to slosh over the side.

'Your second favourite snack is two pieces of bread with salt-and-vinegar chips in the middle.'

I make a kiss sound, pinching my fingers together. 'It's delightful. I stand by that.'

'Strange,' she mutters. 'Very strange.'

'At least I don't dip my McDonald's fries into my chocolate shake,' I shudder, shooting her a repulsed look. 'That's just not on.'

'Excuse me?' she exclaims, outraged, her brows pinching together as she mock-glares at me, her arms moving slowly through the water as she kicks herself around in slow circles. 'It's the perfect blend of salty sweetness.'

'False. It makes the chips soggy.'

'Your idea of good taste is seriously warped.'

'Coming from the girl who stares at the menu for five minutes, tells the waiter she needs more time, only to order a chicken schnitzel every single time.'

'You can't beat it!' she retorts, splashing her arms to further prove her point, making her look extremely cute. In this light, her freckles are prominent, begging me to run my lips over them.

'There are literally so many different things you could get that are so much better.'

'Disagree. *Strongly*.'

'Do you remember that time we ordered half orange juice, half Coke for Zayden?'

She grins. 'And I poured half a packet of pepper in it.'

'He projectile spat across the table, and I saw it land on that woman's head.' I laugh, half grimacing, feeling mildly sorry for the poor woman, but also finding it hilarious to remember Zayden's cheeks reddening as he spluttered and coughed, causing everyone else at the restaurant to send us dirty looks.

'Got him good that time. What about when he filled your potato with wasabi, and you scooped it all onto that big spoon you used to always eat with and ate it all in one go.' She's practically wheezing as she says that last part. Her high-pitched cackle echoes around the patio, and then her infamous snort follows.

I scowl. 'That was so awful, I can't even think about it without gagging.'

'I'll never forget the look on your face.'

I give her the middle finger, and she snickers. Our laughter dies down, and I push off the wall, laying on my back in the water, floating for a moment, staring up at the cloudless sky.

'Can we laugh yet?' I murmur.

'Hmm?'

'Can we laugh yet?'

'About what?'

'About the whole *let's-just-be-friends* conversation we had the last time we were alone in this pool.'

I can practically hear her eyes rolling, and I smirk, turning my head to stare into that pretty face. I feel a pulse of desire clap through me when her gaze darts to my mouth, then back to my eyes. I move towards her, drinking in those long lashes, rosy cheeks and soft red lips. She backs up against the side of the pool, and I stare down at her, placing my arms either side of her, feeling the coolness of her skin.

'Are you sure this isn't just physical, Mase?' she whispers, eyes searching mine. 'I know you think I'm ridiculous for asking, but you had me, and then you left. You took my virginity, and my heart, and tossed it aside like it was nothing but a box you had to tick off your list.'

My eyes flutter closed, and my heart splinters into a thousand tiny pieces, floating around my chest. I lean forward, pressing my forehead to her temple, inhaling the pure scent of Anya. 'I am so fucking sorry.'

'I know,' she whispers, and I feel the weight of her words like an embrace. 'I forgive you. We were young and stupid. I know it was only two years ago, but I feel like we've both grown a lot since then.'

'I agree. It still doesn't change the fact that what I did to you was disgusting and hurtful. You were my best friend, and I fucking ripped out your heart and turned my back on you.'

'I. Forgive. You.'

'How can you?' I ask.

'Because you're proving to me over and over again that you're sorry and this time will be different. I believe you. You're *still* my best friend, despite the distance, and the past.'

'Do you still love me, like I love you?'

'More,' she whispers.

'Impossible.'

She shakes her head. 'I've always loved you more.'

Inching closer to her, my gaze lands heavily on hers. '*Impossible.*'

I comb my fingers through her hair, and she tilts her head back, staring up at me, a slightly dazed expression on her face. 'How will we do this?' she asks. 'With Zayden?'

'If he knows we're all in with this, he'll support us. In the past, he's made it clear you deserve better than me. And you do. I'm just the selfish bastard who loves you anyway.'

'I deserve you, as you deserve me,' she says. 'Me and you. Always.'

'Always.'

'When should we tell him?'

'Soon. I can do it one on one, or we can do it together. Whatever you think is best.'

'Together,' she says firmly.

'Okay.'

'So, this is happening.' She blinks, looking perplexed. 'We're together.'

'Yeah.' I nod. 'Finally.'

'Finally,' she agrees with a soft smile.

Capturing her face between my hands, I kiss her. Long and slow, savouring her taste, exploring her mouth. Every time we've been together, it's been a frenzy of touching and kissing in a rush, like we're about to get caught and time is running out. But now, I know I have all the time in the world.

Anya's phone rings, startling us, and we break apart, a breathless mess. With one last heated look, she turns, pulling herself out of the pool. I slap my hand against her ass as she does, and she lets out a squeal when my hand smacks against her bare cheek.

'Hi, Mum,' she says, still sounding out of breath. She reaches for her towel and awkwardly wraps it around herself one-handed, as she tries to hold her phone to her ear in a way it won't get wet. 'What? Slow down.' She pauses, looking over to me in panic. 'What? I can't understand you.'

Paddling over to the steps, I hurry out of the pool and start towelling off, watching Anya's face as her eyes widen, her hand flying to her mouth.

'Oh my God . . .' She trails off, and my stomach clenches in worry. 'Of course. Of course, we'll go. I'm so sorry, Ma . . . I have no words. Send me the details of where I need to go.'

I hear the front door open, stealing my focus. Zayden wanders inside, his hair messy, his sunglasses still on. He pulls them off, hooking them on the front of his shirt. He strolls out to us, raising a brow, sensing Anya's stress.

She hangs up the phone, all the colour drained from her face. 'Rod's been in an accident,' she whispers. 'A really bad accident.'

I look at Zayden. His face is impassive as he stares at his sister.

'Some scaffolding collapsed, and the four men on it were crushed. They're trying to identify who's been killed, since there's no record of who was up there at the time.'

Rod works a few hours away for weeks at a time. I used to love it when it was just Anya, Zayden and their mum at the house. It always seemed so much more relaxed.

'Is he alive?' Zayden asks, voice cold and emotionless.

She shakes her head. 'If it's him, then no. No one can get a hold of him.'

'Dental records will tell them who's who,' Zayden says, speaking clipped and matter-of-factly, as if he actually knows what the hell he is talking about.

She stares at Zayden, waiting for him to say something, but

he doesn't. 'They need a family member to identify him, and Mum is still on her cruise. She's in the middle of the ocean right now. I said we'll go.'

Zayden's jaw tenses. 'No.'

She jerks back like he slapped her. 'No?'

'No,' Zayden repeats. 'I'm not going.'

Her mouth opens, shuts, and then opens again, but no words come out.

'Zay,' I say softly.

'I'm not going,' he says firmly, folding his arms across his chest. He stares unflinchingly at me before swinging his hard stare back to Anya.

Her lower lip trembles, and moisture gathers in her eyes. 'Why the hell not?' she whispers, looking bewildered.

'I want nothing to do with him or Mum,' Zayden says.

'Whatever is going on between you, don't you think that can be put aside right now? He may have *died*.'

'Good fucking riddance,' Zayden hisses, turning on his heels and stalking inside.

Anya stomps after him, cheeks red, the colour creeping down her neck. My heart launches into my throat as I follow them, anxiety swirling in my chest – I can see where this is going, and I have no idea how to protect either of them.

'What the fuck is wrong with you?' she explodes at her brother's retreating back.

'What's wrong with me?' he snaps, whirling around and slamming a hand to his chest. 'Me? What is wrong with *him*? What is wrong with *her*?'

'I don't understand!' she shouts, tears racing down her cheeks as she stares pleadingly at Zayden. 'This has been going on for ages, and no one is telling me shit! I have no idea what the hell has happened, and I'm sick of being left in the dark!'

'He fucking hit me!' Zayden shouts at her, and she flinches, recoiling, her hand going to the part of her chest where her heart beats. 'He cheated on Mum. I saw it, I confronted him, and he beat the fuck out of me.' Her mouth falls open as she stares at him. Running a hand through his hair, Zayden stares at the ground, then back up at her. My heartbeat is loud in my ears as I look between the two of them. 'He almost fucking killed me.' Zayden stops, turning to the wall, pressing his hand against it as he struggles to get the words out. 'He grabbed me, and he . . . he . . .' He gasps for breath and leans onto the wall for support. 'He told me if I breathed a word of it, if I did anything, he would go to you next.'

My head snaps to Zayden; he never told me that part. My eyes shift slowly to Anya, who looks as if she's just seen a ghost. She sags against the wall, dropping to the floor as she stares up at her brother.

Zayden swallows. 'He held me down by my throat. The next morning, I told Mum everything.' He stops, his jaw ticking. The silence in the room is loud and unsettling. Goosebumps prickle uncomfortably against my skin, and my stomach churns. 'She said that it wasn't true, and I must have dreamt it.'

Anya's hands fly to her face, leaving only her wet, wide eyes to stare back at her brother.

'I showed her the bruises on my fucking neck,' he continues, voice a mere broken whisper. 'My face was banged up. I had bruises all down my arm. I told her what he did to me. She said if I ever spread a lie like that again, she would kick me out of the house. I wasn't a fucking child. She knew I was telling the truth and did *nothing*.' He released a sharp, cold bark of laughter. 'So I saved her the trouble. Never been back there since. Did you notice that whenever he was back from work, I would come home and take you to a friend's? Convince you to crash somewhere else, anywhere else?'

Anya doesn't move or speak. She stares numbly ahead, looking frozen in time.

'You can go,' he says, running his tongue across his teeth, his face returning to its previous stoic expression. 'You should go. Someone needs to. But I'm not going with you.' Pushing off the wall, he starts to walk away, before turning back to look at her. 'I'm sorry, but I can't do it.'

Again, her mouth opens, but no words come out. Zayden shrugs and looks coolly down at her.

'He might have only just died, but he was dead to me long before then.'

31

MASON

Three Years Earlier

LAST NIGHT WAS A BLUR. My head is a foggy mess. Some parts are clear as crystal, but for others I can't quite put all the pieces together. All I do know is that I fucked up. Royally. I ruined Anya's birthday, and Zayden is going to fucking *kill* me.

I need to get out of here. *Now.*

I've been saving for this; I'm prepared. I need to book my flights and go. Everything else can be sorted out later.

Still dressed in last night's clothes, I stumble to the shower and rinse off the essence of her. The pressure in my chest feels like someone is standing on top of me, cutting off my oxygen supply.

After my shower and a strong coffee, I sit down at my laptop and read over my notes. I have everything mapped out: where I'm going and for how long. I just need to arrange the flights and book the hotels and Airbnbs. Slamming my palm into my head, I smack myself once, twice and three times. I can't get her out of my fucking head. Last night, her mouth on mine, feeling what it was like to be inside her, I felt such a burning, intense lust for her that it fried my brain, making me lose all sense of rationality.

Is it all because I'm not allowed to have her? Because there is a forbidden nature about the whole thing? Is it because she's always around and I know how she feels about me? Is it that cat and mouse game we like to play?

No, I think, groaning. *It's a lot more than that.*

I've never met anyone like her.

The ache I have for her is severe and exhausting, and I'm sick of it. I need to go far, far away and clear my head. Start fresh and get away from all this. I can't face her. Not after what I did. I can't handle seeing those round, innocent eyes stare up at me, filled with anger, hurt and betrayal.

I'm a goddamn coward.

The first flight I find isn't ideal. It's long, with two stopovers in random countries, but it's cheap and I can leave tonight. I slam my finger down on the mouse, securing one of the final seats on the plane.

The weight on my chest lifts. The tiniest bit, anyway.

I'm getting the fuck out of here.

32

ANYA

I STARE AT THE EMPTY duffle bag in front of me.

Zayden left. I've been calling him over and over, but it's clear he doesn't want to talk to me right now. To anyone, most likely. The tears on my cheeks have dried, and my skin feels hot and clammy as I pile clothes into my bag.

I was so angry, so helplessly sad, so overwhelmingly shocked that my head was spinning. Now, I feel a strange sort of numbness settled in my bones, driving me on autopilot as I pack my things and embark on a journey I'm sure I'll never forget. The entire situation is fucked up, and I just want to be sick, but there's no food in my stomach to come up, so I'm left with this awful churning sensation that makes me want to curl into a ball and cry, but I'm not sure whether there are any tears left in my body.

I'm so disturbed that the man I call my stepfather is capable of hurt like that. That my brother endured it alone. That my own mother, the woman I love and cherish with my whole heart, turned her back on her son and then never did anything about it. I'm horrified at the entire situation, and I don't know what to think. I'm disappointed in myself for not understanding anything, for being too naive and self-absorbed for any of this to register. My brother has always been incredible at protecting me from the harsh realities of life, but I never knew he was this good at it.

Swinging my bag onto my shoulder, I sweep my eyes around my room, checking to see if I've forgotten anything. A feeling of emptiness echoes inside my body as I open the door and trudge down the stairs, my limbs as heavy as lead.

I feel his presence before I see him. Turning, I look at Mason's face. He stares at me for a moment before opening his arms. I practically fall into him, burying my head in his chest. He holds me for a long moment, and the weight of the world doesn't feel too unbearable in his enfold.

'I'm not going to ask if you knew,' I whisper, sniffling as I step back. 'He tells you everything.'

'I'm sorry,' he breathes, tracing his thumb down the curve of my cheek.

'I feel awful. Sick to my fucking stomach. I don't know if he will ever forgive me for not being there for him,' I whisper.

'Hey,' Mason says sharply, shaking his head and bringing both hands up to caress each side of my face. 'Don't you ever blame yourself. You will not feel guilty about this.'

There is so much on my mind, so many things I want to say, but nothing comes up. I try to get words out, but a sob leaves my lips and my throat clogs with emotion as I bury my face into my hands. Mason secures his arms around me once more, rubbing his warm palm down my back. After a few minutes, I finally get myself under control, choking on my breath as the trembling and crying eventually subsides.

'I'm coming with you.'

I nod, the relief welling inside me almost palpable. 'Thank you. I couldn't do this alone, and the only person I want to be around right now is you.'

He presses a kiss to the freckles on my left cheek, then to the

ones on my right, and his forehead stays against mine for a heartbeat of a moment.

'*Always.*'

It's been a long day. I feel utterly drained. I wish I could transport
back to the moment in the pool when Mason and I both agreed
that we're together, and he kissed me with a fiery passion that
under normal circumstances, would have me kicking my feet with
giddy happiness. But instead, the day has gone on and on and *on*.

I hate that wherever Zayden is, he's alone. Or maybe he isn't
alone, but he doesn't have either of us there. Letting Mason come
with me was another selfish choice, another way for me to prove
I'm not there for my brother like he is for me. My mind is going in
circles, and I just can't think about any of this anymore. My head
hurts, but it's nothing compared to the ache in my heart. We've
been driving for hours, and I tried to sleep. I'm exhausted, but my
thoughts are in overdrive, and the nauseous feeling in my stomach
is only getting worse.

'I think we need to call it,' Mason says, and I turn my head
to look at him. His hand is on mine, and he gives me a reassuring
squeeze. 'Let's crash somewhere for the rest of the night and we
can keep going early tomorrow.'

'Okay,' I agree, a yawn escaping me.

We drive another fifteen minutes before we come across a
vacancy. We pull into the carpark, and I step out of the car, stretching my hands over my head. My legs feel cramped after being in
one position for so long. Checking in to the room happens quicker
than I expected, or maybe it feels that way because I'm in a daze,
like the world is moving around me, but I'm not actually there.

The hotel room is dingy, and its only light flickers. The air
feels stale, and the carpet is so worn down I can see the hardwood

flooring underneath it. At this point, I really don't care. I shower and dress almost robotically, then shuffle back out to the room, my eyes barely cracking open to let me see where I'm going.

When Mason crawls in beside me twenty minutes later, I curl into him, and eventually fall into a fitful sleep in his arms.

The next morning, it takes me a long time to open my eyes, since they're so sore and crusty after crying all night, but I feel a little better after my shower. Poor Mason didn't get a wink of sleep, seeing as I sobbed and sobbed into his chest. He finally drifted off about an hour ago, so I dressed and walked down to the closest cafe. I tried calling Zayden a few times on my way there and, of course, I didn't get an answer. This is how he handles things. He shuts down and goes off-grid. Exactly like Mason used to.

When I open the door to the room, Mason startles awake. He peers around, as if he's forgotten where he is. He rubs his eyes and sits up.

'Morning,' I say, holding up the paper bag and coffees.

'Morning, Blush. Sorry, I didn't mean to fall asleep.'

'You needed some rest,' I reply, sitting on the edge of the mattress.

'Thanks,' he mumbles groggily, taking the coffee from my hand and adjusting his position, leaning back on the wall – there's no bedhead. 'Did you try calling him?'

'Yeah.' I exhale wearily. 'No luck.'

'He'll be okay.'

'I hope so.'

'You know this is how he deals with things.'

'It still worries me.'

We sip and chew in silence, both needing a few more minutes to brace ourselves for the day. I hear my phone vibrate on the bedside table, jerking me out of my thoughts. I look over to it, dread gripping my stomach as I read 'Mum' across the screen.

'Oh, God.' I turn my head away, slapping my hand to my mouth as my breakfast threatens to come back up. 'I can't face her right now. After what . . . after what she . . .' Scrambling to my feet, I bolt to the bathroom and empty the contents of my stomach into the toilet bowl. My knees hit the harsh cold ground. Exhaling, I sag back against the wall, closing my eyes and struggling to draw breath as tears flood my face.

After a minute, I drag myself to my feet and shower once more. I rinse my mouth and brush my teeth. I dress again, push my hair back from my face and go back to Mason.

His shoulders are tense as he paces the room, his right hand doing that trembling, twitchy thing it does when his anxiety is getting the better of him. Walking over to him, I take his hand into mine and press it to my chest.

'Breathe in,' I say quietly, taking a long inhale. He does as I say. The familiarity of this feels like deja vu. I can't count the number of times we stood together, exactly like this, breathing out his panic attacks when he'd come to me after something happened with his dad. Sometimes, it feels like no time has passed between us – we're still just two kids, there for each other, who love each other so deeply, it consumes everything around us. 'Breathe out.' We both exhale, long and hard. Repeating this action, we stay like this for a few moments, until we both feel okay enough to stay upright without the other's support.

'Fuck, I'm sorry,' Mason mutters, raking his hand through his hair. 'I didn't mean to make this already fucking terrible day about me.'

'You didn't.'

'I'm here to support you, not the other way around.'

'We lean on each other. You're a part of my family, too,

Mase. We're in this together. This affects you just as much as it affects me.'

Yanking me towards him, he dips his head low and captures my mouth in his. The kiss is short, but filled with intensity and heat. It wraps me up in a brief moment of bliss before we breathlessly part.

Within a second of our bodies separating, reality hits me, crushing me to the point I almost stagger under the weight of it.

I need to hold it together. I need to get through this.

Silently, we gather our things and head out the door.

The rest of the trip seems relatively quick – maybe because I desperately want the car to just keep driving, with no destination in sight. When we pull up to the address to the morgue my mother gave me, what I'm about to do sinks in. If I had anything left inside me, I'm sure I would be throwing it all back up in this moment.

'Do you want me to be there or stay here?' Mason asks, resting a hand on my knee.

'I don't know,' I whisper. 'I'm not sure anyone that isn't family can go inside.'

'Okay. I'm right here. If you need me.'

'I always need you,' I admit with a small smile.

His grip on my knee tightens for a moment before he releases me.

With reluctance, I open the door and step outside.

33

MASON

I CAN'T STOP THINKING about all of it.

Leaning my head against the headrest, I reach for my phone and call Zayden. After a few rings, the call connects.

'Hey,' he says.

'Hey.'

'Is she okay?'

'No, not really.'

'I don't know what to say to her.'

'She's worried about you,' I tell him, closing my eyes, feeling a headache brewing. 'She feels guilty about not realising what happened, and for not being there for you.'

'I should have known that's how she would feel. She'll think she's to blame.'

'She does.'

'How do I tell her that her not knowing made it easier?' he asks, voice hollow. It tears me in half to hear him this dejected and empty. Zayden is the one who keeps on going, the sunshine in the room. The one who gets the party started and keeps it alive. It's not right hearing this pain in his voice. He hasn't tried to process any of this, and now it's probably hitting him with full force.

'Be honest. Say exactly how you feel. Not hearing from you is making her feel even worse about everything.' I pause, debating whether to continue. 'If I've learned anything from being close with your sister all this time, it's that being honest about shit is the best way to deal with things. She deserves that.'

'I just . . . wanted to protect her from all this, y'know?'

'I know,' I say quietly. 'Your mum called her this morning.'

There's a long stretch of silence, then I hear the slight whoosh of his breath on the other end, letting me know he's still there, processing what I just said.

'What did she say?' he eventually asks, throat sounding tight as he chokes out the words.

'Anya didn't answer. She's feeling distraught about everything. Doesn't know how to process her feelings towards your mum right now. You know, they've always been so close. This has hit her hard.'

'This is so fucked up,' Zayden says, his voice breaking. 'She shouldn't have ever found out. I should have kept my damn mouth shut.'

'No,' I disagree. 'She should know what a monster he truly was. And what your mother did to protect him.' Another pause. 'She needed to know what happened to you.'

'I shouldn't have told her the way I did.'

'It's done now, Zay. We just have to figure out how the hell to move forward from all this.'

'I'm glad you're with her. She needs a good friend right now.'

Guilt floods me, and my heart hurts with each beat. We need to have that conversation, but I don't know how to do it now, with everything going on. I don't want to make anything worse between them when they need each other more than ever.

'She's in there,' I say. 'I'm waiting in the car. Only family allowed in.'

'Jesus. I can't believe I sent her there all on her own.' He sighs. 'Well. Obviously not alone. You know what I mean.'

'She understands.'

I look up to see the door to the morgue opening. Anya emerges, paper-white, and stiffly walks towards the car. Our eyes meet, and she slowly nods.

'Shit,' I say.

'What?' Zayden barely breathes as he asks.

'I think it was him.'

Anya hasn't spoken a word for at least two hours.

Neither of us really feel like going home to face reality, so we decide to book another night at a hotel, though thankfully not the same one we stayed in last night. The things I heard through the walls are enough to make my skin crawl.

After laying on the bed and staring up at the ceiling, Anya finally drifts off to a restless sleep. Her phone has been ringing non-stop. Mostly her mother, but an unknown number as well, which I'm half tempted to answer, but I also don't want to invade her privacy. I spoke with her mum and let her know Rod was in the accident. I will never be able to unhear the sound she made at the news. My ears have been ringing all afternoon.

I have my AirPods jammed in my ears, trying to focus on a lecture to pass the time. For the first half hour, I was able to concentrate and take notes, but now I'm feeling agitated. I need to get out of this room and distract myself with something that isn't so damn depressing. I feel like I can't breathe.

When Anya finally stirs, she agrees that moping around and thinking about all the dark shit that's going on is making us both feel worse. Within half an hour, we are walking into the centre of a small coastal town I've never heard of, with the crisp night air nipping at us. My hand is threaded through hers as we try to find a restaurant to eat at. It's a quiet place, but busy enough that most places have plenty of taken tables when we peer through the window. Anya's stomach grumbles, and I look over at her. She offers me a sheepish smile, placing her free hand over her stomach. She hasn't been able to keep any food down all day.

Deciding on the next closest restaurant, we enter, and it's buzzing with activity. Although a bit outdated, the place has character. The floor is patterned with large black-and-white checks, and all the tables are booths with worn brown leather seats that curve around in a semicircle. A jukebox near the back blares '80s hits, and there are a few older couples dancing on a makeshift dance floor near the bar.

'This place is awesome.' Anya smiles, and my own lips curve upwards at the sight of it. She is the only person who makes my heart feel as if it could stop dead in my chest. She also makes it restart.

'It seems so out of place compared to the other restaurants we passed,' I say in amusement, directing her towards the last free booth. We drop into it side by side, facing the dance floor.

'I hope we have that much fun when we're older,' she muses.

'We will. We *are* the fun.'

A guy who doesn't even look old enough to serve alcohol appears at our table, placing two menus and a wine list in front of us. We each order a glass of rosé, and to save everyone the hassle, I order Anya's meal without asking, because she always orders the same thing. She rolls her eyes, but smiles playfully at me. Warmth spreads in my chest, as she looks a lot better than she did earlier.

'You know, when I was a kid, I wanted to be an adult so bad,' I say, leaning back into the leather and shifting towards her. 'I wanted so desperately to be big and strong, to be able to fight him off.' I don't need to elaborate on who I'm talking about. 'I wanted that independence so badly. Didn't want to rely on him for anything. But now that I'm here, I just wish I could be a

kid again.' I exhale heavily. 'Not go through my childhood again –
God no – but to experience what it would be like to just be free
and oblivious.'

'I get it,' she says. 'I wish I could go back to the time when
shaving my legs before sport was my biggest concern.'

A loud laugh spills from my lips, taking us both by surprise,
and Anya smiles.

'I know I'm studying exercise science, but half the time, I still
don't know what I really want to do after university. Which is
kind of not good, since I'm already at uni, studying.'

'I know. Me too. My degree doesn't even promise me a job at
the end,' she says thoughtfully. She studies me for a moment. 'Did
you know Rod gave me a really hard time about doing a degree
in art?'

I raise a brow. 'He did?'

'He said it's a pointless degree that doesn't promise a good
financial future. He then said I'd better marry rich.'

I shake my head, anger flaring inside me. I never liked the
guy. As soon as Louise introduced him to us all, I had a really
off feeling in my gut. I could never put my finger on it exactly.
Perhaps the lingering stares at us for that heartbeat too long. The
awkward, off-hand comments that rolled off everyone's back, but
seemed to stick in my mind. I've always been naturally observant,
and my intuition was always screaming about him. I wish I'd done
something. *Anything*. I have no idea *what* I could have done, but
it still makes my skin feel prickly thinking about how he treated
their mum, and Zayden, too.

'Well. I don't think his words should be taken too seriously.'

'I'm starting to agree with that,' she mutters.

A waiter brings us our wine and assures us our food isn't
far away. We clink glasses and take a long hearty sip. I never
drink wine, because it always gives me a shocking headache the

next day, but one or two glasses shouldn't cause too much damage to the head tomorrow.

'I feel so sophisticated,' Anya smirks.

'You certainly look it,' I agree with an exaggerated wink.

She snorts. Reaching for my hand, she runs her thumb across my knuckles. I play with her fingers, and then bring her hand up to the table.

'Your scar is looking a lot better,' I observe, running my fingertip across it.

'Yeah. Took a long time, but I barely notice it now.'

Anya always had a large, raised freckle on her left pinky finger. She loathed it. She begged her doctor to remove it, which he didn't want to do. He said it was a beauty spot, and that it was totally normal. Zayden always teased her about it, knowing it would make her react. One day, she convinced the doctor to remove it, and she ended up with four stitches and a pretty decent scar. I don't think she realised it was going to be so sore and leave such a significant mark. But now that years have passed, it's barely noticeable: a slightly raised white line that runs on a diagonal across the bottom of her pinky. One night, when she was upset about how it looked – and I was more than tipsy – I told her that when I proposed, no one will notice the scar, because they will be looking at the big rock on her hand. She blushed a deep red that I swear went all the way to her toes.

When dinner arrives, we order one more glass of wine each. Anya's cheeks are flushed a gorgeous pink, and bits of her hair have unravelled from the loose bun it's in. She's still far from okay, but she has a little bit of her spark back.

'I feel like I need a coffee to keep my eyes open,' I say, rubbing the corners of my eyes.

'Oh my God!' she suddenly exclaims, and I almost spill my drink. 'That reminds me, you know that cafe we used to go to when you finished work?'

'Smooth Brew?'

'Yeah! Well, turns out, it was being run by this guy who started a cult, and he fully used to try and get the customers to join!'

My mouth falls open. 'What?'

'Yeah! I told you the guy with the monobrow was shady.'

I chuckle, shaking my head in bewilderment. 'You did, actually. I remember that.'

'And now, I think about that time he invited us over for tea. He was totally trying to get us to join.'

My eyes widen. 'That is actually creepy as hell.'

'Right?' she agrees.

Just then, her phone vibrates, and we exchange a look of dread before she flips it over. Private number. She frowns, and we both stare at it in silence as it rings.

'I'm getting a bit anxious about this now.'

'I don't think the cafe owner will remember us, Blush. I think we're safe.'

She rolls her eyes. 'Funny. I meant about these private calls I've been getting. I think it might be Dylan.'

I straighten my spine, looking at her in alarm. 'What?'

'I blocked his number, and then got this weird message saying that blocking the number isn't going to stop him contacting me, and now all these No Caller ID numbers keep phoning me. I'm getting more and more each day.'

'What the fuck?' I exclaim, my anger boiling over as I picture Dylan Peterson's smug face in my mind. 'That's not okay. I'm going to answer the next time they call.'

'No!' she quickly argues, shaking her head and shoving her phone into her bag, out of my reach. 'He wants a reaction, and I'm refusing to give him one. He'll get bored and move on eventually.'

'He caused all of this, though, so why would he be harassing you? What does he think it'll achieve?'

She shrugs. 'My thoughts exactly.'

'That dude needs a life.'

'Agreed.'

We finish dinner, then walk around town for a while, trying to keep each other distracted, but my mind keeps returning to the harassing phone calls. I enjoy talking about old times and making each other laugh. The fact that we can make each other laugh right now is a miracle, but it's always been like this with us: easy, effortless, and like the entire world around us doesn't exist.

Anya yawns. 'I think the day is starting to catch up to me.'

Wrapping an arm around her, I pull her close. 'Me too.'

After a loop of the town, realising most places are shutting for the night, we end up back at the hotel. Stepping inside the elevator, I press the button for our floor, and as I step back, I lean over, brushing my mouth across the corner of hers. Her eyes shift to mine, then drop to my lips, and I feel my pulse begin to race.

The doors open, and we step into the hall, brushing hands. I fumble for the card and slide it over the lock, allowing us entry to the room. Looping her arms around me, she presses her lips to my cheek, slowly moving up my jaw.

'I thought you were tired,' I choke out, voice hoarse.

'Not anymore . . .' she trails off, tongue snaking over my skin, making me melt into a puddle of liquid at her feet. 'Are you?'

'Suddenly, not so much.'

I sweep her off her feet, kick the door shut and crash my lips against hers.

34

ANYA

Three Years Earlier

I AM SO ANXIOUS. I'm jumping at every minor movement and sound, whipping my head around so fast each time the door opens that my neck is sore. I've been waiting and waiting for Mason to show up. To return one of my calls. To send a text message. *Anything*. It's been two days of radio silence. My brother has dropped off the face of the earth. They must be together. I don't know what's going on. I have never felt so distant from them. So isolated. So alone.

'Chin up, buttercup,' Phoebe says, running her hand over my hair when she notices me staring at the front door. I keep imagining them walking in, laughing, throwing the football around as usual. Mason's eyes catching mine, his crooked smile lighting up the room, the air evaporating as he walks towards me. 'I'm sure they're just out doing what they usually do. Having fun.'

'It's weird that neither of them has reached out to me. They didn't seem to be acting weird the night of my birthday, did they?'

Phoebe shrugs, her long hair pulled back into a high pony. She loves swishing it around, and today it's driving me nuts. 'I wasn't really paying much attention. You know I don't care for Mason. He's a dick.'

'Can you not?' I grumble, pushing her hand away and getting to my feet.

Phoebe is literally the only other person who knows what happened between Mason and me, and she is going out of her way to be as insensitive as possible. It's almost like she's angry with me for some reason. I'm already so stressed and anxious about what happened, and then about not hearing from Mason or seeing him. I don't need her making it worse.

'I'm just saying, you can do so much better, babe. You have boys drooling over you, stop wasting your time.'

'Maybe you should go,' I say, the tight knot of anger in my chest threatening to explode any second. I can't do this right now.

She blanches at my words, spinning to face me. 'What?'

'You should go. I'm tired.' Getting to my feet, I don't even look back at her as I head to the stairs, climbing up them, my feet feeling heavy.

Two hours later, my phone rings, jolting me from sleep. I lunge for it, seeing my brother's name.

'Where the fuck have you been?' I snap.

'Hello to you, too, little sis.'

'Seriously? I haven't heard from you for two days.'

'I haven't slept. I've been partying non-stop. I just charged my phone. I'm kind of spiralling. About Mason. It was just so . . . out of nowhere.'

My heart climbs up my throat. He knows?

'M-Mason?' I stammer, struggling to get the words out.

'Did you know?'

I pause, brow furrowing. 'Know what?'

'Oh shit, you don't know.'

'Is this a stupid game you're playing with me right now? Whatever it is, I'm not in the mood, and it's seriously not funny,' I huff, exasperated.

'He left.'

The boom of my heartbeat is all I can hear. My throat tightens. My chest constricts. There's a strange buzzing in my head. 'What?' A broken whisper leaves my lips.

'Mason. He left. Packed his bags and . . .' Zayden trails off, ending the sentence with a low whistle. 'Gone.'

Tears swim in my vision as I sit bolt upright. 'He's *gone*? Gone where?'

'Italy. That's the first place on his list, apparently.'

'Are you joking right now?'

'No.'

'Mason can't have just left without saying goodbye to me,' I say, panic welling inside me, making me sound hysterical. 'He didn't even say goodbye to *you*?'

'No, he didn't,' my brother replies, voice firm and wounded. 'I'm fucking gutted. I don't know if something happened with his dad, but he just went all fucking weird and left. I don't know what the hell is going on with him. He's been out of sorts for weeks.'

'I can't wrap my head around this,' I choke out, unable to control the tears and the shake in my voice.

'He'll be okay. He needs to get away for a while, do his own thing, and then he'll be back. It'll be like he never left.'

'Yeah,' I say, my voice sounding far away, unlike my own.

'I have to go. Let's meet for coffee tomorrow. I'll text you.'

My brother hangs up before I can say a word, and my phone slips from my hand.

He left.

Choking on ragged breaths, I wipe and wipe at my cheeks, trying to rid the flood of tears, but it's no use. They keep coming, clogging my nose, my throat, my lungs. I can't see. I can't fucking breathe.

He left *me*.

All of this – years of banter, tension, lingering stares, forbidden touches. All gone after he got his one thing from me. The only thing he cared about.

Every word. Every touch. Every kiss.

It was all a lie.

I'm naive and so damn stupid; I want to scream. He had me in the palm of his hand and tossed me aside once he was done with me. My best friend. The person who consumed not just my mind, but my heart. Gone. No goodbye.

Nothing.

My lungs burn. My chest heaves. Each inhale is like an icy needle stabbing into my heart, over and over. My soul feels broken. Crushed. Demolished.

He promised me we would be together. He promised me this was real.

He promised . . .

Collapsing back into my bed, the tears spill down my cheeks and into my mouth, making me feel like I might just drown in them. Turning, I roll onto my side, staring at the photo frame perched on my bedside table. It's a set of three. In the final photo, Mason has me in his arms, bridal style. He's staring down at me, and I'm beaming at the camera, my hand thrown up into a peace sign. Sobbing, I bury my face into the pillow, letting the pain eat at me until there is nothing left.

35

ANYA

HE KISSES ME LIKE this is our first time together and time is running out. Hard, fast and passionate. All at once, everywhere, claiming every inch of my body with his lips. I groan as he drops me back onto the mattress. Needily, I yank my shirt up over my head and slingshot it across the room, wanting no fabric or material on my body right now. Or on his.

With his mouth on mine, he fumbles for my pants, and I help him, yanking them down my thighs. He peels them off me, tossing them over his shoulder. His shirt is next to follow, and I trail my hands down the hard muscles on his chest and stomach. He shudders underneath my touch, a broken breath escaping him as my hands inch lower. Kicking off his pants, he dumps them at the bottom of the bed. Our mouths move back together in a frenzy; our hands wildly explore each other desperately, but we savour each touch.

'Are you sure?' he breathes, pulling back. His whisky eyes stare intently into mine as he checks to see if I really want this. 'Is this the best time for . . . this?'

'I need to forget everything,' I plead. 'I've wanted this for a long time.' The corner of my mouth lifts. 'Besides, you sort of owe me . . . since last time was so . . .' I shrug, making a face of disappointment.

'Oh, you're going to regret that,' he growls, flattening me onto my back.

I flip us, so that I'm straddling his waist. My lips move to his chest, and I drag my tongue down across the tattoos that cover him. 'Where's my tattoo?' I pant, staring up at him as I continue exploring his stomach with my tongue.

He moves his arm, revealing the curve of his bicep. 'Right here.'

I look up, and my eyes land on the word *Always* written in cursive, tucked between a variety of other tattoos. My mouth drops open as I stare at it. My throat feels tight, and my eyes threaten to tear up.

'Oh my God,' I whisper. 'That was . . . a joke.'

'My feelings for you aren't a joke.' His dark brow arches. 'Been trying to tell you for a while now.'

I roll my eyes, gaze softening as I take in his handsome face, his crooked grin, those smile lines that I see in my dreams. 'I fucking love you, Mase.'

'I fucking love you, too.' His crooked half-smile finally widens to reveal his pure, genuine smile, the one reserved for me. 'Now come here, Blush, and let me give you something to *really* blush about.' Gripping my hips, he drags me slowly up his body. 'Be a good girl and sit on my face.'

My stomach bottoms out at the raspy demand that falls from his lips. I climb up his torso, my heart in my throat. With his hands planted firmly on my hips, he guides me onto his face, and his tongue licks straight up the centre of me, running directly across my clit. An unrecognisable sound leaves me as I jerk in his hold. His fingers dig into my hips, keeping me in place as his tongue darts over me again. A groan leaves me as I begin to rock back and forth, grinding against his tongue, creating the perfect blend of friction. A choked gasp rips from my throat and I fall forward, gripping the bedhead – I'm so glad this hotel room has a bedhead – and curl my fingers around it as I continue my pace, feeling electricity shoot through my body, running straight down to the most sensitive part of me, making me feel like I have a heartbeat between my legs.

'I'm going to—'

I don't even get to finish my sentence as my whimper fills the room, and my orgasm crashes through me with an intensity like nothing I've experienced. My heart thuds in my ears as I move back down to his waist, barely able to catch my breath.

Mason smirks up at me, face completely soaked. Propping himself up on his elbows, he runs his tongue around his mouth. 'So,' he murmurs, his deep voice vibrating from his chest. 'Did that make you blush?'

'It made me see stars,' I confess, recycling the words he threw at me a few weeks ago.

He grins, looking triumphant. Falling off him, I land on my back. He rolls on top of me, and the weight of his body on mine feels incredible. His fingers caress the curve of my hip as he gently moves against me, peppering the length of my neck with hot, wet kisses. His mouth moves to my breast, and he sucks my nipple into his mouth, circling his tongue around it. I squirm, loving the sensation. His other hand moves across my stomach, dipping between my thighs. His finger glides across my slick entrance, and he moans into my mouth, his erection hard and thick, pressed against my hip.

'You're so wet.'

'You're so hot,' I say, not sure if I can even speak English coherently right now. My head is light and fuzzy, and my body scorches with heat and need. The ache to feel him inside me fills me so desperately, I can't think straight. Roaming my hands across his broad shoulders and down the hard planes of muscles,

I memorise every inch of him with my hands, with my eyes, taking in every single moment, not wanting to ever forget how he is making me feel.

'I'm so sorry for last time,' he whispers against my skin.

'This is making up for it.'

He chuckles. 'I don't think anything could make up for it.'

'Shh,' I whisper, capturing his mouth with mine. 'Just kiss me.' I pull back, sucking his lip. Our eyes meet, and I release his mouth. 'And fuck me like you've always wanted to.'

His eyes darken. I move my hand, wrapping it around the length of him and moving it up and down. He releases a sharp hiss, burying his face into my neck and biting me softly. I groan as I continue to move my hand.

Reaching over to his pants, he drags out his wallet and plucks a condom out of it. Bringing the packet to his mouth, he rips it open with his teeth, then rolls it onto himself in one fluid movement. My mouth feels dry as I gaze at him, finding every single thing he does intoxicatingly sexy.

Bringing his hands to my cheeks, he kisses my freckles. 'I love you,' he murmurs, eyes sizzling with electricity as we stare at each other, chests heaving.

'I love you.'

Bracing himself on top of me, he settles between my legs, then gently eases inside me. We groan simultaneously, and I lift my hips, allowing him to sink deeper inside, hitting me at an angle that feels amazing. His hips thrust forward, and my head falls back into the pillows, my fingernails scraping over his shoulders as my legs tighten around his waist, meeting him thrust for thrust. My skin feels hot all over as he moves inside me, stretching me deliciously, making me feel full.

I've lost track of time. All I can focus on is his pace, the weight of him and the way I'm getting closer and closer to the edge of release with each thrust. His thumb rubs circles against my clit as he quickens his pumps, and my moans morph into desperate sounding cries. The orgasm rising inside me detonates, pulsing through my body in violent waves, and I feel like I lose consciousness for a second because everything is bright and white and then suddenly, I'm back in the room, my body ebbing and flowing in my post-orgasm glow, the love of my life devouring my mouth with a deep kiss.

He pulls out of me, and I let out a cry at the loss of contact. Expertly, he flips me onto my stomach and yanks my hips back, sliding inside me all in one movement. A whimper leaves me, this new position feeling even better as he thrusts hard and fast, curling my hair – the bun long gone – around his knuckles. The pain of it, mixed with the intense thrusts, almost makes me feel like I could come again.

'You feel so good,' he groans.

I feel him pulse inside me as he spills his release, thrusting hard one last time before sagging against me, sweaty and breathless. Slowly, he pulls out of me, and we collapse in a tangle of limbs on the bed, neither of us able to form a sentence or breathe enough oxygen into our lungs. Dragging me to his side, he kisses the corner of my mouth, and I bury my head into his chest.

'I hope you know what you've gotten yourself into,' he murmurs.

'Hmm?' I hum, tilting my head back to gaze at him.

'I'm never going to be able to stay away from you now,' he says softly, that crooked smile I love so much back on his lips.

'Good.' I smile. 'I'm hoping you don't.'

36

ANYA

Three Years Earlier

EVERY DAY FEELS ENDLESS and unbearable. I walk down the beach, but it's lacking its golden glow as the sky is grey and dreary, making the sand look pale. My gaze wanders to my left, to the empty space beside me.

How many times did Mason and I walk this very track, hand in hand, talking about anything and everything? Hours upon hours of conversation. Considering how much time we spent together, I would have thought we'd eventually run out of things to say, but we never did. If anything, we always seemed bursting with things to tell each other. Even the most simple, mundane details from our day. We just liked hearing each other talk, watching each other smile and laugh, and just being *together*.

Pulling up his number like I have so many times, I tap my finger on his name and listen to the phone go immediately to voicemail.

'Hello, the person you are calling is unavailable.'

How the hell could he do something like this to me? Did he care for me at all, or was he working some elaborate plan to get his way into my pants? It seems unlikely. How could everything shared between us be fake? I don't truly believe it was an act, but it's hard not to let those dark, insecure thoughts swirl inside my brain. It's been weeks since he left. Well, months, technically.

I thought . . . hoped . . . the pain would have lessened by this point, but in the past few days, everything has seemed impossibly worse.

Turning, I walk towards the ocean. The cool sting of the water is calming as it washes over my ankles. The sun is slowly sinking into the horizon. I look to my hand, which is pressed softly against my stomach. The tears fall down my cheeks as I stare at it, my mind flashing back to the horrible night where everything fell apart.

'Where are you, Mase?' I whisper miserably, squeezing my eyes closed. 'I need you.'

37

MASON

WE STAYED ANOTHER NIGHT. It was a blur of inhaling the same breath, her lips on mine, our bodies entwined. In the bed, on the floor, in the shower. Over and over, every fantasy we'd dreamed about doing with each other, we did.

We stopped every now and then to refuel with food and water, managing to break out of our lust-filled haze to go for a walk downtown and get coffee, but we'd end up back in bed within the hour. When our limbs are tangled together, our bodies closer than I thought physically possible, everything else is background noise. Life, and all its problems, doesn't exist.

But now we're back, and the reality of everything that happened slaps us in the face with brutal force. The house feels cold and empty when we walk inside, and the guilt I've been avoiding plagues me with a sickening pressure.

'He's not here, is he?' she asks quietly.

'I very much doubt it.'

Pulling her to me, I wrap my arms around her and kiss the top of her head. She slides her arms around my waist, and we stay like that for a few moments.

'Maybe you should call him,' she suggests. 'Since he is speaking to you.'

Nodding, I withdraw my phone from my pocket and dial

my best friend's number. When it connects, I immediately tap the speaker and hold the phone between us, so Anya can hear as well.

'Yo,' Zayden answers. There is significant background noise, which makes it hard to hear him. But from that one word alone, I can tell he isn't sober. He's either at a party or some sort of event.

'Zayden,' I say. 'We just got home. Where are you?'

'The carnival. You should come.'

We exchange glances. 'Who are you with?'

'The team.'

'I'm worried about you, man.'

'I'm fine,' he deadpans.

'Yeah. You sound like it,' I say, and notice Anya growing more concerned by the moment as her brows knit together and her teeth sink into her bottom lip.

'Well, I'm at the carnival. I'll see you, or I won't.' With that, he hangs up, and Anya and I wordlessly stare at the phone.

'What do you think?' she asks.

'Looks like we're going to the carnival.'

It's dark by the time we get there, and the car park is packed. Cars are circling the perimeter, trying to find last-minute spots, and we manage to find one after two laps. Since most people are already inside, the line isn't too long, and within a few minutes, we are walking down the aisles of the carnival. It's a complete sensory overload here. People are laughing, talking, and bright lights are flashing before our eyes. I want nothing more than to capture Anya's hand in mine and keep her close, but I need to find Zayden. We need to talk, despite the bad timing. The night air is brisk, nipping at my exposed skin. People bump into me left and right, and I mutter under my breath, growing frustrated.

Anya is furiously picking at her nails, and I rest a hand on her shoulder. Her eyes dart to mine, and I lean forward, kissing her temple.

'It's okay. We'll find him.'

'Finding him is what I'm anxious about,' she admits.

'He sounded like he's been drinking, so let's try the bar.'

Steering Anya in the direction of the bar, we both scan all the faces we pass, trying to find someone we recognise. It's so busy in here, it feels hopeless trying to find him. The neon lights splash across Anya's face, and my heart warms, despite everything that's happening around us.

'I'm so glad we figured it out,' I murmur.

'Hmm?' she says, turning to face me.

'Me and you. I'm so glad it worked out, and we're back to us.'

She smiles. 'Me too.'

'He will accept this,' I say, trying to convince myself just as much as her. 'He can't not.'

'I hope you're right.'

Anya's phone rings, filling us both with dread. We stare at the unknown number.

'Let me answer,' I demand.

'No,' she argues. 'He'll tire eventually.' Declining the call, she releases a huff. Her phone pings, and we both look at the message. She clicks on it, and an image of us appears. I lean in close, my heart hitting the ground at my feet. It's a zoomed-in photo of us in the pool: my arms are around her, and our mouths are pressed together. There's a timestamp with the date in the corner.

'What the . . .' I trail off, my eyes widening. 'He's stalking us? How the hell did he even take that picture?' My stomach churns uncomfortably at the thought of him spying on us. Especially Anya.

'What the hell is he doing?' she exclaims, furious. 'What is his game?'

I shrug helplessly. 'I really don't know. Is he threatening to tell Zayden? Wouldn't he assume Zayden already knows, since we led Dylan to believe we're dating publicly?'

'Unless he's calling our bluff,' she whispers.

Running my tongue across my teeth, I try to slow my racing mind so I can think clearly. The phone starts ringing. Yanking it from her hand as fast as a whip, I punch my finger into the screen and accept the call. 'Listen here, you low-life fuck, if you harass my girlfriend one more time, I'm going to fucking bury you.'

'Hey, Mason.' Pinpricks of ice spear my veins at the sound of Dylan's voice. My insides curl when I hear the background carnival noise through the phone. 'Good to see you again. I'm just here with my friends. You don't happen to think Zayden is here, do you?'

'What the fuck do you want?' I seethe, gripping the phone so tightly I wouldn't be surprised if I cracked the screen.

'I want Zayden to know what pieces of shit you both are.'

'Fuck you.'

'And I think it would be an enlightening chat for everyone. You stab my back, I stab yours.'

'I have no idea what the hell you're talking about.'

'I know you and Anya were together when I was with her.'

'I'm not sure how that's possible, since I was travelling, you moron.'

'I saw your text!' He hisses, and I can almost feel the anger pouring out of him with each word.

'One text, in a moment of weakness, when I didn't even know you were together,' I argue, thinking back to the night I got roaring drunk and was looking at old photos of me and Anya. Texting her one of my favourite pictures of us, saying *I miss this*, seemed harmless at the time. I just wanted to hear from her. 'She didn't fucking respond.'

He scoffs. 'Right. I'm supposed to believe that.'

'What purpose does this even serve you?' I snarl. 'You did this. You broke her heart. You don't get a second chance.'

'Like you did, you mean?'

My heart bangs violently in my chest.

'You hurt her, worse than me, and yet you got a second chance. You walked back into her life like you never even left. You always get everything you want, don't you? Best on the team, king of the school, date the prettiest girls . . .'

'Are you on drugs?' I bark into the phone. 'You've got to be fucking delusional if you think my life is picture perfect.'

'It sure looks like it.'

'You don't know shit,' I seethe, hissing through my teeth.

'Right. Okay.' He says in a huff of disbelief, making me even angrier. 'See you soon, Mason.'

The call disconnects. I pull the phone away from my ear and blink down at it. 'We need to find Zayden. *Now*.'

Clutching Anya's arm, I guide her through the crowd, eyes flitting between each cluster of people. I'm losing track of time, and we seem to be going in circles. I release a sharp breath of relief when I recognise the back of Zayden's dirty blond hair. Nudging Anya, I point at him, recognising a few of the other footy guys lingering nearby in line for the Ferris wheel. A wave of trepidation rolls through me as we draw closer to him. He turns, his gaze landing heavily on us, and a lopsided grin takes over his face. I internally cringe, noticing his dishevelled appearance and bloodshot eyes. Holding his hands in a wide arc, he strolls unhurriedly towards us.

'There you both are,' he says. 'The group is complete again.'

Dark circles underline his eyes, and a five o'clock shadow covers his jaw. Scrubbing a hand down his face, he stumbles over his feet as he approaches us.

'Zay,' Anya says cautiously, looking hesitant to step closer to him. 'Are you okay?'

'*Yes*,' he hisses the word at her. 'I'm *fine*.'

Her lips part, and it looks as if she wants to say something to him, but she swallows her words down, nodding. This is not the time or the place to have any of the discussions we need to. He isn't okay and he isn't in the right headspace.

'Okay,' she says meekly. 'Maybe you should head home.'

'Home?' he echoes, barking out a dry laugh. 'Why would I want to go home? We're having fun. Aren't you having fun?'

'No, not really. I'm worried about you.'

Leaning forward, he grips her shoulders and shakes her lightly. 'I won't tell you again that I'm fine. Lighten up. Enjoy yourself.'

Her lower lip trembles, and Zayden releases her abruptly, huffing with impatience.

'Whatever. I need a drink,' he mutters, turning away from us.

'Hey there, Zayden.'

Hearing Dylan's voice forces a shudder through my body, making my stomach cramp with anxiety. With everything else going on, this is the last thing anyone needs right now.

'What the fuck are you doing here?' Zayden growls, taking a threatening step towards him.

'Just wanted to check in, see all my favourite people.'

'Right. Okay. If you want your face to not be rearranged, I'd suggest you keep moving.'

'Sure.' Dylan smiles, shrugging. Dressed in a casual hoodie and jeans that look two sizes too small, he looks like a total douche. A smug smirk settles on his lips as he glances at Anya, to me, then back to Zayden. 'Just wanted to congratulate the happy couple.'

Zayden's brows rise. 'I don't know what you're on about, but I honestly don't care. Run along now.'

'Oh, I thought you knew?' Dylan continues, the smirk broadening. 'Anya and Mason have been fucking for a while now. Didn't realise it was behind your back.'

My heart drops to my stomach. All the colour seeps out of Anya's face. Heat splashes up my neck as anger uncurls in my chest. The smirk on Dylan's face is cold and cruel. He's enjoying this. He's angry at Anya for walking away. Convinced we were somehow seeing each other when they were together. Furious that I got a second chance when he didn't. It's unclear at this point whether his aim is to hurt me or her. Or perhaps both.

'What the hell are you talking about?' Zayden snaps, jaw tense.

More than happy to supply evidence, Dylan pulls out his phone and shoves it under Zayden's nose. My best friend glances down at it, and whirls around to face me, his narrowed stare hitting me like a bullet.

My jaw flexes. 'Zay . . .'

'What. The. *Fuck*.'

'I need you to take a breath and stay calm.'

'Stay calm?' Zayden laughs, cold and humourless. 'I'm as calm as they fucking come, *friend*. What the hell is he talking about, and what the *hell* is that photo?'

My skin feels hot, but everything inside feels ice-cold. The anxiety is pressing down on my chest, making it hard to breathe. My hand reaches for him, but I pause, and it falls back to my side.

'Well?' he demands, his glare bouncing to Anya. She looks incredibly small right now. Her wide, round eyes are filled with tears as she stares at her brother.

'They've been fucking for years, Zayden,' Dylan interjects when I fail to get words out. 'Didn't you know? They used to have secret dates. Little meet-ups. They fucked the night of her eighteenth birthday.'

Jesus. This is going from bad to worse.

Sweat beads across my forehead, and I feel it drip down the back of my neck. My heart thumps painfully. I can barely even hear the words being exchanged around me.

'He better be lying right now, Mason, I swear to God.'

Gritting my teeth, I stare at the ground.

'Fuck . . .' Zayden chokes out. 'Mase . . . tell me this isn't true. That you haven't been lying to me for *years* about how you feel about her.'

Drawing in a ragged breath, I lift my eyes. 'I'm so sorry, Zay.'

His lips part as his face crumples, the shock causing him to stumble back.

'I'm so happy for you guys, truly,' Dylan continues, wearing a sadistic smile as he looks around the group. 'Like, I'm all for second chances and all, but Anya, like, I'm surprised you took him back after he left so suddenly.'

Anya gapes at Dylan, paper white. My heart hurts to see that pained expression on her face.

'Just go, Dylan,' she sobs, her voice barely audible.

'It's amazing, really,' Dylan continues, ignoring her. 'It's good to see that you've healed, since losing the baby and all.'

My head snaps to Anya's at the same time Zayden's does. She's shaking as she covers her face.

'Baby?' Zayden asks, jaw slack.

'Mason and Anya's baby.' He smiles. 'Phoebe told me all about it. How they slept together, then he left. She found out she was pregnant, but he wasn't returning her calls. It was . . . tragic, honestly. The whole thing.' Shrugging, he places his hands behind his back, a wicked gleam to his eyes revealing how much he is enjoying this. 'She lost it, but hey, Mason's back and they're together. Like a happy couple again.'

Out of nowhere, Anya's words flash through my mind, as if a memory is just resurfacing.

You don't know everything, and it's okay.

'Did I step into some alternate universe?' Zayden snaps. 'None of this better be true, or I'm going to fucking kill you, Mason.'

The sharp bite to his tone has me flinching. There is no oxygen. There is no air. I can't inhale anything. Panic and nausea grip me like a vice, suffocating me until there is nothing left inside me.

38

ANYA

ONE MOMENT, EVERYTHING was fine. The next, my whole life has been turned upside down . . .

How can so many things go so wrong in such a short amount of time?

Those deep whisky eyes bore into mine as we stand under the carnival lights.

'This is exactly why,' Zayden snarls, hands shaking, 'I don't fucking trust men in general, Mase, and with everything you've been through, I didn't even trust *you* with her.' He shakes his head, jaw clenched, a storm in his eyes. 'The risk of her being hurt is why I never wanted you to go there. How the fuck could you have done that to her?'

'It's not like that at all, Zay.'

'Right.' He scoffs.

'Can we just go back home and talk about this?' Mason pleads, looking distraught.

'Nah,' Zayden shakes his head, backing away. 'You two enjoy spending so much time together. Who cares about me?' Turning, he storms off.

Glancing around, I have no idea when Dylan left. I can't even spark any energy to give one fuck about what he is up to now. All that matters in this moment is Mason, and the way he just found out my biggest secret. The part of my life I refuse to let myself grieve or wallow in, for fear it will utterly destroy me. He hasn't looked away from me for a long time, and my stomach is in knots. Tears soak my face. A loud clap of thunder rumbles in the sky, and light drops of rain begin to fall, but neither of us moves.

I've run from this secret for a long time, never stopping to fully process it or let myself understand the true weight of what I went through. I thought this was something I would carry with me to the grave. I have a lot of regrets, and telling Phoebe is number one on the list. I don't know if I made the right decision or not by never telling Mason, but he wasn't here for me through any of it. I never expected our romance to blossom again, after everything. But maybe this secret should have stayed buried, because now he is going to hurt too. His dark hair falls onto his forehead, now damp from the rain. My eyes rake over his sharp jaw, those dark brows, the smoky-brown eyes I adore so much. My heart is tearing in two at the agony in his gaze.

'You were pregnant?' he whispers, voice raspy and deep. My tears intermingle with the rain on my skin, and I slowly nod. 'From that night?'

'Yes,' I say, my voice thick with emotion.

'What happened?' he utters, walking towards me, looking hopelessly sad, making me cry harder.

'I don't know. I'd only just found out. I had an awful pain in my stomach one day, and then I went to the bathroom and there was blood everywhere. When I went to the doctor the following week for my check-up, there was no baby anymore.'

His eyes fall to my stomach. 'Who knows about this?'

'Only Phoebe,' I say, and release a sharp exhale. 'Well, she *was* the only person who knew.'

'You went through this. Alone.' His words ring through to me, and my heart squeezes.

Zayden never told me his story. I never told him mine.

'Well,' I say, a little bluntly, 'you weren't here.'

He stares at me in that intense, scrutinising way he does when he seems to have a brand-new thought about me. The rain streaks his lightly tanned skin, making his eyes appear so much darker. He looks as crushed as I feel. 'When did you find out?' he asks, voice hoarse and desperate.

Swallowing, I shrug. 'A few weeks after my birthday. I was eight weeks along when I miscarried.'

Mason looks distraught, combing his fingers through his hair as if needing to occupy his hands. 'I'm so sorry I left. That I was too much of a coward to handle what was going on between us.' He strides towards me, taking my hands in his. 'I will spend the rest of my life making sure you never go through anything alone again. I'm here for you. *Always.*'

I nod, swallowing the emotion that is threatening to consume me. I squeeze his hands. 'I know,' I say softly.

'I don't think I can ever tell you how sorry I am.'

'It's okay, Mase. It's all in the past now.'

'It makes sense now. Why you were the way you were when you first saw me. Why you were so guarded. So different from the girl I used to know.'

Tearing my gaze from his, I stare out into the distance, watching everyone in motion, laughing, like my entire world hasn't just fallen apart and shattered to pieces. I'm frozen, shivering in the harsh wind, the rain coming down harder now.

'Let's go home,' I say quietly. 'It's freezing, and it looks like the storm is settling in.' Tilting my head to look up at him, I offer him a small smile. 'You're not afraid of them anymore.'

The corner of his mouth lifts a minuscule amount. 'No. Not when I'm with you.'

Curling his arm around my waist, he guides me back through

the carnival and out to the car park. I feel numb and a little stunned. He helps me into the passenger seat, wordlessly offering to drive us back home. I'm glad, because my brain feels like it's malfunctioning.

It's too quiet in the car, despite the low rumbling of the radio and the rain hitting the windscreen.

'I'm sorry I never told you,' I whisper, voice shaky and small. 'I didn't know what to do, and you left. You didn't answer any of my calls. You were just . . . gone.'

'I already feel so guilty about the selfish shit I did back then, and this just makes everything so much worse,' he admits. 'I can't believe we're here right now, talking about this. You really are putting up with me, after everything?'

I offer him a watery smile. 'There is no one else, Mase.'

Capturing my hand in his, he pulls it over to his lap. His thumb strokes my knuckles, and I lean back in the seat.

'The way it all came out . . . Zayden must be reeling,' I say.

'He was already not coping. This has just made everything explode.'

'What do we do? Should one of us stay home and try to call him, and the other go out looking for him?' I suggest, dabbing my fingertips across my skin, trying to absorb the rain droplets.

'That's not a bad idea. Do you want to stay home? So you can have a shower and warm yourself up? I'll go check a few spots he might've gone to.'

'Sounds good.'

'We need to talk more about this,' Mason says. 'But later, when we're at home, where it's less chaotic.'

I nod, agreeing with that.

Before Mason even fires up the engine, my heart stutters to a stop when Zayden appears in the car park, heading towards his car. His white t-shirt is completely soaked through and sticking to his skin. I rush out of the car, my feet sliding across the loose gravel. My eyes flash towards the busy road beside us, and back to him, where his keys are clutched in his palm.

'Zayden!' I cry out, relieved that he's here and he's okay. When he doesn't react, I slow my steps and come to a complete halt in front of him. 'Zayden . . . I understand you're feeling really hurt right now, and confused, and betrayed, and a lot more, probably, but please, I need you to hear us out and listen.'

'Zay . . .' Mason says quietly when my brother doesn't move or acknowledge that either of us are here, or what I just said.

Zayden's chin jerks up, and his cool eyes settle on Mason. 'I want your shit gone,' he says.

I recoil, as if his words have hit me.

A muscle in Mason's cheek jumps, and he nods, eyes shining with regret and acceptance of what the situation has come to. 'Okay.'

'What?' I exclaim, reaching for Mason's arm. 'No.' I turn to face Zayden, staring at him pleadingly. 'I promise you, Dylan made this out to be a lot worse than it is. Please, please just hear us out before you make any hasty decisions.'

'So you haven't been lying to my face for years about your feelings for one another?' he asks, and the calmness in his tone makes a prickle of wariness run through me.

'We tried to fight our feelings out of respect for you.'

Zayden smiles, but it's a smile I've never seen on his face before. Cold, empty and harsh. It doesn't suit him at all. 'Right. So you didn't ever kiss, then? You didn't sleep together the night of your eighteenth birthday? He didn't leave because of it?'

Swallowing, I try my best to get the words out, to plead with him, but nothing escapes my throat – because he is right. We lied to him, and it was wrong, and we only have ourselves to blame for it. 'I'm so sorry, Zayden,' I whisper miserably, peering at him through sodden lashes. I don't know how I can make any of this better. Sorry just isn't *enough*.

'I've always admired our great relationship, Anya. We've always been closer than most siblings. I thought we loved and respected each other enough to be able to discuss something like this. I know I've been unreasonable at times when it comes to my protectiveness over you, but I have good fucking reason,' he snaps, gesturing to Mason. 'Look what he did to you! This is why I didn't trust him to be with you. You deserve someone who wouldn't do what he did!'

I am so sick of crying. I don't know how I possibly have any tears left at this point, but they keep streaming down my cheeks rapidly.

'And *you*,' Zayden says, jabbing his finger in the air, aiming at Mason. 'We would quite literally die for each other, and there aren't many people who I can say that about. You're not just my best friend; you're my *brother*, and I trusted you with my life. I trusted you with *her*. How could you do that to her? And never, not once, speak to me about any of it?'

In two strides, Zayden is in front of Mason. He is trembling, and for a moment, I'm scared of what he might do, but he steps back just as fast, shaking his head, his hands flexing at his sides as he grapples with his anger. My brother is one to throw his fists and think about the consequences later, but he loves and respects Mason too much, and after everything he's been through with his dad, Zayden would *never* lay a hand on him.

The sound of footsteps approaching makes me look up. Shadow covers almost every inch of Dylan as he steps towards us, still looking rather pleased with himself at all the drama he caused tonight.

'Don't mind me,' he says, smirking. 'Just on my way out.'

'What the hell is your problem?' Zayden snarls, stalking towards Dylan, getting almost nose-to-nose with him. 'Why did you do all this? Does it really make you feel better? Huh? Does it make you feel good?' Zayden's cheeks redden, his hands shaking violently. 'You never deserved a moment of her time.'

'Zay!' Mason warns, stepping towards him. 'Don't do this. Be better than him.' Zayden glares at Mason. 'You go on about dangerous men, but you're being one right now.'

My brother jerks back at Mason's words, as if he hadn't realised how close he was to Dylan just now.

'I'm done with all this,' Zayden snarls, stalking towards his car and yanking the door open. He glares over his shoulder at us, swaying, looking far from sober.

'No!' I scream, racing after him. 'You've been drinking. Give me the keys.'

'Don't,' he warns, eyes flashing with a stormy fury that I've never seen before.

'Everything is a mess, I know that, but please don't do this. Don't get in the car.'

Mason appears beside me. 'Listen to her,' Mason demands, sounding a little breathless. 'Don't be stupid. Give me the keys.'

'Fuck off,' Zayden snaps.

Mason lunges forward, and the two slam into the car, falling to the ground in a tangle of limbs. Zayden tries to push Mason's body off his, knocking him down to the ground. The scream that leaves my throat is unrecognisable. I'm distraught and I feel helpless watching the two boys I love wrestle each other. Mason yanks the keys out of Zayden's hand, and in his panic to get rid of them, launches them up into the air. They go flying just past my face, almost knocking straight into me. I rush forward to get them, my eyes filled with tears.

I choke on a sharp inhale as the side of my body knocks against a car I never saw coming. I bounce backwards, slamming into the ground, hitting it harshly. 'Ow,' I moan, clutching my head, black dots dancing across my vision.

'Anya?' Zayden shouts, scrambling to his feet. He rushes towards me as I slowly sit up, rubbing the back of my head.

'You okay?' Mason asks, dropping beside me, touching a hand to my shoulder.

'Yes, fine,' I mumble, wincing.

Zayden releases a breath, relieved, and grips my arm as he steadies himself.

39

MASON

ZAYDEN HASN'T SPOKEN TO me in what feels like a lifetime. There's a weird hollow absence in my chest. It's an adjustment, since we're usually with each other most of the time. Even when I was overseas, we FaceTimed so often it felt like we were catching up regularly.

The world around me moves in a blur as everyone shouts at each other, getting ramped up for the game. I stumble out to the field, the noise of the crowd barely audible to me as I scan the grandstands bordering the footy field, searching for her. My gaze connects with her pretty round eyes and she smiles, waving at me. She's wearing my jersey. Warmth rushes through me. Despite everything, she's here for me and with me. I love her, and it's about time I get to announce that to the world.

A harsh jab to my shoulder almost knocks me off balance, and I shoot a glare at Andy, who seems to be targeting me now that Kai has been suspended from the team. They were very close, so I imagine he's lashing out at me for getting his buddy in trouble. That is the least of my concerns right now.

'Mature,' I say with a sarcastic thumbs up. 'I'm sure we'll win with that attitude.'

Andy ignores the comment, jogging ahead. Zayden briefly meets my eyes and with a tight jaw, he looks away, making my stomach clench. I hate this. I always knew this would happen. My biggest fear has always been that I'd lose one of them.

Mentally shaking myself, I get my head in the game.

The entire first half is a write-off. Zayden and I often play effortlessly together, and we're a deadly combination, but today, he's avoiding me like I have some sort of disease, and the team is suffering as a result. Three times he gets the ball, and I'm ready for him to pass it to me like he always does, but he sends it the other way instead. I stare at him in disbelief when he throws the ball straight towards Andy, who gets tackled the moment his fingers graze it. I shake my head, grinding my molars. I would have got through their defence. They can't catch me, but Zayden doesn't want to give me the power.

'Zayden!' Coach bellows from the sideline, his words weighted with anger and disappointment. 'Pull your head in!'

A few of the rival players snicker at each other, and Zayden glowers at me like it's somehow my fault. I try not to let the frustration get the best of me and continue the game with a clear head, but when Zayden snubs me again, and again, I almost walk right off the field. The first half seems to drag on forever, and by the time I get back to the locker room, I feel dead on my feet.

'What the hell is going on with you two?' Coach barks at us, cheeks reddening in anger as his eyes ping-pong between me and Zayden. Heads swivel in our direction as the rest of the team listens in.

We are both silent.

The air crackles in the room. There is so much energy, so much anger, so much hostility. It's radiating between everyone.

'I expected much better from the both of you. Whatever this is' – he gestures between us – 'fix it, or don't bother coming back out.' With a deep frown marring his face, he stalks out of the room. I heave a sigh, hanging my head in my hands.

'Lovers' quarrel?' Andy spits, eyebrows inching up.

'Can it,' Zayden gripes.

Running a hand through my sweat-drenched hair, I tug on it in agitation before forcing myself to my feet and removing myself from the group. I gulp down the fresh night air and lean against the wall, steadying myself before we head back out to commence the second half.

'Zay,' I exhale as he brushes by me. 'I know you're mad at me, but don't let it ruin tonight. We need this win.'

He continues walking, as if I never spoke.

Closing my eyes briefly, I breathe in, before walking to my position.

Blinking the sweat out of my eyes, I run, I defend, I tackle and I pass. Switching my brain off, I go into autopilot. Weaving in and out of players, I slip through a gap and take off at a sprint. The wind whooshes over me as I pick up speed, until a body crashes into mine, sending me flying through the air. I hit the ground so hard, the air is knocked out of my lungs. I'm motionless for a second, trying to catch up with what just happened, when suddenly Zayden appears over me, his hand extended. Hesitantly, I reach for him, letting him help me up. He pulls me to my feet.

'You good?' he asks.

Swallowing, I nod, pointing to my chest. 'Winded.'

'That was a fucking hard hit,' he says. 'Are you hurt?'

I lethargically wave my hand. 'Fine.'

'Okay.'

'Nice to know you care.' I smirk.

Zayden side-eyes me for a moment, the corner of his mouth twitching with the slightest of movements, before heading back to where he was.

A small smile finds its way onto my face.

*

We scraped in the win.

Just.

I tap my fingers on the steering wheel as I drive. There were murmurs of a campus party, but I'm too tired to be out and about tonight. I don't think any of us are in the mood – even Zayden, which is saying something.

My brows pull together when I recognise Zayden's car pulled over on the side of the road. Swinging in behind him, I get out and wander over. Zayden is leaning back against the head rest, staring out at the road.

'Well, this is tragic,' I say.

Rolling his head to the side, he pins me with a narrowed stare. 'Oh. It's you.'

'It's me,' I confirm, scanning the car, then spotting the very flat tyre. 'Having fun?'

'Loads,' he replies. 'No spare.'

'I did tell you to replace it.'

'I don't really feel like a lecture right now.'

'Fortunately for you, I have one.' Zayden glares at me. 'A spare, I mean. Not a lecture.'

Zayden huffs, and I head to my car's boot. Silently, I get the tyre out and walk over to him, feeling the light patter of rainfall on my skin. Zayden glances up at the dark sky, scowling.

'I got this. Thanks.'

'I'll be quicker,' I mutter.

'Because you're just so much better than me?' Zayden snaps.

'Stop being a fuckwit for two seconds, will you?' I retort. 'I'm here because I love you, man. I miss you, and I fucking hate that this is what we've become. Can you just talk to me, so we can sort this out?'

Zayden stares ahead, stony-faced.

Exhaling, I drop to the ground to begin changing his tyre.

Zayden is silent for a long moment. He looks defeated and exhausted.

'I'm in love with her, Zayden,' I say. 'Like, totally, utterly, sick to my stomach in love with her.' Zayden turns his stare to meet mine, a shadow across his face. 'It doesn't mean I love you any less. You're both my entire world, and I'm not going to ruin anything, I promise. I will always treat her right, no matter what. Her happiness is my number one priority.'

Silence stretches between us, and I sigh, continuing what I was doing.

'You promise me you will never, ever hurt her?' he murmurs.

Pausing, I turn, nodding. 'I promise.'

Swallowing, he nods. 'This has really rattled me. Rod dying, and then seeing Anya almost get hit by that car . . . it's made me realise how fucking easy it is to lose the people you love. Not that I loved Rod in any way. You know what I mean.' He exhales, rubbing his jaw. 'I shouldn't have spoken to you and Anya like that.'

The pressure in my chest uncoils, and I feel air trickle down my body, releasing me from the anxiety and its tight grip on my heart.

'I don't know when I started to fuck up so much. I never had any intention to ruin things between us. In my head, I thought I was doing everything right to prevent things from happening with her. But then I'd see her . . . be around her . . . and everything just went out the window. I tried to fight it so fucking hard, Zay. I left the country to get away from her, and to run away from my feelings and the mess they were causing.' I pause for a moment, trying to catch my breath.

'I love her. So much. It scares me how much I love her. We decided that we wanted a relationship, and we were going to tell you everything. Then Rod had the accident, and everything got crazy after that.' I look at my thumb; blood trickles down it from my picking at it so much. 'There's no excuse for being a bad friend and lying to you. I was so scared of losing one of you. And then there was the thought of losing *both* of you, and I . . . can't handle that, Zay. I really can't.'

'I feel like an idiot.'

Shocked, I look up and stare at him. He's looking right back at me, his eyes such a bright emerald-green, so similar to Anya's, under the soft glow of the streetlamp shining over us.

'I could see it. I knew you loved her. I could see it written all over your face every time she entered the room, but I selfishly refused to let you to do anything about it, because I didn't want to lose you, either. I know relationships often don't work out, and I didn't want that to affect our friendship. I also knew how much anger I had inside me, and I didn't want to risk her being with someone who might suffer from what I do.' He lets out a heavy exhale. 'If you're a bad friend, then I'm one too.'

'I never meant to hurt her, or you. The love I have for both of you is more than I have for anything else in the world. It really scared me, knowing my love could be the reason I lost either of you. I was so scared you would hate me.'

'I can't hate you,' Zayden says quietly. 'And I can't lose you, either.' Hope swells inside me. 'Can you promise me right now that you feel forever about her, and that you will never hurt her like that again?' he asks firmly, his stare landing heavily on mine. 'And that if anything happens between you two, it will not affect us?'

'I feel more than forever about her,' I admit. 'I'm all in this time, and I need your blessing.'

His eyes search my face, staring intently at me for a few long seconds, as if trying to see through me, right to my very soul.

'Okay,' he says.

'Okay?' I repeat.

'If you make each other happy, then you have my blessing.'

Rolling onto my back, I stare up at the stormy sky, smiling softly. Years and years of stress and anxiety, resolved in one simple conversation. Like it should have happened, long ago.

'If you do hurt her again,' Zayden adds, pointing a finger at me. 'You won't like what will happen.'

A small smile tugs at my lips. 'I wouldn't expect anything less.'

40

ANYA

MY HANDS WON'T STOP shaking as I attempt to slide my dress up my hips. Mason's fingers touch mine, and I close my eyes softly, enjoying the simplest of touches from him. My anxiety levels are through the roof today, but having him here makes everything so much better.

'Let me,' he says softly.

Pulling my dress up the rest of the way, he gently eases the thick straps over my shoulders. His warm breath spills across the back of my neck as he inches the zipper up my back, until the dress hugs me tightly.

'Thank you,' I murmur.

Mason was a dream the past two weeks while I mentally recovered from everything. I had a concussion, but thankfully no long-lasting physical injuries from the accident, just some minor bruising. He is the best partner I could have asked for. He's everything I always wanted and more. I can't believe we're finally together, after all this time.

'I know you didn't sign up for this,' I say weakly, gesturing to my glistening eyes. I've been so emotional since the big fight with Zayden, and learning everything about Rod, my mother and what happened between them all.

Running his fingers down the side of my face, he pushes my

hair back behind my ear. Leaning forward, he lightly presses his lips across the freckles on both of my cheeks. 'When it comes to you, I've signed up for everything.'

A soppy grin takes over my face, and a traitorous tear leaks from the corner of my eye. He captures it, smoothing it out across my cheek. The corners of his mouth inch up, offering that sexy, crooked smile of his. My heart thumps loudly when his heated gaze runs down the length of my body.

'I think you get more beautiful every day.'

'Are you saying that because you're the one who brushed and straightened my hair?' I tease, smiling. He is much better at getting it perfectly straight than I am; since it's so long now, it's hard for me to reach.

'Don't go spreading that rumour around campus, I have a reputation, you know.'

I snort. 'Right.'

He grins for a moment before his face sobers. 'Are you ready for today?'

Shaking my head, I heave a sigh. 'No, not really. I don't know how to face her after everything, and I don't know how to process everything Rod did, or his death . . .' Rolling my lips inwards, I softly shake my head. 'I just don't have the energy in me to do any of this right now, but I know I have to. I need to be strong for Zayden.'

'He's not going to go.'

I feel light-headed, and I move to sit on the edge of the bed. 'He needs to.'

'I know he does, but it's going to take a hell of a lot to convince him.'

'Maybe you should talk to him. He listens to you.'

Mason twirls the end of my hair around his finger, looking thoughtful. 'I think we should do it together. We're a team, me and you.'

Warmth spreads through my chest at his words. 'Okay.'

Mason captures my hand, and I let him guide me down the stairs towards the kitchen. My eyes wander to the giant bunch of flowers Cami and Nora bought me. They have been spoiling me with such nice, thoughtful gifts. I appreciate them so much. They are such beautiful people, and I'm very lucky to have become their friend.

I move to Zayden, who is sitting at the kitchen island, a textbook sprawled across the bench as he watches a lecture from his laptop. He looks up, pausing the video. Slowly, he removes his AirPods, jaw hardening when he takes in my outfit.

'Guess you're off, then,' he says, voice bland and emotionless. Despite him and Mason making up, it's still been a little tense around here as he comes to terms with everything. It's also been a bit of an issue that I'm attending Rod's funeral.

'I think you should go, Zay,' I say softly. 'You don't have to celebrate his life or make a statement or anything, but it might give you the closure that you need to move on from this.'

'I'm not going,' he snaps, slamming the textbook closed with a distinct slap. 'He can rot in hell for all I care.'

'You don't think it might help you?' Mason's voice is cautious as he eyes my brother with concern.

Zayden's chin twitches and his eyes slice to Mason's. 'How would it help?'

Mason shrugs. 'I think seeing that fucker be put in the ground could really help you move past this. Seeing first-hand that he no longer has any power over your family. It might feel really good, honestly.'

I glance at Mason in surprise, impressed. He knows how to speak Zayden's language. He just gets him in a way that I can't. My brother looks like he is mulling this information over, and I partly want to roll my eyes. I knew Mason would get through to him, but I'm also aware how monumental this moment could be for him. I want him to heal from this as best he can, and this is hopefully a step in the right direction to start that process.

Zayden rubs his eyes. 'I don't know if I can do it.'

'I get that, man. It's okay not to go, but think about it.' Mason glances down at his watch. 'We need to leave now, but come later, if you're up for it. We'll be right there with you.'

Zayden nods, eyes dropping to his notebook. 'Maybe.'

'Or we can all stay home,' I suggest.

Zayden shakes his head. 'You should go. For Mum.'

My stomach clenches. I've been nauseous for days at the thought of seeing her. She is the woman who raised me, the one who always took care of me. I look up to her for everything. And now, after hearing about what she did, I don't know how I can face her, or how to process it all.

'I don't want you to be alone.'

'I'm not,' Zaydon replies, lazily gesturing to the laptop. 'Me and Mrs Bottom-Cheeks are having a fabulous time.'

'Bottom-Cheeks?' Mason snickers. 'Is that her actual name, or are you doing that thing where you make up stupid names for people you think are annoying?'

Zayden points at him. 'The latter.'

I smile, but it's slow and a little weary. 'Okay. Well, I'll see you later, Zay.'

'Yeah,' he says. Re-opening his textbook, he stares ahead, and my heart cleaves in two at the pain in his eyes.

Wandering over to him, I wrap my arms around him, holding him as tightly as I can. 'I love you.'

'Love you, too,' he says quietly.

As we drive to the church, the sun pierces through the car window, seeming way too bright for the day ahead. I squint, pulling the sun-visor down and settling back into the seat, unable to shake the sickly feeling that has been plaguing me all morning.

By the time we get there, it's nearly starting. The church is packed; almost every seat is taken. I can barely meet the eyes of our family friends and distant relatives, making me grateful we got here just in time.

We head towards the first row, to sit next to Mum. She stands to greet us, looking pale and unlike herself. Her usual golden hair, which often flows down her shoulders, is pulled back off her face, making her features look striking, in a confronting sort of way. My throat feels tight as I look at her. Her eyes widen as she takes in my bruises.

'My baby,' she whispers.

Mason has kept her up to date with everything, but I asked her not to come see me, since Zayden has been by my side so much, and he isn't handling everything that's going on. And I also just needed space to think things through.

'I'm okay, Ma,' I murmur.

She extends her hand to me, pulling me into a hug, and I tense when her long thin arms wrap around me.

'It's so good to see you,' she says, cupping my face, inspecting it with an intensity that makes me uncomfortable. Her eyes close for a moment, and then slowly reopen, a pained look falling across her tired face. 'He told you.'

'Yes,' I whisper.

She nods, stepping back, her hands dropping to her sides. 'I'm sure you're very upset and confused, but we will discuss this later. Okay?'

'Okay,' I say weakly.

'Hi Mason, honey,' she says affectionately, touching Mason's arm. 'Thank you for being here.'

He offers her a polite smile and a stiff nod. Turning, he runs his hand down my back and gazes ahead, towards the coffin. Mum's eyes catch the movement, and they widen when she makes the connection.

'You two?' she asks, motioning between us.

'Yep,' I blurt, and then make a bizarre gesture with my hands. 'We are what you think. Yep.'

Mason gives me an amused look, and Mum arches a brow at my very obvious awkwardness.

Despite the circumstances, a smile breaks out onto her face. 'Finally.'

I barely have time to react before everyone is asked to be seated. My leg is bouncing restlessly, and Mason places his hand on top of it. His warmth seeps through my stockings, and I move subconsciously closer to him, seeking his comfort. My eyes are glued to the photo of Rod at the front of the room. My stomach roils as I stare into his eyes, questioning so many little things he said and did over the years, that at the time, I never realised were red flags. Flashes upon flashes bombard my mind, and I close my eyes, begging my mind to clear them. I can't handle all this right now.

The funeral officiant is mid-sentence when the large wooden doors bang open with a loud screech that has every head swivelling to see who the late guest is. My stomach hits the floor when I see Zayden remove his sunglasses, tucking them into the collar of his shirt as he strides down the aisle, not making eye contact with anyone. He looks handsome, dressed in all black. While everyone else has taken on a formal look, my brother sports his just-rolled-out-of-bed look, but he has the effortless swagger to pull it off. Honestly, my brother could wear a garbage bag and he would still have girls turning their heads as he walks past.

'Oh, God.' Mum's voice is a broken murmur of concern and heartache as she watches her son make his way over to us.

He drops into the seat beside Mason. I offer him a small, encouraging smile, and his mouth twitches. Not quite a smile, but an acknowledgement that he knows I'm offering him support.

I'm on edge throughout the entire service. My stomach is in knots and I feel light-headed, having not eaten or drank anything much for the last few days. I just keep thinking of Rod's hands on my brother, those same hands possibly hurting my mother over and over again, while I was under the same roof, completely oblivious to it all. Other than a few creepy comments here and there, he tended to leave me alone.

When the service is over and everyone stands, Mum reaches out for Zayden, and he stumbles backwards, hitting the pew behind him. Her lower lip trembles as she flinches, her eyes filling with tears.

'I can't do this,' he chokes out, almost falling over his feet to get away from her, his usually relaxed face tense with hard lines. He is looking paler by the second, as if all the blood is draining out of his body and the air is being yanked from his lungs. My heart seems to stop and start again with a painful rhythm as I grapple with getting to my feet, fighting through the anxiety coursing through my body. Mason looks torn with who to reach for at this moment, and it's all happening fast. Zayden bumps into the person behind him, almost sending them flying.

'Zayden,' Mum gasps, her hands flying to cover her mouth.

Zayden turns, fleeing the church, and Mum rushes out after him.

'Fuck,' I mutter.

'Come on,' Mason murmurs, leaning down and collecting my bag, fingers lightly pressing on my elbow. 'We're going with them.'

The number of eyes on us is staggering, but I push forward, unable to stomach meeting any of their curious, sympathy-filled gazes.

Mum and Zayden are outside, around the corner and away from prying eyes. We slowly walk towards them, and my bones feel chilled when I see my brother's pained face and my mother's tears.

'I will tell you everything, Zayden, and one day, I hope we can move past this, but not right now. Not here,' she says on a huffed breath, wiping her eyes.

'I came to you,' he whispers, and my own tears burn my eyes. 'And you turned your back on me.'

'Zayden,' she mumbles, reaching for him, but he steps back just as fast.

'I can't stand the sight of you,' he says, turning away and raking a hand through his messy hair. 'Go back inside. Please.'

'I can't have you hate me, Zayden.'

'You should have fucking thought about that before,' he snaps, whirling around to face her, jabbing a finger in the air, his cheeks reddening. 'But you fucking chose him. He hurt me. He threatened to kill me. He threatened to do the same to Anya. I came to you, I asked for your help, and you failed me.'

'I had no choice,' she whispers miserably.

'There is always a choice. You made the wrong one.'

A hiccup leaves her as she cries, and Zayden turns his back on her, striding away from us with stormy fury.

Slowly, Mum turns, facing us. 'Anya . . .' Mum says, her hand outstretched towards me, but I let Mason tug me along as we try to keep up with a hastily retreating Zayden.

My mouth feels dry, and a strange rush of heat blasts through me. Mason curls his arm around me, dragging me towards a tree that will protect me from the sun's harsh rays. I blink the dots away, swallowing down the nausea, desperate to not make this extremely awful moment for my brother about me.

When I look back over my shoulder, Mum is walking back

towards the church, shoulders slumped, looking like she carries the weight of the world.

'Anya,' Zayden exclaims, reaching for me as I stagger sideways. 'Are you okay?'

'Fine,' I say weakly.

'Let's get out of here,' Mason suggests. He glances at Zayden. 'Come with us,' Mason says. 'We'll get your car later.'

Zayden agrees to this, probably not wanting to be alone right now. We pile into the car, and I rest my head back, feeling exhausted and drained, even though it's hardly even midday. The car is sweltering, and I immediately jab my finger on the button to bring the window down, readily gulping in the fresh air that spills in through the gap.

Later, we are by the pool, ice creams in hand, sprawled out in the shade, and I'm feeling much better for it.

'An hour ago, we were at our stepdad's funeral, and now we're by the pool, pretending he never fucking existed,' Zayden says, inspecting the cone of his ice cream for an unnecessary amount of time.

'We've never been super conventional,' I reply.

'Mmhmm.'

'How do you feel?'

Zayden is silent for a few moments, staring up at the cloudless sky. 'Okay,' he finally answers. 'I have a lot of resentment and anger towards Mum that I'm trying to deal with, but I'm okay.'

'We need to talk to her,' I admit with an exhale. 'She needs us.'

'Yeah,' Zayden says dryly. 'I needed her, too.'

My heart squeezes. 'I didn't mean for that to sound how it did.'

'You're right. She does need us. But I won't need her ever again. I learned my lesson the hard way.' His mouth is tense. 'I don't want to talk or think about this anymore.'

Zayden pushes to his feet, and exchanges a knowing look with Mason, which makes me sit bolt upright, scrambling to get away from them as they both bomb-jump into the pool, sending a giant wave crashing over my legs. I manage to protect my face, but my hair seems to cop the brunt of it.

'Aw, man!' I grumble, looking at my soaked towel. 'You guys are so annoying.'

'You love us anyway.' Mason grins.

My brother and my boyfriend – it still feels so weird to say and think, after all this time – begin play-fighting, as they always do when they're in the water. Settling back on my elbow, I smile as I watch them. They laugh and wrestle with each other, and I tilt my head back, bathing in the warm sunshine.

Everything is going to be okay. Eventually.

When I wake, the sunlight filters through my room, and the anxiety that has been weighing on me so heavily feels like it's lifted. Maybe it isn't completely non-existent, but I certainly feel better.

I spend an hour or so painting by the window in my room, and it makes my heart feel light in my chest. It's so nice to be inspired again. I truly do love it.

Mason's door is open, and when I poke my head inside, his bed is made, the room is freakishly clean as usual, and there's no sign of him. Glancing at the time, I realise he's probably out for his morning run. That man and his routine. The one commitment he never lets falter.

By the time I get downstairs, my brother is there, yawning and rubbing his eyes.

'Good morning,' I say chirpily.

He side-eyes me. He raises his hand, hovering his thumb and pointer finger together, making the movement of turning a dial down. 'Too early,' he grumbles.

I grin. My brother and I are polar opposites. I like to go to bed early, and when I wake up, I'm ready to start the day. My brother likes to stay up all night and sleep until lunchtime. It's like his body doesn't start functioning until after 1 p.m.

'It's not even early,' I say, glancing out the window. Clear blue skies and minimal wind. It looks like it's going to be a gorgeous day. 'Well, early for you, I suppose.'

'Mm.'

'What are you up to for the day?'

'I'm going to go for a swim. Have classes all afternoon,' he says. He eyes my hands. 'Have you been painting?'

'Yeah,' I reply.

'I thought for a while that you'd given up,' he murmurs.

'Me too.'

'You quit when he left. Right?'

Slowly, I nod.

'Hm,' Zayden murmurs, eyeing me for a second. 'Interesting.'

Shaking my head, I lean against the counter. 'I might go grab us takeaway breakfast and coffee,' I suggest. 'I feel like a walk.'

Zayden points at me. 'This is why you're my favourite sister.'

'I'm your only sister.'

'Favourite, nonetheless.' He grins. 'Can you carry everything on your own?'

'I'll be fine.'

'I can drive you.'

'Good point. I'll take the car.'

My brother yanks off his shirt and heads out to the backyard. The drive to the closest cafe is only five minutes, and I lean on the car after I order. The sunlight feels amazing on my skin, and the air is warm.

Mason is back by the time I get home, and I get an excited swooping sensation in my stomach at the sight of him.

'Morning, Captain,' I smile, my eyes catching Mason's as he's mid-strip. He pauses, flashing his handsome smirk at me. 'Please, don't stop on my account.'

Grinning, he removes his shirt, and my eyes rake over his torso. I might have felt it – and run my tongue over it – an umpteenth number of times recently, but it still makes me stop and stare. Those defined muscles, the dark tattoos, his smooth, tanned skin. He really is beautiful. Inside and out.

'Hi, Blush.' Strolling towards me, he captures my mouth with his. I hand him his breakfast and coffee. 'Thank you, my love.' My heart skips a beat at those words, and I feel a little giddy as I place the rest of the items down on the kitchen bench.

Zayden enters, his towel looped around his shoulders, his hair wet. He makes grabby hands at the coffee, and I pass it to him.

'Thank you, dear sister. I apologise for all the times I talked shit about you.'

Mason snickers, and I roll my eyes. 'Yeah, yeah.'

'You want a ride to class today?' Mason asks, taking a sip of his coffee.

I shake my head. 'I'm just going to watch it online. I'm going to go see Mum.'

Zayden stiffens and lowers his cup. He stares at me for a moment before nodding. 'That's good. You should check on her. Make sure she's okay.'

My heart melts at his words. Despite everything that's happened between them, he still cares. 'I feel very conflicted about seeing her, but I know it's the right thing to do. Thank you for understanding.'

'Of course,' he says.

'Are you okay?' I ask.

'Yeah.'

'Promise?'

'I promise.'

'You okay driving back there on your own?' Mason asks. Our hometown isn't very far, but I appreciate his concern. 'Yeah, all good.'

'Okay,' he says, turning to Zayden. 'I thought we could go check out the new golf simulator in town. At the driving range.'

'Oh!' Zayden's face lights up, and I feel relief trickle down my spine at seeing how relaxed and carefree my brother seems to be after everything that's happened. I'm so glad Mason and Zayden's relationship is back to normal. 'Yeah, for sure. Let's do it.'

'Sweet.'

Mason walks over to me, wrapping an arm around my shoulders. He kisses me on the temple.

'Have a good day, Blush. Call if you need me.'

'I will. You too.'

We look over to Zayden, who is practising his golf swing. I roll my eyes before turning to head up the stairs to get everything I need, trying not to think about the day ahead of me.

I walk up the porch steps to the house I spent years of my life in, my stomach churning uncomfortably. The front door opens just as my foot reaches the top step. Mum looks tired. She's dressed in her track pants and a t-shirt with 'Only Judy Can Judge Me' plastered across the front. Seeing her hurts my heart, but when she opens her arms, I fall into her chest. She hugs me tightly before we step inside.

I debated whether to come see her for weeks, but as much as it hurts me to be here, she is my mother. Her husband died, and her son isn't speaking to her. I might not forgive her for what she did, but I would never forgive myself if anything were to happen to her because I wasn't there for her.

'You've been busy,' I comment, taking in the new furniture.

'This place needed a major makeover,' Mum replies, sitting down and heaving an exhale. 'Rearranging the place and cleaning helps keep my mind off things.'

'Does it feel better, having all his things gone?'

'Yes,' she replies, nodding. 'I didn't think it would, but it's been like a cleanse.'

I study her for a moment. There are so many things I want to ask her – about Rod, about Zayden – but I can't get any of the words out of my mouth. Did she suffer, being with him? I never got that impression, but I also never picked up on anything happening between Rod and Zayden, either.

'Are you okay?' I eventually ask.

'I've certainly been better,' she replies, fingers tapping restlessly on her thighs, a nervous habit I inherited from her. 'But, yes, I'm okay. I miss you a lot, and your brother.'

Chewing my lip, I nod. There are so many emotions swirling inside me, I'm unable to decipher exactly how I'm feeling.

'I know things will never be the same, and I don't expect you to understand everything that's going on or forgive me for the things I've done . . . but I need you in my life, Anya. I appreciate you coming to see me today.'

Swallowing the emotion clogging my throat, I nod, not trusting myself to speak.

'I'm going to make some tea. You want one?' she asks, jumping to her feet, as if desperate to escape the tension-filled room.

'Yes,' I force out. 'Thanks.'

As she disappears around the corner, I lean back, pressing a hand to my chest. Feeling my phone vibrate, I pull it out and reply to Mason's text. Noticing a new email, I click on the app and begin to skim through it. My jaw hits the floor as I gape at the screen, not believing what it says.

'What?' Mum exclaims, rushing back into the room.

'Oh my God . . .' I trail off, blinking in shock. 'They want to put my artwork in the gallery show next weekend. They had someone pull out at the last minute and my teacher suggested my piece!' My heart rattles against my ribcage as I read the words over and over, cementing them into my brain until it slowly sinks in.

'Oh, honey, that's wonderful!' Mum beams.

Immediately, I bring up the group chat I have with Zayden and Mason and press the video-call button. Mum's face falls when I step outside. I know she wants to be there when I tell Zayden, but he's not ready to face her yet, and I'm not going to be the person who forces either of their hands.

'What's gooood,' Zayden answers, taking a long slurp of his frozen Coke as he lazes by the pool.

Mason leans in, bumping shoulders with Zayden, his handsome face appearing on the screen. 'Yo,' he says.

The words burst out of me, all at once, and they blink at me at first, unable to understand, so I force myself to repeat what I said, coherently this time.

'No fucking way!' Zayden exclaims, knocking over his drink as he grapples with not dropping his phone.

'Yes way!'

'No surprise there, your art is amazing, Blush.' Mason grins at me, looking genuinely proud.

'Book me a ticket, sis, I'm coming to the show.' Zayden grins, giving me a thumbs up.

'Me too!' Mason pipes up. 'Get tickets for everyone!'

'Okay!' I grin back.

When I tried to make and sell art before coming to university, it had been hard not to give up on my dream. It seemed impossible for me to achieve what I wanted. But now, here I am, my art going into a gallery with amazing artists that I admire and look up to. It seems totally surreal that *my* art is going to be on display. Tears spill over my eyes, and I smile at the two boys I love more than anything.

Everything feels like it's falling into place.

41

MASON

'IF YOU KEEP LOOKING at me like that, we're going to be late.'

Anya's emerald eyes meet mine, and a smirk plays around her lips as she slowly pulls her stockings up her thighs. I track every movement she makes as the sheer stockings ride up her bare skin.

'Then don't look,' she teases.

'Impossible not to.'

Stepping into her boots, Anya performs a twirl, popping her hip.

'What do you think? Does it say "professional artist"?' she asks, planting her hand on her hip as she waits.

Anya's legs look endless wearing her knee-high boots and a short skirt that reveals a generous amount of her thighs. Her shirt is loose-fitting, tucked into her skirt, and her hair falls down her shoulders in a half-up, half-down style, the loose curls framing her pretty face. She somehow looks dressed up while also keeping it casual. She is back to herself now, and that beautiful smile of hers has been on her face almost every day.

'You look perfect, Blush.'

Her cheeks turn pink as she beams at me, running her palms down her skirt. She turns, facing the floor-length mirror on her wall, assessing the outfit for herself.

Tonight is the art show, where the art she submitted for her assignment is on display and up for auction. Considering the struggles she's faced so far in her journey of becoming an artist, I know how big a deal this is for her.

Pushing to my feet, I pull her into me. Wrapping my arms around her waist, I rest my chin on her shoulder, kissing the side of her head.

'I'm so proud of you, Blush.'

Bringing her hands up to curve around mine, she smiles, eyes shining under the ceiling light.

'Thank you, Mase. I'm so nervous about tonight. What if it doesn't sell? What if every other piece sells, and mine doesn't? What if it looks really bad in comparison to the others?'

I shake my head. 'It will look perfect on display, because you did a great job, and they wouldn't have selected it if they didn't think so.' Tightening my hands around her, I give her a gentle squeeze. 'Besides, if it doesn't sell, I'll buy it.'

Leaning back into me, she laughs. 'I love you so goddamn much.'

'I know you do. What's not to love?' I smirk.

She rolls her eyes. 'Okay, we really *will* be late if we don't get a move on.'

Anya gathers all the items she needs, and when we get to the bottom of the stairs, Zayden is already there, shrugging into a leather jacket.

'Ready?' He grins up at her.

Exhaling a shaky breath, she nods. 'As ready as I'll ever be.'

The Uber is cruising down the street by the time we step outside the front door, and we make our way over to it. When I notice Anya's hand shaking, I capture it in mine and kiss her knuckles.

*

When we arrive, Nora and Cami are waiting by the door. They turn, offering bright, warm smiles as the girls all hug each other. I love that she has found them. She needs good friends after everything she's been through.

'Ladies,' I say, when the girls finally break apart.

'Hello.' Nora smiles.

I raise a brow when I notice Zayden staring at Nora for a long moment. She meets his eyes, then blushes, quickly looking away.

My eyes dart to Anya's. Her lips twitch, indicating she noticed the exchange as well.

'Let's go inside, it's freezing out here!' Cami says, wrapping her arms around herself.

There are people everywhere once we step inside, and Anya's eyes widen as she takes in the vibrant art on the walls. There's a vast variety of paintings strung up everywhere. The room is divided into a snake-like walkway, making us loop around the room in an 'S' pattern.

A hum of conversation buzzes through the room, alongside footsteps on the hardwood floor, laughter and the sound of glasses clinking. Most people seem to have a glass in their hand. My gaze shifts around the room, and I notice rows of complimentary champagne lined up along the table. I reach for one, as do the others. A small band towards the back is playing soft jazz music. There's a nice calm vibe in here as people meander about, making idle chitchat as they look at all the paintings.

Placing my hand on Anya's back, I rub in gentle circles, hoping to soothe her nerves. Pressing her lips together, she looks a little distressed as her eyes roam over the room.

'There it is,' I murmur, pointing out Anya's piece.

It looks stunning, the beautiful blend of light blue and purple twisting together. My eyes caught it immediately. I'm not sure if it's because I've seen it before, but it is certainly striking in comparison to some of the other pieces around it.

'I love that you made her eyes the same colour as the background,' Cami comments, moving her glass to her mouth as she takes a quick sip. 'It looks so beautiful.'

'It really stands out,' Nora nods in agreement.

'Thank you.' Anya smiles, cheeks blossoming a pretty red as she takes in everything.

'Let's take a look around!' Cami suggests, leading the way, her heels clicking against the wooden floorboards.

I recognise a few familiar faces – people from campus and some of my classes – and I nod in greeting when we pass them. The art show has drawn a large crowd, and a few times the group gets separated.

When we return to Anya's painting, a couple is admiring it.

'Stunning colours,' the woman says, her lips pursed slightly as she looks at it. 'Just beautiful.'

Casually stepping up beside them, I join them in looking at the piece. 'I've heard this is in high demand,' I murmur, attempting to look a little pensive as I scan my eyes over it.

'Is it?' the man beside me asks, glancing at me.

'I heard there might even be a bidding war for it.'

'You don't say?' the man replies, looking impressed. He turns to the woman beside him, touching his fingertips to her elbow. 'We'd better get our bid in, then.'

'Certainly!' she agrees, and the man writes down the number before quickly crossing the room to where a gallery assistant is standing behind a makeshift counter.

Grinning, I turn back around, noticing most of the group are down a few paintings now, except for Zayden, who is hovering nearby, a crooked smirk on his lips, his hands dug deep into his pockets.

'Well played,' he says, nodding his head at me.

'I don't know what you're talking about.'

'Mmhmm.'

Glancing back, I notice a woman placing a 'sold' sign in front of the painting. Smiling to myself, I return to the group and take a casual sip of my champagne.

42

ANYA

COLLAPSING INTO THE BOOTH, I can't wipe the smile from my face. All night I've been on cloud nine. My first art show was a success. My painting was one of the first to sell, and I've been invited to create a few pieces for the next show in a couple of months.

To celebrate, Zayden suggested we have dinner and drinks at the new bar that's just opened up near Stratton. It's ultra-modern, with black furniture, plush pink booths and neon-pink lights lining the skirting boards. An upbeat pop song blasts almost too loudly from the speakers, and the place is growing steadily busier with each passing minute. It's already become the most talked about bar, as it's quickly becoming known for its incredible cocktail selection.

'What would you like, sis?' Zayden asks, sliding the menu across the table. 'My shout.'

'Ohh.' I grin, perking up a little as I quickly flick over the menu.

'This looks good,' Nora says, pointing to the 'Princess Treatment', a vodka cocktail with baby-pink fairy floss in the shape of a crown.

'Done,' I say. 'One Princess Treatment for me.'

'I'll order one, too,' Nora says.

'Me three,' Cami pipes up.

'And you, Princess?' Zayden asks sweetly, smiling at Mason.

Mason pretends to consider this. 'Hmm. Not right now. Maybe later.'

'Okay, sweetie, just let me know.'

Cami snickers at their exchange. The waitress appears, taking our order.

I'm not sure when it happened, but our group seemed to form overnight, and I am loving every moment of it. The easy-going smile is back on my brother's face, and Mason's eyes don't seem as tormented and haunted as they used to. Cami and Nora have become as important to me as sunshine in my day.

The waitress returns, placing a tray on the table before handing out our drinks. We each reach for the drink we ordered.

'Here's to Anya, and all the success coming her way.' Nora smiles, holding her drink in the air.

'Here, here!' Zayden says.

'And to all of you who stand by me each day. My best friends in the entire world.' I turn my eyes to Zayden, nodding at him. 'My family.'

Tipping his head in my direction, he smiles.

'Cheers!' We collectively say. Leaning forward, we clink glasses.

Turning to face Mason, I place a hand on his arm. He smiles at me, those handsome smile lines appearing around the corners of his mouth. Those whisky eyes meet mine, soft and comforting.

For so long, my heart bled for him, and here we are at last. After all this time, and everything that's happened, I thought Mason and my story was over. Finished. All in the past.

But here we are together, happier than ever.

It's only the beginning.

43

MASON

THE ATMOSPHERE IN THE locker room is tense as we take our seats on the bench. Coach Kennedy enters, adjusting the cap on his head, even though he's indoors and it's nighttime. I've never seen him without it on. He shaved the scruff he's been sporting for the past fortnight – Coach always shaves his beard for game night. The boys love to tease him about it.

I sweep the room, noting the anticipation lighting up the faces around me. Panic jolts inside my chest as I realise one of our star players isn't here.

'Have you seen Parker?' I lean over, trying to be surreptitious, and meet the eyes of Zayden, who is fiddling with his boot.

'He'll be here,' he says.

Parker keeps to himself and is the most mysterious player. All I do know: he is an absolute legend on the field, and I feel a hell of a lot more confident playing a game when I know he is there with me.

The sound of a door banging open somewhere down the hallway meets my ears, and Parker appears, looking sweaty and a little breathless. His hair is tousled, and his jacket is hanging off his shoulder, as if he ran all the way here from somewhere and hardly had the time to get dressed. A few of the other players glance up, and Coach gives him a nod of greeting, but doesn't say anything.

If anyone else was this late, they would get their ass kicked. I'm sure Coach and Parker have some understanding about whatever is going on, and I don't mind if he's late as long as he makes it to the game.

A week ago, the news of me becoming captain was announced, and thankfully everyone has been supportive. The main offender – Kai Adams – has been removed from the team and is awaiting his court date for what he did to Anya. With everything else that went down recently, I'd almost forgotten about him. In his absence, the team seems so much more cohesive and like a real squad. I didn't realise how much influence he had over some of the other players. It's a much better environment with him gone.

After the mess of everything, life has resumed. At first, I wasn't sure how either Anya or Zayden were going to handle it all, but they have, because life simply keeps going, and they need to move forward with it.

'You lot are a strong team,' Coach Kennedy says, voice booming with a level of loudness and confidence that effectively captures the attention of everyone in the room. 'You're fast, you're ethical and you know their weaknesses. This game should be a walk in the park for you. Play fair, listen to your captain, and work together.' His eyes scan the room, and when they land on mine, I give him a reassuring nod, which he returns. 'Good. Now get out there and make me proud.'

Whoops and cheers bounce off the walls as everyone leaps to their feet. Zayden claps a hand on my shoulder, grinning at me. His easy smile is back on his face, and he seemed more like his normal self these past two weeks, which is a relief. We've been throwing ourselves into training for the game, to keep up our strength and maintain a healthy distraction for Zayden, since falling into partying is something he does all too frequently.

We've eased back into our comfortable ways as three best friends. I thought it might make Zayden feel uncomfortable or awkward knowing that Anya and I are together now, but honestly, it feels just like it used to. It's such a relief, and my anxiety is the best it's been for as long as I can remember.

'See you out there.'

My best friend runs ahead of me, catching up with Christian and Parker, who are leading the rest of us out. I hang back, focusing on my breathing for a few moments before I start running. As we jog out onto the field, I see the stands are full, and the roar from the crowd is deafening. I spot her almost immediately. Beaming back at me and dressed in my jersey – as she should be – she blows me a kiss that sends warmth racing through my body.

Exhaling steadily, I returned my focus to the field, as the game is about to begin.

I can't help but grin as the crowd stamp their feet and scream our names.

We beat them. The South West Stingrays.

No, we *annihilated* them.

As arms circle around me, pulling me in a bunch of different directions as everyone leaps and bounds in excitement, I track Anya rushing down the steps. I weave in and out of the team as everyone starts spilling onto the field. The place is packed, and there are people everywhere, but all I see is her.

Running towards me, she jumps, and I circle my arm around her waist, yanking her to me. She wraps her legs around my waist, and I dive towards her mouth. My free hand combs her hair from her face as I kiss her passionately, not caring in the slightest that there are probably hundreds of eyes watching us right now.

This is it. This is what I've been craving. The longing that's been building in my chest and climbing up my throat for as long as I remember.

We're here.

We made it.

Threading her fingers around the back of my neck, she breathlessly pulls back from my lips and presses her forehead against mine.

'Good game, Captain,' she purrs, smiling in that slow, sexy way she does so well. She could send me into cardiac arrest with the way my chest feels when I'm around her.

'Thanks, Blush.'

'I love you,' she says, emerald eyes glistening as she blinks up at me under the bright lights of the field.

'I love you more.'

Setting her on her feet, I let the team drag me back towards them, still celebrating our win.

The next couple hours after the game are a complete blur. We end up back at Christian's house for a party to celebrate the absolute thrashing we gave the other team. As the new captain, I couldn't be more thrilled that my first game was that one. Everything went smoothly, we won by a huge amount and the team played together the best they have since I joined.

It hasn't been a big deal that Anya and I started dating – apparently most people assumed we already were. Since we're always around each other, that makes sense. Probably no one realises the years of pain we endured, and Zayden's involvement.

I'm leaning against the wall, sipping my beer and watching Anya as she dances with Cami and Nora. Her long hair cascades down her back as she moves to the beat, her smile lighting up the entire room. With everything that's happened, seeing her so happy and carefree in this moment feels like breathing in fresh morning air.

'Yo yo,' a familiar voice says, and my eyes bounce towards Christian, who strolls over to me. We do the one-armed shake we always do when we see each other.

'Hey,' I reply. 'Your place is awesome.'

'Thanks. My sister owns it with her husband, but they live out of state,' he says. 'I never congratulated you properly, by the way, on becoming captain. Well-deserved, my friend.'

'Thanks, Christian. Appreciate it.'

'You're officially with Anya now, hey?' He smirks. 'That was obvious to literally every single person. Ever.'

I roll my eyes. 'It was not.'

'Okay. Keep telling yourself that.'

After taking another sip, I lower my voice. 'Do you know what's up with Parker?'

Christian shakes his head. 'Nah. He keeps to himself.'

'If he didn't come to practice and the games, I would never see him.'

'Yeah. I think he works a lot.'

Christian and Parker are the two guys on the team I'd love to hang out with more, but Christian is often away camping on weekends, and Parker is basically a ghost. He has no social media presence, and I don't even see him on campus or in any of my classes.

Loud cheers break out across the room, and I turn my attention to Zayden and Andy, who are competing for beer funnel records. Zayden has been doing well, considering everything, but he is partying hard these days. He's always partied hard, but now it seems more frequent and more reckless. Christian makes a sound in the back of his throat and glances at me, as if having read my mind.

'Is Zayden all good?' Christian asks, forehead creased as he observes the scene in front of us, much like me.

'Some days yes, some days no,' I admit.

'He seems to be hitting the drinks hard lately.'

'I was just thinking the same thing.'

Christian and I stand in silence for a few moments longer before we begin mingling once more. After an hour of jumping between groups, I feel myself growing a little bored and tired.

'Hey, Captain,' a silky voice murmurs, and I twist to face Anya, who has those pretty lips tilted in a flirtatious smirk. 'I'm wondering if you'll escort me to the after-party?'

'The after-party of the party?' I raise a brow. 'Tell me more.'

'It requires a limited amount of clothes.'

'I see.' I grin, glancing around us. 'Where is everyone?'

'They're all playing a game out the back. I've already told them we're heading out.'

'You just knew I'd agree, did you?' I ask playfully.

She leans forward, her breasts pressing into my chest, her lips touching my ear. 'I have some moves I've learned recently that I would love to show you.'

Meeting her eyes, I flash her a grin and finish the rest of my drink. Collecting her hand in mine, I drag her towards the front door. It feels surreal to be together out in the open like this, showing the world that we're partners. It's been a long time coming, and it feels so right.

The Uber arrives within a few minutes and the ride home is short, as Christian's house is less than ten minutes from ours. The house is dark and quiet as we stumble through the front door, her arms around my neck, my hands on her waist. We land on something – the lounge – and she straddles my hips, pinning me. We're both breathing hard as we stare at each other.

'Don't move,' she demands, and her lip twitches as she fights the smile threatening to take over.

'Yes, Ma'am.'

Pushing to her feet, she drifts towards the cabinet, where the speaker and the light switches are. She flicks on the switch that Zayden set up, which coordinates the TV and the speakers, matching the lighting with the sound. Switching it to red mode, she presses play on her phone. Turning to face me, she unzips her dress, and it falls from her shoulders. My eyes widen and I prop myself up on my elbows as I drink in the lacey red lingerie she has on. It's a two-piece set; the top half barely covers her breasts, and the lower half is completely see-through. She begins dancing to the beat, moving sensually and slowly. I adjust myself in my pants as I take in every movement.

'You're making me lose my damn mind, Blush,' I whisper, feeling breathless as she drops to the ground, crawling towards me.

Never breaking eye contact, she shifts to sitting and pushes herself back, moving her legs into the air and exposing every inch of delicious skin, plus the part of her that has most certainly put a spell on me. Making a fist with my hand, I bite into it as she moves, her long legs fanning through the air. Moving to get on her knees, she arches and curves her back in ways that has me groaning.

'Come here,' I croak out.

'Not until the end of the song,' she taunts.

'You're killing me.'

My gaze is locked on her as she continues. When the song ends and rolls onto the next, she strides towards me and sinks down between my legs. Reaching for me, she unbuckles my belt, yanking my pants and boxers down my thighs. I hiss when her hands wrap around me, rubbing up and down my length.

'This is mine,' she says, moving her hand faster. 'You're mine.'

A groan leaves my lips and my head tilts back. 'Yes,' I breathe. 'Take everything, it's all yours.'

A breathy moan escapes her, and she pushes to her feet. Leaning forward, I circle my arms around her, kissing her bare stomach. Gripping the edge of her panties between my teeth, I inch it down her legs. She gasps when my nose skims the sensitive spot between her legs. I tug her forward, and she falls on top of me, straddling her legs over my waist.

Skating my hands over her hips, I move my finger to her entrance. 'Fucking soaked.' I smirk. 'Always so eager for me, aren't you Blush?'

She squirms, applying pressure to my finger as she grinds against me, chasing the friction to settle the ache I bet she's feeling, since I'm feeling it just as strongly.

'Yes,' she whispers.

'I need to get a . . .' I trail off, looking to see where my pants ended up.

'I'm okay without, if you are,' she murmurs breathlessly. 'I'm clean and on birth control.'

My gaze snaps back to hers, and we stare at each other for a moment. My eyes travel down her smooth body. 'I'm clean, also. I'm game if you are.'

'Yes,' she murmurs.

As she raises onto her knees slightly, I shift underneath her, positioning her on top of me. She sinks down my length, and we simultaneously let out a groan. The feel of her clenched around me is otherworldly. She curses, glancing down at where my body meets hers, taking her lip between her teeth as she adjusts to my size. After a moment, she begins to roll her hips, and I move with her, finding the perfect rhythm together.

Securing her with one hand, I bury my face between her breasts and thrust up inside her. She chokes on her breath as she continues to ride me, matching me thrust for thrust. Her hands roam over my chest and slip around my neck as she leans down, kissing me hard. I continue to move inside her, feeling us both grow slick with sweat and breathless from the exertion. Her fingers tangle through my hair as she rocks forwards and back, pulling harshly on my scalp, and it feels fucking amazing. Slipping my thumb against her clit, I rotate it, applying pressure in the way I know will have her crumbling. She quickens her pace, both of us moving feverishly. I feel her tighten around me, and she lets out an incoherent sound. I thrust harder and deeper, and she rides out the wave of the high for a moment. She sags against me, breathless, a dazed expression on her face.

Recovering quickly, her limbs loosen, and she releases her tight hold on me. I use this lack of control on her behalf to yank her off me and flip us off the lounge. We fall to the floor, and I slam back inside her once more. She releases a half-cry, half-moan, arching her back as I pump in and out of her. Leaning forward, I sink my teeth into her shoulder, enjoying her cursing in that breathy way I love so much. My hand moves to her throat, lightly tracing its slender curve. I meet her eyes, and she nods. My hands tighten around her throat as I fuck her hard and relentlessly.

'Harder,' she gasps.

'Of course, Blush,' I grunt. 'Anything for you.'

I tighten my hold a little more, and she whimpers, eyes rolling into the back of her head. Seeing how much she loves this is such a turn on.

'Touch yourself,' I demand, sweat dripping down the back of my neck. 'I want you to come again.'

She almost sobs as her hand moves to her sensitive clit. My hips thrust forward one last time and I feel myself explode inside her. A gasp leaves me as she cries out my name, twitching and jerking against me as she also climaxes. I pump again, long and slow, draining every last drop before I pull out of her, and we collapse in a sweaty pile on the floor.

'Fucking hell,' she mutters.

'I'll say,' I agree.

Turning to face her, I draw her towards me, and plant a kiss on the side of her head. We both sit in a breathless silence. I feel as if I almost blacked out from the pleasure rolling through me at the end. Curling my arms around her, I bury my face into her neck and hold her to me.

It's the best feeling in the world.

44

ANYA

WHEN I BLINK AWAKE, I stare around in confusion for a few moments as the world settles, and I realise where I am. Mason is beside me, lying on his stomach, his arm slung over my abdomen. His tanned skin and dark hair looks perfect among his pale sheets. Reaching out, I run my nails lightly down his back. He releases a soft groan.

'Waking up beside you is my new favourite morning routine,' I say.

Slowly shifting, he gazes up at me. 'Me too, Blush.'

After spending an hour rolling around in his bed, and then in the shower, we finally manage to detangle from each other long enough to get ready. I just can't get enough of him. The feeling of his mouth on mine, his skin on my skin, the way he moves in and out of me. I sigh blissfully as I pull my brush through my hair.

Trotting downstairs, I see Mason is already there. Two mugs of coffee sit on the bench.

'I'm cooking eggs on toast,' he announces.

Walking over to him, I wrap my arms around his waist and press my cheek against his shoulder. 'I love this,' I whisper.

'You love what?'

'This,' I say, tightening my hold on him. 'You. *Us.*'

Twisting so that our lips can meet, he pecks his against mine. 'Me too.'

Plopping down onto the seat, I wince at the pain between my legs. I lost count of how many times we ended up on top of each other over last night and this morning, but the soreness in my legs will remind me of it all day, I'm sure.

'Have you got your results for the art assignment yet?' Mason asks. 'I'm assuming you have, since it got selected.'

I nod. 'Yeah. I aced it.'

Grinning, he turns to face me. 'I knew you would. It was awesome.'

'Thanks. I was so nervous about it, but it all worked out, thankfully.'

'You're a complete natural at painting.' Wandering over to me, he kisses my forehead. 'I'm proud of you.'

Warmth blossoms in my chest at his praise.

The front door swings open, and Zayden enters. His hair is dishevelled, his shirt is on backwards and so crumpled it looks like it's never been washed before. He winces when he removes his sunglasses.

'Fuck, turn the brightness down,' he mumbles.

'Of the sun?' Mason snickers, gesturing to the light filtering through the kitchen window. 'Sure, just give me a second and I'll get right on that.'

'Close the blinds, motherfucker,' he mutters.

'No way. It's a gorgeous day,' Mason continues. He whistles as he flips the eggs, and Zayden clutches his head. I grin in amusement, feeling thankful that I'm not hungover like he is right now.

Zayden glares at Mason. 'I don't have the energy for you right now.'

'Sit down, sweetheart, let Mason take care of you.' He smirks, pointing his spatula to the empty seat beside me.

I love watching Mason in the kitchen. He pours fresh juice for Zayden, alongside a glass of water. Popping two pain relief tablets onto the bench, he slides them across to him with the glasses. 'For the head,' he says.

'Cheers,' Zayden thanks him, eyes closed.

'How was the rest of your night?' I ask.

'I don't really remember it. I woke up in the backyard, in the hammock.'

'Oh my God.' I release a snort of laughter. 'You're a menace, Zay.'

He rubs his face, looking exhausted. I peer at his neck.

'Were you alone in the hammock?'

'I think so.'

'You have some' – I point to my neck – 'little love bites. Everywhere.'

Zayden groans. 'Fuck. I don't even remember kissing anyone.'

'Dude.' Mason grimaces, leaning in to survey my brother's neck. 'Looks like you fucked a vampire.'

'I need to quit drinking,' he mumbles. Using his phone camera as a mirror, he winces, running his fingers down his neck. 'Goddamn.' Lowering the phone, he hangs his head in his hands. 'What did you guys do after the party?'

Mason and I exchange a glance just as Zayden looks up. He places a hand over his mouth.

'Oh hell nah, wrong question. I'm going to be sick.'

'I'd like to point out that the copious amount of alcohol you consumed is what's making you sick, not us,' Mason says.

Zayden gives him the middle finger as he rushes to the down-stairs bathroom.

Shaking my head, I take a sip of my coffee, settling back in my seat.

'There you go, my love,' Mason murmurs, handing me my plate. 'Breakfast is served.'

I beam up at him. 'Thank you.'

'Fuel up,' he mutters darkly, leaning forward. 'I'm not done with you yet.' He takes a bite from the corner of my toast, pushing back from the bench.

Heat races down my neck, and a shiver of excitement rolls down my spine.

I could get used to this.

THANK YOU

THANK YOU SO MUCH for reading *Break the Rules*. I really hope you enjoyed Anya and Mason's story. I love writing romance stories with emotional, angsty characters that draw you in. I had so much fun exploring the sports romance genre, and I always love revisiting one of my favourite tropes: second-chance romance. I hope you enjoyed it as much as I enjoyed writing it.

ACKNOWLEDGEMENTS

FIRST AND FOREMOST, I'd like to thank the readers – thank you from the bottom of my heart for picking up this book and embracing Anya and Mason's story. Thank you for your love, encouragement and reviews. I will be forever grateful for your support.

I really enjoyed writing this book; I adore these characters and I loved exploring this side of the romance genre!

Thank you to my friends and family who dealt with endless questions and ideas and offered me much appreciated feedback.

This book wouldn't exist without my best friend, Becka. My rock, my ride or die, the yin to my yang. Thank you so much for all your help and guidance whenever I embark on a new story idea. I appreciate all your help, advice and everything in between that you do for me.

I will always thank my beautiful friend Genicious, who supported me so much when I first began the journey of self-publishing. If it wasn't for her and all the help she provided me, I would never have taken the plunge and ended up with the deal of my dreams from Penguin.

To my beautiful friend Nicole, who is also subject to my long voice notes of rambling thoughts. Thank you for being such a kind, generous and wonderful friend to me. I am so glad we found each other, even though we live on opposite sides of the world!

My amazing 'Team No Sleep' girls, who have given me feedback and crucial advice that has helped shape me as a writer and has motivated me to be where I am today – thank you Kenadee, Jess and SJ.

Jordan – my wonderful beta reader, advice giver, editor and creative genius – who is always down to work on my next project with me, always knows the best way to word things, always has a new idea or title in mind when I can't think of one. I really look up to you and rely so much on your advice. I've been a fan of your writing since I was in my early teens, and I'm honoured you've become one of my closest friends.

Thank you especially to my amazing friends Haley, Chloe and Tamika for always listening to me, offering me advice, and always being there for me.

Thank you to my amazing book club for supporting me! I am so thrilled to have found such a wonderful group of people to share my bookish adventures with. Creating our online book club gave me the confidence to be bold with my reading and helped me take the dive to branching out on my own Bookstagram.

To my wonderful friends, Jane, Rachelle, my close friends who have always given me help when I've asked, and always gone above and beyond to support me, by turning up to my book events, telling so many people about my books and so much more. I love you girls. Thank you to Marnie and Tyler. Thank you for all your help with positions, team names and brainstorming titles! You contributed so much to the planning and plotting of this book, I really appreciate your input!

To all the bloggers, reviewers and BookTok accounts that shower me with support. To anyone who has followed me on Wattpad and been a part of my writing journey. I can't ever tell you thank you enough.

Last and certainly not least, a massive **thank you** to the amazing team at Penguin Books Australia for your support and the incredible opportunity you have given me. Chris – you are wonderful. I appreciate how kind you are, how supportive you've always been, how prompt you are to answer or follow up any questions I have, and everything you've done behind the scenes to make this the most perfect experience. I will be forever grateful!

Powered by Penguin